BELOW

NOT YOUR PLATYPUS PUBLISHING

www.notyourplatypus.com

Sensational Stories from NOT YOUR PLATYPUS

☐ **THE FINAL TRANSMISSIONS OF A DOOMED ASTRONAUT by Joey Rodriguez.** Seven crews had come before her, each one trusted with the same mission. A substance, a source, a beacon of light, growing somewhere in the universe. There were warnings, collateral damage on a massive scale, and the oppression and opposition that came with this new discovery. They had chosen her out of necessity from the dust that had settled after fear and anxiety had run high. Now, out here in the void of space, she must fight to survive against the elements, her inexperience, and those who wish to protect the universe from her mission. **$9.99 (PAPERBACK) / $0.99 KINDLE**

☐ **TERMINATION DUST by Joey Rodriguez.** The dust had fallen recently, a larger deposit than the prior season. A great indicator of how harsh the winter will be, tales were told that these early flakes were born from spirits who have been allowed to pass on without proper burial, those who ascribed to a life of greed, of thievery, of boiling pitch. Ila had returned home, a native daughter of the North, just west of the border. It had been nearly a decade, but she sought refuge now to clear her mind of the fog-swept bay. The judgment from a pistol deep in the tundra, however, forced her to forsake all that she had chosen to forget about her past. Alone and without direction, each member of her pack that ventured out into the wilderness that early morning faced the rising tide of the spirits of the forest. **$9.99 (PAPERBACK) / $0.99 KINDLE**

☐ **WITHIN THE SPACE OF SEVEN BREATHS: PART I by Joey Rodriguez.** Civil unrest plagued the minds of the higher court, a need to revert to the old ways of honor and misguided power. The samurai class had been slowly choking on its own suicide, every faction blaming the other for its downfall, a voice unable to rise above the pitch and declare a new chapter. The memories of the past, of misdeeds, of vengeance, of lust and greed, did not stay buried; the stories of youth, of creatures and demons as thin as air stealing the very souls of the unlucky; they were not meant to mix. The unexplainable had always been there, but the veil was now torn, a resistance brewing on all sides, intent on reigning supreme; all while keeping the unwilling worlds of life and death from shattering into one another in a violent chaos perfect for cultivating a horrifying new order. **$9.99 (PAPERBACK) / $0.99 KINDLE**

Buy them on **Amazon.com**; visit **NotYourPlatypus.com**
for our full catalog of amazing books; or use this handy coupon for ordering*!

Please send me the books I have checked above. I am enclosing $_____ (please add $10.00 to this order to cover postage and handling). Send check or money order—no cash or C.O.D.'s. Prices and numbers are subject to change without notice.

NAME _____

ADDRESS _____

CITY_____ STATE_____ ZIP CODE _____

Allow 4-6 millennia for delivery.
*This coupon is not an actual valid coupon, please purchase our books online!

NOT YOUR PLATYPUS
PUBLISHING

BELOW

JOEY RODRIGUEZ

NOT YOUR PLATYPUS PUBLISHING LLC
www.notyourplatypus.com

Dedicated to all those under the spell...

"With six eyes did he weep, and down three chins
Trickled the tear-drops and the bloody drivel.

At every mouth he with his teeth was crunching
A sinner, in the manner of a brake,
So that he three of them tormented thus.

To him in front the biting was as naught
Unto the clawing, for sometimes the spine
Utterly stripped of all the skin remained.

"That soul up there which has the greatest pain,"
The Master said, "is Judas Iscariot;
With head inside, he plies his legs without.

Of the two others, who head downward are,
The one who hangs from the black jowl is Brutus;
See how he writhes himself, and speaks no word.

And the other, who so stalwart seems, is Cassius.
But night is reascending, and 'tis time
That we depart, for we have seen the whole."

Dante's Inferno: Canto XXXIV

TABLE OF CONTENTS

SOWER OF DISCORD

I

At least thirty variations existed in the mountains and vibrant hills of the North, but the intricate differences mattered little in the throes of the silent hunt. A protruding, confident chest inhaled, hide retreating down to the bone. Loose tufts of caramel fur detached into a passing, tepid breeze; the seasons were fading into one another and the dead flakes must be shed.

Delicate hooves of charcoal had calloused; little rivulets formed from constant scraping against the obstacles of the forest floor. The pliable lips of the native beast quivered as it latched downward onto a leaning patch of brimming pasture that had grown around the base of a stark, red maple, chewing with no sense of satisfaction, simply elements that must be swallowed in order to swallow the next.

It was far from sacred, a lost buck navigating a solitary path, attempting to keep its belly full, its senses honed, and its antlers ornate and dense. A mate would satisfy it; a duel for her honor. It would prance and huff, snorting frost as it tangled with the others, beating back the naïve opposition to plant its seed.

Its jaw ground sideways, chewing the soft plants between flat teeth, head straight as it surveyed the maze of birch, sweetgum, and deflowered dogwood. They grew in no discernible pattern, the result of seeds spread by ravenous, winged scavengers for centuries; frightful gales from churning storms blowing the small offspring to and fro. Wet trunks slithered in front of one another, sparring with thicker branches below, each trying to tip their crown to the sun.

Bubbling clouds of gray had crashed into one another like massive titans, the early afternoon muted, the downpour to come later in the evening. There would be no nutrients for the starving giants.

The deer took a second helping of the watered-down grass, noisily munching until it had formed a paste over its tongue, easy enough to swallow. A thickness bulged in its throat, legs unbalanced.

It stumbled, knocked aside as if by some fellow, warring male. The front hooves crossed over one another in a delicate ballet, a gurgling whine cursing the heavens. The arms of the forest swirled as it could no longer bear to stand, collapsing upon its partially eaten meal.

The gunshot seemed to triple as the echo carried it skyward, the *crack* chasing the projectile in futility, never to catch up with the fire and light. The hunter lowered his weapon, removing his eye from the mounted scope, the buck so close only moments before as he had leaned heavily onto a cluster of fallen, white birch. He wrapped the sling of the rifle around his shoulder and approached his prey with leisure.

It stirred with pain, hind legs kicking in futility as if it would only have to rise to its feet to gallop back into obscurity. The bullet had sawed through the base of the neck, opening a flowing gash that coated the soil, pumping in waves, the buck's heart unable to prevent its rapid expulsion.

The hunter was reserved to wait, fetching a crude cigarette from a filthy, drawstring bag. He struck a dry match against the butt of his rifle and sucked the rolled end of the homemade relaxant. Whipping the flame into the air, he tossed the smoking wick into the wet brush, presiding over the helpless eyes as they begged for forgiveness.

A quiet drag enveloped his lungs with the fragrant tobacco, his adrenaline thanking him for the boost of confidence. He exhaled, allowing the deer to seize, the muscles stiffening, a horrible *bleat* escaping through its wound. Saliva foamed at the tip of the tongue as it wheezed into a deadly silence, suddenly falling still.

From deep within the labyrinth, the Messenger watched.

He would never admit to the debilitating effects of aging, though he lacked actual experience in the matter. He had once discovered graying stubble weaving just like the mismatching inhabitants of the forest, giving him the appearance of winter's sudden onset. He shaved it off immediately.

In the mornings, his bones would crack in thunderous applause, forcing the pent-up air from between the joints. In the afternoons, his muscles would mutiny, no amount of heat and ice to loosen their vice. He would attempt to disprove his own theories, forcing himself into feats of relevancy and strength, but nothing more would come of it, save for bruises and exhaustion.

The blood phased him little, the healthy buck wrapped around his shoulders, his hands clustering the hooves together like a sweater over his neck. He knew the trails and the overgrowth, he would not be confused by the obfuscation. Adjusting the prize, he reseated the deer, relieving a sharp pain in his left shoulder.

The hunter, nor his father, nor his father's father, had built the modest cabin. In his mind, it had simply always existed, a refuge from the terrors of pollution and noise. The backs of ancient red pines had been felled and stacked to create the exterior, dulled now into a shade more black than brown. A masonry chimney had been fashioned on the far end with flat, colorful stones, pressed forcefully into gray mortar. Water and sun had dyed them earth tones and chipped away at their respectability.

He had left a lantern burning in the window, replenished with butane before his routine had begun earlier. The beacon drew him forward in the waning light, pushing in the front door with the heel of his muddied boot.

The catch was deposited on a carving table, the feeble, oak legs wobbling under the weight of the creature. The rifle was stowed against the wall, his hands free to load a few pounds of kindling into the fireplace. The warmth *crackled* as the cabin absorbed the heat, allowing him to shed his top layer. The overcoat had been his father's, from the first war; thin, field gray, it had served him well in business and pleasure, accompanying him now to fight back the chills of the waning fall. Edging the cuffs of an emerald, wool sweater back, he rummaged through the bulky bottom drawer of a writing desk, removing a roll of leather.

A well at the rear of the cabin provided fresh water, the axle squeaking as the hemp scraped between the rusted flanges. He placed the bucket into the base of a deep, steel sink, unfurling the leather roll onto a butcher block next to it. The instruments had been given their own pouches, a buckle of copper locking them in place. He freed a chisel first, gripping the juniper stock delicately, inspecting it for inaccuracies.

Dipping a white rag into the frigid water, he lovingly rubbed the dried blood from the flat face of the beveled metal. He had nowhere to be; he would take as much time as he needed.

He draped the crimson rag over the edge of the sink, wiping his wet hands across the front of his sweater. A pair of rubber gloves slipped over his fingers as he jammed his interdigital folds together to ensure their compression.

The buck was laid on its back, legs heavy and folding at the joint, waiting patiently for rigor mortis. He inserted a stubby blade into the white, wisping fur, slitting through the thin membrane, careful to keep the knife elevated, allowing the skin to guide it across the belly. The tautness of the hide relaxed with each inch, revealing a bloated, marbled belly. Short, shallow strokes pierced through the abdominal tissue, his free hand tugging at the weakened muscle, separating the ends and allowing imprisoned blood to slip over the edge of the table and down between the rotting floorboards.

He continued his incision to the hollow junction of the neck and chest before setting aside the knife. Balancing the edge of the chisel against the first rung of the rib cage, he tapped the base gently with a wooden, tenderizing mallet, ensuring his accuracy. He raised the hammer and slammed it into the handle, plowing through the bone, stopping himself short of puncturing the heart.

The creature's twelve barricades broke easily as he climbed the calcium ladder. Fully loosened, he wrenched apart the ribs, the severed ends snapping and collecting in his palms.

Tiny, bloated fingers sprung from between the organs, pale and drenched in a thick mucus. The hunter reeled, stepping back quickly from the field dressing. The hand curled sleepily into a fist as if caught in the midst of a pleasant dream.

To the knife roll, grabbing a cleaver to hack away the suffocation.

He pivoted to the buck, but the anomaly had vanished. He had not witnessed whether the hand had slipped back within the confines or if it had simply been his own distraction.

A step towards the corpse, boots heavy on the hardwood, distributing dust below. Easing his hand forward, he slipped the cleaver above the lung, lifting the heart, searching for the prisoner.

The deer *squealed*, honking a gasping knell that racked its frame with a violent burst of animation. It bicycled its legs as it rolled from the carving table, crashing to the floor and driving the hunter to the edge of the sink. The creature whined, beating the air with pain as it stood, emptying its contents, intestines unspooling in a wet slap.

Swatting its antlers, it hurtled towards him, depositing a stream of blood in its wake. He shielded his face, raising his arms and resisting the twisted spears. The fearless buck tore through the wool, slitting his flesh in thin strips as he flailed the cleaver.

He connected with the snout, digging deep into the bone. Using the leverage, he flung the deer aside, releasing his grip on the knife. Stumbling, he crashed down upon the kindling, tripping into his rifle. He racked the iron bolt backward, the chamber loaded with a fresh cartridge by the action. The buck could not shake free the embedded blade, but it charged nonetheless.

Bolt returned, he raised the rifle to his shoulder, forsaking the scope. The barrel roared as smoke vomited, masking the impact. The corpse obeyed, head pounding the wood, offering no final request. The hunter chambered a new round, prepared to fell the bastard a third time. His forearms stung, the tickling sensation of blood dripping down to the elbow was too irritating to ignore, but he kept his weapon trained.

The child had matured.

A thick fist punctured through the remaining vitality, opening like a blooming wildflower, palm slapping the sloppy mess. The head emerged, a bald field traced with pulsating veins of black. Skin had fused over the eyes in a layer of stitched scar tissue, the nose flat, nostrils ripped open to allow bile to leak. A mouthful of razored calcium crisscrossed, forming a sea of sharp rocks, no need to eat, for the others would feast on its kill.

The hunter did not allow the being to free itself fully. He hugged the trigger, dousing the wall in black. The wound was precise, the entry point a calculated hole near the top of the head, the exit a gaping mess. But the pale vision continued to emerge, unaffected, snarling in a tone that suggested a foreign tongue. The hunter leapt upright, stomping through the door, slapping it aside as he led with his shoulder. Into the darkness, he retreated, swinging his elbows wildly as he hobbled over the skeletons of fallen birch.

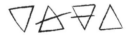

Bony, wooden fingers scraped his face as he plunged into the forest, unable to gauge depth and distance. His knees rose furiously, in danger of jabbing his chin as he overcompensated. His boot lodged between a spiraling root, tugging him forward.

The hunter tripped, jabbing himself in the gut with the butt of his weapon. His speech curdled as he wheezed, releasing a pathetic whine that teased his sense of masculinity. He swung his head back towards the cabin, only a dim bulb in the distance, shrouded by five-fingered leaves and dry needles.

He could not feel the hot breath, nor the uncomfortable claustrophobia, that usually accompanied such intimacy, but the whispering had already commenced. It was gibberish, a chorus of hushed, fragile, prepubescent prayers. They began as a dull ache, water filling the canal, swelling until he could not escape the infernal chanting. Hacking away at the tree's vein, he freed his boot and lumbered further from the buzz of his quiet retreat.

The voices increased, another layer filtered through the churning gut of chaos, accompanied now by a burning, sulfur-like stench. The children dispersed, the wail of a centuries-old evil screaming threats into the back of his skull. The hunter added to the choir, howling into the black atmosphere. His knees buckled as he fell once more into the soil, clutching his ears, sealing them off with his dirty palms.

The elongated skull shimmered in the darkness, briefly, as if the hidden moon had swept over it. The Messenger remained silent as the hunter filled the night air with his own painful echo.

Mud had spilled into his mouth, his throat gagging on the refuse as he attempted to expel it before he swallowed it completely. The skies had opened, drenching the forest floor in an increasingly rising tide. He pushed his hands into the slop, finding solid earth, enough to force some sort of balance upon his heels.

Clawing at his eyes, he cleared away the muck, flicking his wrists to cast it back. He pivoted in the liquid, unable to fully wipe the black ink from his vision, blind to the deafening rain. Listening carefully, he waited to be purified, perhaps another layer of grime to be shed before the thicket would part its wooded imprisonment and allow his pardon.

Fire curled in an enormous explosion of phosphorus, thick streams searing the necks of the towering pines. Hastily shaved branches had been positioned at the base of a haphazard stone ring, leaning against each other in a wide funnel. The blaze had erupted from within, the flames licking the droplets from the sky, but refusing to give in to their cooling touch.

He knew the invitation was meant for him, the clarity returning to his eyes. His boots released a thick kiss as he fought against the suction of the mud. He reached the edge of the orange glow, back hunched, weighed down by the unceasing storm.

Hands outstretched, he attempted to transfer warmth, but none came.

A panic painted his face in disbelief. He curled his fingers into his palm, he could feel his own skin. The wrinkles, the blisters, the crusted ridges of time. Once more into the heat, nothing to transfer as the dermis began to bubble, blistering into a black crust as a riverbed of veins burst, leaking down his wrist. He felt no pain, no instantaneous state of shock pumped placebos to relieve the stress. His charred hand continued to flex, the skin loosening and sliding away from the muscle.

He bellowed, unaware of what atrocity he had committed that would encourage this punishment. Turning his back to the flames, he watched the first set of paws emerge from the border of the darkness. The lips curled, peeling back to allow dripping fangs, hunger heightening the wisping condensation as it streamed through the frigid air.

Two more slinked forward, their matted, black fur thick and pointed despite the rain. The trio of wolves released a guttural huff in unison, the one to his right launching a single, furious bark to punctuate. Whether it was a warning to submit or retreat, the hunter did not know.

He swung his rifle from around his shoulder and dragged the bolt towards him. His charred fingers ripped, freed from the burden of his palm.

The pack closed in, running their tongues along their gums, anticipating the meal.

The hunter whimpered as his index and middle finally tumbled into the pitch below. Shoving the mechanism back into place, he funneled a new round as tears streamed from his bloodshot eyes. His lungs inflated, but he felt no sense of relief, a guilty stone overcoming his gut as he would not survive.

There would be no time to incapacitate all of them, the barrel snapping down the line.

He chose the middle wolf, its bravado sneaking it ahead of its siblings. The beast whelped as the bullet tore through the gaping mouth, *snapping* the head back. As it crumpled, the others pounced, tackling the hunter and pinning him against the black sea. They bared down upon his neck, sinking into the soft flesh and ripping his arteries free. He was forced to swallow the fountain of blood that spewed from the ragged wound, muffling his cries for his mother.

The Messenger hobbled from the confines of the forest, his burlap robe soaking in the expulsion overhead, though burdening him no further. He watched quietly in the flickering light as the wolves ate, the precious screams of the hunter frightening him.

▽△▽△

The hunter awoke to the blessings of a cloudless sky and the filtered tone of the morning sun. Pine needles had stuck to the filthy perspiration of his cheek, his chest cold against the still, muddy waters. He sucked the crisp delight of the tinted air, choking quickly on the purity.

He rolled upon his back, eyeing the giant stalks as they swayed in a breeze borrowed from the distant lilac peaks. Shielding his bleary vision with his right hand, he found comfort from the stinging light.

Scar tissue had decimated his fingers and palm, winding around each joint in a pattern of chaos, as if his skin had been sewn back together simply to close a festering wound. It was not swollen, rather, emaciated, from what he could recall from the night before. He could move each instrument individually without pain, but he rejected the flesh itself. It was unbecoming. Convincing himself it was his own would be impossible.

He remembered.

The memory was ensnared in his concentration, suddenly running his fingers along his neck as if predicting his next scar.

He rose clumsily, beating back the stiffness in his calves as they locked. The cluster of birch ahead revealed no hidden reconnaissance. He knew unequivocally that he had been abandoned here.

The rifle was not far; muddied, yes, but operational. He inspected the chamber: a single round to accompany him. It could last him indefinitely, the daylight its own form of ammunition. He left nothing behind, the news of his death trapped in the darkness of the prior evening's madness.

▽△▽△

He trusted his eyes; truth and uneasiness did not deter their observation, reserving his internal compass to set the course. Yet, his deterioration had begun to sting him with thin barbs of uncertainty.

The sockets had been doused in black, absorbing the river of blood that bubbled from beneath the black habit and emptying it down the sickly visage. The mouth lay agape, the skin below unencumbered by clothing. If it spoke, it did so in a whisper, locked behind the thick pane of the cabin window. The distance allowed little clarification as the vision retreated and he was left to ponder his solitude, convinced that the shadows of nature had conspired to make mischief.

He stood quietly in the doorway, running his hands along the broken hinge. His tools remained on the butcher block, the spoils of his hunt bloodied and lifeless on the dusty hardwood.

Aging typebars pecked at the onion skin paper, providing a wet slap as they stamped the black ribbon. Each letter was deliberate, using only his indexes proving laborious. He had amassed a sizable stack of finished pages, two inches thick and growing. Most of it was original, a few copies to be distributed when the time was right.

> To my fellow congregants,
> An hour is upon us. Not the opus we have come to pray for these terror-filled nights and anxious days. Temptation may steer us from our duty, and it has the right to, but we must return to the tasks presented. Trust, more than any act, has been bestowed upon us, we must wield it with responsibility.
> A war is raging, and we have chosen wisely, protected our souls with sacred texts and blessed charms, but we must hide no longer. Have you done your civic duty? Have you done as you have been asked? I know that I have. I know that my place in this eternal kingdom has been secured and that you too will find a place next to me.
> Take heed, as there are forces lurking within our commonalities that have been disenfranchised, that side with the Others. They are bred to punish us, to prevent us from our final calling. I have documented the final solution, included for your perusal. This shall be the only copy, ~~this shall be the only copy, this shall be the only~~

His knuckles massaged his wrinkled eyelids, forcing a bit of moisture to cure the painful, arid blinking. Unlocking the fingers, he twisted the release valve and raised the message to inspect his mistakes. A drop of collection fluid slid across the duplicate phrases, his hot breath curing it.

Reseating the page, he hunted for the appropriate letter across the circular field of symbols.

> *This shall be the only copy, one which will guide you to the swollen fields, to the entrance. There you will find the gaping mouths of disease and the pestilence of the unclean (though, they are worthy of our usage). You shall be welcomed and enter into his kingdom, a privilege that we proud few must cherish and execute before we blanket the cities in blood.*
>
> *We will all bathe in putrefaction, present to him that we are leveled, that we are clay, molded into the hammer, spear, and flame of justice. He will rule once more, through us, and only ~~and only and only~~*

A mental block.

Had he more time, he could expand, but he would need several hundred more copies. Those waiting with swollen tongues and bitter throats required his guidance. He too found his mouth afflicted, unable to call moisture to calm himself.

He opened a thin drawer in his writing desk and rummaged past broken pencils and straightened paperclips. A sheepskin-bound notebook, the fluffy wool edging on gray, his name embroidered in bright blue thread, proved cumbersome. Casting it aside, he shook the drawer, hoping to dislodge his suppressant. A rosary slid from the back, his flask following.

The swirling, crimson beads crumpled upon the crucifix, his withered and scarred hand reaching first for the sacred charm. But his homebrew called him, the flask embraced, the drawer slammed shut.

He could barely inhale, his lungs tightening, crying out for help. The stool beneath him tipped as he stumbled away from his sermon, the lid of the vessel opening and the warm liquid spilling into his esophagus.

It was not the fermented potatoes of the locals, the thickness oozing, slapping his tongue with the intensity of copper. He vomited, ejecting blood across the small confines. He released the container as his face slammed into the floorboards, another cough releasing thick droplets. His pupils shrank as the room spiraled in agony. He could not command his eyelids to shield him from vertigo, his lips mouthing an impromptu prayer.

Delicate fingers slithered between the planks. The cracked and bruised nails dug themselves into what remained of his hair, dragging him downward.

The cellar door had been left open, the rug roped aside, giant iron ringlet twisting gently in the breeze. He had slumped his rifle as he always had, next to the fireplace and the kindling. Refusing to remove his coat, he snatched the weapon and took to the top riser, staring, wavering between fear and idiotic bravado.

A poor, antiseptic light snuck through the slits in the floorboards above, illuminating infrequent patches of hope, but it was still much too dark to see, unless his patience would allow his eyes to adjust.

The face. Snarling in the darkness, framed by a stone archway, begging him to follow. He could see it clearly, snapping at him, then dissipating into the black absence. He knew fully this could be no coincidence. It had led him into the cabin, beckoning him from the window, fooling him into venturing into his own dead end.

His boots scraped the errant dust and pebbles that had accumulated over the century, announcing his intentions. Descending deeper into the cellar, he passed under the curved threshold, a musk tickling his nose. Mold had festered here, perhaps; bales of hay once entombed a bounty of ice blocks for the summer heat.

Disappearing into the pitch, he was welcomed by the miniature echo of his strained wheezing. He could not control the blockage in his lungs, his nostrils sickened by the tone. He turned from the empty storage space towards the meager drippings of light behind him. The arch yawned as it seemed to have stretched infinitely into the distance.

Motioning towards the familiarity and freedom of the cabin, he paused. His feet had merely pivoted but had somehow elicited a dry slither, sweeping debris in its path. He made no further attempt, listening as the limping began to echo in the chamber.

It crept with speed now, displaying no shadow to interrupt the limited light, no chance to sneak an inaccurate shot.

Behind him now.

A hiss. Far from snake-like, it snuck between sewn lips, a cry of help and of hunger.

The hunter's head cocked to the right, finding nothing in the darkness. His peripheral blurred the figure as it stood in the archway, caressed by a ray from above, the disgusting light flashing over her bare chest.

Rifle bashing into his shoulder, he spun towards the stalker, releasing a volley. The muzzle brought a brief clarity, the raucous scream blotting his ears. The bullet burrowed into a wooden beam at the rear of the cellar, splintering into a dry shower. Her muscles had not expelled any sort of inertia, she simply did not exist anymore.

The organ bellowed a holy hymn.

He was left with little time to mull the vanishing corpse as the sudden interlude sunk its claws into the base of his spine. Thundering, a punctuation of eight notes, a shivering bass and a dizzying almost electric warble of angelic highs, he was once again drawn into the darkness.

What once had been merely brick and ancient mortar now parted in voluptuous velvet. Curiosity drew him to part the curtain.

A diffused, powder blue filtered through the massive walls of curving, stained glass, showering the congregation that had amassed in the darkened cathedral. He was not greeted as he entered the hallowed ground, venturing no further than the curtain, his fingers clinging to the inviting fabric.

Copper pipes intertwined like outraged vines, bursting through the organ's skull and attaching themselves to the wall. Bloodied hands and feet snuck through the openings in the maze of the wailing pipes as the damned moaned for forgiveness. A hooded organist kept the festivities marching onward, slamming his frail fingers into the keys of misshapen bone, playing from memories past.

A font of dark liquid marked the last bastion of cleanliness. A ripple surged through the center, casting a wave to the edge of the basin where is settled peacefully. He angled his head, guided by the monstrous marble columns, to the sacrifices overhead. They had been hung by their ankles, tethered to a rounded chandelier of blue-flamed candles, throats slit, the last drop of essence filling the station as they themselves collected the falling wax.

The ceremony began.

The silk robe was virginal white, layered atop a black lining that draped over the feet like the proud dress of a nubile bride. It offered no impediment as the figure ascended the spiral towards the pulpit, clutching an ancient tome. A pallium of red wool had been draped over the neck, inverted crosses dotting the length as it hung against the chest. The weight of a four-tiered, iron tiara, encrusted with the plaque- and blood-stained teeth of wild mammals, dipped the head of the holy orator forward. If it caused any discomfort, it could not be discerned by the curtain that masked the ancient face: a crimson cross following the curve of the nose, two slits allowing some semblance of vision. Setting the book down on a lectern, it opened of its own volition, the charred flesh stretching as the indiscernible instructions were presented.

The organ cried out its last note, the echo of the enchanting melody lingering like a lost frequency.

With arms outstretched, the voice commanded. "Be seated, my son."

The hunter was drenched in embarrassment as the congregants shuffled in their oak pews. They too had protected their anonymity, hoods of white, black, and red silently judging him.

The curtain in his sweaty grip had become a jagged knob of crystal, the sanctuary doors locked. He backed away from the futility, suddenly pawed and admired by the hooded audience. They guided his arms forward, relieving him of his rifle. He could not command his legs to resist, forced to take in their rotting flesh as their masked faces certainly hid hunger and lust.

He was deposited to a gilded hassock, a hand on his shoulder bringing him to his knees. The others dispersed, taking their seats once more.

"It has been foretold," the sermon commenced, "of a resurrection. A period of a thousand years of forgiveness." The voice was of a distinct vintage, a male brimstone of centuries past, but still worthy of reverence. "As we gather, we cannot, *shall not*, be granted this luxury. For *you!*" The edge of his fist *cracked* the wooden lectern. "*All of you!* You have not convinced Him. You have not bathed in your sacrifice. You have not slaughtered the lamb, nor offered a seat at the table of privilege.

"There can be no mistaking the tragic failure of our cowardly and insidious people. We stand on the precipice, overlooking the river that beckons us to the capital city. Pray, tell me what you have done to part the seas of sin?"

The robe of the blessed shimmered as he pointed forcefully at the hunter.

"Yes," came the whispers. "What have you done?"

"Tell us." A field of quiet anger began to boil.

"Yes," they continued. "Tell us. Tell us. *Tell us.*"

Perspiration squeezed through the pores of the unprepared, tickling his neck as it dribbled down his back. His anxious knees conspired to seize, forcing his calves to cramp, his only escape to finally address the question.

"*I don't know!*"

They reacted only with a deafening hush, the hemp above *creaking* as the bodies swung gently against the weight of the chandelier.

"This poor, wretched soul," the preacher branded, "he has come so far, has served so valiantly. Yet, he has humbly rejected progress. We will not except your modesty. You have done exactly as you were instructed. Yet..." The sacred textbook closed slowly as the pastor caressed the withered skin. "Yet, you shy away from what is expected of you now. You run. You believe that by finishing your *errands* you have been discharged from continuing forward. There is but one path to the resurrection, my son, and you must not disobey. The *consequences* have already been showered upon you, have they not? They continue to drive iron through your flesh. You know in the eternal, black depths what you must do now."

The members of the dark bowels rose ceremoniously as the organist fiddled across the thick keys, blessing the room in a ghostly wail. But they did not stand to offer prayer. Instead, they shuffled down the aisle, arms outstretched.

The pastor tugged at his cloth mask, ripping it unevenly from the grip of the tiara. His face had undergone a ritualistic mummification, the skin shrunken against the bone, following every sharp curve, pieced together from varying tones. A black ink had infected his eyes as his lip curled high above infected gums.

"Do not defy Him!"

One by one, the masses strayed from their hoods, their faces beset by famine, pestilence, war, and death.

The hunter found fluidity in his legs, rising quickly, spinning his back to the altar. But the horde was upon him again, swallowing him into the madness as they snarled and hissed. He could do no more than protest in the agonizing yelp of a bruised animal.

"A pathway has opened!"

He was slammed into the aisle, a forearm around his neck to prop his head towards the sanctuary doors as they eased open. The hooves of an ashen and yellowing beast *clacked* as it entered the arena, the Messenger gripping the saddle, his cloak depositing soot with every gain. The horse huffed condensation, shaking its head, the loose skin barely covering the exposed jaw bone, flapping freely.

"No!" the hunter resisted, swinging his arms against the handcuffs of the gathered. He could not release his fate as the Messenger's jagged blade scraped against the carpet, tearing the gentle fibers. "No!" he screamed again, slurring the long vowel as he flailed. The beast trotted purposefully, the gold-buckled reigns *twinkling*.

"You have not cured your envy! You repeat the mistakes of the past! In doing so, *you must be received into His kingdom of torture!*" the pulpit blared.

The hunter mustered a final resistance, his mouth agape, beaming an angry howl. The congregants could sense the tremor, their legs suddenly defying their orders, dragging them skyward, arms outstretched, clawing for safety as they collided with the ceiling. Freed somewhat from the vice, he slammed his eyes shut as the horse galloped. He curled forward, hunched in a prison of his own making. Tears dripped from beneath the tight seal, the creases of his lips beginning to bleed as he opened his mouth wider and wider.

As the last, vile hand left his flesh, as the guilty swung upwards, he attempted to banish them forever.

The seam ran in thirds, scored with dull bone, easily folded to fit within the envelope. The typewriter's ribbon had run dry, but there was little time to return with fresh ink. His tongue, too, had lost its own ink, the self-adhering glue becoming a poison in his mouth.

A wicker basket held the completed instructions, the addresses typed, the only evidence of his handwriting the signature he had scrawled at the bottom of each note, a wide consonant followed closely by nonsense. He tossed another sealed envelope into the basket, no need for a return at the top left, he knew he might not be alive to receive it.

He spread the mouth of the next sleeve and inserted a copy of the letter. Sliding his tongue, he curved it around the glue, activating the binding chemicals, sealing it forcefully as he dragged his hand across the back. He flipped it over, studying the addressee.

Exhaustion blanketed him, his fingers shaking as the letter attempted to slip away. He held back, placing the unsettling matter on top of the desk, a hand through his hair to massage the insects that crawled across his scalp.

His lips curled, chin ruffling as he clenched his jaw. He could not prevent his eyes from leaking, a distant pain compelling him to resist and end the madness. Sobbing into a cupped hand, lest the entire forest know his emotions, he forced the letter into the desk's drawer, jabbing it back into place so he would no longer have to shoulder the shame.

BELOW

He had slept peacefully for most of the night, dragging himself to the straw-stuffed bed as the sun had slipped behind the last greedy branches, swaying for one last dose. Having little time to comfort himself before slumber took hold, he had lost consciousness face down, a blanket barely unfurled to warm him.

The mattress buckled, folding in the center and sinking quickly. His torso entered first, stung by the bite of frigid water as it gurgled from below, leaking over the sides of the metal frame and onto the floor. He awoke in a panic of pain and blockage, coughing violently to expel the sudden lump. His balance had been enveloped by the liquid; his arms and legs flapping to fight the current.

His confines slipped away as he plunged into the void.

Had he opened his eyes? He must have.

A murky pain wrinkled his vision, forcing him to retreat. Fabric caressed his face, blubbering like a jellyfish, a thick, rough caul. It irritated him, but he was unable to swat away the nuisance.

His hands had been bound at the wrist, crossed behind the small of his back. Oxygen would level his anxiety, but the depths of the lake only filled his throat, begging him to choke. He twisted like a fresh catch, fighting the reel as he chomped deeper on the angler's bait. The burlap sack gave way, bringing the safety of light above as it drifted to the sanded floor. He kicked his legs furiously, flopping towards the shimmering, frosted surface.

Though the water sloshed and tumbled around him, he knew his escape would end here, below the thick layer of ice. His vigor did not deflate, an ingenuity fueling him to spin, planting his feet flat against the ceiling. He curled his knees into his chest and ignited a sharp kick.

A seam appeared, snaking across the surface. Not impenetrable, but certainly resilient. The impact forced him deeper into the water, requiring a recalculation as he wriggled upright, swimming upward and repeating the strategy.

His right foot punctured through the ice. Seized immediately by the frigid temperatures, he was wedged in the constricted wound, his foot unable to fold into a proper angle. Hanging limp, his lungs dissolving in heat, he rapped the layer with his left foot, stomping viciously, the chunks *cracking* like bone.

The lake buckled as a shard loosened, dropping into the water, freeing his locked foot but collapsing upon his chest, weighing him into the depths. He rolled, allowing the icy boulder to drop freely. His vision had begun to darken, the edges blurring, fading towards a pinhole, just like in the films of his youth.

Suddenly, the sensation intensified, the mountain air scraping his chest as he breached. He swallowed the freshness, coughing through the taste, though grateful for its presence. Whipping his head, he surveyed his surroundings, caught now in the middle of a massive lake, ringed by row upon row of white, dusted pine. An unfamiliar range of rock towered over the northern tip, giving no indication as to how far he had navigated off course.

The Messenger appeared to him.

Clouded by shavings of snow and ice that whipped alongside a lost breeze, he approached.

"*I have done as I was told!*" the hunter assured.

An unsatisfactory answer as the Messenger continued his lumbering, his cloak soaking up water, his staff *pinging* as it chipped the ice.

"*I wish to be released! You cannot hold me against my will! You promised!*" He fought to release his handcuffing, swinging side to side as his wrists began to chafe. "Do not come closer!" he pleaded, cheeks flush with color as fear and resistance inundated him.

But the Messenger stood before him, a beast of agonizing height, long streams of condensation seething from bony nostrils.

"Leave me *be*!" the hunter sobbed. "You cannot speak. You cannot guide me. What have you left to give me?"

The prayers had begun.

Whispering children, their hot breath seeping into his ears, overwhelming him in a brutal tongue. His head dipped below the waterline of his own volition, a scream escaping in a wrath of bubbles.

Tarred and oozing hands crawled up his chest, wrenching his collar upward, pushing him towards freedom. He spat the noxious water at the Messenger's feet, cursing under his shallow breathing.

The heads of other loyalists had emerged, their necks fused with the ice like a stockade, unable to twist, unable to address their peers, winding from the center of the lake in a concentric circle, row after row caught in the same horror. Below the surface, their arms and legs gyrated, banging against the frozen layer, unable to break free. Two men had been imprisoned side by side, the taller of the two gnawing on the open skull of the other, chewing slowly on the bloody matter as his victim hung limp.

The hunter knew he was to be called next. The Messenger knelt before him, offering a gloved hand, palm flat.

Sets of yellow eyes blinked in the water around him as the black hands of loyalty overcame him, dragging him, drowning him in the depths below.

HÄXAN

II

She wrestled the white beads between thumb and index, rolling over the smooth, manufactured surface, reciting internally her penance. A pause, the words monotonous, the order becoming tenuous, like drying honey. Droplets jiggled on the window, forced back by the speed of the vehicle, each one clinging tenaciously, leaving a mucus-like trail, just little snails trying to make a living.

Staring out at the empty streets, the residences choking the narrow throughway, she kissed the crucifix at the bottom of the rosary. She would complete the rest in the evening.

Her driver made no attempt to communicate, he knew she would not respond in kind. Not because she was rude, she simply needed to concentrate. A sigh of exhaustion, perhaps desperation, escaped. She knew not what to expect when she arrived, only that she need not appear weak.

The wound across her cheek leaked under the pressure of the dirty handkerchief. She removed the cloth, inspecting the blood seeping through. It had slowed considerably, the initial flow staining her wimple, the splatter forced up and across the side of her coif.

They had allowed her a dusty, four-paned window overlooking the front of the precinct, the rain still dousing the city in apocalyptic sheets. She thumbed her rosary once more, squeezing until it had made a soft indent, her anxiety flowing through her silent chanting.

A *squeak* and the ragged, metal door to the interrogation room popped open, an exhausted paper-pusher entering, lugging a reel-to-reel recording device. He set the beige and caramel machine in front of her and connected a bulbous tabletop microphone to a quarter-inch adapter.

"When will I be-" but she was cut off as he promptly departed, avoiding eye contact. The door slammed shut.

She returned the handkerchief to her cheek, biting through the pain, hoping to pressurize it and prevent further discomfort and worry. Hushed voices in the hallway and a cluster of shadows assembled in front of the door.

A curse. An apology. Subtract a shadow.

Two entered. They lacked the Prussian blue, starched, and poorly slimmed uniform of the *Polizia di Stato*. The shined dress boots had been replaced with muddy loafers, their blazers hung around the backs of their desk chairs, their sleeves rolled to the elbow, the edges caked with dried sweat and rainwater.

"Sister Cecilia?" one of them inquired.

"Yes?" she whispered, failing to realize how parched her throat was, despite bathing in the downpour.

They stood timidly behind the opposite end of the table, nervous hands folded over one another, concealing a bit of the stomach that was forming from bad habits.

"I am Inspector Petrosino," spoke the youthful one. "My partner, Inspector Battiato." A nod, a closed fist to cover an awkward cough.

"Am I being charged with a crime, inspectors?" she asked. "I find it rather disrespectful that I should be kept here against my will if I am not being formally reprimanded."

"Uh..." Petrosino stumbled, "May...may we sit?"

"I do not have authority here; do as you wish."

Battiato crossed behind her, grabbing a loose chair for himself as his partner sat, placing a second, smaller recording unit onto the table. They huddled around her, a damp mixture of mud and adrenaline spewing from their underarms.

"We must apologize, Sister," Battiato began, snapping a cigarette to his lips and striking a loose match. "May I?"

She nodded. He primed the tobacco, inhaling deeply. He scratched his scalp, navigating around the greasy comb-over. "You are not being formally charged, Sister. We have brought you here as a precaution. And to ask you a few questions in order to better understand what happened this morning."

"This conversation will be recorded," Petrosino declared, engaging a maroon recording flap on the larger of the two machines. He positioned the microphone in front of her as the first reel labored around its circumference, pulling the unused tape at three and three-quarter inches per second. They had inserted a fresh roll; she suspected she would be here for quite some time.

"You have blood on you," she interjected, pointing towards the blotch on his striped dress shirt. The young detective craned his neck back, angling for a better look as he held out the material.

"It must have transferred when I inspected the body," Petrosino remarked.

"Have you been looked at by a doctor, Sister?" Battiato wondered.

She shook her head.

"I promise, we will make this simple. Then we shall send for someone. Can I offer you something to drink before we begin?"

"No, I simply wish to return home."

"Very well." He eyed Petrosino, encouraging him to ask the most obvious.

"How was it that you came to attend the funeral of Annamaria De Sio?"

She placed the stained handkerchief on the table so they could witness her sacrifice. "I did not know *Signora* De Sio personally, nor her family. I did not attend out of sympathy, only my professional duty."

The courtesy knock allowed her to finish tidying. She smoothed the top blanket of her bed, folding back the hem to synchronize the white bed sheets with the gray wool.

Another knock, a bit more frantic.

"Just a moment!" she returned, shoving a copy of *Borstal Boy* into her nightstand. She pulled open a large bureau and stood before a square mirror mounted to the back of the wing. She adjusted a bobby pin that secured a chestnut bun to the back of her head before wiping perspiration from beneath her bottom lip.

A fellow devotee burst into her room, drenched in anxiety. Cecilia jumped, unprepared for the introduction.

"Sister," the nervous youngling burped. "The telephone, you must come, quickly."

Their heavily soled loafers clacked against the polyurethane-slathered hardwood as they trotted down the dormitory hall. The phone had been left off the hook atop an ornate bistro table flanked by two plush armchairs.

BELOW

Cecilia picked up the receiver and brought the static to her ear. "*Pronto.*"

$$\triangledown \; \vartriangle \; \triangledown \; \vartriangle$$

Petrosino nodded, rubbing the remains of a few days of black stubble. "You can attest that you had no prior knowledge of De Sio?"

"I cannot deny that the name is familiar, it does show up in the papers from time to time."

"Of course," he smiled. "But you know nothing regarding her family's business dealings?"

"Are you suggesting that I contribute to *Signore* De Sio's empire?"

Battiato waved aside the line of questioning, sucking down his cigarette to the filter. "What is it that you do for the church, Sister?"

"I am in charge of the historical curriculum for our students."

"Among other things," he insinuated.

Her calm demeanor seethed as she narrowed her brows low over her disrespected eyes. "*I do not know what you are referring to.*"

"Do not lie to me, Sister. This...*man* was *unwell*. You have cured cases such as this. You have acted, on occasion, as an *esorcista*?"

Her thighs were beginning to stiffen in the stubby, metal chair, forcing her to roll her shoulders and adjust her rear.

"I cannot hide the work I have done," she sighed.

"So, it's true?" Petrosino pressed.

"Yes. I have worked with many to displace the evil that has infected them."

"And you believe that is what transpired this morning?"

She remained quiet, staring down at her hands, clasped together, trembling from the memory she tried desperately to deflate.

"You shy away," Battiato noticed. "Are you ashamed?"

A tear marched down her cheek as she held the tide back. "No, inspector, I am *afraid*."

He snubbed the finished cigarette and positioned the portable reel-to-reel unit in front of her. The Geloso-branded recorder had seen better days, the multi-colored paint on the operations panel rubbed practically clean by countless interviews.

"We acquired this from a reporter employed by *Il Messaggero*. He had been tasked with recording several interviews at the funeral.

He witnessed the occurrence before you arrived and was able to capture what you accomplished."

He shoved his fat fingers onto the machine and it sputtered to life. Silence poured from the miniature speakers as the tape squealed with each revolution.

"Eh?" He fumbled with the device, twisting the braided dials west to east. A horrible screech burst from the recorder, shoving Cecilia against the backrest of her chair.

"Jesus!" Battiato cursed, leveling the volume.

She had tried to erase the sound of the creature's voice, enough to be able to continue the rest of her duties and avoid becoming lost in its volcanic timber. It emanated from the back of the throat, screeching in a high tone and backed with a gurgling bass. The voice hissed with each response, huffing like a frightened animal, cornered and prepared to fight.

S. CECILIA ZAMPA:	Why do you fear the rosary?
ANTONIO DE SIO:	Why, why, WHY...
S. ZAMPA:	Yes, why?
DE SIO:	BECAUSE IT...
S. ZAMPA:	Because?
DE SIO:	BECAUSE...BECAUSE...NO! I will not speak it. [screaming]
S. ZAMPA:	Hold it! Hold it in your hands!
DE SIO:	[screaming] [unintelligible] *Mangia merde e morte!*
S. ZAMPA:	Hold him down!
UNKNOWN MALE #1:	He's slipping!
S. ZAMPA:	Restrain him, now!
DE SIO:	I have planted my seed! I have raped the precious loins of my blood!
S. ZAMPA:	In the name of the T-[unintelligible]... in the name of the Most Blessed Virgin Mary, tell me the truth! Are you he who speaks the words of Lucifer?

The mahogany casket had already been lowered into the three-foot by eight-foot by six-foot hole, the heaven's slathering the dirt walls and leaking onto the lacquered lid.

Cecilia stood defiantly, a black umbrella keeping the wind and fury at bay. The afflicted had been brought to his knees, two of his kin placing pressure on the shoulder, his arms spread out for all to witness the black indentation of rosary beads infecting his palms.

"I will not ask you again!" she threatened. "Are you he who speaks the words of Lucifer?"

"He has come, has he not!?" Rain dripped past his eyes, inverted into a milky white, a festering sore running diagonally across his face as if the punishment for cheating at an unfriendly game of cards. The color had run from his body, a sickly hue replacing it, a spoiled green infecting his veins. Blood began to spill from his earlobes, a pumping wave dripping down his cheek. "I will create. I will create disorder amongst us all!"

"Why have you come to this innocent man? Have you no better mischief to reap?"

His arms flailed as his restraints buckled, the frightened men fighting the slippery eel until he succumbed to the mud.

To the reluctant kin, she fished, "What is this man's name?"

The possessed squirmed at the question, "You dare not speak thy name!"

"Antonio," one chimed. "De Sio."

"Antonio De Sio," she repeated. "I call upon thee to speak!"

"I have *cleaned* the bastard! *Cleaned* him!" The demon screeched. "I have pumped this bastard's cock free of seed. My spawn will rise, an army of princes to lead us to victory. Your child will be amongst them."

Cecilia reached into the depths of her habit and removed a small, tin flask. Antonio licked his lips in anticipation.

"Drink of that vile poison. Course! Course through your *loyal* veins."

She approached carefully, kneeling to his level, his family holding him firm. Her umbrella enveloped them in a protective bubble of secrecy. She studied him as he hissed at her, his gums swollen, teeth seemingly too big for his gaunt cheeks.

"You have committed a grave sin, have you not?" She poked.

"I am the father that comes into the daughters of man. You sin in the eyes of only one."

She pulled the umbrella aside, turning towards the hushed crowd of mourners that had gathered to lay the dead to rest. Hunched under their own army of parasols, the women gawked with open mouths as the men stared, wide-eyed, unable to blink.

"Your family is watching, Antonio. Do you not think it proper to return to those you love?"

He snapped forward, their noses in danger of breaking, but he held fast, flapping his tongue. "I am loved! I am loved by *all*. I have siphoned him, though," he whispered. "There is nothing left to love. I suppose I shall infect your womb next!" A playful grin sprinted across his lips.

She stood quickly, uprooting the flask and dumping a clear liquid across his smugness. "I command you to speak the truth!"

He writhed, pitching his chest straight out, *cracking* his ribs in defiance. "Scum water!"

The flow burned a painful path across his eyes as she crossed her wrist, slapping him with the purification. "The power of Christ compels you to release Antonio! You have no worth here, you have no persuasion! *In nomine Patris et Filii-*"

Antonio severed the chains of his human captors, arms contracting as he dove, shoving his head into Cecilia's chest. She slid against the mud, heart thundering against the walls of her skull. Her stomach shrank, sucked up into her esophagus as she braced for the impact. His knees straddled her, burnt palms pinning her wrists into the rippling sea of refuse. His kin flopped in the rain, slipping as their dress shoes refused to grip the malleable soil.

"That shit scum water," he snarled, lips creasing her own. "You have only harmed my vessel."

He bared his teeth, the wild beast within tearing into her cheek and wrestling a portion of fat between his fangs. Like leather, her flesh tore with difficulty as he swung his head, his neck bulging from the exertion. Cecilia howled against the pain, rainwater seeping into her throat as he savored her. The wound pumped down her cheek and across the purity of her habit.

Suddenly, he departed, his eyes unsure of the force which called him back. The two men had torn him loose, launching him into a heap, his face smeared with dirt and blood.

A pistol sprung from a holster, the more impatient of the duo marching with a declaration of "*a fanabla!*" Antonio faced the barrel, unimpressed with the feeble attempt at bravado. Cecilia begged for a reconsideration, her fingers twinkling as she reached for the poor soul. The handgun erupted in the rain, opening the back of Antonio's head in a viscous stream.

UNKNOWN MALE #2: *Figlio di puttana!* [gunshot] [gunshot]
UNKNOWN FEMALE: [scream]

The thin, white tape unspooled the last of the revelation, the collection reel slapping the loose tail against the center gears. Petrosino mercifully stopped the racket.

"What happened next?" he pushed.

She returned her handkerchief to her cheek, finding the pain renewed, her hellish scream on the recording transporting her back into that moment when his teeth sank deep into her flesh.

"The sirens," she whispered, swallowing to moisten her throat. "The sirens of the police. They arrived, almost immediately. After the shooting."

"Did you know the deceased?"

"No. As I said before, I am aware of the family."

"They had gathered this morning to bury Annamaria, Antonio's sister," Battiato informed her. "Her corpse was found outside the city limits, her internal organs harvested. Do you believe that Antonio was responsible for her death?"

"That is a question that I do not have the authority or knowledge to answer."

"Sister," Petrosino began, sighing in a huff of frustration. "You have seen cases such as these, cases of extreme mental illness, delusion-"

"I am to think that you do not believe what has been recorded?" offering her hand across the evidence. "I understand, Inspector, that you may be skeptical of what has transpired, but I would be the first to admit I was lying."

"And you are not lying now, Sister?" Battiato sneered.

"I do not understand your insinuations," she confessed. "This man, this Antonio, had been corrupted, devastated by the death of his sister. Any one of us could attest to moments of weakness. Any one of us is susceptible to persuasion and power. This young man is no more guilty than you or I."

"He attacked you, did he not?" A new cigarette mounted for confidence.

"He was driven to it!" she snapped. "You do not understand the toll that is taken on the body. He was steered by an evil presence, by a-"

"Lucifer?" Petrosino smiled.

"You believe this to be a simple farce?" She turned away, disgusted.

"He was suffering from mental illness, Sister!" His fist clanging against the table, he had her attention again. "He butchered his own blood! He tried to cover himself in innocence, but the sight of his family poisoned him with guilt."

"How can you write him off so easily? Have you no respect for the dead?"

"How else do you explain what happened this morning?"

"*I told you*, his mind and body were being controlled."

Frustrated, Battiato pounded the recording device, pausing the confession. He massaged his forehead with vigor, ignoring his wasting cigarette as the ashes plummeted. "I can understand, Sister, how you might interpret his behavior. After all, they summoned you first, not us, correct?" He wiped his mouth, the anticipation giving him too much joy and hunger. "I am truly sorry that you had to be put in a position of vulnerability, but we cannot allow you to float such fanciful and outrageous claims. This...*freak* is responsible for his sister's death. Just as he is responsible for the others. He was ill, Sister. Very, very ill. Do you not think it noble to conclude this case, so that these families can sleep at night, eh?"

"And what if more bodies appear?" she demanded.

"We have had our share of homages in the past. We will take care of it."

"Are victories that hard to come by?"

"*Enough*," Petrosino demanded. He pointed towards the recorder. "When I turn this back on, you will swear that Antonio De Sio was under the influence of his own mental anguish, that he was disturbed. You were called to administer last rites. Do you understand?"

"What of the man who shot him? Will he not be prosecuted?"

"He is a hero!" Battiato shouted. "He single-handedly took down this bastard. We can easily overlook the weapons charge."

"And what if I refuse?" she asked.

"There has been quite a bit of backlash against your kind, has there not? Especially in connection with the De Sio family."

"I would not know anything about that," she barked.

"Sister, there is no need to lie. Suppose myself or Inspector Petrosino saw you leaving the De Sio household."

She found herself crumbling, the hardened soul losing the tiresome mask. "That would not be a crime, gentleman, I make house calls often to attend to the sick."

"Just like the others, we might have observed...more."

"How dare you!" she screamed. "I will not be treated in such a manner!"

"You are young," Petrosino smirked. "Slender. Tucked behind such clownish robes. You fit a mold, certainly not your fault entirely, but we can make things difficult for you and the many inhabitants of St. Benedict's."

"You would punish children simply for your own gain?" she stammered, eyelids shivering as she fought to keep them from clearing away the saline that lined the rim.

"It is the gain of the community, Sister. A murderer dead, a city safe from torment. Do not tell me that is worth nothing." He engaged the recording lever and edged the microphone closer to her mouth.

Confidence vanished as the wooden divider slid into its recesses, leaving only a dark, latticed screen between her and the profile of her supervisor. She spread her palms and clasped her hands back into prayer, allowing a bit of air to wick away the nervous moisture.

"Forgive me, Father, for I have sinned. It has been...four days since my last confession."

"Sister!" he chimed happily. "I was beginning to worry about you."

"I apologize for my absence. I have been away; attending to a few matters."

"The children will be most pleased."

She could determine his wide, white smile through the screen, one that brought her a bit of joy as well.

"Please, continue, Sister. I did not mean to interrupt."

Night had come, the rain continuing its lashing of the city stones. She stared at the filtered and octagonal colors that bled through the droplets, magnified by the headlamps of passing vehicles. They had removed the reel-to-reel unit, leaving her with a cup of stale and lukewarm coffee.

A nurse had cleaned the wound efficiently, applying a layer of bandage and tape to relieve her paranoia of having to pressurize it. She unpinned her coif, opening it carefully over the knot in her hair.

She knew it would take a blistering boil to remove the blood and dirt, but there were far more pressing matters than her dress.

Unfurling her bun, she combed her tired fingers through the bunched, chestnut strands, loosening them away from their habit of entangling themselves. She spiraled the long locks carefully, angling them upward, wrapping them around the base until a pin could lock the shape, just small enough to fit under the conservative covering. It had been some time since she allowed such pleasures outside of her designated quarters.

She raised her rosary, prepared to continue her penance, never taking her eyes off the still-breathing city. Her fingers slid over the beads, smearing the burnt flesh of Antonio De Sio.

Her cubby had been filled with well-wishes, handmade cards from students: colorful flowers and incorrect grammar. She treasured their support and would read each in her own time, a suitable gift of sweets in return for their concern. A letter of inquiry from a sister church; a collection of missed phone calls; note after note; it overwhelmed her. Only a few days absent and things had turned upside down. She tossed the haul onto her desk, seeking refuge on her undisturbed bed, her face buried in the single pillow.

An inconvenient knock attacked her door.

A sigh of frustration, smoothing out the wrinkles of her blanket and her habit.

"Come in," she ordered.

The door creaked, a small slit appeared.

"Sister Cecilia?"

"Father Endrizzi, is something the matter?"

He smiled, taken aback, but far from offended. "Of course not."

"Oh," she returned, sheepishly, "You do not normally venture to this side of the facility."

"True. A regret due to my schedule. I did not mean to disturb you. Do I pose an inconvenience?"

"Certainly not," she grinned, offering him her desk chair.

He closed the door behind him and sat casually, his leg crossing over the opposite knee. She returned to the bed and addressed the hem of her dress as she waited for him to continue. An uncomfortable silence rose between them, their eyes meeting, suddenly parting, unaware that the other was to begin.

"I..." he began. "I must confess that this is rather unorthodox."

She stood, "We can meet in the dining hall if you would like, or the sanct-"

He waved his palm, clearing the notion. "No, no. Meeting here is of no discomfort, I must make more time for you and the others. I have been neglecting my duties towards your concerns. That is a sin *I* must atone for."

She slowly retreated to the mattress, unsure of where this thread would unravel.

"I have thought about what you said this morning, in regard to your confession."

"I must apologize," she offered, fumbling with her hands as she tried to express her guilt. "I was very upset, and I should not have used that tone, nor should I-"

He paused her yet again. "Sister, you have done nothing wrong. I have thought about what you said. And, I have come to beg for your forgiveness. My words were not proper and the penance I suggested unjust."

▽△▽△

"Without any hesitation," she sobbed, refusing to wipe the river that ebbed from her eyes. "He executed him as if he were a mere nuisance, an insect nagging at his ears. I do not understand the cruelty that one must commit to be so numb to this evil."

"Did you attempt to stop this transgression?"

"Yes. But I could do little from my position."

Father Endrizzi mulled over her response. "Do you believe that the Devil had possessed this man?"

She stared down at her knees on the plush velvet. "I cannot be sure," she muffled into her chest. "Something evil drove this man, whether it be the Devil or his influence."

"You have a unique position here, Sister. I must confess that even I would be incapable of handling this burden that you seem fit to carry. As in all professions, we must fail. It is a natural order, is it not? We spread the gospel to those who will listen, save those who open their hearts, but we cannot lament those that do not follow. God will speak to them in time."

"And what of those who speak to the Devil? Who are corrupted by his tongue?"

"They too need our assistance, do they not?"

Though she heard the door open, she preferred to continue her prayers, waiting as the two sets of exhausted loafers shuffled inside. Petrosino laid a typed confession near her empty chair, unclipping a fountain pen from his breast pocket.

"We can offer you a ride home, Sister."

"No, thank you. I'd rather like to wash away this nightmare."

"I understand your insistence on retreating for a few days," Father Endrizzi offered, shifting against the hardwood of the confessional bench. "You know that myself and the others love you dearly and that we are certainly capable of shepherding you through any trauma that might still be lingering."

"I know, Father. I...I simply needed a moment to quell my fears."

"Have you spoken to the police? Certainly, they might be able to shed more light on the prosecution."

She swallowed her sins.

Her penmanship was perfect as she elongated the loop of her Z. She returned the cap to the pen and placed it on the stinging metal table.

"No," she lied. "I believe they will handle it in due time."

"O-oh," he stammered. "An inspector had dropped by the front office, only a few days ago, looking for you. I had thought for sure that you had spoken to him regarding this matter."

"What was his name?"

"I did not have the chance to inquire. He did leave a card for you, I believe. Perhaps it will put you at ease to know they are going to proceed in the right direction?"

"Yes, Father."

"I cannot abide by the methods of your sudden absence, though I understand fully now why. You must atone for the sin of abandoning your duties, Sister. I ask that you pray the rosary until you feel compelled to rid yourself of guilt. A visit to the children would also rest their worry."

She had abandoned her umbrella in the cemetery, the inspectors shooing her into the night, slamming shut the precinct's wide, pine green doors without thought to her safety. The cobblestone streets made quick work of her balance, each step ending and beginning with water filling her simple, black shoes.

Her coif protected her briefly before it absorbed the cold weight of the storm. She was miserable, regretting her decision to proudly storm off into the darkness on her own. Street lamps buzzed with golden beams, but the hour meant that traffic too slumbered.

"*Minchia!*" she cursed, wrapping her arms around her chest to stave off the chills.

A neon invitation flickered against the downpour.

She had no choice, ducking down a stoop into the establishment. Their judging eyes froze her, the patrons of the bar unsure of what had just washed ashore. They were the miserable, the tired, the half-drunk, and always drunk. She nodded with embarrassment, awkwardly approaching the bar, her shoes echoing against the backdrop of a pop song.

The wider conversation awaited her involvement. The bartender advanced tentatively, wrapping a towel over his shoulder. "Can I help you?"

"Y-y-es," she spat, staring at the swollen jaw of the elderly proprietor, his hair flush with grease. "I need to call a taxi. Can I use your telephone?"

"Customers only," he replied.

Water dripped from her soaking form into a puddle at her feet. The song ended; time's up.

"I'll buy you a drink," waved a hand down the bar. She was older, a tight leather jacket of canary wrapped around her shoulders, cut just below her breasts. She waddled towards Cecilia in thin heels.

"What's your pleasure, Sister? Wine?" followed by a hearty laugh. The dwellers returned to their empty conversations as someone had taken the bait, and the burden, away from them.

A smile, Cecilia understood the joke, it had just grown stale. "Wine would be fine."

The woman shook the ice in her empty glass as a reminder, the bartender retreating towards the end of the liquor, dusting off a bottle of red.

"Lost?" the woman asked.

"N-no," Cecilia assured. "I just need to get home."

The cork popped like an injured mouse, the glass gurgling as he filled it halfway. He set the drink in front of her, "*Grazi.*"

He selected a bottle of gin, a carafe of vermouth rosso, a large vial of Campari, and set to work.

"I am Giada," the woman offered, extending her hand.

"Cecilia," accepting.

"I hope you do not mind my appearance." She gestured towards her revealing outfit, adjusting a tight, strapless top of black and white stripes.

"I am unfamiliar with much of the day's fashion, but I do not judge those for trying."

Giada smiled, "You *are* pretty, in a plain sort of way. What happened to your face there?" She shoved a finger to the bandage as Cecilia pulled back.

"Just an accident, a scratch really."

The bartender shaved the peel of an orange and drooped it over the side of a fresh glass. He slid it towards the half-drunk and she obliged. "Don't forget about the phone, Salvatore."

He grumbled, expecting a big tip for his hospitality, but gave into the paying customer's demand. A beige rotary phone was offered to them. "Local only."

Cecilia picked up the receiver and hung her index in the numbered guide, searching for a sequence. She hung up, laughing nervously. "I do not know who to call."

Giada polished off half of her drink before swinging the phone to her ear. "I'll get you home. I should have this number tattooed on my arm!"

Father Endrizzi leaned forward in her desk chair, clasping his hands around hers. "Your penance was harsh, Sister. We all face adversity, and sometimes we must face it alone. Do not feel obligated to complete the rosary at my request, you have nothing to be guilty of. The world did not set itself ablaze in your absence. I am sorry and regretful for the way I interpreted your truth."

"I do not know what to say," she admitted.

"Rest, my child. Be sure to see Sister Raphaela to inspect your wound, I would hate for you to be in any discomfort."

He released her hands, rising from the chair. "I must be off. Will you promise to speak with me if the need arises?"

She looked up at him, nodding. "I will." She stood as he exited.

"*Buona notte*, Sister."

She painted a smile as he closed the door, leaving her with her own guilty thoughts.

The soap seemed to do little under the near-scalding flow. She adjusted the petaled valves, calling for a harsher pour. She scraped the dried mud and plasma from beneath her short fingernails, rinsing them in the plugged sink.

A bloated horse-fly fluttered past her, attaching itself to the mirror above. It dragged its legs across its mucus-spewing mouth, cleaning its tarsus, inspecting the minute flavors. A second buzzed, staking its own claim on the mirror. The inquisitive pair danced, roaming aimlessly. The chorus of their brothers and sisters rose as she witnessed the cesspool of vomit and feces that gurgled behind her.

She plunged her face into the sink, washing free the stain of her failed exorcism. She breached the surface, sucking in the putrid stench. A gaunt figure stood behind her, within an arm's length. Flies cavorted across his bare chest, drinking the fresh blood that dripped from the incisions of a thorny crown. A heavy wave of vinegar joined the fray as the vision opened his toothless mouth. Her eyes began to fill with ink, sloshing violently as he stared at her with an equally soulless expression.

She awoke, screaming violently, toppling her chair as she

slammed her back into a chalkboard. Her students roared with fright, curling away from her terrifying ejection. She continued her fear, collapsing to her knees as tears exploded from her eyes and she could hold on no longer.

The congregation of peers huddled at the threshold of the nurse's station. They whispered concerns of insomnia, malnutrition, and psychosis. She pretended not to hear them as a thermometer dug under her tongue.

"Don't speak," she was ordered, lest her temperature provide a false positive.

A defiant clearing of the throat drew the gossip from Cecilia to Father Endrizzi. "I believe the pews need to be restocked."

"Yes, Father," they chimed, disappointed.

He watched the gaggle until they had cleared the corner, stepping into the examination room, dragging a somber disposition.

"Mph mmph whmph ymph thmphng," she mumbled.

"Don't speak!" the nurse repeated, slapping Cecilia across the knee. She ripped the thermometer free, dragging a thin line of saliva. "She's fine. Blood pressure is normal. Breathing is a little erratic, but otherwise fine, Father."

"May we have a moment to speak?"

The nurse nodded, stowing the instrument in a jar of blue antibacterial fluid.

"I am fine, Father."

His eyebrows practically soared off his face, his incredulous expression holding back judgment.

"I just need some time," she muttered.

"I agree wholeheartedly."

She turned toward him, curious as to whether this led to expulsion or redemption.

"Sister, you have been under a tremendous amount of stress lately. I can see that it has taken its toll. Sister Carlotta tells me you haven't eaten in over a week."

"My stomach..." was the excuse.

"I am strongly urging you to take a sabbatical. I received word this week that our mission in Venezuela is in need of help. Perhaps the tropical climate would suit you."

"Perhaps..."

He placed his hand upon her quivering shoulder. She withdrew, the weight seemingly endless, pressing her flat against the green and white tile. Realizing his faux pas, he restrained himself.

"Cecilia," he promised, "weakness is not wholly weakness. It is our way of strengthening ourselves, hardening what makes us incomplete."

"I am afraid, Father!" she faced him, eyes bloodshot, corners leaking down to her chin. "I have seen the face of the unholy, I have felt his jaws. What is to prevent my own soul from being swallowed?"

"You have performed exorcisms before, under supervision and on your own. What do you believe has changed?"

"What if the innocent are not to be forgiven? What if this is a conjuration of their mind? Are we filling our heads with nonsense? Covering our own insecurities and avoiding the truth?"

"This man who attacked you, do you believe he was possessed? Or, do you simply think he was purposefully evil, without intervention?"

"I cannot say. He spoke like so many others, with such vitriol, as if sulfur churned in his stomach. But does the world care? Do we need a scapegoat to pin these sins upon?"

"That is what Satan represents, does he not?"

"But does he pull the strings, or do we pull them?"

"That...I cannot answer, only God can reveal his true purpose. It would behoove us to pray, will it not?"

"I do not have the heart to speak with God."

He was of no help to her now, standing quietly, watching her sob into her pooling palms.

"I suggest you retire to your quarters," he said flatly. "I will have Sister Elena conduct the rest of your classes. We will discuss your leave of absence in the morning."

He pivoted, marching back into the hallway. The nurse approached, hands folded in front of her stomach. "Can you prescribe a sedative?" he whispered.

She nodded, squeezing his forearm with assurance.

Cecilia wept.

Dehydration had set in, yet she continued to cry, curled into a helpless ball, facing the back wall of her quarters. She had left the orange bulb of her table lamp burning bright, a companion in the sudden unfamiliarity of the room.

The shadows played peculiar shapes: elongated triangles, rhombi intersecting in chain-like patterns. It appeared above her, rushing from the darkness, just a face: blood vessels under the eyes popped and pooling beneath the skin; teeth sharpened like an abhorrent prehistoric miscalculation; a pale blue and white layer of flesh; eyes wide and piercing black; lips flush with old fuel.

It spread its cloaked arms, dousing the light.

Like shattering glass, day had broken. She sat upright, her lower back bearing the brunt of the exercise. Slowly she surveyed the room, beating back the notion that she was being observed. She feared Father Endrizzi would burst through the modest wooden barrier and toss her from the bell tower at any moment. Fleeing was not an option, he *wanted* her to take care of herself, but his tone and his insistence felt more like a padlock upon her life's mission.

Rubbing the dried mucus from the corners of her eyes, she shambled to her desk, picking through the previous day's mail, hoping to find something to preoccupy her. The children had been most understanding, the cards of encouragement and prayer filling her with pride and a sense of security.

GEt well.

we mis Yuo.

We love you veery mutch.

Positive symbols flourished in flowers and hearts, their internal filters far from forming. They spoke truthfully and without hesitation.

She ran her thumb over the logo for the Abbey of St. Bartolomea Capitanio, creasing the simple book, propped open so that a crucifix could emerge, backed by a rising, ringed sun. She set the correspondence aside, selecting a yellowing envelope beneath it.

There was no return address, just her last name, hastily scrawled across the front. She turned it over, finding a blank white card attached.

She peeled back the fibrous material, fighting against the glue. It had been greased by a sticky material, honey perhaps, or an unclean hand. The business card proudly sported the *Polizia di Stato's* coat of arms: a lion furiously clawing with a silver sword at the book of law and the torches of peace.

The Inspector must have left it, the one Father Endrizzi seemed so keen on her meeting. She threw open the door to her quarters and rushed into the hall, paying no mind to her appearance, her nightgown fluttering, collecting dust as she tried to raise it above her ankles.

She fumbled with the receiver, spinning the rotary and keying in the number printed on the card. She prayed this was not a coincidence, but a sign. As the line rang, she was caught in Limbo, afraid that the gates of Hell would answer, forcing her to acknowledge and accept her divine fate.

EVERYTHING REDUCED
TO ONE PLAN

III

The road simply vanished.

Asphalt dribbled across the edge of the tree line, thick oak and ochre larches huddling in row-like patterns begging drifters to lose themselves within. Rain had continued to fall, the atmosphere a blanket of peace and war. A loose rumble of thunder softened in the distance as he dragged on a damp cigarette.

It had been decades, but the landmarks remained the same: the crumbling lean-to; the channel that ran parallel to the road, disappearing into the mouth of a stone sewer as it snaked beneath the forest. He cocked his head towards the motorized *thwump* of his vehicle's windshield wipers and nodded.

They would disembark and continue on foot.

The iron bell clattered nonstop, the receiver swiped, the message stored or forwarded, then silence. For a moment.

The phone rang again, the piercing tone vibrating forcefully between his ears, his palms mashing together, trying to funnel his anxiety away from a crude comment. He adjusted his thin, black tie, smoothing it over his wrinkled dress shirt. The leather bench was rather comfortable, but his watch warned him he could not appreciate it much longer.

A parade of chattering, young students marched past, coordinated in an inky blue, led by an elderly nun, cane in hand, stomping from carpet to wood.

"Inspector?"

He raised his head over the children, eyeing the towering priest, his hand outstretched.

"I am Father Endrizzi," shaking forcefully. "I must apologize for the wait."

"I had requested Sister Zampa," annoyed, the lobby's incessant hymns of nuisance boiling his patience.

"Yes, I am afraid that she is indisposed at the moment. May I be of service?"

"Unfortunately, your Holiness, I must speak with her. A private matter."

"Of course. If you would be so kind as to leave your information, Sister Elena will make sure she receives it." He offered his hand once more, a reluctant single pump and the conversation faded with his echoing footsteps.

"Do you have a phone number or address that you would like to leave, inspector?" Sister Elena asked.

Into the pocket of his overcoat, fumbling for the stack. They were stained and unprofessional, a former meal sticking to the face.

"Uh...here."

The Sister nodded, placing the card in the empty cubby.

Why could he not find the *b* key?

"*Porca miseria!*" he muttered, finally pecking the letter into his tedious weekly report. "I cannot stomach this shit anymore."

"Mmm?" his deskmate cooed from behind the safety of a fanned newspaper.

"These reports are driving me insane, I'm simply repeating myself week after week."

"Just an excuse to cover everyone's asses, make sure we're not wasting taxpayer time."

"I should be wasting my time canvassing houses, trying to make arrests."

The thin, recycled paper fluttered as the uninterested continued his journey into national news.

The typewriter *clucked* once more, back to hunting for the grammatically pleasing adjective to describe his unproductive shifts.

"Fuckin' let go of me!" The cry ripped across the station floor, drawing the attention of those with little to do.

Two uniformed officers struggled as a bleeding street rat resisted their advancement.

"Fuck you!" he writhed. "I'll fuckin' kill all of you!" Though handcuffed, his shoulder produced enough force to knock back one of his handlers, pitching him to the tiled floor. The suspect rammed the still-standing partner, plowing him back and denting the thin drywall. A nightstick roared across his knee, imploring him to genuflect. A crack across the skull and the perpetrator slipped unconscious, his head *pounding* the ground.

"Get this bastard into containment!" came the instructions, another two added to help drag the body through a set of double doors and out of mind.

"That's the kind of shit I should be doing." Nobody heard him. Nobody cared, really. Enough crime solved itself, it did not need a boost by the apologetic and uninspired.

His desk phone screamed for his attention, his finger slipping, adding an *i* instead of an *o*. He savored the vitriol he unleashed under his breath at the damned machine. Scooping up the phone, he sighed, "This is Zampa."

"No return address still?" he asked, flipping the open envelope, inspecting for curiosity.

"Nothing. Just like the other ones."

The office was a disaster: bookshelves lined haphazardly with the works of peers; knickknacks from the well-intentioned; stacks of manila folders vomiting with paperwork, leads, transcripts; a corkboard of ideas, football scores, photos of *mafiosos*. He had been in this cave many times, the blinds always drawn, though somehow the randomly placed desk lamps provided enough to see.

"You have to let me print this, Frankie."

"Would that not be taking away from the news regarding Pio XII?"

"What news?"

Frankie held his hands out, "Tomasso, please," adding a smirk.

"Half the fucking paper is dedicated to a retrospective. It's fucking boring. You know there are other letters."

"Then print the goddamn thing!" He tossed the unread letter across the desk at the editor, knocking aside his nameplate.

"Don't you think I'm trying to help you?" Tomasso shot back. "I brought you the others! I deserve a little credit for finding those bodies."

"*You* didn't find them."

"And you would have?"

Frankie could not deny the assistance provided. A frustrated sigh zipped through his clenched jaw. "Why print this? Why now?"

Tomasso dug under the refuse piled atop his desk, snatching a folded copy of *Il Messaggero* and flinging it at him. "That's why," he pointed.

The headline had the all the components of an immediate demotion: *Slain De Sio Heir Revealed as Countryside Harvester*. A stark photograph of the shooter standing bravely over the slain and bloodied son came equipped with a caption of its own: *Marco De Sio [left] intervenes as his cousin, Antonio De Sio [right], confesses to murders.*

"Bullshit," Frankie whispered. "Bullshit! What is this, huh?"

"My contact says it's true."

"Did this story run?"

"You're looking at the nightly edition, just about to head to print."

"Then you don't need the letter."

"One would think, but you and I both know little Antonio can barely string together a few sentences, let alone a sermon's worth of hate and introspection." He offered the letter back to Frankie. "A bit too calculated for my taste. The sister falls victim to this madman and the brother conveniently takes the hit? Throw in his little tirade at the funeral and you have a dosage fit for consumption. *Guilt* overcame him."

Accepting the letter once more, he excised the thick folds within, unfurling them.

"This isn't over, Francesco," Tomasso urged. "Maybe not enough evidence to find the real bastard, but enough to reverse this falsity."

Lost in the typed correspondence, Frankie barely looked up. "Let me think about it."

"I can keep my floor manager at bay for another few hours, but I *will* print this."

"Just wait for a statement, will you give me that at least?"

"Fair is fair." Tomasso stood and extended his arm.

Frankie accepted. "May I keep this?" indicating the letter.

"You know that's a copy," he smiled.

We will all bathe in putrefaction, present to him that we are leveled, that we are clay, molded into the hammer, spear, and flame of justice. He will rule once more, through us, and only one shall be chosen.

A final gift has been presented to the Father, the vessel needed for transmogrification. There is little time for transportation. In my condition, I cannot guarantee its safety. I call upon thee to settle this affair with care and diligence. You will find it wrapped in linen, as ritual dictates, stored beneath the ground where the harsh elements cannot penetrate so liberally.

I am afraid I cannot allow myself to further participate in such a fashion, I have completed that which I am indebted. I have satisfied my Father's request, and I have stolen the rotten and the despicable from the soil in his honor. I have been called to a higher purpose now, one which will bring torment to those who did not believe. Blood shall vomit from the soil, the sun shall be draped in sackcloth, the seas will putrefy, the heavens will seethe, and we shall worship at his feet. The final sacrifice has been prepared, allow the ceremony to commence, allow our Father to plow the rewarding fields of society and reap what he is owed. I am but a humble servant and-

"More?"

He disconnected from the haunting lines and stared blankly at the waitress. The pot of steaming coffee beckoned him.

"Yes, *grazi.*"

She topped him off, spinning daintily as she attended to other empty cups.

Frankie thumbed through the pages, finding numbered instructions, a crude map, more ramblings. Soda water sloshed underneath his skull, his foot tapping an anxious beat.

He dug through his overcoat slung around the café chair, extracting the newspaper draft. He began reading the sensationalism, cooling off the rim of his cup before slurping the black liquid. Tomasso had done well with his limited information, the poetic prose drawing him in like the pulp novels of his youth.

He recognized the name immediately.

The cup missed the saucer awkwardly, spilling the excess over the lip. A few ruffled bills would suffice, tossed onto a napkin. He gathered his things and folded his coat over his arm, dashing for the exit. It had been several years since he had spoken to his sister, but he supposed the circumstances warranted his intrusion.

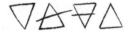

He had lost count of the number of cigarettes he had lit, choked down, and stamped out in his rage. His fingers burned enough to ignite the tobacco on its own, but he held off from releasing any fury, conserving it for the-

The driver's side door practically exploded as he burst out, whipping it shut. He allowed a blue sedan to glide past, splashing him lightly with the collected water of the potholed avenue. Marching, overcoat loose for maximum reach, he crossed under the arch of the station entrance, flashing his badge to a patrolman who lazily waved him through.

The duo was strolling towards an issued patrol car, a uniformed officer beckoning them from the passenger window.

Petrisone spotted him as he rose from the chamber of his lighter, dragging back and issuing a crass smile. "Zampa!" he offered warmly, arms outstretched.

Frankie greeted him with the back of his service revolver, cracking him across the nose. Petrisone erupted in a fountain of blood, crashing to his rear, belting an agonizing whimper as he clutched the broken cartilage.

The weapon spun in Frankie's hand, the hammer slammed back, barrel shoved into Battiato's unprepared expression.

"What the fuck!?" Petrisone bleated.

Frankie shifted, aiming at the stuck pig. "Shut up!" Back to Battiato. "*Antonio De Sio.*"

The uniformed officer attempted to de-escalate the situation, opening the passenger side door. Frankie kicked it shut, bruising the heavy-set intervener's arm. "*Don't you fucking move.* Antonio De Sio! Why did you lie?"

"What are you talking about?" Battiato asked.

"You pinned the Harvester murders on this fucking slug. You know he didn't kill those people."

"We got a signed confession from that cunt," Petrisone coughed.

A boot to his jaw released a string of splintered teeth. "Then how do you explain this?" He tossed the yellowing envelope to the still-upright partner. "Another letter. Instructions on where to find another body. Directions, ingredients for a black mass. We both know that fuck De Sio could barely cut his own fucking food. He's a spoiled, rich *monello*, not some religious zealot."

A crowd had formed, bunched together like asparagus at the entrance to the precinct, an unattended phone blaring within.

Battiato threw the paperwork back at Frankie. "We caught the fuck and his cousin put a bullet in his head. He was insane, Zampa. We beat you to it. He flipped out at his own sister's funeral from the guilt and confessed. Don't tell me you're defending his father!"

The barrel burrowed into the aging detective's cheek. "I've worked this case for months. De Sio? *Figlio di puttana!* I would be no better than him, pinning this shit on his son. You want to bust him? Want to make him suffer? Hit his heroin distribution, the bordellos, where he makes his money. You wanted to pad your collars and you fucked up." He backed off, keeping the revolver trained. "He's still out there," pointing arbitrarily into the distance. "Another body turns up? *Dio non voglia!* They will come for *you*."

He holstered the weapon, shutting the flap of his overcoat. He wiped Petrisone's blood against Battiato's cream button-up. "You ever call my sister a cunt again, it'll be more than just your teeth you're gonna lose."

Frankie would not entertain a retort, he had resolved the small vendetta. As he stomped back to his vehicle, the heaven's ripped further, dumping a flood upon the street. The car started just as angrily as he commanded, zipping around the corner and barreling head first into the storm.

The electricity in the warehouse had been severed, the breaker's ripped from the walls, the attending investigators forced now to navigate by flashlight.

"How old is the body?" Frankie asked, following the beam of the coroner in front of him. The narrow staircase moaned as they ascended, spiraling around a central tower, filing one at a time.

"She's no more than eighteen, maybe nineteen."

"That's not what I asked, Alphonse." He tiptoed around a snaking rubber cable that had been run up the risers.

They disembarked near the top floor, two uniformed officers guarding the double doors, already roped off with cautionary tape.

Alphonse paused and faced Frankie, pushing against his chest with his gloved hand. "This one..." His voice faded with a hint of reflection. Perhaps it was just the harsh glow of the flashlight, but moisture formed in the corner of his eyes. "I'm a religious man, Francesco." He poked him now with each syllable. "I cannot abide by what has happened here today. This girl..." His lips shivered, his voice cracking against the horror that he had witnessed. "This girl did not deserve such ceremony."

Frankie could not recognize the significance of the statement, his eyes turning towards the crime scene, preparing solely on the recommendation of his coroner. "Stay here," he cautioned.

Nodding to the uniformed officers, they gripped the copper handles and swung the doors inward.

She had been suspended above the floor, rusted hooks, capable of stringing up massive sides of beef, had punctured through her wrists, pulling her wingspan apart. The process had been repeated through her ankles, linked chains running taught to the ground. She had been dissected, the incision running from the base of her neck down to her crotch, the skin folded back, secured with more chain. Beneath her, a makeshift altar had been constructed of pallets and cloth, soaked now in her blood.

Like a lotus, she bloomed, her organs completely removed, an empty cavity bearing itself to those who came to genuflect. Hundreds of candles still flickered, their once tall and angelic towers collapsing within as the wick burned optimistically and the wax poured over the rim.

Her head lay limp, mouth bloodied, eyes wrapped in jagged, black fabric, stolen from the altar cloth.

Frankie ducked under the cautionary tape and swept his flashlight against the loft. He avoided a heavy streak of red that had spilled from the body and spread to the doors, abruptly ending and curling back into the room in a wide circle. The age of the building allowed the city air to funnel through the rotting, planked walls. The chains rattled against their tension, raising and lowering the body subtly as if the poor girl were trying to escape her fate.

An ornate chalice had been discarded on the altar, overturned, the contents dry. A distinct imprint of a bottom lip had been left behind. Despite the incessant rain eroding the city, he heard the soft whispers. He checked her mouth, the flashlight stuttering, but she had not moved.

The altar.

He crouched beneath the links, avoiding disturbing the sacrifice further. She had been tattooed along her spine, just like the others. It was Latin, confirmed by a scholar at Sapienza, though a mixture of symbols that would need translation.

An inverted crucifix had been slathered in greasepaint, the carved depiction decapitated, hung on the wall behind her.

"We've got power!"

The muffled declaration signaled the awakening of tripod-mounted work-lights stationed at the back of the room. The high-intensity beams blinded him, his unstable footwork frightening the inhabitants beneath the altar.

Gray and white wings fluttered in hysteria as a flock of pigeons released themselves. Frankie shielded his eyes as he collapsed in the whirlwind, losing his flashlight. The diseased birds took refuge in the trusses above, cooing softly as they congratulated themselves on avoiding defeat.

"Jesus!" Alphonse called. "Everything all right?"

"Yeah, yeah," he waved, turning over onto his knees. "Fucking rats." He fumbled for his lantern, blasting the high beam across the nesting grounds overhead. A catwalk had proved the perfect height for their refuge. He traced a ladder from the far edge down to the floorboards.

He snapped his fingers towards Alphonse. "Camera. *Camera.*"

The coroner retreated to a white, plastic case, removing the thirty-five-millimeter body from a foam core. He attached a tele-photo lens to the mount and handed it to Frankie.

An errant drip traveled from loose shingles to cracked beams, sneaking its way downward, pelting the already slippery rungs of the ladder. He traversed the nuisance, wiping his hands dry periodically against his already wet overcoat. Popping his legs over the side of the catwalk, he dismounted. The pigeons seemed to pay him no mind as he handled the length of the walkway, positioning himself in the middle of the room.

He cocked the advancement trigger and placed the viewfinder to his eye. The flash ignited, and his feathered companions exploded in fright once more, rushing through a battered hole in the ware-house roof.

$$\triangledown\,\,\triangle\!\!\!\!-\,\,\triangledown\!\!\!\!-\,\,\triangle$$

He would never claim to be artistic, the flash barely enough to caress the floor, but the developer had done a commendable job, enhancing the brightness, revealing the gigantic pentagram scrawled in the victim's blood. It was the first appearance of the symbol; the inverted crucifix, the chalice, the tattoo, they had been tested in victims past.

Spreading the photographs he had acquired across his already overfed desk, he studied the empty corpses in no particular order. No two were similar in their minutiae. The perpetrator had been overly cautious at first, each body free of external injuries. He had stalked them, making sure he funneled them perfectly. No struggle, no need to crease the fine leather. Men, women, children, he had preyed upon all of them, relieving them of their mechanisms. This was far from sexual, the lack of penetration hinting at a sadism that bathed in the joy of butchering.

Using a codex watermarked with the Università di Roma's insignia, he carefully translated the symbols of the latest cryptic branding: *fornix*. He cycled through a rubbery legal pad, searching for his collection. He wound the excess over the top and slid his pen down the two columns. He had seen this word before: *proditor, tristitia, moechus, limbus, infantium, bestialitas, luxuria, gula, avaritia, ira, invidia, superbia*.

No, he must have been mistaken.

The borrowed banker's lamp stacked atop the pile of dossiers poured a harsh blanket of light across his materials, the hour late, his eyes burnt and his stomach threatening to secede. The swing doors *creaked* as a peer joined him, the early shift in danger of encroaching on his solitude. He cocked his head to acknowledge the early riser but was left with only the flapping of the hinges.

The bastard had become sloppy, his methods hasty, mistake after mistake, none glaring enough to reveal anything more. His victim's struggled, saw the eerie figure lurking in the shadows, shielded themselves from his wrath. Either way, they ended up on Frankie's desk, his neck buried in witnesses with poor vision, telephone tips, and an increasingly tenuous relationship with–

"*Minchia!*" he blurted.

The attending officer at the front desk gawked for a moment at the tired soul that hurried to his post.

"The evening edition, you still have it?" Frankie asked.

A shrug. Digging in the wastebasket.

The officer slid him a wet and soiled copy of *Il Messaggero*. "All yours," he huffed, attending to more pressing matters.

Final Letter from Countryside Harvester Raises Doubt on De Sio Confession. It was bulky but ultimately true. He skimmed through the unapproved copy, his name appearing several times, as was the harrowing phrase, "No comment." He knew this would run again in the morning, perhaps with more embellishment.

The faint bell of his telephone drew him from the bad press, trotting down the hall, and through the swing doors.

"Zampa," he answered, tossing the paper with the rest of his case.

"They said you were working late, I did not believe it, personally."

"Have you read the paper, Alphonse?"

"I had nothing to do with that."

"Well, perhaps we can bring some clarity to this hearsay."

"I just received the toxicology reports. We found trace elements of ketamine and a benzodiazepine sedative, midazolam." Papers rustled as Alphonse clarified his statements. "There was a small insertion just above the collarbone, possibly from a needle. This kind of concoction is generally reserved for animals, though."

"He tried to correct his mistake," Frankie theorized.

"Possibly. Chloroform can be effective at close range, but the risk involved his certainly much higher."

"If he didn't approach her in person, how did he inject her?"

"My guess would be a dart from a considerable distance. The injection site was pretty bruised, which would account for weight and distribution method. A rifle could provide that kind of speed and intensity."

"She was on holiday," Frankie remembered, "near Gran Sasso."

"She ventures off into the woods, he tags her with enough sedative to bring her to his sanctuary, and *here we are*."

"Anything else?"

"Yeah, another first," he sighed. "She was pregnant."

"Jesus," Frankie leaned forward, palm to his head to beat back the horrific thought.

"From the distention of the belly, the size of the breasts, and the swelling along the ankles and wrists, she was about thirty weeks along."

"Fuck." Some time to reflect in the darkness of the cruelty. "The baby?"

"You know I can't answer that. She was in the third trimester, if he removed it before he killed her, it's entirely possible it's still alive."

"That wouldn't match his motive."

"He's self-correcting, Frankie. Anything is possible now."

His eyes fawned through the physical world around him, glazing over in sad futility and a retrospection of deep hatred and protectiveness.

"Get some rest, Francesco," Alphonse suggested.

Called from the daydream, he blinked, releasing a tear, a reaction to his drying eyes. "Yeah," he whispered. The receiver bucked into the cradle as he regretfully turned toward the unorganized mess, slipping his face into the comfort of his palms.

His own haggard handwriting had stuck to his cheek, the drool of exhaustion fusing the legal paper to his skin. The toll of his phone has shocked him into a dazed coherency. His deskmate, masked by the morning's paper and Tomasso's fear-mongering headline, offered no nicety. The sun had risen painfully, Frankie's eyes wholly unprepared.

The phone refused to retreat, the internal bell chiming happily, pleasuring in its duty. The bare minimum distance between the receiver and the plunger would silence it. His hand hovered. He expected to be reprimanded.

The speaker slid against his ear, waiting to be clued in.

"*Buongiorno?*" It was phrased so timidly, the female timber unrecognizable.

He cleared his throat, ripping the stuck page from his cheek. "This is Inspector Zampa, how can I help you, *signora?*

"Francesco?"

"Yes?"

"It...it is Cecilia."

"Jesus! Oh, shit," a smile. "I apologize. Cici, my God. I-Where are you?"

"Sister Elena, correct?"

The young girl nodded as she guided him through the rectory. They preceded down a set of carpeted risers, the landing leveling into a series of private quarters lining each side, the stubby, arched doors barely tall enough to duck under. Frankie admired the stained wood, the poetic craftsmanship of each carefully selected piece. Wrought iron decorations lined the ornate entrances; crucifixes and religious iconography splitting up the monotony of stained glass that funneled in a prism's worth of beauty on a sunny day.

"Sister Cecilia, she has lived here long?"

"Several years, I believe. I started only this past summer."

She dropped him in front of the correct room. "Thank you." He handed her a wad of damp currency, her instinct to awkwardly accept and provide a courtesy smile. "For the poor box," he clarified.

"Of course. Have a blessed day, inspector."

He nodded, waiting for her to grant him some space.

Whether it had been the money in his pocket or his anxiety, his hands had become drenched. He dried them against his trousers, shaking them like a shaggy mutt. He gripped the accented lever, prepared to enter.

"It is customary to knock before entering a private audience."

He cocked his head at Sister Elena as she had paused at the end of the hallway, providing the suggestion with the utmost respect.

He smirked, wrapping his knuckles across the center of the door. Footsteps hurried from the opposite side of the room. The tumbler rolled into place as his sister's face, framed by the security of her coif, greeted him.

They did little to foster the joy that would normally be reserved for a moment such as this. Her eyes welled, her fingers to her lips to prevent the ugly curl that would erupt if she allowed herself to give in.

"Cici," he whispered with much amazement. "Or is it Sister Zampa now?"

"Did you ever think I would be so proper?" She squeaked.

He could not hide his smile. "I never thought we'd see you again."

"Inspector, hmmm? A revolver too?"

"Yes, but barely. They considered me for marksman school, I had to talk them out of it."

"You and David always had such keen eyes."

"I'm an old man now," he chuckled. "Not much for these eyes to see."

She broke the chatter, embracing him. His arms flew outward, unprepared. He finally settled, returning her squeeze as they reconnected in the middle of the empty hallway.

$$\triangledown \, \bowtie \, \triangledown \, \triangle$$

He admired a photograph of Cecilia enveloped by the smiling

faces of her students.

"They must adore you," he commented, turning towards her as she sat on the edge of the mattress.

"I taught them during a mission trip to Honduras. The children here are wonderful, but they talk back," she joked.

He had removed his overcoat, his sleeves rolled to the elbow, airing his perspiration.

"I apologize that I cannot offer you anything to drink."

He swatted aside the notion, "Just like Papa, I've got to moderate." He spun her desk chair, carefully taking a seat against the unforgiving wood.

"Do you know why I'm here, Cici?"

She lost her smile, nodding in a long arc. He produced the unprinted draft of *Il Messaggero* and handed it to her.

The blotted image of De Sio's corpse flung her back to the cemetery, the weight he had applied as he pounced, his teeth sinking into her flesh, the warm ejection boiling her as the cold rain drowned her.

"What happened that day?"

She broke from her memory. "Do you know what I do, Francesco?"

His brows furrowed, taken aback by the question.

"When I first joined the church, I would make pastoral calls to the sick. I would anoint them, pray with them, hear their concerns. I offered comfort during difficult times; when we are the most expectant of God's interference.

"It is considered tedious by the other sisters, something to keep the youngest busy and humble, but I rather enjoyed my conversations. In Honduras, I was called to the bedside of a young woman in the throes of a disheartening illness. She was in considerable pain, wailing for hours, her bed soaked with sweat."

$$\triangledown \,\, \triangle\!\!\!\triangledown \,\, \triangledown \,\, \triangle$$

"*Yo beberé la sangre de la perra!*" The raven-haired invalid flopped violently against the straw mattress, her hands bound to the posts of her bed with torn sheets. Perspiration bulged from swollen pores as she arched her back, peeling back her lips, screaming in the guttural howl of a demonic presence.

Cecilia stood at the back of the room, frozen, as the poor girl's family attempted to restrain her.

"*Este coño es mío! Es mío!*" She gargled in a baritone impossible, punctuating the vowels with an ear-splitting shriek.

A hunched, elderly woman shuffled past Cecilia, a ceramic bowl of water and a dirty rag filling her care. She dunked the cloth, swimming in the clear liquid, breaching, squeezing, unfurling. The cool relief touched the burning forehead, releasing a series of resistant howls. The bed stomped the modest stone floor like a judgment gavel, plumes of dust rolling towards the corners.

The mother approached, placing her hand on Cecilia's shoulder, averting her gaze.

"What is wrong with her?" the unprepared nun asked. She shook her head, realizing her mistake. "*¿Qué está mal con ella?*"

The brave woman could crumble at any moment, yet she remained transfixed on the performance, her daughter to break the seal as long as she was by her side. She dared not look away, but she answered with conviction, "*El diablo la ha poseído.*"

"I prayed. I blessed…I blessed her with oil and water. I read her scripture until my voice faded. I sat for days, comforting this girl. She spoke of despicable things, claiming to be Beelzebub, a prince of Hell in Satan's direct service. He would flay sinners inch by inch, removing their skin, keeping them alive until only muscle and bone remained. He promised to do the same to me.

"He would denounce God, declare how he would assault him, assault the gates of Heaven and rid the world of all that praised him. She was a shell, Francesco, a shell filled with an unimaginable presence that drained every ounce of strength from her.

"Holy water burned her flesh; the crucifix drove her insane. The room would freeze and boil without explanation. It was patience that saved her, sitting with the demon, taking away his power, proving that you were unafraid of his threats.

"The family and I prayed around their daughter each night as the girl shrieked and struggled. Soon, the beast could take no more and he departed. She died the next morning from dehydration and malnutrition. Her skin had no elasticity, each bone poking through the skin.

"I saw this same reaction in the cemetery. Antonio De Sio… he was simply a vessel. He loved his sister, but he was frail, that is when the Devil strikes."

"What about the confession?" Frankie pressed.

"That is a lie. I saw his cousin shoot him, right through the skull." She pressed her index to the impact point. "He was dead, Francesco."

"What did you tell the police?"

"Exactly what I just told you!" She was bordering on agitation, her hands curling into fists, unsure of whether to rap her knee or swing mightily for his head.

He stood, palms outward in a peace offering. "I am not doubting you, Cici."

"I am sorry," she sniffed, wiping at her eyes before her own weakness revealed itself. "I am under a lot of pressure and I am not sure how to cope with it." She stared down at her busy fingers. "I've never talked to you on the phone before, I did not even recognize your voice."

"I slept at my desk," he laughed. "Rough night."

"Me too."

He popped a cigarette from a busted packet, asking for permission. She obliged. He offered her one of her own. She hesitated. "Come on, we're not kids anymore."

A nod, she accepted, his hand quick with a bright flame from a matchbook. Her veins sang with joy as she inhaled the familiar, sticky taste.

"Reminds me of the old railways," she said.

"And David with his little mustache that Mama would stencil." He drew a preteen pencil thin growth over his mouth with his finger.

"*Vaffanculo!*" they both shouted, giggling furiously, their eyes practically closing. Frankie imitated a wide gallop as if he were a gangly child suddenly attempting to fill oversized trousers.

"He always played the dragon or the talking animal!" He sucked another mouthful of smoke, tempering his giddiness. "I thought you people weren't supposed to curse?" he kidded.

"I'll bumble through a few Hail Marys perhaps, that should be sufficient."

He cocked his head, searching for an ashtray. Ignorance took hold for a moment as she rummaged through her nightstand. She removed an old makeup compact, dumping the sponge and tapping her loose ash into the imitation tray.

"I have no use for it," she lamented, Frankie unsure if that was self-deprecating or not.

He joined her, clearing the edge of the cigarette with his index. "If what is in the paper is not true, why are they saying you confirmed it?"

"They threatened me," she whispered, cleaning the lining of her nail with an opposite one, avoiding his inquisition.

"How?"

"They kept me in a room for over twenty-four hours, Francesco. I just wanted to go home."

"So, you signed?"

"What choice did I have? They told me they would concoct some sort of story that involved me and the church and the De Sio family."

"The bordello."

"Hmm?"

"A *capo* in the De Sio family was bussing in girls dressed as nuns into one of their bordellos."

"*Bastardo.*" She flicked the tip of her cigarette, ceremoniously kicking the inspectors off the cliff. "They said the boy was mentally insane. They blamed his poor brain." She tapped her temple for emphasis.

"You don't agree?"

"Of course not!" she scolded. "Do you not believe me?"

"I am not a religious man, Cici, that was all Mama."

"I have seen dozens of similar cases, all spewing this-this-evil. Men and women who live like you or I completely enveloped by a higher power. It is the Devil, Francesco, nothing more."

He shrugged. "I don't doubt you."

"You were always very procedural."

He pointed to his heavily bagged eyes, "My divining rods."

A smile creased her lips. "David did always write the part of the hero for you."

Frankie surveyed her cramped quarters, eyeing a suitcase half-tucked beneath the foot of the bed. "Going somewhere?"

She leaned forward, spotting his observation. "Father Endrizzi believes that I should take a sabbatical."

"Huh?"

"A forced vacation. Things have been very difficult for me and I am beginning to worry the others."

"So, they feed you to the wolves." He smashed the filter into the compact. "You're staying with me tonight."

"No, I cannot impose, I–" She did not want to argue and his shimmering, charitable expression was impossible to ignore. "Just for a night."

He held up his palms, "It's all I ask. It will be good to catch up." Tapping his breast pocket, he seemed lost, digging through his trousers. "I have to work today, but I can meet you later? Tonight?" He shuffled towards her desk, grabbing a pencil from a collection and sorting the clutter for a clean space to write.

Yellowing; creased from water drying the thin pulp. *No return address.*

He cleared the handmade children's cards, allowing the envelope to sit unencumbered.

"Where did you get this letter?"

She craned her neck towards the question.

"Have you ever received anything like this before?"

Cecilia joined him, studying his fascination. "No? Is something wrong?"

Francesco rubbed his suddenly flush face with his hand, wicking away the anxious perspiration. He retreated from the desk, fingers through his hair. He patted his upper lip. "Open it," he directed.

"Not *now*," she shot back. "Why are you acting like a child?"

"Just open it!" He was a little too loud, preoccupied with the contents rather than his tone.

Frightened now of his jittery state, she fetched a letter opener, turning the envelope sideways and scoring the dull blade across the top. She extracted the thick bulge within and set it aside. "What now?"

His stomach gurgled, threatening to upheave his meager breakfast. Uncertainty drove him forward as he carefully unfolded the paper, straightening it, commanding it to lay flat.

Typed, the ribbon wafting between thick and thin applications, it did not begin like any of the others.

Dearest Cecilia...

"*Merda,*" he whispered.

Daylight snuck through the drawn, dust-coated shades of the disheveled bedroom. The sheets had been flung askew, a pillow tossed to the ground. Unpacked boxes formed a dresser of sorts, hangars with wrinkled dress shirts draped over available surfaces.

The key rarely worked, the lock's age fighting against the copper youth. Frankie nudged the door in, Cecilia in tow, her bulky suitcase making it over the lip of the doorway.

"Kitchen's to the left," popping on the murky overhead lamp.

He led them down a crowded hallway, more boxes stacked along the walls, gushing with field work and an endless supply of report copies.

"Did you just move in?" she inquired.

"Something like that."

Into a dark living room, his hand searching for a table lamp. The ignition partially revealed his obsession as he navigated the chaos towards another source of light.

A couch had become a filing cabinet; the opposite wall blocked with an oversized map, pushpins indicating points of interest, supporting photographs and handwritten notes. Manilla folders created a web of paranoia across the floor, each stack indistinguishable from the next.

Finding a switch, he brightened the room further, though, much to his chagrin. "Can you tell I bring my work home with me?" he chuckled, embarrassed. "Uh..." stepping towards the bedroom, picking up the discarded pillow and fluffing the sheets. "You can take the bed tonight; the couch will be fine for me."

"*What is this*, Francesco?"

"Ahh," he sighed, trying to swat away the conversation he would inevitably spring on her in a moment. "A drink? To start?"

"What am I doing here? What is with you?"

His mind whirled with possible responses, but he would need to start from the beginning. He whipped off his overcoat, tossing it atop a cardboard box. "Why don't you sit?"

He removed the clutter from one of the couch cushions, dropping it carelessly onto the floor. She abandoned her suitcase and indulged him, shedding her own coat.

"The letter..." he clapped his hands together. "De Sio!" he was getting similarly frightened and excited to share his theories. "The De Sio girl. She was a victim in a series of similar crimes."

"I read the papers sometimes," she admitted.

He took to the evidence pinned to the wall, removing several photographs. "The bodies...they were all discovered with their organs removed."

Cecilia inspected the stack, flipping through the lifeless, gored corpses, their interior linings blackened with rot as their chests had stiffened, pried open like a fresh oyster. "I remember reading the letters," she said softly, her sensitivity to the malicious behavior remaining high despite the exposure.

"At first, we suspected jealous lovers, poor business dealings, but it amounted to bullshit. Three bodies within a week, six more over the next month, fifteen by summer, another twenty since then. No discrimination, n-no sexual intent. We had no leads, no witnesses. Then..." he marched to a tall stack and skimmed through the titles written along the filing tabs of the manila folders. He ripped out a letter sealed in a plastic sleeve. "A letter. Typed. He sent this to every newspaper in the city. No return address on the envelope. He would target an editor, a reporter, any name that popped up in the paper that might be able to spread his message. They printed this before we had a chance to stop them."

He turned the wrinkled declaration over to her.

To my fellow congregants,

I have risen! My collection has begun, and the rats have no doubt fed on the scraps I have provided. My Father has risen, feeding on the flesh that I have procured. I am optimistic that you too will join me soon, in any capacity. It is with much regret that we must stay silent, cloaked with mask and dagger. with mask and dagger with mask and dagger I have done as my Master commands. I will continue to do his work and praise him. I have savored the blood that will fulfill his resurrection. In time, so will you all.

Frankie layered another letter over the first. "His second sermon."

To my fellow congregants,

I banish this scum water! Vile, putrid liquid putrid liquid. Coat yourselves in this sick? You are unworthy. I own this vessel.

"They became increasingly hostile, page after page of vanity and horrifying descriptions of torture. He would tell us where he had left the corpses. Not a trace of any involvement, as if he were discarding waste into a garbage can."

"He fancies himself a preacher of sorts," Cecilia theorized.

"He certainly held an audience captive."

She accepted a pile of correspondence to inspect, organizing it on her lap.

"These are not even a quarter of the amount that we received. There were some imitators, some rather convincing, but it was rather easy to distinguish."

The ramblings overwhelmed her, the text cryptic, blasphemous to an egregious point.

> *God will feel my throbbing flesh and choke on the blood of his enemies.*

> *They must tear out this abortion, they must!*

> *...conducting themselves like whores!*

> *...they throw their doctrine before sows to eat. So, this is dragging out, that's enough now!*

> *The human vitae is vital. Vital. Vital.*

> *...he belongs to me!*

> *...he belongs to me!*

> *...belongs to me!*

> *...belongs...*

$$\triangledown \, \not{\triangle} \, \triangledown \, \triangle$$

"He belongs to me!" screamed the harbinger, spitting blood onto her face.

Cecilia wiped aside the disgusting ejection, shoving a crucifix into the pale grin. She averted her gaze momentarily to the open scripture in her opposite hand, the thin pages flapping against the wind, taking her momentarily out of place.

"In the Name of Jesus Christ, our God and Lord!"

"Do not speak his name to me! Do not speak!" His teeth bulged as if a creature were attempting to exit through his mouth, releasing the bone from the gum to avoid injury. He squirmed, eyes locked shut.

The grated elevator car buckled as he shook the chains binding him to the fence, slipped through the links that surrounded them. She turned to the mass of concerned peers, their overalls covered in soot, their faces masked in black dust, their headlamps casting a purifying glow on the unwell foreman.

"We must move him," she insisted. "He will disable the elevator if he has to."

An intrepid miner spoke up, "It took several men just to subdue him, *signora*, we cannot risk further injury."

"Giuseppe?"

It no longer held the gurgling contempt of magma and heat. She cocked her head towards the back of the elevator. He struggled for air, waiting for the demon to pump more through his puppet.

"Giuseppe?" he called again, lifting his head. "Please, release me. My throat...I need..."

His loyal men inched forward, the disgusting scowl erased, the malice cast into the darkness.

"Do not approach!" Cecilia roared. "In the Name of Jesus Christ, our God and Lord!" She thrust the crucifix towards the sheepish foreman. "Strengthened by the intercession of the Immaculate Virgin Mary, Mother of God..."

"What has become of me?" he lamented, tugging at the chains. "What have you done, Sister?"

"...of Blessed Michael the Archangel, of the Blessed Apostles Peter and Paul and all the Saints..."

"Untie him!" came a call from behind.

"...and powerful in the holy authority of our ministry! We confidently undertake to repulse the attacks and deceits of the Devil."

"Sister," the foreman wept, "I want my family. I have done nothing wrong!"

"God arises! His enemies are scattered and those who hate Him flee before Him. As smoke is driven away, so are they driven; as wax melts before the fire, so the wicked perish at the presence of *God*!"

Blood poured from his mouth, a seizure rocking his body in galloping waves. The car could not contain the vibrations, a cable *thwacking* as the spine ripped and Cecilia plummeted with the possessed. An emergency break rang as a metal clamp squeezed the remaining line, pausing them in the darkness of the damp mine. She was forced to the corner, head throbbing from the impact.

The foreman panicked, barely inhaling before his lungs wasted the oxygen, matching the ferocious beat of his heart. Cecilia rubbed the swell forming above her temple.

Boots rushed to the edge of the shaft, beams of lights stinging her eyes through the cage. "Sister!?" they cried, the car gently swinging from its sudden halt.

A tepid droplet splashed against her forehead, her finger smearing the crimson vitality between her thumb and index.

"There is company in the darkness," the foreman whispered, his voice hoarse. "I will take the child of God into the depths and we shall all feed on her flesh as we steal her innocence. She has tasted the sweet freedom of her own kind. I will inject her with righteousness. I am Lucifer. I am the Lord of Flies."

As the miners above frantically strategized, their lanterns splashed against the demon's face, his smile drifting between the darkness like a Cheshire cat.

Cecilia held her crucifix upward, facing it towards the suspended. "Give place to Christ in whom you have found none of your works; give place to the one, holy, Catholic and apostolic church acquired by Christ at the price of His blood!"

"Futile, little bitch! Futile!"

"The power of Christ compels you to leave this vessel!"

"I will feed on the sins of your children!" He fought against the shackles, swinging the car, ramming it hard into the jagged shaft wall.

"The power of Christ compels you to leave this vessel!"

"I am no prince! I am King! I shall cast my seed across this kingdom!"

"The power of Christ compels you to leave this vessel!"

"I have come for you all! I will rise and reign for all eternity."

...I have come for you all! I have come for you all! I will rise and reign for all eternity...

The memory had manifested in the mistyped, plastic-sheathed message.

"This...man," she began, "he is not simply..." Looking away, she tried to gather and compose. "I have heard this vitriol before, Francesco. This man has aligned himself with powers stronger than you and I."

"That bullshit," he sighed.

"Do not belittle me!" she fought back, showering him with the manic letters as she stood. "You have not seen what I have seen. This man is frightened. He is being controlled."

"He is possessed? Huh?" he mocked. "The Devil sneaks in through his window and plays with his strings?"

"Is that so hard to believe? Is it so hard to imagine that the disturbing things he says and does might be committed by his hands but not by his soul? That someone is whispering to him, forcing him to obey?"

"Then who do I arrest? Who is blamed for this?"

"You know the answer to that," she scolded. "Can it simply be the reason why rather than how?"

Frankie considered it. "Highly capable, then?"

"He is more sentient than what I have encountered. Perhaps he can control his actions, perhaps he merely speaks through a conduit."

"And he speaks to you." He presented her with the final letter. "Read it."

She ran her tongue over her chapped lips, swallowing with difficulty. She slipped the envelope free, finding the couch cushion once more.

> *Dearest Cecilia,*
>
> *I write to you in my hour of need. You cannot possibly know me as I am now, the distance too great, time too dry. But it has come to my attention that your skills in eradicating the unwanted hosts of men has garnered much attention. I have followed your holy endeavors closely, have seen the bravado that you exude.*
>
> *Prayers, though, cannot help me now. Vile water blessed by the greedy hands of men cannot save me. It is you. Your blessed hands must touch my burning and festering flesh. You must free me from my prison. from my prison from my prison I have performed an illegal black mass. It was the only way to save you, to prevent you from the punishment that I have witnessed.*
>
> *I have pleaded with many others for assistance, my cries falling on deaf and ignorant ears. I pray that you will heed this misfortune and flock to my aid as the mighty shepherd you have become.*
>
> *Do not worry about Valentina, she is safe with me. My disobedience will not be forgotten. Follow the instructions I have included. The others, they have received similar instructions, nonsense to fool them, to draw them from*

my trail. I request your presence. You must bring your gifts, cleanse my flesh so that I may draw fresh breath, so that I may no longer drown in an eternal lake of ice. ~~an eternal lake of ice an eternal lake of ice~~

The final page blared like a struck match, her flesh searing, fusing with muscle and tendon. Her hand shook violently as she stared into the harsh pencil drawing. To others, it was a scrawl of a happenstance encounter in the maze of birch and maple. To her, it was a reminder of what they buried that day.

The drawing of her father's cabin plucked an off-key chord that seized her spine. She had chosen to forget that image, nestled between the canopies and the mountain. But it had resurfaced, crawling with bloody claws to publish the truth once more.

Tears cascaded from her lashes, skiing down the sides of her nose and resting on her chin. As each droplet forced its way out, it nudged the previous from the precipice down upon the thin paper. The impact spread as the material tried nobly to contain the liquid.

"Do you remember..." she whispered. "Do you remember...in the summers? Mama and Papa would leave for work in the morning, before we had even stirred. We would spend the day pretending to save our home, from dragons and beasts, knights and princesses venturing into unknown lands. He would write things for us to say. He would write them down on the backs of Mama's cloth napkins when he ran out of paper. Do you remember, Francesco?"

He too sensed the very ledge of emotion, his heart crawling into his skull as it hurried. His eyes fluttered against the building saline as he turned towards Cecilia.

"He would write things for us to say, and when he could not write...when he could not write he simply repeated himself. He would repeat the last phrase until he made himself sick. Then...only then, could he continue..."

Frankie plugged his mouth with his hand, muffling his sobbing, controlling his throat's insistence to vomit.

"He would make you fall in love with a maiden. He would make you fall in love with a valiant princess. He would...he would only make you fall in love with...*my Valentina.*"

"No!" Frankie rejected the notion.

"It is him, Francesco..."

"No! No!"

"It is David..."

Frankie grunted in frustration, flinging his arms across a stack of evidence, coating the room in his tireless efforts. "Papa is the one we blame," he snorted. "He was the one who raised his fist, not David. *Not* David."

She shoved the drawing of the cabin into his hands. "How did you not see this? The letters, Francesco. How did you not see this?"

"I was supposed to suspect him!? How, Cici? How? Huh? Because Papa hurt him he is automatically disturbed?"

"It is not David who is doing this," she reiterated.

"Who!? The Devil? His *minions*?"

"He *needs* help. This is a cry for help."

"And the bodies?"

"You cannot be sure he is responsible."

Frankie huffed, knowing she was right. "Then, what? Hmm?"

"We have to find David."

A crushing wave of emotion sewed his lips shut, his head turning to blink free more tears. He feared his own hands would secure the handcuffs against his brother's wrist, or worse.

Frankie hurried down the dormitory hall, clutching Cecilia's letter and ripping the receiver off the communal telephone. His fingers whipped the rotary against its axis.

He had forgotten the number.

Beating the toggle, he reset the line, waiting for the dial tone. He tried again.

"Yes, I'm trying to reach the offices of *Il Messaggero*."

Mumblings.

"*Grazi.*" Paranoia refused to allow him to concentrate, his head cocked towards both ends of the seemingly infinite hallway.

Finally, a connection. "Inspector Zampa for Tomasso Oscuro." He tried to interrupt but settled for listening intently. "Pull him out then, I need to speak with him." His hand gestured wildly, using the letter to punctuate his logic. "No, no, I need to speak with him now, I have something he must run in the evening edition." His eyes darted. "I don't care if you lose your job, do you want another body to turn up!?"

"Is everything all right?"

He whipped towards the interjection, fearful he would not have enough hands to draw his revolver.

Sister Elena stood at a safe distance, fingers clasped together.

"Inspector? Is something the matter?"

He entered a state of composure, folding the letter and stuffing it in his back pocket. "I'll call him back," he muttered into the phone, returning it gently to its cradle.

"I heard shouting, I thought something must have happened."

"No!" he overcompensated. "No, Sister Elena, I was trying to reach an old friend. I apologize if I frightened you."

"I do not frighten easily," she smiled, biting her bottom lip as she drank him in.

Frankie coughed, unsure of what to make of her expression. She approached, coyly, reaching for his thin tie, straightening the mess. "Can I get you anything, inspector?"

The request befuddled him, his response a noisy chatter of teeth and embarrassment. "N-n-o, thank you, Sister. I-I-" Cecilia stood in the doorway of her quarters, suitcase in hand, his overcoat draped over her arm. "I must depart, Sister. I have a...several matters I must attend to."

He slid her hands from his tie, breaking the seal of her charm. "Of course," she whispered, eyes drowning in lust.

Frankie nodded, delicately pushing past her. He accepted his coat from Cecilia. "When we were children, they used to just slap our knuckles with a ruler."

He pulled the door shut, the shadow of their feet fading from beneath the sill.

A hand emerged slowly from beneath her bed, the cuffs of its black robe spewing grains of sand across the hardwood.

The jug gurgled as he filled his stubby glass. A swish towards Cecilia and she declined, her own cup still half-full.

The kitchen had been slathered in an olive green, tiles of light yellow intermixed with white. A folding card table had served him well, most meals spent in the living room or at the precinct.

"You must tell your supervisors?" she asked, staring at his need to swirl his cup to dispel his anxiety.

He leaned forward, massaging his arid eyes. "If this *is* David..."

"Would they kill him?"

"If he resisted."

"Would they kill him anyway?"

"I can't be sure." He stuck a cigarette in his mouth, igniting it, sucking hard on the antidepressant. "Do they want to? Naturally."

"Certainly, Petrisone might."

"Who?" he perked up.

"Inspector Petrisone. He was the one who coerced me into signing the confession."

Frankie seethed with internal hatred, keeping the boil to his blood.

"Do you know him?" she asked.

It took him a moment to snap out of his vendetta. "N-no, no" he lied.

"Oh...well, him *and* his fat ape of a partner can rot," she spat.

He reached forward, cradling her hand in his.

"And what will become of us?" she asked.

He exhaled, unsure. "Do you always wear your hood?"

She ran her fingers along her vail, realizing that it still entombed her. "Oh." She reached behind her head and untangled the loose thread, unwrapping the fabric.

"I did not mean to suggest that you remove it," Frankie corrected.

"It is fine," she assured. "I am on sabbatical, Father Endrizzi cannot see me here." She unhooked the crown band from her forehead and slid from the embrace of her coif.

"I can't believe they let you keep all that hair," he chuckled.

She scratched between the layers that threaded backward into her frayed bun. She grabbed her glass and downed the sweet wine, crossing herself in reverence and leaning back in her chair.

"Is it sinful to want to hide?" she asked, perhaps to her own amusement.

"It depends," he shrugged. "From who?"

"Everyone."

"I suppose not to you, but to the others, maybe."

"We must define our own sins."

"If that suits you."

"What if David is responsible?" avoiding even more sensitive topics.

"David as we know him? Or the David you theorize he might be?"

"His flesh, Francesco, the physical being we know."

"In the eyes of the law, he is guilty. In the eyes of morality, he is even more guilty."

"What if it was not his hand?"

"There is little difference. He would be tried as a murderer, the reasons why matter little, only the act itself."

"Then we need not go," she sighed, reaching for the wine and helping herself.

Frankie could not shy away from her reversal of duty. "Do we not owe it to David to attempt to clear his name?"

"He was always a recluse! We were his only friends. Papa beat the joy out of him and he retreated into his mind. He barely spoke until we took him to the hospital. There is no doubt that these letters came from David. Mama would drag him to church and the Fathers...they would beat him too. He writes like they spoke, with a pulpit always at their chest, ready to broadcast their ego."

"Then why kill? Why dismember and parade and brag?"

"That is what concerns me. He was always theatrical, but it was never real."

"Not to us."

"We must define our own sins..." She lost herself in thought, focusing her eyes on the minutiae of the air as she swallowed another glass of nectar. "After they released David, I just...I gave up. He did not try to contact me, so I assumed the worst. Or, perhaps, the best.

Frankie paused, refusing to drink further. "Released?"

"I called the hospital, many years ago, they did not have him listed as a patient."

"Jesus," he rubbed his face, trying to sober himself. "Cici, *David escaped.*"

She offered confusion.

"He-he killed a doctor. Bashed his head in. At least that's what they claim."

She pushed the wine from her reach.

"The locals, they lost sight of him. They tried to track him with all manner of dog and aerial photography, but they never found him."

She leaned forward, unable to comprehend the egregious oversight. "When did they tell you?"

"*Not for three years.* Mama's old address was still listed on the hospital records. When her landlord finally passed away they found letters addressed to her amongst his belongings. They were from the hospital director. An officer, a friend of mine, still working our old neighborhood, recognized the name and passed them on to me."

"*Cazzo,*" she sighed.

"I too called the hospital, threatened them with everything I could throw at them, but they would give me little information without jurisdiction. They weren't willing to admit they had failed him."

"Him? Or us?"

He filled his meager class to the brim, tossing it all back at once in a wave of shame.

"*Fornix*," Cecilia whispered, running her fingers along the tattoo captured in the grainy photo. Frankie's car bucked as it absorbed the shock of a shallow pothole, showering dirty water across the sidewalk.

"It's Latin," he informed her.

"It means *arch*."

"Like the aqueducts?"

"It can also be a euphemism for women of low moral fiber and where they pedal their goods."

"The De Sio girl might have been pregnant, but she was far from a whore."

"He was punishing her?"

"She was not married, but that hardly constitutes a crime."

"You told me yesterday that her family would disguise women as nuns."

"She paid for the sins of her father."

"His writing is the antithesis of the church, even by standards past. Sin is of infinite value to those who speak like him."

"He wrote similar judgments on his other victims. Hardly beneficial to eat your own, no?"

"I cannot pretend to know what he is thinking."

Frankie eased on the brakes, pausing outside the convent. "Gather what you need," he said, "I'll be back in about a half hour."

"Where are you going?"

"Just an errand I need to run," he smiled.

He had unholstered his revolver, angling it downward. The rucksack across his back was cumbersome, but he dared not complain. They had walked in silence since leaving his vehicle, tiptoeing through the dew-soaked vegetation.

"I don't remember so many weeds," Cecilia observed.

"Papa kept the trail relatively clear in the summer. He would disappear in early May, sorting the branches and the rocks, making sure we wouldn't trip."

Two frail lines of hemp had been draped over the flexing arm of a low branch, the ends tied to dirty swatches of green, little pieces of wet paper pinned to the material. Frankie used the barrel of his weapon to lift the dangling oddity, its placement to predict the trail ahead.

The rain had dissipated, the droplets now falling from tired limbs and needles, plopping into the outstretched leaves of the bottom feeders. A clearing had appeared, the crowns above letting in a decent clarity.

"It seems rather odd that he would walk this area with such uncertainty," she wondered.

"Perhaps he hasn't arrived yet."

Wet debris *snapped.*

Frankie spun, revolver thrust outwards towards the disturbance. The forest had shifted, the trunks shuffling positions, distributing themselves unevenly in the path they had followed.

Another misstep, swinging his weapon south. The low-hanging leaves of a maple swayed in the wake of the predator.

The mask appeared first. Spherical eyes of glistening black; a long, protruding beak warbling as the hooded figure leapt over a felled trunk; bare feet wrestling with the mud. The flailing arms came to a heaving rest as the unannounced halted at the barrel's explosion.

"*Polizia!*" Frankie shouted, lowering the revolver from the heavens straight at the intruder.

Blood-stained hands rose, implying innocence.

"Take off the mask," he instructed.

Shivering from the frigid weather, the beak rose, the frightened visage of a youngling's teary face replacing the Middle-Aged veil. The cloak slipped from the girl's head as she held the mask at her side, refusing to drop it.

"Cerberus," she sobbed. "He has opened his jaws." She pivoted her torso, pointing deep into the labyrinth. "He will rise...he has-"

The *crack* of the rifle was apparent in the echo, not the initial ejection. The girl's head rocketed to the side, her collar severed as it broke free of her spine. She spewed, blanketing the weeds as she collapsed onto their bed.

Cecilia stood in a puddle of her own fear. Frankie wrapped his arm around her shoulder and rushed to the safety of a hulking trunk.

"Get down, get down," he whispered, forcing her into the dirt. He peeked around the girth of the mighty forest dweller, scanning the camouflage.

"Do you see anything?" she croaked, head pressed up against the slick bark.

Frankie retreated, kneeling to condense himself. "It's a fucking maze, he could be anywhere."

"David!?" she screamed; a repeat muffled by Frankie's dirty palm.

"What if it's not him?" he argued.

She glared at him from beneath his muzzle. "Mmph-mmm..." He removed his hand. "He wanted me to come here, did he not?"

"*Cazzo*," he muttered, stealing a peek into the distance, the sniper tucked and invisible. "We have to search the girl," he lamented.

"Is that wise?"

"She obviously knew something."

"What do you suggest, then?"

"I will provide covering fire, together we drag the body."

He stuck out his hand. She wiped the wet soil from her fingers against her jacket, accepting his help. "Is this the heroism men like David fantasize about when they are children?"

"Usually their sister isn't part of it."

"You'll be right next to me?"

A nod. "After the first shot, okay?"

The lip of the barrel scanned the forest, jittery, impatient for a hint. A low cluster of tangled branches heaved, his revolver blowing smoke and fury as he unleashed a single round.

"Now!"

They slipped from behind the trunk, keeping each other abreast. Cecilia grabbed one of the limp arms as Frankie fired a second round. He fumbled, finally locking around a wrist. Together they pulled, dragging the body through her own blood and matter, leaving a third shot as a parting gift.

Slipping back behind the maple, Frankie kept his face pressed to the husk, waiting for a response. "Search her," he said, refusing to seek coverage, lest he miss his opportunity.

Cecilia gagged at the raw scent wafting from the girl, her eyes beginning to sink into the back of the head. Her hands shook violently as she pawed at the neck of the robe, unraveling the center. She peeled back the cloth, revealing the girl's nude form, a rosary of black dangling between her breasts.

Frankie stole a glance, "Take the robe."

"Why?"

"Young girls don't parade around the forest by themselves dressed like that. There will be more."

"What about David?"

"He hasn't fired a second shot. Perhaps it was just a warning." He holstered his revolver and began disrobing the girl. Her wound squealed as blood spilled from his jostling. He propped her onto her side as he slipped the sleeve from her arm.

He inspected her back, finding no markings or wounds amongst the pale skin. Balling the robe, he handed it to Cecilia. "If we head through this gap here," he pointed, "we can use the trees as cover. We run until we hit the base of the mountain, then we can follow the ridge to the cabin."

"What about her?"

"The others will come for her, eventually." He removed his revolver and popped open the chamber, eyeing two remaining rounds.

Cecilia cleared an errant hair from her face, looking into the star-struck eyes of the innocent girl. "*In nomine Patris et Filii et Spiritus Sancti.*" She crossed herself, kissing her thumb.

"Go," he urged. "*Now.*"

Tucking the black mess under her arm, she tore through the forest, ducking under the gnarled arms of dead wood. Frankie spun from behind the maple, his revolver barking.

"Sister?"

Cecilia whirled past reception, Sister Elena in her wake waving awkwardly at her trot.

Back to the mahogany door, inhaling the musk of the room, her habit soaking from the constant tears raining over the exhausted city. She threw open the top drawer of a dresser, grabbing a handheld compartment case.

Popping open the iron buckles, she revealed a velvet interior, molds imprinted for miniature vessels of holy water, Eucharist, sacramental wine, and anointing liquids, a gift from her time in Honduras, the lid signed by her students with appreciation.

She would need to refill and replace.

To her bureau, shifting aside the many tedious and similar layers she had worn throughout her tenure. A black garment bag had fallen to the base of the chest; she reseated the hanger and unzipped it.

It had been the last outfit she had worn.

She buttoned the wool slacks, rolling up the cuffs over a set of high-tops. Hiding her rosary under a white, men's button-up, she smoothed a thinning, gray sweater over it, popping the collar beneath. A navy jacket completed the set, her reflection a far cry from what had entered the room, now and fourteen years ago. A distaste furrowed her brow as she slammed the bureau shut, snatching the consecration kit.

Reaching the sanctuary proved simple, the doors closed to the public until noon. She hurried down the center aisle, avoiding the glaring eyes atop the crucifix. Scurrying to the right, she entered the sacristy through a swing door.

A steel dispenser dripped excess holy water into a basin to prevent waste. She tugged on the valve and the tainted liquid dribbled into her flask. The refrigerator hummed as she opened the sticky door, selecting a jug already in use. She matched the lip with the vial from her set, refilling the sacrament. Pressing the bottle back into the mold, she pulled herself into the center of the chamber, eyeing the many drawers lining the wall choking with accessories, texts, and clothing to be worn during each holy mass.

She tugged the ivory knobs of the top layer: donation baskets. The second drawer: antiquated hymnals. The third-

"Sister Cecilia."

He must have come from his office, but the stairs bellowed like a wooden ship.

She spun to meet him, "Father Endrizzi," embarrassed, trying to collect her things. He stood at the base of the staircase, hands intertwined behind his back.

"You have returned." A step forward, the rosary around his belt jingling.

"Yes, Father. Just for-only for a moment. To collect a few things."

"Will you be partaking in a bit of pastoral care?" encroaching further, pointing to her kit.

"My brother...he is ill, I wish to visit him, give him some comfort."

"Dressed like this?"

She blushed, fussing with the wrinkles. "It is all that I-" her head rose as his palm sailed across her cheek, pounding into her jawbone. The sudden thrust forced her to the ground, elbow singing as it broke her fall.

"He contacted you, didn't he!?" he screamed, reaching for her hair, his bony fingers intertwined in the long threads. He brought her to the surface of the dresser, pressing her face into the frigid, polished wood. His free hand curled into a fist, his knuckles pounding against the still-healing wound on her cheek. The stitches ripped, bleeding through the gauze as he launched another strike.

"First they want you for themselves. Then they want you to disappear. *You will not become his savior.* The Lord shall inherit his flesh."

Her arms fought against his grip, nails sinking into his flesh, but he did nothing to resist the pain.

"Do not concern yourself with matters beyond your understanding, Sister. You will no longer thin our herd."

She snagged his rosary, ripping the beads loose, the excess clattering to the floor. The distraction allowed her to punctuate his robe, her hands gripping his flaccidity, twisting unnaturally.

Not even he could ignore the searing pain that gripped his crotch, loosening his hold upon her hair as he attempted to creep backward. She rose, grabbing her consecration kit and jamming it into his temple as his eyes widened. The blow ejected in a burst that slathered the wall in a red so crimson it appeared black in the dim light of the sacristy.

Releasing him, Cecilia backed away, yelping as she dropped the box. Father Endrizzi railed, stumbling from the sudden lack of clarity. He tripped over his own feet, crashing into the dispenser of holy water. Together they plummeted, littering the floorboards with a frothing mixture that bathed him in his last rites.

His chest began to twitch as he seceded from his body's best interests, his head pumping a steady pulse into the river. Cecilia retrieved the kit and searched the remaining drawers, stealing a column of eucharist wrapped in wax paper. She shoved the components in their respective molds. Father Endrizzi's fingers twinkled as he reached for her, his mouth inhaling the bloodied water as he gagged.

She bolted from the sacristy and made haste down the aisle towards the sanctuary gates, the inverted eyes of Christ mocking her as she clung to what remained of her faith.

Engaging the gear shift, he rammed his car into park, slipping into a nasty puddle. The sidewalks outside the cathedral were empty, the rain driving all the rats indoors. Leaning into the passenger seat, he rolled down the window, fighting against the squeaky knob. Cecilia had not returned.

Eyeing a bank of payphones, he returned the window and exited, stomping quickly into the unattended booth. He shut the folding door and searched through his soaking pockets. A few coins to spare, enough to deliver a request.

He paid his dues and dialed.

"Yes, the offices of *Il Messaggero*, please."

He watched through the glass as a vehicle navigated the blinding storm, its headlight barely puncturing through the haze. Blood still lingered on the outside of his hand, Petrosino's nose proving more fragile than he had expected. He wiped the excess against his overcoat.

A connection. "Tomasso Oscuro, please. Inspector Zampa calling."

He was on another call. Would he perhaps hold for a moment?

"I'll stay on the line."

Silence now, the heavy droll that inspired confidence that the line had not disconnected.He turned towards the towering church, admiring the hand-carved spires that punctured the sky. Centuries had passed since its inception, yet the stone had not deflated from weather or war. Thunder rolled towards the north, the storm shifting with purpose.

The rectory's extravagance had fused with the sanctuary, a hallway adorned with stained glass connecting the two structures. Tall, arched windows had been given to the upper floors, curtains of satin bordering their frames to block the sun in the most trying of times.

A figure stared down at him, expressionless.

He knew him. The tall zealot who had shooed him away when he had first come to see Cecilia. Wings dripping of black mucus embraced the Father, swallowing him into the recesses of the room, the curtains gently wafting in his wake. Frankie rubbed the building condensation on the glass with his sleeve, eyeing the perch again. It remained empty.

"Francesco!" always pleased to receive a headline or two. "I've got a staff meeting in about ten minutes. I've run dry on the De Sio story, please tell me you have something."

"How's that retrospective shaping up?"

"Bah! Nonsense. We will all forget about the Pope when they

choose the next one."

"Tomasso, you didn't receive any other letters, did you?"

"From who?"

"Our friend from the country."

"Not that I'm aware of. Why? Do you have something?"

"Yeah, I might. I need you to bury the story for now. Understand?"

"It's suffocating from a lack of information, Francesco. What else am I supposed to do? I've already got your friends threatening to arrest me for libel."

"I've got to leave the city for a few days. Head up north. Just keep this nonsense quiet, buried behind the lifestyles. Don't let those bastards scare you, they can't arrest you for bullshit like that."

"What are you up to? Going to play the role of the honest officer? The country roads safe with your intervention?"

"Maybe."

Between the angular sheets of rain, he saw a frantic shape approach his car, tugging at the passenger door. They knocked on the window, uttering a mumbled, "Francesco!"

"Francesco?" the receiver tickling his ear.

"Just don't print anything until you hear from me, or I'll arrest you myself."

He returned the handset and curled the door back, stepping from the phonebooth cautiously.

"Cici?"

She turned, cheek oozing blood from beneath the gauze.

"What the fuck happened?" He approached, reaching for the wound.

She smacked him aside, "We have to go, *now*, Francesco." Her eyes plead for him to stow his questions until they had left the city in their rearview.

He nodded, keys releasing the door's lock. She crawled into the dry leather as he slid into the driver's seat.

"Just drive, please," she begged.

The ignition sputtered as the windshield wipers cleared away the torrent as best it could. He did not bother to check his mirrors as they darted back into the street, tearing through the lonely morning.

Her hands surrounded her mouth as she shook, sobbing painfully, unwilling to share. Frankie's eyes darted from the road, assessing her wound, the gauze peeling away from the medical tape, the blood mixing with the rain as it wept down her cheek.

"I think..." she stammered. "I think I killed him."

"What?"

"Father Endrizzi...I...I hit him."

He cocked his head, unsure.

"H-he approached me. He accused me of being in contact with *him*."

"Who?"

"I think he meant...David."

"Christ. What did he do?"

"He started hitting me. He pinned me down. I-I took my kit and I...I"

Frankie removed a hand from the steering wheel and squeezed her knee. "Cici, it's okay."

"No! He was bleeding! He was shaking, Francesco. He said that I will not be *his* savior. That the Lord will inherit *his* flesh. He spoke just like David. Just like *him*."

"Are you sure?"

"Francesco, I killed him! I struck him in the temple. He was trying to stop me. He was trying to stop *us*."

"What are you saying?"

"David was writing to his fellow congregants. A man of high stature in the church does not refer to himself as a congregant."

"He bows, then, to another? Father Endrizzi?"

"I don't know. He spoke from a subservient position."

"*Jesus.*"

"We don't have to go back, do we?" her eyes were painted in bright veins, leaking rainwater and tears onto her jacket.

"No," he empathized. "No. Of course not. If David is responsible for this, then Father Endrizzi is a guilty man." He tried to draw her away momentarily, slow her anxiety. "Your wound," he directed.

She touched the gauze, pulling back fingers dripping with watercolor. "There is extra, in the bag."

He angled his arm behind the passenger seat, digging through a rucksack. The white tape pulled on the minute pores of her skin; the slower she dragged the more the pain radiated around the swelling, purple and blue impact. She removed the opposite side and tossed the bandage onto the dashboard. Frankie stole a glance, the crust of the scabbing crease dotted with yellow and brown as it healed. It had begun to peel slightly, the image of Father Endrizzi's fist smashing into her cheek tightened his grip around the steering wheel.

"Here," he offered, loaning her his handkerchief. "The glove box too."

She popped open the compartment, an ice scraper and a single brown glove rattling alone together. Shifting them aside, she saw the flask, removing it. She stared at the familiar initials, running her thumb over them as she had not done in many years.

"I can't believe you kept it," she said.

"I'm not proud of it. It belongs in those woods too."

She unscrewed the cap and dotted the handkerchief with alcohol, pressing it forcefully against the pain. Taking a swig of the strong brew, she offered it to Frankie.

His mouth had gone dry, he needed to rehydrate. Even over the roar of the storm, he could hear the liquid sloshing in the metal container. He accepted, but with reluctance, savoring the harsh aftertaste and the warmth his bones contracted.

Cecilia followed him, gulping another dose of bravery.

"David, David, David," Frankie whispered, drowning his thoughts, tossing the flask into the back seat.

The slow descent of the sun was upon them. Despite the heavy blanket above, they knew daylight would slip from their advantage soon. They had met the heavy crag of the mountain several miles back, using the ridgeline to guide them south.

Popping in the distance, a rifle issued another warning to those who ventured too deep. A birdsong flittered past, the creature eager to flee the madness of the forest. Frankie turned towards the echo, allowing the wave to die.

"Papa was always a good shot," Cecilia reminisced.

"Mama too," he teased.

She scolded him with her eyes.

He turned back towards the south and continued onward. "Are we going to bury the memory too?"

"And pretend it never happened? That's naïve. I think we should just drop it. I don't need that fear clouding my judgment... and I don't want to lump David in just yet."

The thought had never even jockeyed towards the forefront of his mind, the possible outcomes pausing his progress as Cecilia stole the lead, leaving him in solitude as he contemplated the difference between love and duty.

The tree line had been shoved back from the cabin, forming a wobbling semicircle of a clearing. A cluster of raw wood had been stacked decades ago, the beginning of an addition, never quite started and never fully realized. A clothesline dangled between the side of the cabin and a steel pole driven into the infertile ground, its only burden a stained, white sheet. It remained as it had been, the days and nights flooding back, superimposed over the grim display that greeted them.

The front door had been left open, top hinge torn, the interior painted in darkness. Frankie and Cecilia stood at the gateway between the forest and their inheritance, refusing to move.

"It's so small," she whispered.

"*We* were small too."

He opened the chamber of his revolver and replaced the empty cartridges.

As they pressed their soles into the familiar domain, they could not help the weight that befell their shoulders. Frankie reseated his grip on the stock, rubbing his index along the curvature of the trigger.

Slowly, they closed in on the cabin, circling around the roofed well in a wide arc, zeroing in on the doorway, eyes to the wide window, waiting for foreign movement. The barrel entered first, passing a copper still, its pipes assembled together in a pile fit for travel. Frankie carefully scanned the interior, his boot scraping against the floor.

A knife roll had been left open atop a butcher block, the adjacent basin filled with a bucket of stagnant water. Dried blood layered a carving station, a tuft of fur stiffened and glued to the surface. Stains and loose thread littered a fabric sofa in the corner of the room, a stack of books acting as a fourth leg. Their mother's rocking chair, a basket of dust-covered yarn at its side, sat unused. The room was heavy with cold air, the fire dissipating long ago. There was kindling, neatly stacked, a poker to shift the burning stock.

Frankie lowered his weapon as he fully crossed the threshold, entering the once-promising days of their youth. Cecilia stole her own inspection, marveling at how little had truly changed. She snapped to the blood across the carving table.

"Oh my God," she crossed herself.

He ran his fingers over the crimson blemish, unable to collect a simple sample. "Hopefully, just a mistake from a past meal."

"Papa's desk," she admired, running her fingers along the hand-carved pulp. It had been cleared of memorabilia, only a copper mug and a cluster of unsharpened pencils left behind. She reached beneath and slid out a wicker stool. A short, baby blue canvas bag had been laid on top, a black stripe running down the middle, meeting the dual zippers as they kissed. "Francesco?"

He turned from the knife roll, his fingers caressing the dusty outline of the missing tools. He holstered his revolver and picked up the bulky unit from the stool, placing it gently on the desk. Unzipping each side individually, he lifted the loosened flap and allowed the typewriter to breathe.

"*Merda*," he whispered, keeping the disappointment from Cecilia's ears.

An envelope had been left, stuffed between the rows of clean keys. No return address, just his name. She reached for the letter, but her wrist stiffened, Frankie's hand preventing her from disturbing the possible ensnarement.

"I think it would be wise to handle it carefully."

He allowed her to slip free. "Will this become evidence?"

"Possibly."

"Or are you superstitious? I can bless you if you'd like?" she smiled.

He snatched the letter, confining the typewriter once more, locking the steel teeth together, sealing the evil. "No." Frankie marched to the sofa, tossing his rucksack into the springy cushion.

"I was simply teasing," she confessed.

Though he could not bear to face her, she knew emotion had overcome him. She took to his side, rubbing his back.

"Can you free him?" he mumbled, voice cracking against his insistence that he was not upset.

"What do you mean?"

"He is poisoned, isn't he?"

"I cannot be sure."

"This is what you do. You...you free men of this influence."

She knew her skills were not defining in any sense. Her duty was to follow instruction and rule, patience winning out over talent.

"We will find him," she assured, "and we will release him of whatever has driven him to this."

His finger slid under the glued flap of the envelope, ripping it open. Uncurling the single page, he met the frantic plea.

Frankie,

Continue south. The creek, the imaginative raging

river of our youth, is but a vein. Coursing now with timid-ity, it shall run rampant in due time. Follow it east, there you will find the mouths of Cerberus. The congregation is set to arrive, but I have faith that you will arrive much earlier than expected. Cecilia has ignored my cries for help. I fear that my lucidity will crumble before the ceremony begins. They torment me, brother. They torment me with bleeding flesh, with nightmares of my own sacrifice. They control me, move my fingers, slide the knife, spill the poison. I do not want I do not want I do not want to die, Francesco. They have taken Valentina from me. They have taken my love! Please, Francesco, do not lie to me again. Do not abandon me again. Not again.

- David

Tears pelted the single-spaced letter, acceptance the only path now, denial an injection of bliss that only rotted the vein.

"Pray with me," he choked.

As the sun finally lost hope, careening behind the mountains and down beneath the horizon, they recited the Our Father, hoping it would protect them as night fell.

WOLF & MOUSE

IV

The maniacal laugh bubbled from his brother's mouth, a hand cinching his collar as the ringlet on the floor popped open, revealing the descent to the cellar. A tin colander fell to the surface of the desk, no need for it during the intermission.

"Frankie," he appealed, his hard soles tripping over the treads as the game continued, the rules defined by everyone but him.

"It's your turn," Frankie insisted, planting him in front of the stone arch, the light streaming between the floorboards refusing to grant clarity down the dark passage.

"Five minutes," he was told.

"No!" He fought against the stranglehold. "Papa said we're not supposed to be down here!"

"We all had to do it, David."

"Cici never did it!"

"Of course, she did, before you were born."

"I don't understand why I have to."

"Don't you want the strength of a bear? Hmm? The eyes of a wolf? Bravery, David, that is what is down there. You think Papa got so strong because he eats meat?"

The void beckoned him.

"Five minutes?" he asked timidly.

"Just five minutes." Frankie slithered away, his boots tapping toe first, gently squeezing the heel, careful to fish for the railing.

"Then we get to finish? Right? You promised we would finish." David did not look back, fixated on the unknown.

"I promise, we'll finish. The brave knight needs inspiration, this will help you write an even better ending. Just...don't forget... *beware the Striga*!" Frankie yelled, howling with delight as he bolted to the surface and slammed the cellar door, layering the maroon rug on top.

David rushed towards the staircase, "Frankie! FRANKIE!" His weak fingers threaded between the slats, his arms unable to shift the lid, the chime of the ringlet beating a rhythm between his horrifying squeal. Tears came, soot splashing his face as he pounded his fists.

His sharp terror echoed in the tunnel as an arc of light split the air. The snout huffed, shaking a necklace of twinkling bone. He turned towards the disturbance, slowly lowering his arms. He watched the oily, black wings unfurl as they left the stone confines of the alcove. David whimpered, his trousers darkened as he released his bladder, the urine dripping past the risers and pelting the floor.

The sunken face burst from behind him, claw-like fingers clamping his mouth shut as he screamed.

Peeling back the rug, the cellar flew open, his father's gruff, staccato accent calling his name, "Da-vid!"

Curled into a ball at the base of the stairs, he wept, reciting, "Papa...papa," into his chest.

He squirmed as his father kneeled, lifting him. "No!" he fought. "Let go of me! Papa!"

"Settle! Settle!"

Frankie knew his lapse in amusement would reap no benefit.

His father rose from below, his face expressionless, the color flush in his cheeks. David shrieked and flailed against his massive arms as he deposited him onto the plush, artichoke-shaded sofa.

"What happened, Papa?" Frankie asked, attempting to distance himself from the prank. With intent, his father turned, screaming towards him, his hairy fingers curling around his neck as he choked his son.

Up against the wall, his head emphatically chimed as his vision curled in a white blur.

"Have I raised a cockroach? Hmm?"

Frankie's face emptied into a purple pool at his neck, his pale lips begging for air.

"Papa, no!" David cried out, stumbling towards the one-sided bout. A backhand *cracked* the sprinting child across the nose, his balance sucking him towards the cellar, his spine singing as he bent over the staircase and collapsed upon the numbing, stone floor once more.

"Look what you made me do, you disobedient rat!" The epithets rained as a tone invaded David's ears, a piercing ring that drowned his attention and forced his eyes to disconnect, the blurry beams of angelic light shifting into octagonal chains. He watched a shadow overtaking the cabin floor as blood poured down the joists.

Cecilia adjusted the pathetic inferno with an iron poker, shifting the split logs and tossing a handful of twigs to keep the flame chewing. She had shed her jacket, keeping herself busy rummaging through what David had left behind. Frankie had found some semblance of sleep, overcoat draped over him like a wool blanket as he curled on the couch.

She sat at her father's desk, running her fingers along the canvas typewriter case, the horrible words spewing from the ribbon into the ears of those who refused to listen. She opened the single drawer, a loose sheet of typing paper left behind, glued to the interior with dried correction fluid.

Maneuvering the drawer proved difficult, the recesses lining up improperly and refusing to close. She jiggled the knob, trying to the loosen the rigidity. A crimson-beaded rosary slid forward, tangling pathetically at the edge.

He had lost track of how many glasses he had consumed, but the headache signaled a truce. He set the empty cup down, a bead of wine shimmying down the edge, back to the base.

"You can take the bed," he repeated, his chair wincing as he stood.

"I would prefer the couch, actually," she admitted. "I sleep better when there is something at my back."

He held his hands out as if to agree, but the offer still stood. "*Bene*," he smiled. He kissed her forehead, "There are blankets... somewhere," swatting the air left and right.

"I'll manage, Francesco."

"*Buona notte*," he slurred, shuffling from the kitchen like an elder, burping and scratching his irritated scalp.

She unbuckled her suitcase, unthreading the long leather straps, unzipping the circumference. Her uniform was all that she had thought to bring, the blasphemy worthy of the strictest penance. Beneath the many copies of her habit, she retrieved a white envelope.

A glance at the closed bedroom door and the dragon-like snore pushed her into the bathroom for some privacy. The boomerang lock *clacked* as she engaged it, running the faucet loudly, the sink gurgling.

She lowered the lid on the coral toilet and sat, exhausted from the effects of the wine. It had been some time since she had ingested so much in such a short period. Clearing the cobwebs from her eyes, she flipped the letter from the Abbey of St. Bartolomea Capitanio and tore through the crease. She knew their decision was moot, but perhaps the fantasy of what could have been, what ultimately should have been, could sustain her.

They had accepted her proposal, the child to be transported upon the clearance of the hospital's head administrator to the Abbey. Full visitation rights. Around the clock care. An education at their parochial school.

> *With much appreciation, we thank Annamaria and the whole De Sio family for their generous donation. We trust, Sister, that this child will flourish and be provided the utmost care and consideration.*

Ripping the letter in half, then halving it again, again, again, she released the insignificant scraps, weeping under the heavy drone of the faucet, begging silently for her love to return.

The eyes were black, surrounded by shrunken muscle, the flesh damp and without proper color, a banshee's wail escaping the exposed teeth and receding gums.

Frankie awoke, hair disheveled, lips pursed, drool dripping from the corner to his chin. He wiped his face, smearing the leakage aside. His vision refused to focus, the heavy glow of the fireplace crossing from left to right. He pressed his feet to the hardwood as he righted the tattered ship, shaking his head forcefully to engage his engines. Cecilia had fallen asleep next to the fading fire, his rucksack at her back.

A bright disturbance had plastered itself against the grimy panes of the window. The reflection of the flames, at first glance. He sauntered towards the basin, resting his hands on the lip as he glared through the glass.

The rubber had been shaped like a plump hog, a flat snout

protruding outward under a slanted jaw. The stiff ears elevated the black hood, visible only by the raging torch it held in its naked hand. A shotgun appeared from beneath the robe, belting a cluster of buckshot. The glass shattered, Frankie dove, covering his head as he was draped in fragments.

Cecilia bolted upright, turning towards the gunshot.

"Stay down!" he urged, crawling to the sofa, probing for his revolver.

The front door of the cabin buckled as a stiff heel took advantage of the loose hinge. A leathery Wolf glared at Cecilia, eyes hidden behind reflective lenses. The barrel of a machine gun rose, finger to the trigger.

Frankie's barrel howled at the Wolf, the head snapping, coating the door with a violent spray. The automatic weapon discharged, pelting the ceiling in a syncopated pattern as he slumped to the ground. Cecilia retreated as Frankie leapt past her, yanking the machine gun free of the deadly grip.

The Pig motioned the cavalry onward, the darkness suddenly ripe with the flames of bursting torches, the tree line flush with robed beasts basking in the flickering light.

"Avē Satana!" the Pig spoke.

"Avē Satana!" the congregation repeated, the chorus riding the open mountain air.

Frankie stood in the doorway, tucking his revolver into his waist, swinging the automatic's stock to his shoulder.

"The bitch!" the Pig pointed. "We have come for her."

"Fuck you!"

"We do not engage in such petty negotiations, inspector."

He cocked his head at the formality. With a slight turn towards Cecilia, he issued commands. "Grab your things. The cellar, when I say so."

She nodded, creeping away from the discussion, securing the rucksack.

"Where's David?" he shouted.

"He has served his purpose."

Cecilia peeled back the rug, tugging on the ringlet and easing open the cellar door.

"Where is he!?"

"Such anger! David learned well from those who have steered him from naivety."

"Vaffanculo, pig fucker." Frankie hugged the trigger, pumping the swine up the middle, cutting a bloody swath. The torch dropped to the dry grass, the flames feeding on the delicious kindling.

The congregation stormed the castle.

He shut the cabin door, no real protection offered by its pathetic strength, but a roadblock nonetheless. "Go!" He ripped the robe from the Wolf, the mutt nude, just as the young girl. Cecilia sought shelter below as he pulled the mask free, stuffing it against the small of his back.

He knew this man, or what remained of his face. The door sheared practically in half, gasping its last breath as the creatures flooded inward. He opened firing, spraying the brave. They collapsed, arms spiraling, tripping those who foolishly stood too close.

A Stag dove through the window as Frankie slammed the lid, rushing into the basement.

"This is a dead end, you idiot!" she whispered angrily.

The door above squealed as light flooded onto them, a scurrying Rat training the Pig's shotgun downward. Frankie emptied his magazine into the growling lust, tipping the body down the treads, the door slamming behind him. As the corpse came to a rest, he stole the pump-action, firing two rounds into the ceiling, beating back the advance.

"Back up, slowly."

She led him towards the far end of the cellar, hand on his shoulder, the shotgun stock massaging the aching muscle. Footsteps multiplied above as shadows began to blanket the beads of cleansing light.

"She is needed alive!" came the cries.

"Keep going," he whispered.

"Where?" she panicked. "There's nothing back here."

"The sewers."

"What?"

Another attempt to breach the cellar, this time with strength in numbers. The trio of mountain dwellers pounded the staircase.

The shotgun exploded, ripping the arm off the encroaching Bear. The stream of fire and fury ignited the cellar briefly, their position comprised. "Kneel, kneel!" Frankie ordered. They pressed down into the seemingly ancient mold, the return volley scorching the walls behind them, the aim off.

He tugged the pump, loading a fresh round and expelling the spent cartridge in a whirling ejection. The next blast peppered the remaining duo, their heads *smacking* the unexpected stone below.

"Up, up, up." They stood, pushing towards the arch and the depths of the darkened hallway, a constant nightmare in their youth, now a possible savior. He cocked the shotgun again, allowing the shell to ping off the narrow walls.

"What sewers?" she pressed, but an impediment met her back before the explanation. "There's something here."

He dug into his back pocket and handed her a matchbook. She dragged the stick across the sandpaper as he returned his grip to the base of the shotgun. She waited until the initial deep breath of the flame had exhaled, allowing her fingers to peel back and avoid a nasty bite.

The carcass had been propped upon a butcher's hook, a length of hemp around the wrists, keeping it snug over the metal curvature. The face had been stripped, the skin removed down to the neck. The muscles had remained hydrated in the moisture, shimmering in the limited light.

Cecilia froze, shaking the small torch as she tried to control her fear. The mouth opened, the meat sucking in air with a terrifying gurgle. The flame reached her pinched thumb and index, burning her in a screech that echoed up to the cabin proper.

Frankie spun as Cecilia lit another match, proving her reaction was justified. "Jesus..." he whispered.

The corpse gyrated subtly as shock overwhelmed the malnourished experiment. In the darkness, Frankie could make out the gap below the swaying feet. He grabbed the match from Cecilia and bent down, shining it across a grate.

He shook the flame free. "Stand back. Cover your ears."

She obeyed, creeping past the heavy, futile inhalations. Frankie aimed at the ground and cleared the grate with a rousing blast. He pawed at the metal, the jagged ends searing with heat. He slipped his fingers through a clean edge and yanked it free, tossing it back towards the wider cellar.

"Don't worry, there's a ledge. Just go slow, slide if you have to."

"Where does this lead?"

"It empties out near the lake, from there we can follow the streams to the east."

"Give me your hand."

She extended, allowing him to guide her downward, her arms slipping through the hole. He stuffed the rucksack behind her, jabbing it with the butt of the shotgun.

The cellar roared with encroachment, more congregants joining the fray. He flung his revolver, belting a retort that eased back the black robes as he jammed himself into the sewers. His boots scraped against the decline, guiding him down into ankle high, watery refuse.

A torch swung through the hole, a Lion's head poking out behind it. His hand pointed in the dim light at Frankie, the excitement lost in the echo of the shotgun. The mighty jungle king's head stained the sewer walls as his limp torso wedged itself into the frame, dangling upside down, the torch slipping free.

Frankie watched the flaming club bounce off the curvature, waiting until it rolled to his feet. He retrieved it and spun his heels.

"Cici?" he whispered.

The Lion's dead weight heaved as his fellow beasts attempted to free him.

"Cici!?"

A black form shivered, the robe soaking up the bacteria-infused water as it huddled, creating little ripples among the debris.

Frankie sloshed towards her, crouching to comfort.

"Francesco?"

It was a whisper too, but clearly from his rear. He swung the torch toward Cecilia, her clothing caked, a smile buzzing across her lips as she adjusted the rucksack on her back. Her eyes leapt passed him, transfixed on the contorting mass. The hood flapped back, a Mouse, hair stripped by eager and malevolent scissors, pounced upon Frankie, knocking loose his instruments of war.

She pinned him, stuffing his head beneath the water, turning the cheek so he could inhale the putrid liquid. In the glow of the torch, Cecilia reached for the butt of the submerged shotgun. Frankie stabbed the edge of his palm into the Mouse's chin, pushing her upward, trying to create distance and vulnerability. "*Annegare! Annegare!*" the rodent repeated.

Cecilia aimed the soaking pump-action at the little scavenger. Her own scream accompanied the blast as the woman's neck ripped, leaving a muscular hinge as the head rolled onto her back. The thick, arterial expulsion splashed Frankie in the face as he rose to the surface. His gasp included a mouthful of the vile blood, encouraging his stomach to empty, cocking his head aside as he vomited.

Frankie tossed aside the practically headless, wiping his mouth.

"Her h-h-*head*," Cecilia stammered.

"Up there!" Frankie directed, a pair of boots slipping through the grate's frame.

She lurched towards the kicking legs and pulled the trigger.
Click.

"Cock it!" he shouted, sorting the garbage, trying to locate his revolver.

The pump complained, scraping against her wishes, but she muscled through, the shotgun spitting the used shell as she primed her attack. The round gored through the fleshy calf, shredding the muscle. Frankie found his waterlogged revolver and added the torch for a bit of clarity. Though it had soaked through, he slung the dirty robe of the Wolf over his shoulder. Pressing down on the top of the skull, he freed the Mouse's mask and added it to his collection.

Cecilia's adrenaline had been dumped, overdosing her system, a tingling effect rattling her brain as she cocked a fresh round and pumped the spray into the belly of the congregant. The pathetic scream filtered past the hole, flooding the sewer.

She was prepared to saw him in half, but Frankie's hand paused the unnecessary waste.

"Cici, come on, we have to reach the lake, we cannot stay and fight."

Her wide-eyed fury could only nod as he dragged her into the infinite darkness, the mob chattering as they regrouped, launching a pointless counterattack into the small waves of their escape.

Punching the clock on its next shift, the sun had stretched its fingers above the horizon, a flutter of gold and violet hues. But gray and shiftless cotton had already marched forward, providing a dreary topic for the forest's early risers. The lake had once formed naturally over the course of the mountain's evolution, carving a niche from volcanic activity and the erosion of wet and wintery millennia.

Man had widened it, clearing thousands of war-ready logs, to expand the fresh water into a dumping ground, a habitat for those seeking shelter, should the war escalate, and the cities be razed. The massive body had been diluted by carelessness, the inhabitants forced to evolve or perish in murky waters. The mountains that towered above chuckled at its pathetic poisoning, their peaks lost in the clouds like a retreat for the Gods.

The sewer mouth sloped downward, borne out of a cliff that had been separated from the giant crag of the main formation; another misfit. The torch had jabbered enough, barely a tepid heat emanating to burn his fingers. Frankie tossed the useless club as they shuffled into the grass. Cecilia released the rucksack, collapsing into the plush bed of dry blades, shotgun at her side.

"I know why Papa never took me down there," she chuckled.

"I'm baffled as to why he would take anyone," Frankie mused. "I guess he was proud of his work." He took to a moss-stained log and made a perch for himself, easing the pressure from his legs. "Imagine," he wondered, peeling a packet of cigarettes from his stiff back pocket. "Shipped out to the front, constantly transferred between dodging mortars and digging holes in the mountain?"

"Sounds like a nightmare," she moaned sleepily.

He selected the most intact of the cigarettes, tossing the rest into the lake. He slapped his front pockets, his breast.

"You still have those matches?"

She reached beneath her sweater and held the packet up in the air for him to retrieve on his own.

"Toss it over here."

A limp wrist and a pathetic attempt forced him to stand up, stomp forward, and fish for it himself. He struck the bulbous head, sucking on the filter as he ingested a bit of relief.

Cecilia motioned for a chance, reluctance almost denying her, but he knew this would be his last, might as well share it. She squeezed an intoxicating inhalation, slowly releasing it in a dull cloud between them.

"Papa told me something," Frankie began, "when he took me down here."

"Another life lesson?" She returned the cigarette.

"No," he laughed, staring back at the lake, drinking in its interpretive beauty. "He told me...he was sorry. He told me he did not mean for the things he said and did to surface. That he loved me. He told me he was weak, he told me he was not to be trusted."

She squinted in the daylight, "Papa said that?"

He nodded, taking a small drag. "You believe that? You believe that he was something other than our father?"

"How do you mean?"

"You think he might have been..." his implication allowed him to be free of uttering the words.

"By alcohol, perhaps, but not by anything more than his own rage."

"The war certainly sunk its talons into him."

"He's a bastard, Francesco. He succumbed."

"We must define our own sins," half mocking her.

"Do you blame Papa or the alcohol?"

"Papa, of course! If David is part of this-this cult, then do we blame David for killing those people, or these freaks?"

She huffed, frustrated she could not answer the question. "Will you protect David?"

He handed her the final puff, clapping his hands clean. "I must define sin on my own terms, I suppose."

Flicking the butt, she reached for his assistance. "Are we lost?"

He tugged, bringing her upright. "David wanted us to follow the streams east, but everything ends up here. If we head west we might have a better chance of meeting up with..." he snapped, trying to remember the word. "*Cebris?*"

"Cerberus."

"Right," he hummed. "Right." A bit of unknowledgeable silence. "And what is that exactly?" eyes narrowing for effect.

"He was the guardian of the gates of the underworld. A monstrous dog of three heads."

"You love dogs!" he joked, throwing his hands up into the air.

"Tone, Francesco," she scolded, eyes threatening him. "Don't turn this into one of your routines."

"David always did know how to write specifically for me."

She cocked the shotgun, making sure the spent shell rolled into his chest.

"You sound like Mama now," he gambled with a smile.

She pushed past him, following the gentle trickle of a stream that wormed its way through clustered pine, the bushy towers trembling in the wind as their home had once again been invaded.

"Across the bridge, past the evil thorns, into the black forest, the knight rode!"

The brave hero paused in the swept trail, "Do you have to narrate so loudly?"

David stood, brushing aside the plentiful boughs of a juniper bush, shutting his sheepskin binder. "How else are we going to know what's happening in this scene?"

Frankie adjusted his helmet, a colander purloined from his mother's cupboard before they had departed. "It's confusing me."

"Is this where I come in?" Cecilia asked.

"No!" David shouted. "The knight hasn't even wandered for a hundred years yet."

"People don't live that long," Frankie explained.

"He's right," she added, pulling on a fake wig of collected moss.

"It's just a story," David whined.

"What if the knight is cursed by the old witch?" Frankie suggested.

"That's not how the story goes."

"We can make the story go in any direction we want. Maybe the knight has a partner who helps him defeat the dragon?"

"*Vaffanculo!*" David shouted, throwing his binder at Frankie, his rear tucking in as it avoided him.

"David!" Cecilia chastised.

"I want to do it my way," he muttered, arms crossed as his face steamed into a beet hue.

Frankie retrieved the book, dusting the wool of dead leaves and clumps of dry soil. He handed it back to his brother.

"*Grazi,*" he seethed.

"Where is the brave knight off to now?"

David sighed, popping open his script. "He became lost in the branches and could not find his way home."

Frankie feigned fear, chopping at the low hanging arms of a stripped birch with his cardboard sword of arguable strength. "Where am I?"

David giggled at the enthusiasm.

"Mama! I am so lost! Will I ever find my love? Will I ever find my long lost *polpette*?"

The ad lib delighted the playwright to no end, his giggling practically buckling his legs.

"*Polpette!?*" the knight called, hopping to a lazy stone perched beneath a swaying maple. He danced in the filtered sunlight, calling for the dinner staple, dodging imaginary monsters.

"A hundred years have passed," David read. "And the knight has not found his way out. There are no signs of the dragon and no signs of his love, Valentina."

"Does this have a sad ending?" Cecilia interrupted.

"I don't know yet."

She threw the hood of her black robe over her head and crouched, waddling towards Frankie as she hissed, imitating the creaking sound of her old, evil bones.

"You are lost, brave knight?"

"I am just lost," he admitted. "I am not brave."

"I will make a deal with you. Bring me the flower that is protected by the wicked dragon and I will show you a way out of this forest."

"I cannot defeat the dragon on my own."

The witch fluttered around the knight, throwing dirt into the air, concealed in the tiny pockets of the inner lining. "I know all kinds of magic that can help you. I have an elixir that will defeat the dragon. All you must do is drink it, and you will be able to defeat one hundred dragons!"

"Throw in a *polpette* and you have a deal!"

"*Frankie!*" David chided.

Cecilia broke character, her stomach tickled by the still-running joke.

The quiet mountain retreat rumbled with a high-pitched release, the guttural, low frequency galloping right behind it. Their performance ceased as they exchanged concern.

Frankie bolted towards the disturbance, his siblings in tow, no need for a word spoken. They rushed past the crudely constructed dragon of balsa wood, papier-mâché, tattered blankets, and too much green paint, bursting through the thicket, leaving it to twist in their wake.

They cleared the stream, hopping over the flow; David carefully traversed using the flat, elevated stones that had greedily poked their heads above the surface. Finally, into the clearing, they found their mother, kneeling, head hung low. She turned towards their commotion knowing the creatures of the forest would not cause such an obvious racket. Her shotgun fumed, coughing smoke from a successful launch.

She waved them forward. Trotting over fallen branches, they approached cautiously, a gasping, curdled wheeze hiding amongst the growth below.

The deer shut its eyes, ashamed, wishing it would not have to perish in the comfort of such a unified and captivated audience.

The lasting pulse of a rifle forced them to stop, her fingers curling away from the shotgun, drying her anxious palms.

"Others must be escaping," she said.

"Which means we must wait for him," Frankie observed.

"For how long?"

"Until he is finished hunting."

The forest returned to its intoxicating droll as they continued. Above the swaying crowns, a flock gathered with wings extended, caught on an updraft, soaring in a wide circle. They begin to break

BELOW

formation, diving into the brush, tweeting in a pulsating screech.

The curved, orange beak *cawed* as the first waldrapp stumbled to the needle-scattered ground, backing Frankie away from the sudden introduction.

"You love birds!" Cecilia teased.

"*Scio! Scio!*" he insisted, flapping his arms. The three-foot bird cocked its thin head, muttering, the translation lost between them. Its face had been plucked, a leathery, pink and red splotch drifting across the forehead. Black feathers shimmered like motor oil as it strutted, pecking the ground for morsels. "*Scio!*" Frankie yelled again, kicking his boot wildly.

A second, curious peer found a perch on the twisted arm of a knotted oak, joining a chorus as the flock disappeared from the sky, taking refuge under the canopy, surrounding Frankie and Cecilia.

They spoke out of sync, crowing their own agitation in squealing soliloquies. The conversation turned sour as they began the hunt, pecking at the tentacle-like branches of dogwood and birch. Breaking through the thin bark, the trees began to bleed as the thin bills pierced deep into the muscle and fat. Viscous pitch oozed from the bulbous burls, lumps suddenly appearing: arms, legs, fingers, faces twisted in agonizing positions, frozen, waiting to be feasted upon.

Cecilia stared into the wooden, empty eyes of a woman reaching from one branch to another, her torso folded into the bark, her hands leaking as a waldrapp stabbed at her knuckles. Francesco too saw the trapped souls, their final acts captured in the tallest boughs, fodder for the hungry sentries.

"Mama...?" She stared at the effigy, arms sprawled above her head, eyes closed in peace. Her wrists had been slit, moss spilling from the suicide, growing, fluttering, covering the base of a maple, its roots poking through the soft, pliable soil.

"Cecilia?" Frankie called, watching as she approached the trunk, fingers extended.

A scream tore them from their mother's sin, the lips of the damned above now revealed by the hungry flock, free to call to those in earshot. Forgiveness and penance did not spill forth, but pain and fear. Beaks descended, ripping the instruments and muffling the sounds with blood.

"Mama..." But a pair of wings intervened, locking its claws into her mother's face, snapping at Cecilia. She screeched her own call, flipping the shotgun in her hands and ramming the stock into the avian skull. The mask of bark tore, strands of sap clinging between the pelt and skin, as the bird was cast aside, stunned into a ravenous seizure, but far from dead.

Her mother's eyes opened, her nose barely able to breathe, still plugged with pulp. The incisions from the eager waldrapp oozed as Cecilia dissected around the mouth, exposing the dormant voice.

Francesco had let his revolver drop to his side, slowly dragging his feet in the odds and ends tossed aside by the meals above. He watched as Cecilia caressed his mother's head, tears streaming from both of their eyes.

"Mama!" she wept, her hands stained by the oozing pitch.

"Why am I here?"

"I-I-don't know. I-"

More lamentations exploded from the dead, distracting the reunion.

"Francesco," his mother called.

He was afraid.

He was but a child, no more than twelve. Why was he tasked with finding her? Why was he the one who had to summon those who could attend?

Fighting back a loss of color, a tear slipped through the defenses. "No!" he screamed, dragging the ferocious denial. The preening ceased, those in attendance swallowing what had been clenched in the corners of their rostrums. "You left us!"

"*Francesco!*" Cecilia fired back.

"No; you abandoned us. You took what you wanted, you completed your vendetta and you could not stand to fight anymore."

"Leave her alone!"

"This is not real, Cici."

His mother could barely move, tears mixing with her wounds as she tried to bite through the pain. "Francesco, forgive me..."

"*You are not my mother.*"

"Francesco!" both women delivered the same disappointed, impassioned tone.

"What the fuck...?" his hands rubbed free the blur, the moisture swirling with flakes of bark and pollen.

"I am sorry," his mother sobbed. "I cannot begin to explain what led me to this decision."

"Easy, huh? For you? Just let us fend for ourselves."

"Do not think that I abandoned you because I rejected you."

"What else am I supposed to think?"

"Let her speak!" rang a voice from the heavens.

"Allow her to explain," croaked the branches of the oak. "Hold your tongue! We have eternity, you do not."

"Shut up!" Francesco snarled.

"Frankie...I am sorry. Papa, he stole what was left of me. Ridding him from this earth did little to cure what was left behind. I kept my emotions rigid, I could not cry, I could not smile. I broke, Francesco. I simply broke. Can you endure pain? Can you endure it when you close your eyes in the middle of the day, when you are so far away from what caused it, yet it digs into your flesh, reminding you of the nights spent nursing your wounds? I could not. I would not. I still loved you, I still cared for you, but I decided that your life would be better without my pain. I had to leave. Can you imagine a life watching from a distance as I deteriorated? What would you have done? It was not your job to save me. I would not put that burden on you, or Cici, or David. I alone carry that. Me, Francesco. I forgive you. I forgive you for thinking that you were the only reason why. I forgive you for being angry, I forgive you for the suffering, the sadness, the discovery. You three are all that matters. I gave you a way out. You did not realize it, but you seized it, you climbed out of the pit Papa created. I have rectified my decision; will you do the same? Will you forgive me?"

Frankie knelt before his mother, patches of sweat reforming under his arms as he fought through a nervous fever.

"I..." he mumbled.

"You could not save me, Francesco. Not then. But I have no purpose without my children. Please, do not turn from me."

"Mama," his hand hovering over the bark. "I..."

"Erase this pain. Clear this guilt from our minds."

"I....I...forgive you..."

She choked, head stuttering as the moss streaming from her wrists wilted, the vibrant green aura immolating strand by strand.

"What's happening?" Frankie shouted.

"Mama?" Cecilia cried, voice *cracking*.

Their mother's head stiffened as the flames crawled over her. He was forced to retreat, watching the funeral pyre helplessly.

"What's happening to her?" he asked again, facing the gathered wooden souls.

"She is returning," came a hoarse explanation.

"Where? To where!?" he shouted.

"To Limbo."

"To blessed freedom, to await further judgment."

"Her guilt has been cured, but she must wait, alone, far from here. Far from those who are still being punished."

"Her cleansing can now begin. She has released what she has

held on to."

The flock tired of the proceedings, mocking their sympathy with cackling honks as they pumped their oily wings.

"They will return," the sinful regretted. "To feast and digest our own guilt when it has hardened across our lips."

"Why must she be judged?" Frankie protested. "She was innocent!"

"All are judged. All must be vetted. Perhaps she will find solace that her own torment has ended, and hope will rise if she should be declared worthy."

"What about *my* torment!?" he screamed, saliva spewing from his anger. "Bring her back!"

"Here, we are boiled down to our sins, nothing more," they lamented.

"Bring her back!"

The deer had been hung by its neck, the organs placed into an overflowing bucket for sorting. The shotgun she had used to down the beast had been kept just out of reach, so curious hands did not dabble. A stubby knife hugged the marbled layer between flesh and fur, the gentle sawing separating the pelt.

"Mama?" Cecilia asked, flexing a pair of feathered wings attached to her back, the shoulder straps tucked underneath her arms. "Why do we need to take its fur. Can't we let him keep it?"

"He does not need it, Cici," she assured. "It will keep us warm in the winter."

She nodded, shifting atop the stump, her black robe thrown over the surface to keep her dress dry, the strands of white moss dangling over the edge of the hood. She remembered her mother being much older, perhaps her own inability to accept how young she had been when she had succumbed to her own pain. The dark locks of the elder's hair had settled beneath a cream raffia, the cut relatively short, the pesky strands no longer in danger of meddling with her work or her vision.

Her mother cleared away a line of perspiration from her forehead, rubbing the healing bruise a bit too hard. The edges had yellowed, the center throbbing in blue and purple.

"Careful not to tear it again, we need the whole thing intact if we want any chance at warmth." Her father would not be satisfied by any action that did not involve his hand. He passed them, refusing to make eye contact, a yoke balancing on his shoulder as he carted water up towards the cabin.

"Is the well out again?" her mother asked, retreating to a familiar timidity.

"It's always out," he barked.

Frankie had emerged from the cabin, kicking loose rocks down the incline, watching them flop into the forest.

"Francesco," her father called, waving him over. His shyness barely hid his guilt, but their father simply needed assistance and was relatively unsuspicious. "Take a bucket, bring it 'round back." He unhooked the heavy handle, but the transfer slipped, the water wasted on the dry grass.

David's frantic squealing pumped her father's legs, knees in danger of smacking his chin, taking the small hill with ease as he burst into the cabin.

Her mother grabbed the elongated shotgun, snapping the break-away, only one barrel still loaded. "Stay here, Cecilia. I will tell you when it is safe." There was an unnerving lack of panic in the order. Her mother fished into the folds of her dress, *snapping* the sturdy chain free. She gave the crimson rosary a disgusted scowl and tossed it to the ground.

Cecilia watched the checkered skirt ascend, Frankie slipping out of sight, towards the internal commotion.

A breeze caught the flayed buck, twisting him silently as Cecilia remained, following the instructions diligently, her feathers fluttering as she adjusted their fit. Free to dawdle, she approached the discarded necklace, bending down carefully to touch the perfect beads.

The gunshot drew her back to the cabin.

"Francesco?"

Cecilia cradled the pump-action in her arms, staring, delusions of flight edging her towards the emerald maze behind her.

Frankie paced, tearing follicles of hair from the root as he bellowed. "Bring her back!"

"Francesco?" she called again, timid, trying not to inflame his fury further.

A damp spoil had colored his face, perspiration soaked into his collar. His bloodshot eyes studied her. "Where did you go?"

"I'm right here. I haven't left."

"Mama...she was right here." He stomped towards the base of a moss-covered maple, digging his fingers in the dew-kissed vegetation. "The birds..." his head craned to the monochrome sky. "The-they were here. The trees, Cici. You saw them?"

"I haven't seen anything, Frankie."

He stepped away, waking from one nightmare and tumbling into another. The only reaction remaining was to laugh, tears stewing with his drunken cackle. "She-she was right here," he used his revolver to identify the sight of his mother's plea. He could barely speak, giggling between words. "I...I...forgave her...she made me forgive her...and then she-sh-she left us again."

A gunshot stifled his criticisms, a dull ache floating up Cecilia's back as she had assumed that Frankie had released a bit of steam, the crest of the echo enveloping them. He checked the barrel of his revolver, no heat and smoke to speak of. Free momentarily of his descent, he continued west, knocking aside the spindly branches of a birch.

Cecilia allowed him several paces, trotting behind the inspector's sense of duty. He slid to his belly, collecting rotting leaves around his chest. The forest had formed a ridge, perching it above an isolated valley littered with ochre and maroon fronds. Rocks of forgotten cliffs poked through the soil, time giving them the appearance of being stacked by the Gods of the forest. Frankie had found the edge of the bluff, the advantage allowing him to look down on the entire, vulnerable scene.

A ditch had been dug from the base of the rock wall, fanning out, following the curvature of the rim. Like the victims of a plague, they had been dumped, unbound, atop one another, decomposing into the body below. A viscous soup formed at the bedrock, fuming with maggots greedily devouring the sacrificed flesh.

At the top of the ditch, a fresh addition laid face down, rolled unceremoniously by a fellow black-robed congregant into the compost. The Racoon adjusted his mask, spitting a wad of mucus onto the ground before he rejoined a stringy Possum. He stood above a mutilated stump, the surface ruined with hundreds of bloody incisions. A sobbing sacrifice had laid his cheek onto the splintery chopping block as the Possum spun a woodsman's axe in his hands.

Cecilia edged closer, seeking camouflage behind a cluster of bushy laurels.

"For the crime of attempting to schism our beliefs, for the

crime of inciting revolt, brother, you have been condemned to be-
heading!" The Racoon took his position, pinning the helpless congregant in place.

"No! No!"

The executioner raised his blade, swinging his arms as if splitting logs for winter kindling. The axe chewed through the bone,
disconnecting the nervous system, spraying the Racoon in a liberal
wave. The bottom of the blade caught the stump but had not completely severed the guilty. Wrenching it free, a second attempt finished the surgery, dumping the head into the leaves.

"Fuck!" the Racoon cried, flicking his hands free of blood. "You
couldn't do a clean cut?"

Cecilia knew that voice, it's annoying cadence searching for
a match in her memory. There was a liquidity to it, a clench that
forced each word to be spit past stretched lips.

The Possum shrugged, his purpose simply to end the life, not
make it elegant. His uninterested response conjured a pistol from his
bloodied partner, the barrel oozing as he ended the executioner with
a bullet to the head. The axe slipped from his hands as he fell peacefully into the sodden earth.

The Raccoon holstered his weapon and proceeded to stow the
bodies in the festering pit of the guilty.

Frankie slithered away from the edge of the ridge, working his
way towards Cecilia. "I know that voice," she whispered.

He glanced around their perimeter, clearing them of interlop-
ers. "Wolf or Mouse?"

$$\triangledown \, \text{A} \, \triangledown \, \triangle$$

He had wedged himself between the tub and the toilet, his legs
straight, left shoe untied, his usual urge of kicking them off in the
entryway somehow curbed this afternoon. The shower curtain had
been pulled halfway around the clawfoot, porcelain womb, a tempo-
rary shroud to those seeking relief from bladder and bowel troubles.

Frankie reached into his trouser pocket and retrieved the folded cardstock. His first two trimesters had been ridden with scathing
reports of *sufficiente* and *respinto*, scattered in alternating fashion
across *artografia, canto, geografia, storio e cultura fascista*, the pen
bleeding over from frustration as he barely attended any class other
than working with his hands.

He had been excited to show her the remarks of his instructors, how he had sharpened his mind, praises of *distinto* littering the final column, the red angry pen replaced with black ink and encouraging exclamation points. The texture ripped easily, the work and excitement wasted. He sprinkled the scraps into the toilet, laying his head back against the tiled wall. Reaching for the pack of cigarettes on the lip of the tub, he stole one, lighting it and dragging a cloud into his lungs.

His mother's eyes had remained open, staring at him as if he himself had handed her the razor and carefully placed in the attached soap dish. The dark water covered her breasts, her neck in danger of slipping below the surface. Her right hand had fallen by her side, her left dangling over the rim, droplets lingering on the edge of her fingertips, *plopping* into a puddle below. He had left bloodied footprints as panic had set in, but he supposed that now would be an inappropriate time to clean up. No need to hide it, until-

"Frankie!" The familiar whine of the front door closing forcefully, the sill unshaven, preventing it from simply shutting from its own weight. David marched down the hallway, a harmony in his strut.

Frankie tossed the cigarette into the bathtub, eyes leaking as he tried to adjust his focus, preferring to blur himself from the world. As the tobacco sizzled in the murky water, a small plume of smoke rose, signaling its last gasp.

David opened the bathroom door.

She had not raised the shotgun, allowing perhaps for a bit of repentance.

Frankie's vision had remained clouded, turning against his father's fist towards the angel in the doorway, bordered by the shimmering light of the summer afternoon.

"I waited..." she whispered, hands balmy, the stock slipping slightly. "I waited for you to change. I listened to your tongue. I sat by your side, I waded in the trauma you brought back from the war. *All to be judged by your fist.*"

Frankie tried to open his father's grip, peeling the fingers back like the rind of a rotten fruit, stiff and wet.

"You speak like a woman mad with fever," his father scolded. "Alessandra, you must put it down." His eyes lowered towards the shotgun, he knew she would have no trouble dropping him.

"*Let him go*," she barked through grinding molars.

"Alessandra–"

"*Now*, Paolo!" The barrel rose, flush with his forehead.

He nodded, half-mocking her as he released their son. Frankie's feet found the hardwood, his mouth sucking a serving of freedom. He rubbed his neck with shivering hands making sure it remained attached.

Paolo raised his palms, admitting defeat. "And now?" he smiled, a gap where a tooth had been pulled.

Thunder crashed as the shotgun crowed, the flash of light tearing through his skull as it separated below the nose. The buckshot spread, peeling back the skin like a popped balloon as it shredded the meat into a cloud of thickness, smearing matter and bone against the walls of the cabin. His tongue wriggled, tapping the bottom of his jaw, as what remained abandoned through the opened veins. The body slumped to the ground, leaking through the slats, flooding the basement.

Frankie could barely exhale, his throat impenetrable once again. Heat rose up his back, perspiration bulging down the follicles of his unkempt hair. Alessandra stood tall against the smoke of her vendetta as her eldest screamed with what little his lungs could provide.

▽△▽△

The Racoon wiped the blood of his former brothers across his robe, groaning in disgust. He had waltzed from the mass grave, far from concerned about his vulnerability.

A limb *snapped*.

His bulging lenses whipped towards the disturbance. The creatures of the forest had all but fled the inner density, seeking water and shelter from nefarious noises and sleepless nights. Deciding that the trees were old bastards, unable to keep their bones tended, he continued onward.

The Wolf and the Mouse waited for him, embraced in black. He paused, unsure of their intentions. "What the fuck are you doing here?"

They turned towards each other, sharing a silent conversation.

"You just get here?" The Racoon pried. "What's with the rucksack?"

The Wolf raised a shotgun and pumped a shell into the unsuspecting Racoon, the blast carrying him some distance, punching him hard into the soil.

The Mouse raised his mask. "Jesus! I didn't say kill him."

Cecilia removed the hungry Wolf, "You can't just aim this thing, it sprays all over the place!"

The Racoon moaned, fumbling for his chest. They shared a look of opportunity and rushed the fallen creature. Frankie retrieved the loose pistol as Cecilia prepared a new round, aiming for the incapacitated head.

"Don't move," Frankie cautioned, spreading the black robe. A rusted iron plate had been fashioned around the congregant's chest, the power of the buckshot burrowing deep into the vest, not enough to puncture.

Cecilia grabbed the top of the leathery mask.

"Ow! Ow!" he pleaded, her fingers gripping bits of his hair as she slid the visage free.

"Zampa!" he spat, wires running between his upper and lower jaw, clamping it shut so his wounds could properly heal.

"Jesus! Fuck-what the fuck!? *Petrisone?*"

"That's him," Cecilia seethed.

"Who?"

"That's the bastard who forced me to sign the confession."

"I didn't force anything!" he pleaded, slurring his consonants, saliva spilling out of the corners of his mouth. He squinted, his mandible flaming from the intensity of the pressure.

"Who do you think gave him the broken jaw?" Frankie smiled.

The revelation forced appreciation from her own cocked grin, a bit blasphemous.

"Grab him."

Cecilia followed, slipping her hands under the corrupt inspector's underarms as they hoisted him upright.

"You should have told me you were a lost soul," curling his lip to allow air past the metallic studs.

"We're not part of this shit," Frankie shot back. "Then again, you were never the observant type."

"You're actually cute without your nunnery costume," pointing at Cecilia's face.

"Oh my God, *he's an idiot,*" she groaned.

Frankie forced the newly acquired pistol to Petrisone's forehead. "What did I tell you about talking to her?"

"You said don't call her a *cunt*! I didn't call her a cunt."

"He's not wrong," she agreed.

"What are your people doing out here?" Frankie asked.

"What the fuck do I know?"

Frankie bashed the side of his head with the butt of the pistol, knocking Petrisone back into the grimy deposit.

"You're a cop, Zampa!"

Frustration dowsed the interrogation.

"*Stronzo*," Cecilia muttered. "We saw you kill those men."

"Are there other graves?" Frankie inquired.

Petrisone struggled to remain in control of his pain tolerance, shaking his head to shed the cobwebs. "Of course, there are others! Up and down the mountains they've buried bodies."

"Why do they kill so many?" she pushed.

"They are merely pawns. Sacrifices. Rituals require blood, Sister."

"Why did you kill the executioner?"

"He got blood on my fucking robe! Filth is a sin, you should know that; using that mouth like a good, little *zoccola*."

Frankie popped a round into the ground at his ear, showering Petrisone with mulch, adding a second and third above his head as he closed in for an execution of his own.

"Francesco!" Cecilia screamed, wrenching his hand back, ceasing the intimidation.

The cowering Raccoon curled into himself, whimpering, snot dribbling from his nose as he balled. Her eyes insisted to shed the moment, that the words alone would not hurt her. Frankie relinquished, lowering the pistol.

"Fucking Zampas!" Petrisone screamed as best he could. "Making me come out to the middle of this fucking swamp. Wear a fucking mask made of fucking skin. I can practically see Austria from here!" He thrust his elbow out, crawling slowly as if his anger required solitude.

Frankie looked at the rubbery Mouse head in his hands. The stitches were not merely thread, the pockmarked flesh of similar, but not exact, tones. Those in the sacrificial pit had been dissected to create the next one's anonymity.

Frankie fished into the rucksack and pulled a set of handcuffs from a buckled pocket.

"Our Lord will fix this," Petrisone continued, slithering like a worm. "He will devour you for threatening one of his ow-OW! *OW!*" His wrist bent behind his back as the cold sting of the interlocking metal pressed against the bottom of his palm. His free hand plunged into the earth, gripping the malleable dirt, but Frankie's strength tore the soil, securing his hands in the restraints.

Pulling back on the linked chain, the prisoner was forced to his knees, then to his feet, offering much resistance and pathetic mewling.

"Don't kill me, please," he begged, flecks of dirt staining his cheek.

"I'm not going to kill you," Frankie assured. "She might," turning towards Cecilia, "but not if you talk."

Her grip on the shotgun inspired little confidence, but he nodded furiously.

"What are you doing out here?"

Petrisone swallowed, trying to control his urge to sing. "There's a ceremony, planned for tonight. The resurrection of our Lord and the coming of his son. We've been waiting for thousands of years for an opportunity like this."

"You wish to resurrect Satan?" Cecilia clarified.

A nod. "We have assembled the necessary ingredients from the sinners. Tonight, they will inject the virgin and sacrifice the newborn blood. The Father will speak the incantations and we will kneel before the birth of our Lord as he is reincarnated."

"Jesus," Frankie spat, a metallic salt drying his tongue.

"How will he be reincarnated?" Cecilia asked.

"In the body of the vessel."

"Who has been chosen?"

Bewilderment spilled across Petrisone's face. "You came all the way out here for this, didn't you?"

"David..." Frankie muttered.

"*Avere i coglioni!* This kid. Nothing behind the eyes. Kills for fun."

"That's why he branded them. He was tagging them, not chastising them."

"There are many sins in this world, Francesco, a treasure trove of those who may be sacrificed."

"Antonio De Sio," Cecilia interjected. "Why did he become possessed?"

"You're asking the wrong person. David was finished with his task, the murders needed to stop, buy us more time. Little Antonio was known for his outbursts, his low mental capacity, it fit the narrative and we ran with it."

"But the papers exposed you, David wrote another letter," Frankie reminded him.

"Nobody believes that shit! David had to be controlled. He was believing in a cause that splintered from ours. His last letter was a gross oversight, but Pio XII's death overshadowed all of it. The world mourns, Francesco, for a man in a gilded crown with power dictated by his fellow men, not for some pregnant *pompinara*. The politics matter with the fringe of our society only."

"Why David?" Cecelia asked.

"Because he is weak. Because he is impressionable. *A mezza sega!* He does as he is told without a fight, without disrespect. I envy that."

"Why you?" Frankie wondered.

"Because this world is shit, Francesco. It is utter *shit*. This system is broken. These people are broken. *We* will rain fire and blood onto the streets and *we* will drown those unworthy. Our Lord will thresh the fields that these inglorious heathens have sown. A new world order will form, and the chosen ones, the souls lost now, will be found. *We* will have a place at His right hand. *We* will be rewarded for our efforts. You pray for empty promises, you repent against your vanity, but you return each time to the sewer you have flooded. This experiment is over. And people like you will be His puppets. He will eat your flesh, He will drink your blood, and He will mock you for eternity as He *fucks you*."

"Do you feel him kicking?"

Cecilia's ears filled with the whirling winds of the ocean's current as she pressed herself to the swollen belly, rubbing her hands along the top of the dome.

"I think he's sleeping," she joked, smiling.

"Not much longer until he will be up all night," followed by a concerned, attention-seeking sigh.

Cecilia straightened herself on the bed and laid her head atop a damp, feathered pillow. "The Abbey will take care of him," stroking the worried face.

"Have you heard from them?"

"No, but I suspect with the donation they will have no issue."

"I'm afraid they will reject him."

Cecilia placed her hands once more on the nude belly, rubbing clockwise. "They know nothing more than you cannot keep him. Frankly, they need improvements to their rectory and the money will certainly help."

"What about us? We cannot remain so secretive forever."

"I will leave when the time is right."

"Why not now?"

"I cannot abandon the children."

"As you abandon ours?"

"You know that we cannot raise him here. Not in this epicenter."

"He will see his mothers when time permits, then? What kind of life is that?"

Cecilia sat up, shifting her legs to the floor and turning her back. "Are you regretting this already?"

"No...no. I'm just...*afraid*."

"Do I not stand to lose something as well? The church will go as so far as to hang me."

"You know they won't resort to that melodrama."

"Once he is born, things will be different."

"I know. I am simply tired of waiting."

Cecilia turned, leaning in, lips slowly enveloping as their tongues probed.

"Anna!?" the siren came from the foyer, the double doors shutting with an urgent echo.

Cecilia broke towards the sound.

"Antonio," Anna worried, scooting towards the edge of the bed. She leaned away from her belly, pressing down hard upon the mattress as her knees pumped, raising her straight, careful to ease her back into the motion. She waddled towards the door and peeled back a sliver. "Just a moment!" she called, shutting it. "You must go."

Cecilia had already begun to redress, slipping herself into a black habit as Anna stared at her bare breasts, following the flowing tunic downward as it shrouded the gaunt outline.

"Have you been eating?"

She paused, coif halfway over her face. "Now I am too skinny?"

"I just worry."

A concerned knock, tapping like a woodpecker.

Anna struggled as she donned a plush, emerald robe, cinching it tight around her waist. Cecilia pinned her crown band to her coif and layered a veil over her head, masking herself in piety. Quickly, to her blood-red rosary and creased Bible, clearing her throat.

The door opened and she humbly exited, pretending to catch herself before bumping into the spectacled brother. "My apologies," she bowed.

"Again, with this?" furrowing his brows.

"You remember Sister Zampa?"

"*Signora*," he nodded, finding a bit of restraint. "This *bastardo* is going to slide out a priest if its blessed one more time."

"There is nothing wrong with reflection and prayer," Cecilia reminded him. "I hope to see you both at service this Sunday."

"We have a family engagement out of the city," he huffed, unraveling a billfold and counting out a month's worth of donations. "For the poor or the sick, whatever you need."

"*Grazi*," she grinned, accepting the alms. She turned to Anna and slid her mother's rosary into the hands of her love. "Until next week?"

"Thank you, Sister."

"*Signore*," she nodded, shuffling past the impatient sibling.

The pair whispered as she descended a gilded staircase, her short-heeled shoes *clacking* on the marble treads. The servants had been occupied, preparing an afternoon meal of fruit, cured meats, and aged cheese sliced into perfect cubes. The palatial entryway of pastel blue *cracked* its jaws as it labored open, allowing sunshine to spill across her smile.

"Sister?"

She paused, pivoting towards the balcony, eyeing Antonio as he leaned across the railing.

"Would you like one of our drivers to escort you back to the church?"

"No, thank you, *Signore*. It is such a beautiful day, I think I will walk."

She continued into the pleasing warmth of the golden light, a chill suddenly digging its claws into her shoulders. The illumination ceased, the mansion of stolen wealth bathed now with the trappings of a blackened, cramped stairwell, her shadow sucked into the void.

The hustle of trays overflowing with maggot-encased innards and gravy boats of viscous drippings found their place at a banquet situated at the far side of the dilapidated loft. A final supper had been prepared, the chef's perspiring back shielding his busy and stained hands. The wailings of trauma floated from the carved surface as he ripped the bloody boy from the womb, forcing Anna to vomit against the sensation, reaching helplessly for Cecilia.

But she was so far away, clueless as to what she had done to deserve such penance.

▽△▽△

The photograph had not been adjusted for depth, the focus of the face blurred as the cheeks rose and the baggage of sleepless nights began. It was obvious to her, though, the death mask that Anna had worn when she was first discovered.

Cecilia stared at the flimsy print, somehow desensitized to the open wound. Hung like a butcher's prize, ready for pelt to be separated, Anna looked so much wider than she remembered, her flesh sagging, even in her third trimester.

The car jolted as the poor maintenance of the country road began to rear. Frankie handled the bump, bringing the steering wheel straight, sighing under the beat of the windshield wipers.

She had promised herself she would not attend the funeral, it would seem suspicious, especially from her nosy brother. If she had not answered the phone, if she had simply stayed in her room, feigned illness, hid in the reaches of her bureau, then she would not be in her brother's car, shoving years' worth of silence into a six-hour road trip.

"What happened to her baby?" she asked, shimmying the photographs around the official police file.

Frankie took his eyes of the road momentarily, offering a bit of disbelief. "How did you know?"

"A woman's body changes, Francesco. I worked in the mission hospital in Honduras, there is very little that I have not seen."

He understood that he was to keep his prying to a minimum. "They never found the baby."

"I see," she whispered, disappointed, but fully prepared for the truth.

"They never found the baby..." he whispered, trying to decipher the brake lights several hundred meters down the road.

Cecilia had not been distracted by the awkward urination, her back turned, watching the ebb of the mixed-species forest.

"Move the robe!" Petrisone shouted. "*Cazzo!* Now I smell like piss!"

"Maybe you should think about a pair of trousers underneath, eh?" Frankie teased.

"Easier to fuck with nothing in the way," he cackled.

"*Jesus,*" Cecilia sighed.

"Done?" Frankie pressed.

"Yeah, yeah."

"How much further?" she asked, turning towards the now robed and decent.

"Half a kilometer, maybe a little less."

Frankie wiggled the pistol, instructing the prisoner to take the point position. They kept several paces behind him, their voices lowered for privacy.

"What happened back there, Francesco?"

"He wanted me to hold his fucking cock while he took a piss!"

"No, no," she clarified, "What happened between you and Mama?"

Several meters separated the siblings now, Frankie's eyes caught in the blur of a memory, suddenly feeling the heat of the burning moss. Cecilia cocked her head, the distance a bit too extreme. She released a sharp whistle, pausing Petrisone, his annoyed expression accentuated by the bulge in his mouth.

"You were there," Frankie muttered.

"You kept shouting for Mama."

"You did too."

"I never spoke a word. You went on and on about birds, swatting the air like a maniac, I thought you were just trying to act like a fool."

"She was there," he insisted. "Carved into the tree. You peeled away the bark and she was there."

"Francesco?" Her anxiety churned the soil into sand, threatening to swallow her.

"You were *there*," he pointed, accusing her of lying. "The birds ate the bark, ate their skin. They were screaming, you heard the screaming. They said Mama went to Limbo, that she was to be judged again."

"You were hallucinating," she said, palms out, trying to calm him, approaching carefully. "We are both exhausted."

"She told me that I could not save her," his lips pursed, eyes glazed over in a tidal wave that needed only his encouragement to wash down his cheeks. "She asked me to forgive her. For what she had done."

"Mama killed herself because she was broken. She did not kill herself because she did not love us. She could not bear the pain of living a life that she did not believe in."

"It's a sin!" Frankie screamed.

"No. No, Francesco. It is not a sin. It is a choice. A choice that we must live with. We cannot bring Mama back. The most you can do is forgive her. To forgive yourself. You own no guilt. She rests in peace because she knows that her children will not carry resentment and guilt for the things they have no control over."

"Why did I have to find her?"

"There is no answer. It could have been me, or God forbid, David. But it was *you*. You cannot possibly change that now."

"I forgave her," he nodded. "I forgave her because I saw how much pain she was in, locked inside that fucking prison. The birds... the fucking birds were ready to eat away at her soul; waiting until she regrew...feeding again. I could not bear to see her like that."

"Now you understand," Cecilia smiled. "That is all Mama ever wanted, was for you to understand. She did not need our permission."

She wiped the unintended tears from his cheek, smearing the trickling river.

"Yeah," he squeaked. "but why must we carry her pain?"

"Only you can determine what is pain. To you it is pain, to her it is freedom. It is not written that you cannot feel sympathy."

"She was sad, wasn't she?"

"There is no description for her sadness, Francesco. She could not return from where she was placed."

"A better place..." he whispered.

"I hope so," she smiled. "The pain will fade, with time. That memory will remain, but you can strip it of guilt. Blaming yourself will only make you more susceptible."

"He's escaping," the tone still lingering in his sadness.

Cecilia cocked her head as Petrisone galloped over a sunken trunk, already putting a considerable distance between them.

"He won't get far," she assured, facing Frankie, offering a smile, a private joke now between them.

A gruff exclamation of stupidity and the escapee tripped, consuming a mouthful of dirt.

"I think he *might* need our help," she whispered.

Petrisone wailed like a spoiled child, arms bound behind him, rolling from his side onto his back. His ankle had snapped, the bone pressing against the skin, already swelling with purplish delight. They seized his robe and yanked him from the earth, careful to apply extra weight to the injury.

"*Cazzo!*" he piped, sweat spewing down his temples. Through the wired jaw, he wheezed, attempting to stave off the fire in his lungs.

"How much further now?" Frankie asked.

Huffing through a cycle, he winced, keeping his foot raised above the ground. "Just beyond the thorns."

The forest had suddenly abandoned its perplexity. A wall of thick vines, hardened by time, siphoned of vital nutrients, had sprouted armor. Coarse and jacketed thorns poked through the calcified flesh, running an impenetrable weave across the face of a man-made, stone wall. Tall pines, stripped of their precious needles, shivered behind the barrier, praying that soon they would rejoin their separated brethren.

Playing the reluctant role of crutches, they ferried Petrisone to the edge of the tree line, pausing in the tilled throughway of a once blossoming field, now relegated to a single aisle.

Those who had attempted to scale the wall, whether in or out, had been hung against the embrace of the thorns, jabbing into their skin, making small incisions, the number multiplying as they thrashed. Several congregants had yet to be removed, their skin bleached and oily, waiting for the sun to bake them into powder so that they may finally slip free.

Axled carts, wheels fractured and imperfect, had been abandoned along the stretch, the improvised road slipping into the fog. Flies buzzed over spoiled meat, shoving the maggots aside for a taste of the inner-cities. They stumbled into the middle of the pathway, avoiding a late model car, often seen petering down the narrows streets of their home. The windows had been broken into, blood soiling the entry point, the driver violently pulled through.

"You brought us to the gates, didn't you?" Frankie scolded.

"I need to protect my investment, don't I?" Petrisone grinned.

A corpse had been crushed under the weight of a spilled cart, her arms gasping for assistance, the fingers bony, a memory of flesh still coating them. They avoided the grisly final moment, maneuvering around the supplies of the faithful.

"Why hasn't this been cleaned up?" Cecilia asked.

"Failure is to be mocked. The doors do not simply open for anyone."

Frankie angled the limping annoyance against the side of a sedan, a missing wheel driving it slightly downward as if kneeling to a higher power. "I've had enough of this cryptic nonsense!" he shouted. "How does a fucking moron, a pig, like you, end up in this shit? Huh? Your father was a cobbler and a drinker, he didn't have the time or the stamina to be involved."

Petrisone shoved his shoulder against Frankie, trying to set aside space. "My grandfather was a lost soul! You want to point fingers? Your father was a drunk too! Not to mention a wife-beater! He laid hands on you too, you—"

The back of his head *snapped* against the passenger door, skull throbbing as Frankie met his pissing contest. "You know *nothing* of my father, even if he was a piece of shit."

"For all his flaws, I still admire Paolo."

"What?" Cecilia cocked her head, her guard lowered.

"*We all love him.*"

Frankie stabbed Petrisone's gut with a balled-up fist, a mouthful of air choking him momentarily. His eyes welled as he bent into the pain. "*Bastardo.*"

"Paolo Zampa is dead," Frankie barked through his own clenched jaw.

The defenseless Raccoon stuttered as he attempted to laugh between his injuries. "I suppose David brought you here to speak with him. Don't give me any of that emotional shit, like you've removed him from your heads."

"A shotgun ripped him apart, I was there. Took his head practically clean off."

"One of your vendetta fantasies, perhaps?"

Frankie shoved him forward, forcing him to hop. "Keep walking!"

Petrisone cocked his head, "Paolo assumed you might be angry, but these family issues...they tend to work themselves out."

As he pogoed away from the siblings, Cecilia grabbed Frankie's arm. "What is he going on about?"

"He's psychotic. Only a thick-headed bastard like him would fall prey to a bunch of Devil worshipers in the middle of the goddamn woods. Who knows what David feeds them."

He broke from her concern, catching up to Petrisone, allowing her to stand amongst the refuse alone. She reached into her robe and thumbed through her jacket pocket, removing her mother's rosary. She rolled her fingers slowly over the beads, reciting the holy words of penance, handed down to her by Father Endrizzi.

"*Pater noster, qui es in caelis, sanctificetur nomen tuum.*"

Petrisone paused, shaking his head, a bubbling sensation filling the back of his skull, a concussion setting in.

"*Adveniat regnum tuum. Fiat voluntas tua, sicut in caelo, et in terra.*"

To his knees, shivering, a pale blue injected into his lips. Condensation streamed from his mouth as he hyperventilated, ice water clogging his veins. His eyes gagged, pupils rushing backward.

Frankie bent his arm, scooping up Petrisone to reset him.

"*Panem nostrum quotidianum da nobis hodie, et dimitte nobis debita nostra, sicut et nos dimittimus debitoribus nostris.*"

"No!" Petrisone resisted, bumbling towards a stack of wooden crates.

"*Et ne nos inducas in tentationem, sed libera nos a malo. Amen.*"

He slumped over the vineyard-stamped balsa wood, pawing at the loose lids as the cases tumbled on top of him, pinning him onto the ground, the bottles ringing like a wedding toast.

Cecilia looked away from the cheap jewelry as Frankie stood above the Raccoon, steering his eyes away momentarily to deliver the bad news: "He's dead."

$$\triangledown \; \not\triangle \; \triangledown \; \triangle$$

"They never found the baby..."

Kerosene, rice paper, sweet wine, a pine box or wooden container.

The country road wound to the right, skirting the edge of a vineyard's plush yield.

Prepare thine faces with sackcloth as to spread anonymity. The Lord shall know you by your wretched stench. Until the moment of dedication, it is wise to remain solemn and participate as a nameless, faceless ghoul.

The Mistress is to strip nude, lay upon the altar, and receive the seed of those who wish to call upon the Lord.

Frankie rubbed under his chin, drawing away his exhaustion towards the electric *thwump*.

The sacred symbols shall be drawn as such. Salt shall ring the circumference to protect those who chant the incantations.

An offering of money shall be burned along with the intricate flesh to signify the absence of greed.

Anxiety tightened his collar, a bead of sweat tilting down his neck. He felt like coughing, expelling the lump in his throat.

> *The child shall be raised over the bride, its throat slit with a blessed dagger. The bride shall bathe in its blood, the excess to fill the chalice and all those in favor to drink from it.*

"The child..." he whispered. He remembered the letter, not the first, but an innocuous one, much later. Filled with little information, more ramblings, but a second and third page had contained the instructions. The De Sio crime scene had been staged, the most complete in the series.

"A ceremony," he blurted. "It was a mock ceremony, a trial. But he had no bride because she was with child."

Cecelia had fallen asleep, head propped between the passenger door and the edge of her seat, uncomfortably bobbing to the stresses in the road.

"At least no evidence of one," he trailed off. "She would have laid on the altar. He wouldn't have sacrificed the child without the proper materials. He needed it alive. He needed it for the final performance. He wanted something else. He followed the directions."

"Needed who alive?" she muttered sleepily, adjusting her neck.

"David...he has the De Sio baby. It's alive."

"Hmm?" furrowing her brow, trapped between clarity and lucid follies.

"For his final ceremony. That's what his last letter alludes to. *Present to him that we are leveled.* It's still alive. It's still alive..."

Cecelia chose not to engage, pretending to sleep through his theories. Droplets of rain smeared against the window as Frankie's foot weighed heavy on the accelerator.

A tear worked its way down the curvature of her cheek, the possibility of life overwhelming her.

There was no reason to wait.

A discarded plank had been fetched, wrapped in a shred of the bloodied clothing, doused in kerosene, illuminated. They repeated the process until they had enough to banish the creeping darkness. The body had been shrouded in linen, what some of them had shared the night before, still dotted with sweat from the summer humidity.

Alessandra had set about the tools, gathering what she needed, though a shovel would suffice. They had trekked through the night, torch at hand, ropes dragging the body until they felt the distance was plausible, the earth here moved by creatures of habit rather than the revenge of man. The malleable dirt succumbed easily to the head of the shovel, tossing aside insects disturbed from their nest. The children sat together, embraced by the light of the ceremony, watching their mother dig their father's grave, comforted by a hulking marker of crisscrossing branches and wet hemp.

They stared, not out of fascination, but of necessity. They could not close their eyes, lest they remember the blood, the expulsion, or the echo of the blast. The flames lifted black smoke into the open air, shrouding the stars they desperately wished to call out by name. Instead, they sat quietly, glazed over, becoming inept at processing the events, crumbling them, and burying them in the backs of their own forests.

The body fit snugly into the hole, the knees slightly bent, forgetting to compensate for his height. No time to course correct. Alessandra dumped the loose soil back upon her husband, covering the white sheet, dying the blood black and brown.

The Messenger waited on the outskirts of the darkness, watching as the shovel speared the excess, depositing the grains into the grave.

"How can you tell?" she asked, glancing at Frankie.

"He's definitely dead."

Cecilia poked Petrisone with the barrel of her shotgun. Not even a grin from the rib-tickling. "What happened?"

"H-he just collapsed. I tried to pick him up and he fell. He must have hit his head or something." He pivoted the lifeless expression, switching it this way and that. "The Wolf," he realized.

Cecilia waited patiently for him to explain.

"The man who came into the cabin; the mask I stole. I had seen him before. In the chaos, I lost the connection. But I remember him. He's a police officer too. He was there when I confronted Petrisone and his partner about the false confession."

"Did he say anything to you?"

"No. I had never seen him before, until that moment."

"If the police and the clergy have been summoned here, who

does that leave?" she wondered.

"The politicians."

He began to slip free the blood and piss-stained robe, unlatching the buckshot-chipped iron plate from around the chest. They stood, clearing their knees and backs of tension.

Frankie looked down at the discarded wine bottles that had tried to prevent Petrisone's downfall.

"Thirsty?" he asked plucking a bottle free. No label, the cork loose, starting to swell.

"I hardly think this is the time for such things."

He struck a match, stuffing the remaining three into his back pocket. Curling the chugging flame around the neck, he used the heat to squeeze the cork through the taut mouth. The bottle *popped*, bubbling the top layer of the wine, an almost transparent mist quickly dissipating. He sniffed, snorting the sweet fragrance. "Seems okay." A swig and a satisfied palette emerged. "Sacramental wine," he teased, easing the bottle towards her. "I don't see anything wrong with that."

She could not resist, trying to shuffle her annoyed expression to the forefront. The wine soothed her parched throat, the vintage encouraging her brain to pulse pleasantries. She handed the bottle back. He continued onward, filling his belly. She crossed herself before Petrisone's body, hoping that some peace would come of his horrible actions.

"How long will we follow this trail until we decide we're heading in the wrong direction?" she asked, catching up with him.

"If David is to be believed, then the stream runs directly into Cerberus. I'm hoping at some point these two intersect."

"David seems to say many things," she observed. "What do you make of Papa?"

"You mean that babbling? David must be feeding them lies. He never accepted Papa's death. He was there that night, he knew exactly what happened."

"He was six years old, of course he did not understand."

"I'm not blaming him. He would talk to his collections until he was seventeen! The doctors had to pry them from his hands. He liked to make up stories, he liked to pretend. He is pretending again."

"But these men are real, Francesco."

He could not agree more, failing to admit he might have been wrong.

"He is not the center of attention," she continued "but he is being driven there."

BELOW

Frankie tried to mask his anger with another mouthful of wine.

The protective border wall seemed to falter here. A symbolic tower once activated a sense of intimidation, shrouded by the tall stalks of pine. It had collapsed within itself, now, spilling onto the trail, preventing most modes of transportation from venturing further. They stumbled up the uneven stones, lodging their feet into the tight corners of circumstance, shaking them free only to find more uneven footing. Frankie offered his hand, boosting Cecilia up to the modest peak.

The wall ended.

Meeting the mouth of a massive arch, it became clear that the trail had not been man-made, but a dry riverbed, ferrying fresh water onto the grounds before time and intervention could no longer prevent its evaporation. The sewer system had been plugged by the collapsing parapet, staving off the direct flow, the subterranean entrance clogged with a mountain of yellowing bones.

Hooks had been mounted to the underside of the arch, a length of rope connected, wrapped around the necks of hooded figures, stripped of clothing, hands and legs bound with green hemp. Two corpses had been installed on either side of a scrawled message: *Bella ciao.*

Hungry pests crawled through the refuse below the condemned, munching on what remained of the jerky, giving the bones the eerie appearance that they were vibrating.

"*Nonna* used to sing to us..." Cecilia remembered. "I always assumed it was to prevent Mama from becoming a *modina* like her."

"*O partigiano portami via, o bella ciao, bella ciao, bella ciao ciao ciao...*" Frankie mumbled, off key. "The gangs in Naples would bind the hands and legs of suspected thieves within their own organization with dead snakes. They would strip them of their eyes and teeth, remove any tattoos or identifiable marks, stuff their mouth with coins and drop them at the doorsteps of their enemies."

"They have stolen, thereby we will steal their very identity."

"They had become greedy, wanting only for themselves."

"Just like Satan."

"Then why punish them? Isn't that what he wants?"

"No one likes being stolen from. Not even the Devil."

A moss-tinged staircase had risen from the moat, running alongside the intact wall that still held the arch in place. It disappeared high into the greedy branches, a way forward, without risking injury amongst the thorns.

Navigating the crag, they descended the awkward rubble, approaching the collection of rebels who had rotted on the vine, only for their skeletons to collapse into a heap, unable, now, to be recognized. Shreds of clothing had not yet decomposed, velvet and cotton wisping in the gentle breeze, the rich and poor congregating.

"How long has this been happening?" she wondered.

"Forever," he muttered, angling his head towards the scarecrows. "We've followed the water as far as it can go."

Cecilia took the initiative, rubbing her shoe against the damp moss, testing the strength of the exposed staircase. Using the wall as a guide, she slid her hand against the cool stone, each step calculated.

Frankie bent down, shuffling the bones aside, inspecting the teeth marks of those who had feasted on the scraps. He buried the image, wiping his hands clean on his trousers and returning towards the endless journey.

Cecilia had disappeared.

"Cici?" he called, stepping towards the treads. He leaned into the pathway of the staircase, staring into an enveloped tunnel. A hole of bright hope had been bored at the summit, whether it was flat or relevant could not be determined from such depths. He was certain she had not scaled the sticky branches of maple and birch that hugged the claustrophobic ascent.

"Cici?" he called again, taking the first step forward.

She heard the commotion, looking back down the slope, finding nothing but the black, crashing seas she had crawled from. Swirling wind rocked her like a ship in the midst of an ancient swell, the rucksack dragging her towards the funnel of languishing souls that surrounded her, leaving her little room to stand straight.

They held hands, lovers of all creeds, of all races, of all sexes, endlessly circling the staircase, masking the valleys and trees that had thwarted her only moments ago. Flowing as if underwater, their movements were regulated, agonizing, simply blinking took centuries, their clothing wafting with equal difficulty.

Occasionally, a hand broke the invisible barrier, splashing the risers with water, as if they had found the surface, only to slip back into the depths.

Cold, salted liquid crashed against her neck as she tripped, plunging towards the treads. A hand gripped her rucksack, pulling her into the swirl, the shotgun falling from her reach. The burlap absorbed the water quickly, weighing her down, but the clothed hand reeled in the elusive catch without much effort.

More water spilled from the torrent, rushing across her face. A wrinkled fist shot forward, wrapping its tendrils in the fibers of her hair, pulling her head back, a beacon of pain radiating from the base of her neck. She slipped from the bind of the leather strap, freeing herself momentarily, sinking her nails into the vice attached to her head. Blood squirmed from the incisions and the hungry soul limped away to lick its wounds.

Cast back to her knees, she rolled onto her back as she scooped up the pump-action. Aiming at the drifters proved useless, she did not want to hurt them, she wished only to pass safely. The wind whipped against her wet skin, pushing the droplets between her pimpled pores.

The couples hissed as they swam passed, circling the ascent, drifting towards a darker punishment, though it flashed brilliantly like a collapsing star.

From the crowd came a waterlogged call.

"Cecilia?"

Her head snapped to the right, her name lost in the bubbles.

"Cecilia?"

To the left now. Only a crowd of unhappy.

"Cecilia?" She returned her head straight, waiting patiently as the flowing, amber hair cleared in the flow, Anna's face beaming with happiness beneath. Cecilia's heart collapsed, unable to beat. Synapses had fired too much electricity, her vision fading.

"Where is my child?"

Cecilia's mouth moved, lips mimicking the correct words, but there was too much blockage, too many memories that confused her network, preventing the right order. Anna's fingers broke the clear caul, dripping ocean water onto Cecilia's chest. They caressed her cheek, pulled her forward, leading her into the guilty sea.

The liquid filled her mouth as Anna's lips met hers, the gales picking up, in danger of freezing their kiss. They enveloped one another, the suction fighting for dominance. Refusing to break, water drooled from the nooks of air that appeared as they adjusted.

The affection broke as she could no longer swallow, her eyes popping open into Antonio's manic, wailing expression. He had found her neck, his left hand squeezing tightly, shaking her back and forth, condensing the bone. From beyond her diminishing vision, she spied the intertwined hands, brother and sister doomed to a lifetime of intimate attachment.

A look of regret had been sewn to Anna's face, a hopelessness that could not be redeemed. Her fate had been sealed.

Rage boiled in Cecilia's muscles, her shoulders squaring as she leaned back, pulling Antonio through the barrier into her world.

She shook off the wave that broke through as the blisters on his face began to peel, seared as it had been that day in the cemetery when she had doused him with holy water.

"I am the father that comes into the daughters of man," he barked. "You sin in the eyes of only one."

With her remaining adrenaline, she commanded the shotgun to his chest.

"The power of Christ compels you..." she whispered from beneath his anger, closing her eyes as she released her flames.

His belly erupted, pouring across her as the force jettisoned him back, shrouding Anna in a cloud. The gentle balance between reality broke, the ocean collapsing upon her as she sank upwards, past the sinful audience, floating towards the putrid bottom of the blood-tinged water.

"Are you a decent inspector?"

He laughed, caught momentarily in a stupor. "W-what?" he chuckled, glancing between her and the storm as he eased away from the accelerator.

"Are you?" Cecilia asked again.

"I-I suppose so. I don't know if I understand the question."

"Are you like those men who questioned me? Do you bully people to get what you want?"

"No, of course not! You want to know if I am crooked? Not how many cases I have solved? Or maybe how hard I've worked to become an inspector?"

"Have you ever taken a bribe?"

He cocked his head, slightly annoyed. "Always looking for a confession," he teased. "Does alcohol count?"

She thought a moment, "Just money, I suppose. Or power."

"Did you see my apartment?" he smiled. "I *have* taken..." he cleared his throat. "Well...I won't say."

"What?" she pressed.

"It's nothing. No. Just...next question."

"Tell me!" She slapped his arm playfully. "I'm not prudish."

Impossible to hold back his amusement, he folded quickly under the interrogation. "I was offered sex...and I took it."

"Oh my God!" she mockingly crossed herself. "The Knight is not so pure!"

"It was one time!"

"Just one time!?"

"Well, twice, but it was back to back."

"Francesco! You are a...what do they call it?"

"*Sporco.*"

"*Yes!* Yes."

Rather proud of himself, he tried to hold back the feeling of becoming too comfortable in the moment. "What about you?"

"If I told you anything, I'd have to go to confession."

"So, there *is* something!"

"No! There's nothing."

"You've never taken some of that poor box money? Maybe bought yourself a little wine? Maybe you forgot to bless it?"

"Your only ammunition is wine and bread, you know as much about me as I do about you."

"It's true," he laughed, mixing it with a sigh of realization. She slapped his arm, a childish fit of giggling overwhelming her as she could not let go of his sexual exploits.

They had borrowed the car from his mother. A relic of the 20s, it had once been his father's, but after his passing she had no use for it, keeping it in the garage for when the grandchildren wished to ride up to the cabin.

Alessandra drove slowly, the headlights akin to no less than two candles. Barely enough of the backwoods road could accommodate one vehicle, the edges bordered by irrigation ditches, but she persevered against the terrain and her exhaustion. A sense of dread forced her eyes to the rear mirrors, but only darkness chased them. The children huddled together next to her, caught in the warmth of pleasant dreams, their eyelids fluttering as they slipped deeper into unconsciousness. Cecilia tightened her fist, pressing the beads of her mother's rosary into her delicate flesh.

Again, she checked the mirror. She made a promise to herself that she would not return to the cabin. That she would run from his family.

David stirred, groaning, wiping sweat from across his brow and smearing it against his tired eyes.

"Mama?"

"Yes, David?"

"Where is Papa?"

The mirror held freedom within its rusting frame; though it refused to release the night, it was still freedom nonetheless. At that moment, she did not realize her answer would exit so harshly. She knew what they had witnessed, but this would be the first of a lifetime of explanation, an eternity of repeating the words, knowing they were true, knowing that her children would remember this night and they too would soon repeat it.

"Your Papa is dead."

The shotgun's familiar blast tore through the peaks of the huddling forest, rocking their necks in a rush of heat.

Frankie caught the movement, peering back into the darkened staircase. His revolver glued to his hand, he took the slippery ascent two at a time. The errant fingers of clumsy branches nicked his arms, as he swung past, ducking slightly to avoid the intertwining ceiling.

A lump of shadow laid up ahead, his hands fumbling over it, turning it towards him. "Cici?"

But the rucksack would not acknowledge him. He grunted, throwing the supplies over his shoulder, lumbering up the steep incline. "Cici!?"

He fought against the perspiration, the grinding pain in his joints, the anxiety brought about by his denial, the wine settling nothing. Finally, to the landing, allowing him level ground. She lay slumped upon her side, her weapon cradled against her chest.

"*Cazzo*," he huffed, sliding to his knees. He shook her with passion, slapping her face gently for effect. "Get up, Cici."

She would not respond in kind. Stowing his weapon, he shed the rucksack, rolling her properly onto her back. He slicked back his hair, wiping the grease against his dress shirt. Hesitating, working his hands around the body, he could not decide where to start.

He propped open her mouth and dug his fingers inside, fishing towards the back of her throat. Nothing seemed to be obstructing her breathing. He mumbled to himself, positioning his head over hers. He licked his lips nervously, unsure of how to proceed. He whipped his arm out as if preparing to handle hazardous materials, fingers twiddling the air. He plugged her nose, pinching hard.

In. Out. In. Out. Slowing his heart, clearing his lungs. Inward, a long hold on the crisp mountain breeze. Over her mouth, he locked, breathing out forcefully.

She remained still as he pulled away to inspect. Another deep breath and he transferred the hot intake.

Nothing.

"Cici! Wake up! Huh? Wake up!" He tapped her cheek, leaving only small patches of reddening skin.

A huff of anger and he returned to her mouth, blowing furiously. The expulsion came upon him immediately as she turned from his resuscitation. She cocked her head and ejected sea water, a layer of bile and vomit following, running a river into the wet soil.

Frankie fell to his rear, spitting in reaction to the sight and smell, covering his nose as she coughed.

"Anna..." she moaned.

"It's Frankie, Cici." He crawled to her side as she recoiled from the sickening puddle.

"She was there..."

He retrieved his handkerchief from his back pocket, using the already bloodied cloth to wipe free the mess dribbling across her cheek.

"Francesco...she was there. They were both there."

"It's all right. Just, don't talk. Breathe. Just breathe."

She coughed again, her throat gagging against the aftertaste of alkaline and her last meal.

He sopped up her discomfort, tossing the handkerchief and its horrid stench into the brush. Strands of hair needed to be smoothed out of the way, but she cared little. She reached for him, holding tight his own quivering and sweating hand.

The sky wept for their reunion, little droplets pelting the ground in random order, far from flocking together in the sheets that had pelted the city. He looked up to the sky, opening his mouth for a morsel of the fresh water. As he craned his neck, he saw the entrance for the first time. The trees had infested the corridor at the peak of the staircase, leaving a wide berth between each pocket of trunks, luring them into a dead end. A stone wall had been built here too, another arch interrupting the flow before it faltered into the maze of giants.

A passionate Prussian blue, the wooden gates flexed their centuries' old dominance, luring Frankie towards them. Embedded iron decorated each panel, bulbous lumps connecting long brackets, cinching the beams together, compacting them so as to unburden the hinges.

He could not break away from them, tripling his height, perhaps more. The kingdoms of royalty and knighthood, the legends of his boyhood books, settled beyond the gates, his curiosity driving him forward.

"Frankie," she moaned, her arm skyward for his attention. He collected his rucksack and tightened the leather strap against his chest. He slid the shotgun between his back and the burlap, making sure it would not squeak free. Shoving his arms underneath her, he cradled Cici, lifting her from her discharge.

Towards the entrance, they marched.

Like an ancient troll, the doors groaned with disapproval. Frankie paused in the growl. The hinges *cracked*, spewing flecks of rusted iron and collected pollen, bending as the massive entrance began to open its jaws. Scraping against the thick earth underneath, they revealed the remnants of those who had traveled just as far.

The path led only forward, straight into the gaping mouth. Eclipsing the gates in size, the first head held the distinction of a decaying, black mutt. The bottom jaw had been buried, the fangs spearing through the dirt, an unfortunate soul impaled on the jagged point. Its snout, leathered with calcium, leaked a pulsating, black stew that emptied below, streaming into a ditch that encircled the muzzle. Thick fur protruded through infected pores, the strands coated in the debris carried by the mountain's gust. The expansion of the mouth had ripped against its capacity, widening it into a cave of malnourished gums, oozing pus as flies greedily lapped. Its eyes sat high, towards the back of its head, shrunken into the sockets, bloodshot, soulless, unable to move, forced to stare ahead at its meals as they were lead to the slaughter. A cadre of crows perched themselves on the curvature of its flopping ears, holes of hunger poking through as the flock had become peckish.

Mimicking the Trinity, it had been fused on either side by the hideous, gasping profiles of a rat and a goat, their faces elevated by an incline littered with plague-starved corpses. The disease-ferrying rodent too had had its mouth torn, stretched past its tolerance, ballooning, tent-like. Row upon row of gnawing teeth dropped from the roof, its pale tongue limp, indented from the boots of men. Smoke poured forth from its nostrils, a light blazing in its throat as the odor of sulfur twisted elegantly into the afternoon sky.

The goat's rectangular pupils welled, the gigantic tears pouring down its cheek and soaking into the already muddied ground. Shaved and split horns bore through its skull, installed due to a lack at birth. The upper gums had been punctured by thick chains, ornate chandeliers of searing candles dripping hot wax into obese stalagmites that formed over its bottom teeth, the blistering and bloody lips sagging as they allowed access deep into the cavern.

Within the gaping throat of the dog, they could see the makings of the sanctuary, pillars propping up the fleshy walls, stained glass held in place by dried blood and scar tissue. Ancient wax infested the arms of disorderly pews as new candles burned atop their adornments. The aisle stretched forward, under the watchful eyes of the inverted, swinging by their feet from circular candelabrum. The crimson carpet met the dirty marble chancel, the altar sitting atop, draped in black velvet.

Frankie swallowed what little resolve he had stowed, completely shrunken in the eyes of the feral beasts. He stood before the sickening holes, hoping Cecilia would not wake, that she would be free from witnessing the Devil's playground. Their entrance was cause for celebration, though, as the howl of a pipe organ exploded from the mouths of the once loyal, the soldier of the horde, and the sheepish, hungry, blind follower.

RITUAL

V

The ashes of those who had fallen on their journey curled towards Frankie as air poured through the intertwining copper pipes, the adept, gloved fingers keying the phrasing of a shrill melody. Cecilia stirred, awakening to the spewing mouth of the mutt, their eyes meeting, a frigid spell cast. She bucked, freeing herself from Frankie's care, jabbing her knees into the dirt. An inhalation of the smoky fog, preparing to alert the congregation with terror, but his hand muffled the shriek, an arm extended over her chest to keep her wriggling to a minimum.

"Don't-don't-don't," he whispered as her eyes darted across each of the spewing mouths, her feet scrambling, trying to push herself backward, finding no security in his shadow. "Cici. Cici!" tugging at her head, trying to make direct contact. She refused to break free from the empty pupils. "Look at me. Look at me, Cici." She shivered as if she had just plunged through a thin surface of ice, the water trapped below unable to harbor warmth. "I need you to look at me." Finally, she commanded her neck, easing towards him, the eerie hymn behind them blaring.

"This is Cerberus, isn't it?"

She nodded ferociously. "David...David is in there."

"I am beginning to hope he is not. Let's get off the road."

They slipped from the path, ducking behind the spokes of a carriage, its roof sheared from the supports, leaving the lid of a coffin askew, a leg frozen in rigor mortis peeking through.

"It's just like the riverbed," Cecilia observed, shaking her head clear. "They just abandon their belongings."

"Tributes?"

"I can't be sure. They just leave them to rot."

"Gilded and opulent above ground," he mused.

She stared at him, knowing his insinuation was more than partially accurate.

"What did you see?" he pressed. "On the climb? You were soaking wet."

"I...I must have fainted from the heat."

"You saw something," cutting through the obfuscation.

The tears spoke for her.

"Just like Mama," he offered solemnly.

"I cannot...I cannot tell you what I saw."

"And I will not ask anymore."

The Prussian blue gates sang to the accompanied organ, their rusted bones rubbing hard against the pulp. As the middle parted, a cadre of hooded congregants marched inside, each holding a chain connected to the shame of a shuffling prisoner. A red cloth had been wrapped around its oblong, cylindrical head, a tattered emerald green sweater covering its midsection, hands bound in steel, feet bare.

Frankie peeked through the carriage's underbelly, the silent escort making no attempt to escape as a Stag, a Woodpecker, a Dog, and a Cow gave him ample lead. A slender Eagle at the rear, delicate fingers dragging a cigarette in tow, had slung a bolt action rifle over her shoulder, looking back briefly to make sure that they were sealed within the grounds.

As they passed, they paid no mind to the dilapidation, the sight familiar, almost banal.

Cecilia snuck to Frankie's side, attempting her own assessment. "Fresh meat," she whispered. "What do we do?"

He reached into his robe and retrieved the masks from the small of his back. "Wolf or Mouse?"

She grabbed the rodent, slipping it over her head.

"We need to ditch the pack."

He unbuckled the rucksack and dug through their supplies, removing Cecilia's consecration kit, the corner still sticky with blood. The manila folders choking with his work, the painstaking investigation, would need to be discarded, no use in rehashing the evidence. He shoved it to the bottom of the sack, tussling the change of clothes they had brought, his fingers scraping against the iron plate.

He presented it to her. "You should put this on."

They held it together, unsure if she was worthy of donning it.

"What in the hell are we doing here?" she asked, attempting to analyze their surroundings further.

"Maybe we deserve it," he thought. "Maybe this is our punishment."

RITUAL

"David left us. Didn't he?"

"That's not how I remember it."

He released the armor, busying himself, adjusting his revolver and Petrisone's pistol in his waistband as she slipped into the iron vest. Satisfied that they had extracted the essentials, he removed the extended leather strap from the bag, tying it tightly to the stock and barrel of the shotgun, looping it over Cecilia's shoulder.

"Tuck it under the robe."

She did as she was told, zipping up her jacket, her kit bulging under her breasts.

The Wolf slid over his eyes, the robe cinched and buttoned. He tossed the useless supplies into the carriage and leaned against the bumper, watching the prisoner and his guards descend towards the sanctuary.

Frankie walked carefully, each step rehearsed, as if he had been indoctrinated, no reason to be afraid. She took to his side, striding reluctantly towards the festering warmth. The organ continued its introit, the fires of the rat increasing with each key change. A horse carcass had belched at the belly, spilling outward, a crow stabbing at the midday meal. It seemed unconcerned as they approached, the routine all too familiar.

Stone wells sat flush with the earth on either side of the path, concentric circles spiraling towards a reservoir of black, shimmering against the gray light. A bubble of frightened air burst onto the surface, splattering what grass remained along its circumference.

The snout of the mutt hung high above them, dripping mucus into a pit that funneled underneath the mounds dominated by the rat and goat. The gap had been considerable, the fangs of the dog guarding two stone spans that circled around the odorous flow, leaving the congregants dry as they crossed onto the tongue. The impaled soul had bled down the length of the tooth, his hand limply pawing, as if to release himself with one effortless push.

Though the throat was dark, the flickering wicks of the ceremonial candles brought a clarifying glow to the subterranean church. They each took a bridge, marveling at the pulsating, fleshy walls, veins bulging as the living creature remained buried in the rock of the mountaintop. Below, the slop flowed willingly, a steady churn whipping it. White flecks appeared suddenly, popping like hidden predators in the murky swamp. Blank, milky eyes stared, lips protruding.

"Just one more drink," they whispered.

"Another bite, I must tempt fate."

"Just between my lips. To hold it. The smell..."

Grimy hands waved for their attention, addiction driving them to beg. They stumbled over themselves, pushing one another down below the surface.

"I must fill my belly," they echoed. "My veins."

An arm swiped the stone bridge, the face of cherub chasing it, dripping with viscosity. She pleaded with Cecilia, "I must have more." Her opposite shoulder rose, flayed from the elbow down, the meaty strips swinging against her movement. "The needle does not hurt. Not anymore."

Her leg suddenly shot back into the mud, her face disappearing below the orgy of attention as she was dragged into suffocation. Frankie and Cecilia quickly scurried from the hunger, each soul forcing the next back into the stew, never gaining a steady foothold.

The protruding buds of the flattened tongue sprouted delicate posies, each mound encased in a thinning moss. Gasping corpses cradled their wounds as the white flowers burst from their chests, eyes, and loins, becoming one with nature, beauty achieved. Frankie tiptoed around the decorations, keeping his eyes from wandering.

Those who had been hung above swayed to the final verse of the ceremony's introduction, all eyes watching patiently as a white-robed cleric climbed the spiraling ascent towards the pulpit. He reached a lectern, setting down a leather-bound grimoire, his hands folded lovingly on top. He nodded towards the organist across from him, the fanfare of the intertwining pipes fading, the whispers of the dead trapped between the folds of the humming copper pipes left behind.

Raising his arms, he addressed the hundreds standing in attendance, the kingdom of nature represented in animals of hideous scowls and black, empty lenses. His Holiness too had been shrouded, a simple white hood adorning his head, a flap loose over his face, dipping down past his chin. A crimson cross followed the curve of the nose, two slits allowing some semblance of vision.

Frankie and Cecilia stole themselves into a pew at the rear, keeping their wits narrowed, blending in as a child does in a crowded classroom. Praise did not bellow from the orator's lips, his fist curling, slamming the closed text in front of him. "Damn thee!" he screamed, slurring his speech, far from drunk, an impediment in his tongue, somehow. Frankie turned towards Cecilia, expecting the horde to revolt against them. The priest pointed stiffly at the souls who ferried the blindfolded prisoner as they processed down the aisle. "Disrupting a holy ritual is an active sssssin!"

The four bounty hunters found their knees, genuflecting quickly, seeking to explain. "We have retrieved what you have requested."

The cloth spun free from the victim's head as David faced the pulpit, a cage encasing him, a padlocked vice squeezing his neck. He fought the chains that had led him into the spotlight. "No! No!"

Cecilia squeezed Frankie's hand, contracting her calves as she clung to the pew.

David was subdued easily.

"The tool of ssss-eremony has returned!"

"*Veni, omnipotens aeterne Diabolus!*" the collective shouted in return.

"Silence!" the holy scolded. "We must not invoke his interference, a mere hiccup in our return to the stage of the black lights! Be seated! Be silent!"

They obeyed, the rush of cloth and air muttering under the *creaking* pews.

"Rise!" he commanded to the quartet. "You have been granted this opportunity. Have found yourself autonomous in your duties. And, you have performed them well. The resurrection has been guided by your grace. My resurrection born from your dedication. The hour is late, though darkness has yet to fall. Patience must come to thee. Soon there will be no reason to flee. There will be no reason to resist. Stow him beneath the cloisters, prepare him for this evening."

The loyal bowed, dragging the resistant pawn towards the chancel, disappearing through a doorway to the right. The Eagle paused for one last moment of surveillance before allowing a wooden layer to *clang* behind her, muffling David's frantic cries for help.

"But a mere distraction," the priest waved, wrenching back the cover of the holy text, his fingers running along decaying pages. "I had planned on a reading of triumphant victories, of blood spilled, but I will not wrestle with such hyperbole. I have risen. The works of my father and his father cut short, the lineage snuffed. But, there is hope. You have assembled here, you have all done your part.

"You have hidden in the shadows, not an easy task. You have sacrificed your flesh, your blood, your very souls. You have defied the cities, have defied organization, you have left your families, your loved ones. You are on the right side of history, a participant in the sacred ritual that will allow us to feast side by side with our Lord. To be granted forgiveness from the sins we have not yet committed.

"You will bathe in lust this very night, you will bend, and you will hail and turn your soul over to Him. These ceremonies are not unfamiliar to you, the decoded truth for your eyes only, drawing you to the mountain. You have seen the path of those who did not contain the strength to rise to our elevation. Left, now, in the gnarled wood, to rot. They are to be missed, perhaps, someday, resurrected to begin again in the ranks. Because you are here does not mean you will survive. When I stand on the mountain and command you, you must obey! If these instructions cannot be followed, then I will move upon it."

An accusatory index poked the air, fingering the guilty.

"The Bull!"

The masked congregant turned to his peers, meeting the deadly stares of betrayal. They grabbed him, shoving him face first into the aisle.

"Papa, no! No! It was not I!"

They led him to the altar, a Stag snuffing his protest with a jab to the gut.

"This traitor has broadcast information damning to our cause," the holy officiant bellowed. "He has spread lies, not for our gain, but to sabotage, all in the hopes of furthering his insignificant career."

The congregants lifted him to the flat surface, propping his neck over the short edge, dangling deliciously. Off with the mask. Frankie whispered the name of an old friend.

"*Tomasso.*"

Cecilia cocked her head. "You know him?" she whispered.

He put his hand on the rim of the pew in front of him, prepared to storm the gathering. She gripped his wrist. "NO," she breathed. "He is one of them."

"He does not deserve to die."

"Neither do you," she reminded him.

"Papa! Please, I beg of you! I have done all that you have instructed!" Tomasso wept.

"Yet you turn against me. You jeopardize our mass."

Cecilia thumbed the beads of her rosary, whispering against the heat of the inside of her mask.

"*Áve María, grátia pléna, Dóminus técum. Benedícta tū in muliéribus...*"

"I call..." the priest muttered, a spell of exhaustion suddenly weighing him down. His hood shook as he cast aside the human limitations. "I call upon the Messenger to render judgment!"

From the vault of the arched roof came a swirling, feathered mass, a barrel roll employed as he opened his wings and hovered above the sanctuary. The decomposing head of the goat huffed as he softly docked behind the altar, allowing his burlap robe to kiss the cold marble. The *clucking* bones that hung around his neck bristled as his wings folded tightly.

"*...et benedíctus frúctus véntris túi, Iésus. Sáncta María, Máter Déi...*"

"It is not his place to cast judgment!" the Stag reminded him. "*The Messenger must not sin.*"

"I have not sinned either! I have done no wrong!" the editor squirmed, riding the tails of his brethren's explanation.

"The Messenger must set aside his own hesitations," the priest commanded. "He obeys the slaves of our Lord. He will render judgment henceforth."

The Messenger did not have cause to understand, his scythe's blade unfolding as he slammed the base into the chancel, cracking the fine stone.

"We turn thee over to the heated pits of falsification! The rat shall devour your headless corpse as the crown shall be promoted in effigy against those who wish to commit similar sins."

"*...óra pro nóbis peccatóribus, nunc et in hóra mórtis nóstrae. Ámen.*" Her fingers moved to the next bead, her breathing shortening as she began anew. "*Áve María, grátia pléna, Dóminus técum.*"

The Messenger lowered his weapon just over the connection of spine and neck, measuring for accuracy. Tomasso could not turn towards the execution, the point of impact to come when he least expected it.

"I...I have..." The holy voice wavered as his vision clouded.

"*Benedícta tū in muliéribus, et benedíctus frúctus véntris túi, Iésus.*"

"*Avē...Satana...*" he croaked, stuttering backward and plunging down the spiral staircase. The Messenger ceased his duties, unable to continue without direction. A pack of Wolves galloped towards their leader's slumping form as the congregants cried out from their pews. Tomasso, suddenly unburdened, leapt from the altar, streaming down the aisle as stunned hands snapped at him. He beat them back, freeing himself.

"Stop him!" shouted a Wolf as he stepped away from the limp body of his Master.

"*Sáncta Mar-*"

"Go, go, go," whispered Frankie pushing Cecilia into the aisle as Tomasso streamed past. They sprinted in his wake, ascending the staircase to the field of posies, watching him weave between the sprouting taste buds.

BELOW

"Tomasso!" Frankie shouted, reaching his arms out, swiping.

A yelp of terror fueled the sacrificial lamb as he took to the stone bridge, avoiding the gluttonous hands of the thick river. He circumvented the debris of the road, pounding his fists into the gates of blue.

"W-where–" He searched for handles, but the interior lacked an escape route.

"Tomasso," Frankie burped, fighting for oxygen. He lifted his mask, allowing a glimpse.

"Frankie? What the fuck...? What the fuck are you doing here!?" He bled anger and confusion, tugging on the ends of his hair, trying to find a coping mechanism to calm himself. "You're here to kill me. Fuck!" He paced in a short track, kicking dirt aside. "Fuck! You could have told me, you know!"

"Tomasso! Shut the fuck up and listen to me!"

"You were right there. You were right there! You looked me in the eyes!"

"Would you listen to me!?"

Cecilia glanced over her shoulder, the back of the dog's tongue now layered with the concerned gawking of the congregation, their presence soon to investigate the delay. "Francesco," she whispered, nudging him towards the deadline.

He agreed, offering his hands to Tomasso. "We're not part of this shit. We need to talk to you. Run, to your right, behind the truck." He nodded towards a farmer's transport leaning against a decline, the engine not strong enough to bring it level against the pathway. Its open flatbed had been filled with loose straw, a border of wooden planks surrounding it to keep the herd from falling out.

Tomasso saw the trotting souls in the distance as they closed the gap. He agreed with a tilt of his head, leaning hard to the right.

Cecilia and Frankie followed, bolstering the ruse, feigning confusion as they ducked behind the bed. Frankie layered his palms into one another, boosting Tomasso into the yellow stalks. Using Petrisone's pistol, he released an errant shot into the woods, stowing the weapon quickly underneath his robe.

A squad rounded the side of the truck, finding Cecilia pressing hard against Frankie's thigh as he groaned in agony. "Into the woods!" he directed, pointing furiously. The others nodded in unison, hopping over the weeds as they ordered themselves to spread out.

They waited for the creatures to blend in with the desolate network before ending their unrehearsed scene. Frankie dug into the flatbed, slapping Tomasso's leg. "Come on, come on."

He sprang upright, fluffing his hair free of the hay. "I have to get out of here."

"You need to take us to David," Cecilia ordered.

"Who's this now?" he gawked, slightly offended.

"Shut up, Tomasso," a tender slap to the face to gauge his attention. "The prisoner they brought in, the one with the cage around his face. We need to find him."

"Why?"

Frankie swung his open palm again, applying pressure, "Where is he, Tomasso?"

"Jesus, Frankie," rubbing the burgeoning bruise. "I don't know where they keep him."

"But, someone does."

Annoyed, Tomasso knew he would have to return to the depths in order to escape it. "Yeah...yeah. *da Medicina.*"

An extending hand of assistance and he hopped to the ground. "We have to enter through the western wing," he reported, throwing the hood of his robe over his bare face. He poked his finger into Frankie's chest. "Stick close and don't talk to anyone unless I say so."

Cecilia nodded along, keeping pace as they glided along the outskirts of the road, taking the slope to the left and approaching the weeping goat. Tomasso leapt over the throbbing lip, condensing himself as he navigated the maze of dripping wax. Each droplet splattered the sharp point of the budding stalk below, growing by minute, by hour, until floor met ceiling and a grotesque column formed, only a modicum of heat to topple the entire structure.

An inverted cross dangled like a uvula, hovering above the helical path that contorted down into the black gullet. Candelabra had been neglected near the entrance, their stalks snapped. Tomasso ripped a candle from the holder and handed it to Cecilia, taking one for himself. Frankie retrieved his matchbook; three left. He struck the flimsy, flat wood, breathing life into the wax cylinder. The flame transferred easily between them all.

Down into the spiral, hands against the walls as they kept themselves balanced. Through the center of the staircase, they witnessed further levels, the bottom impossible to gauge in the limited glow.

They kept silence between them as moisture plopped in hidden puddles, the earth moist and perspiring. Without incident, they exited onto the upper level of a circular arena, wide arches providing a glimpse into the center of the pit. The curvature below had been embedded with iron gates, sectioning off cells. Bedding had been provided, a wooden crate for contemplation. The barely audible groan of the imprisoned rose through the darkness.

"The Mistresses," Tomasso explained. "They are pumped full of sedatives until they are needed for sacrifice or breeding."

"Who keeps watch over them?" Cecilia asked.

"There is no need. They do not run because they cannot even stand. The drugs have polluted their systems."

He urged them onward, rounding the path, pushing through an unlocked, square door. A fireplace had been recessed in the far wall, a healthy chunk of kindling burning uproariously as bulbous cast iron pots boiled above the flames. They ducked below the threshold as they entered a blistering heat

Instruments of preparation hung from the bordering brick; a grilled rack swinging from the ceiling contained even more cookware. Barrels of salt had been stacked atop containers of wine and liquor, bags of flour and meal splayed across the stone floor.

A sharp metal *thwap* turned their attention to the far corner, a wrinkled form clearing away bone with a hefty cleaver, a rubber apron surrounding his waist as he wiped blood free from his hand. Buckets of entrails and discarded flesh buzzed around him, the upper half of a tortured face stared out with dull eyes.

"da Medicina?" Tomasso inquired rather meekly.

The elderly prepper set his tools aside, slowly shuffling to face them. A gash across his neck had healed improperly, the tissue scarring in a crooked pattern, little veins splintering off to find deeper reservoirs. His nose had been removed, the unclean remains jutting outward, the oblong holes sucking in the putrid air. He removed a pair of copper goggles, waving them forward in the bright stream of the fireplace, his eyes squinting past the haze. He applied a black leather strap around his ears, a mold of a former nose giving him a healthier appearance.

"da Medicina," Tomasso began. "*David,* I need to see him."

The old man scoffed, huffing and flapping his arms. He pulled his index across his throat.

"No, no," Tomasso assured him. "He was at mass. They brought him home."

A smile, a celebration! To a cloudy bottle of wine, he shimmied, downing a healthy gulp before offering it.

"Where do they keep him? Where are his quarters?"

da Medicina crossed himself with inversion, kissing his fingers. "With Papa?"

A nod.

"Why?"

Shrugging, taking a sip of wine. He pointed towards a folded set of white sheets, a washcloth, and a bucket of still water.

"*The washing.* da Medicina prepares the Mistresses, he bathes them for each ceremony and he...separates them when they have no longer become useful. David will be brought here to be thoroughly cleaned before tonight's ritual."

"What happens tonight?" Cecilia asked.

"The final resurrection."

"Of who?"

"*Satanus.*"

"Why, Tomasso? Why did you fall so easily?" Frankie pressed.

"I didn't willingly choose this! They came to *me*. They knew I had connections with you, influence upon the press. They wanted to keep you far from the trail. They were going to kill me, Frankie."

"Why didn't you come to me then? I could have protected you!"

"From them!? No-no-no-no. There are thousands of them, all corrupting the system. Their network is too vast to run from."

"But you became greedy," Frankie pressed.

"I had a story! A story that I could run with. You know I've been kept from a promotion for years now. You helped me break this thing, the others were eating out of my hand!"

"Why did you print the retraction? Why did you keep the case in doubt?"

"We could have solved it together. I would have given you David! Can you imagine the heroics? The-the-the fucking *attention* we would have received?"

"Why did they choose David?" Cecilia asked.

"They did not come to him. He came to them."

"I don't understand."

"This was *his* idea."

"Jesus..." Cecilia whispered. "David..."

"But they've imprisoned him," Frankie reminded them.

"He came with a proposition," Tomasso explained, "but it was Papa who orchestrated everything."

"Who is he? Who is Papa?"

"Frankie, I–" he was interrupted by a vice around his neck, Frankie's fingers drumming against the windpipe.

"*Who?*" eyes swelling with rage.

da Medicina reached for his cleaver, but Cecilia flapped her robe, threatening him with the shotgun.

The grip was too tight, Tomasso choking further than Frankie had intended. He peeled back and allowed oxygen to squeeze through the battered windpipe, but he refused to let go completely.

"*Your father.* Papa is your father, Paolo."

Petrisone had simply babbled, but this was confirmation.

"Paolo Zampa?" Frankie clarified, already knowing the answer, blinking over and over to moisturize against the tone of the room.

Cecilia removed the head of the Mouse.

"*Cazzo!* You must be the nun," Tomasso squeaked. "They are looking for you too."

Frankie tossed him to the floor, wiping his hand against his robe.

"You are mistaken," he corrected. "My father is dead."

The chatter exceeded an acceptable level, echoing in the catacombs with youth. They were ecstatic, the night upon them, their efforts forming an edible conclusion. A barnyard of congregants ferried David into da Medicina's workshop, *hawing* about the gifts in which they would be showered with.

"*Medi!*" they cried in unison, happy to see the polite, old man. David slumped, an unintended stupor slowly fading, his participation only half invested.

"For tonight!" a Cow howled, shoving David forward, seizing the chain that attached to his neck and yanking him back. The prisoner coughed, unable to massage his neck.

da Medicina shooed them off, his own private ceremony to commence.

"You," a Pig snorted, pointing at the young Rooster, a spiked red comb popping from his head. "Stay behind, make sure the old bastard hurries."

They turned their back on the youngling, the top of his hand flicking the bottom of his chin in disgust. He found solace on the edge of a crate of wine, lifting his sleeve to check the time.

The elder wheeled a steel preparation table into the middle of the room, applying rubber brakes to keep it in place. He tapped the flat surface and encouraged David to sit. With difficulty and the incessant rattling of his chains, he perched himself on the frigid metal.

da Medicina inspected David's fingernails first, shaking his head in disappointment. *This would not do.*

"I will not survive this night," David whispered.

da Medicina scoffed. *Everything will be fine.*

"For you, perhaps. I am afraid that I will hurt others. That I will hurt you."

Me? No. Rubbing his neck. *My voice will return. Papa has promised. We will talk through the night!*

"No, no." He grabbed the wrinkled, vein-tattooed, hand. "I forced the scar upon you. You warned me, and I did not listen. I am going to die tonight. I will become the vessel and I will be no more."

"Shut the fuck up. Fuck!" the Rooster crowed.

Ignore him. Youth!

"You would be wise to treat da Medicina with some respect," David countered, the lock around his neck loosened, the cage lifted free from his shoulders, a painful indent remaining.

"I'm not the one who is about to get an ass-full of *sborra. Testa di cazzo.* Papa will be the one who drinks. You will watch. *Bastardo.*"

The old man begged him to pay a little respect. *This is not the time to bicker.*

The Rooster lifted his mask above his nose and bit into a cigarette, torching the tip and inhaling. "*Segone.* At the end of the night, I will be buried in *mona.* And this asshole? Dead. Fucking piece of-"

The cigarette leapt into his throat as Frankie clamped his palm over the Rooster's mouth. He squirmed, the smoke choking him, the burning embers blistering his tongue.

Cecilia rose from behind a barrel of olives, shotgun trained on da Medicina. "Easy now." Tomasso snatched a cleaver, scuttling up to the old man.

"What is going on?" David swung his head from the Wolf to the Mouse.

Frankie removed his mask, tossing the Rooster aside. He spit out the cigarette, retching a thick, gray mucus. Cecilia followed, slipping free from the timid Mouse.

"F-f-frankie?" The child that had been buried for so long, returned, his cadence cresting like a wave, his pitch squeaking higher. "Cici?" He bounded from the preparation table and almost tackled his big brother, weeping in a somber, forgiving tone as he transferred his joy. Before Frankie could respond in kind, David had brought Cecilia in for an embrace.

"I-I can't...What are you...How did you find me?"

"Your letter," Cecilia explained.

"My letter?"

"You wrote me a letter. You said you needed my help."

His smile peeled away from his lips. "No," he corrected her, smirking in confusion. "I-I didn't write any letters."

"You wrote hundreds, David," Frankie assured him. "You sent them all over the damn country."

The child hid, replaced with the conscience of an indoctrinated butcher. "Five seconds and you're already trying to convince me I'm insane!?"

"David!" Cecilia exclaimed, reaching her hand out. But he pulled away, disgusted. "You wrote to me. You told me that you had Valentina, that she was safe. You wanted me to wash you, to cleanse you of what ailed you."

"No!" he backed away. "I said no such thing! I am here for a purpose. I have done what they have asked. I refused to become the vessel, but it is my destiny!"

His siblings shared concerned glances, approaching the frightened woodland creature, offering morsels of truth.

"David," Frankie insisted. "Whatever has happened, we can help you. We came to help you."

"No-no-no, that is not the order! You have not come here to help me. You have come to help *him*! He brought you here, he turned you against me."

"*Love.* Isn't that what has assembled us?" The siblings turned slowly, the revelation slurred, but with a familiar accent.

Paolo stood in the doorway, flanked by an entourage of congregants. Drenched in white, his hood remaining, he opened his palms. "My children, *together*."

Cecilia wasted no time, pumping a fresh round into the ghostly presence. His robe tore as gunpowder and buckshot thrust him to the ground. A Lion to his right furrowed his robe, producing a carabiner that returned the outburst, pelting her in the chest.

David stepped in front of Frankie, his arms outstretched. "No! Don't!" The bodyguards flexed their firepower, aiming their weapons on the youngest.

Cecilia coughed, rubbing her chest, suddenly unsure as to why it remained flat and rusted.

Paolo, chest bleeding profusely, his ceremonial robes peppered with black holes, rose with the help of his followers. "I am beyond flesh, my child. I am so much more than a shell." He lifted his vail, the features of his face reconstructed from old skin, the dermis unable to stretch appropriately, bone exposed underneath drying muscle. He had been stitched from the dried and pockmarked remains of others, but he appeared wholly their father. His jaw bulged and clicked as he wheezed, sucking in the right amount of pathetic molecules to speak his truth.

Frankie unsheathed his revolver, pressing it to David's temple, his opposite hand steadying his shoulder. "You are a monster!" he cried. "You have corrupted David. I am going to set him free of your influence."

"I have corrupted nothing, Francesco," Paolo hissed. "David is his father's son. He will listen to me. He will take his rightful place. Your mother accomplished nothing in her attempt to silence me. She, in turn, could not handle the silence and ended her life. She could not bear to live in a world with my spawn."

"No!" Frankie barked. "Lies! *You hurt her.* You made her what she was."

"My poor boy. Such a delusion. I provided, I spread my seed. And in return I received *nothing*. Ungrateful bastards who sucked my essence dry. *This* is for you, my son. For David. For Cecilia. This is a new era. My debt...our debt has been repaid. Now, we call upon a new proposition." Paolo stepped forward. "You will witness the transmogrification. You will bleed for our Lord, and you will inherit his power." Another step forward.

"No! I'll shoot! Cici, shoot him!"

She rammed the pump back, lining up the barrel with her father's creeping form. The trigger *clicked*. Empty.

"Francesco," Paolo whispered, an echo of a thousand tones bursting through Frankie's canal. "Francesco," churning, sulfuric, an itch he could not scratch.

He could no longer bear to keep David as his hostage, the gun falling from his grip, his palms slapping his ears shut. Paolo's eyes burned a hole through his resolve as he stood over him. He opened his mouth in protest, but no sound came of it. His eyes clamped, plunging him into darkness, yet he could still see the eerie linger of his father's piercing eyes.

"Join us."

Between the staccato inhalations, he had little time to curse. His leather, shin-high boots had been tied too tightly, each stride pooling more blood at the bottom of his feet. His vision rose and fell with the elevation, funneled through the tinted goggles buckled across his eyes.

BELOW

He had soaked the multiple layers of gauze of his beak-like mask in sodium and potassium carbonate, adding what remained of his canteen. The stench was rotten but preferable to the chlorine smoke that wafted from the canisters as every third man pulled the pin on their respective ordinance and tossed the gas into the field.

The trench had been crude, the darkness providing enough cover to crouch and prepare. The enemy had dug themselves in with skill and efficiency, boring into the mountain's side, planting anti-aircraft artillery on the higher bluffs.

He crossed himself, praising God for allowing him safe passage this far. His rifle sat on the lip of the trench, his platoon mimicking, waiting for dawn to break. Thunder pulsed high above, the sun due, but shrouded by the curtain of a nasty brew. The rain came with much pomp, lightning ripping large swathes through the furious storm, striking the ground at the base of the crag.

A tap on his shoulder, "Zampa."

A death sentence.

Skipping a man.

Another tap. "Giancana."

Skip another.

"Rossi."

He reseated his hold on the barrel of the bolt action rifle, tugging the fixed bayonet, ensuring its security. The muddied field grew fingers, shoveling dry dirt and grass into its whirlpool. The tree line would protect them until they rose, crossing the pasture of dead in the crossfire of the enemy, their foreign backs to the mountain passes and an easy retreat.

His countrymen would be slaughtered.

The whistle sounded, the smoke already released, his feet sucked into the muck. The first volley activated, the enemy's rifles belting like fireflies behind the curtain, zipping past his helmet. A hand-cranked, emplaced machine gun opened to his right, the steady beat mowing down a cadre of charging brethren, clouds of red mixing with the white.

He found the seam in the smoke, stumbling into the concrete trench, crushing an adversary as he broke his fall. Others fared better, firing wildly, thrusting with their bayonets.

A peer rushed past him, screaming from beneath his gas mask. "*Tedeschi! Tedeschi!*" He looked down at the moaning soldier he had crushed, the wool coat field gray, hemmed with red. The brimless cap had been lined with a black band and pinned with a circular button of white, black, and red.

"Artillery..." he whispered. "German artillery!"

The rock face above erupted in a shower of dust as a massive round punctured through the mountain. The screech deafened him momentarily as the treads of a tank burst through the tree line at the far end of the enemy trench, concealed cleverly in brush and branches. The Iron Cross of Germany greeted him as it swung its barrel upon his comrades on the opposite side of the field, igniting the impromptu position. Not even the driving rain could diminish the harsh, hungry flames.

Hundreds of German soldiers spilled from the forest, refilling their own trenches, slaughtering those that had crossed the line.

"Paolo! Paolo! Go!" screamed a ranking officer, pointing towards cover. His neck sheared as a bayonet sliced through the artery, splashing the concrete walls.

Paolo steadied his rifle, the barrel *cracking* as he felled the crude German soldier, the path becoming clogged. He scrambled to his feet as the trench walls ricocheted with powder and debris. The tank belched once more, earth raining down upon him as he crouched beneath the surface.

The hypnotic rhythm of warfare *pop-pop-popped* as he navigated forward. Another machine gun awoke in front of him, the operators unaware of his presence as the spotter held a tail of ammunition, pointing towards the ones who must die. Paolo pressed his back to a short wall, peeking around the corner as the weapon *clacked.*

The pincer of troops closed upon him, chasing him with vigor. Caught now between the unaware and the salivating jaws of Germany, he could not count on God's blessings. He fired his rifle at the charging, single-file cluster of grays. The soldier at the head of the column collapsed, his face twisting as his cheek fluttered, vomiting a dark stream.

With nary enough time to cock the bolt, he reached into his belt and ripped his sidearm against the button flap. He rounded the corner and pressed the barrel to the back of the machine gunner's skull, emptying his mind across the muddied waters. He turned it quickly to the spotter, pumping two rounds into his frightened expression.

Taking control of the automatic weapon, he turned it towards the still-charging Huns as they leapt over their dead brother. But the tripod base would not allow him to fully turn, a simple bolt preventing his ingenuity. He cursed as he strained to unseat the weapon, the burdensome construction tipping back, forcing him into the bottom of the trench. With the machine gun on its side, he hugged the trigger, erupting erratically, shaving off the leg of a leaping German.

Screaming in delight, Paolo embraced the trigger with madness, watching a river engulf the trench, the elongated rounds, chewing through the flesh of the enemy. It took several casualties before the attack slowed, a new strategy to be devised. An artillery round breached above, pushing him off target momentarily.

A rallying cry echoed across the field, for the country he loved had disabled the blasted tank, the final shot pushed off course.

Similar declarations, in ferocity only, rang out in the forbidden tongue, a boy, no older than he, clutching the pulsating organs of his stomach as blood pumped through his throat. Paolo reseated the weapon properly on the ground and laid upon his stomach, setting his eye on the stock and peering down the iron sight. He wiped the droplets of milky dust and rain from his goggles, keeping his focus on the small gap in front of him.

Metal rattled with a distinct, hollow *plink*, the sound multiplying rapidly. An oblong German grenade landed in front of him, another tucking itself beside his feet. The position compromised, the heavy weapon useless, he found his footing and ran deeper into enemy territory.

The ordinance had been cooked, though, the timing almost perfect. Paolo felt lighter, lifted suddenly upward as the bulbous heads blossomed. The heat flowed up his right leg, tickling him as it found comfort in his knee. The force shuddered the material of his trousers, the seam tearing as shrapnel dug into the muscle. He landed face down, his back dotted with tiny embers of metal.

Turning over, pain appeared, a blinding realization that he too was fragile. His leg vomited in waves, the charred, mangled flesh of the amputation soaking up the rainwater. The severed limb twitched as he stared at the freed hunk of meat, his boot still strapped.

The Germans persisted, approaching slowly, materializing from the fog. Paolo could not remember how to breathe, a wheezing burp spewing from his mouth. His vision rumbled as he blinked through the slow, euphoric sensation of shock. His pistol in his hands, his fired into the thirsty ghosts, beating back their advance as more blood joined the fray.

He cocked his head, the end of the trench calling him, a crooked ladder extending into the canopy of pine. Canisters bounced forward, his comrades closing in, the chlorine gas refilling the battlefield.

Digging his elbows into the coarse concrete, he boosted himself forward, his exposed bone clapping against the growing pool of rainwater. Smoke enveloped him, his memory slapping an image over his goggles. Each gain released a whimper of exhaustion, chased by a squeal of pain. Rifles signaled all around him, a propeller buzzing overhead as unidentifiable aircraft swooped low, releasing hand grenades onto the chaos.

Paolo put his back against the ladder, using his arms to lift himself upright. He squeezed the railing, bending his knee and stomping onto the next rung. The process repeated, his hands soaring higher.

Boiling in his mask, the pain dulled in the phantom limb, he rolled from the top of the trench into the fallen needles of the swaying deciduous forest. He pulled the ladder free and propped himself up, the crude construction of broom handles and hemp acting as a crutch as he limped from the skirmish and swung himself under the boughs.

The hounds of war chased him, the radiating tones of his country's rifles bouncing around his skull. Though he continued to put distance between himself and the sacrifices behind him, he could not escape the whistle of–

The mortar sunk halfway into the soil before it announced its presence, the shockwave throwing him into the trunk of a pine. His back seized, the feeling of foam injected between the discs of his spine. A chunk of the metal tail pinned his forearm to the tree, blood leaking down to his elbow. The once serene thicket danced skyward as both forces fired for effect, carpeting him with focused artillery. The goggles protected his eyes from the spectacle, the crowns of the trees disintegrating, the rain joined by singing needles and shards of bark. The sky became a river of flame as the forest buckled under the shelling, the fire spreading quickly, twirling from branch to branch.

Paolo fished into his uniform and tore out his necklace. He stared angrily at the silver crucifix, tossing it into the oblivion. "I reject thee!" he screamed over the din. Matching his wail in time with the explosions, he covered his face, deflecting the aftermath.

Finally, mercy exposed itself, the thunderstorm continuing, though. All that remained was his laughter, his chest vibrating as he chuckled, his senses lost, his face flushing the color onto the ground. "Why...?" sobbing now, his emotions shuffling like an unwieldy deck. "I will die here! I will die here and this...this is your fault! Give me this chance..." he huffed, whispering now, head drooping onto his chest. "My country will not...will not fall. Do not trade my life for failure."

Flesh, suctioned to the bone, snaked for his chin, the pale

fingers lifting it gently.

"My son," clicked the tongue. "Your potential is so perfectly wasted, here, in this...*Hell.*" The voice was soothing, manageable, so clear in his ears.

Paolo stared into the portal created by the black hood, locking eyes with a malnourished visage: bloody bags beneath the piercing black pupils; a lack of facial hair; teeth filed into jagged stalks, clumping towards the middle around bruised, black lips. But the figure turned from him, shuffling around the mortar-tilled earth, refusing a longing glance.

"Perhaps, under a new umbrella, you will find some semblance of power; of opportunity. The others? They have potential, they have made progress to be sure. But I need virility. I need plump thighs, a fertile womb in which to plow."

"What do you want from me?" Paolo muttered, lowering his head once more.

"Alessandra," the snake hissed. "She is young, is she not? Breasts of fine cream. Lips that beg for your release."

"*Vaffanculo.*"

Face to face now, wrapping around the trunk of the tree, the potent odor of sulfur curling from the decaying mouth. "If I have my way, I won't have to. Give me your wife's womb, allow me a child and you will find the use of your leg and arm quite familiar."

"I...I..."

"Allow me to spill my burning seed, allow me an heir so that I can one day shed this crooked form and rule with the strength of my kin."

Paolo pawed for his crucifix, buried now under the churned and scorched earth. The bony arms leapt towards him, shoving the shrapnel deeper into his forearm, drawing a curdled wail.

"Give me her womb!" pressing harder now, twisting, reigniting the flow.

A timid branch coated in whipping flames tumbled beside him, the heat pouncing towards the already shedding needles.

"Y-yes..." Paolo whispered. "Yes!"

"Say it!" the voice no longer tender, as unforgiving as the inferno.

"Yes! Her womb is yours!"

The robed salesman released the hilt of a knife from Paolo's belt, sliding it quickly across his pale palm. "Drink, my son. Savor even a droplet of my blood and you will be freed from pain." His fist tightened, drawing a healthy flow, angling it high.

The patter splashed Paolo's face, his jaw fighting to remain closed, fearing he would perish despite the nourishment. A satisfying smile crossed the evil lips, his eyes wide, savoring the victory.

Finally, with reluctance and the *clicking* of his mandibles, he opened his mouth, swallowing the crude plasma.

Hell rained down upon him as the sky fell once more, the young soldier screaming in the chaos, alone again, but whole.

The elderly man.

Another in a never-ending chain of butchers, she suspected, carving flesh, for one day he would be relieved, put out to pasture and allowed to live.

He appeared in a haze of liquidity, smoke surrounding him. From the darkness into the reach of the fireplace. The needle stung at first, entering the vein, the tightness around the upper arm fading as the rag loosened.

Cecilia blinked through the sheen, dripping saline down her chin.

She wiped the nuisance free, straightening her tunic in the oval mirror.

"Are you crying?"

She cocked her head, "Just a bit of dust." She returned to her ritual, keeping an eye on the couch behind her, clearing her cheek further.

"Why Anna?"

Cecilia met the woman's inquisitive reflection, blinking nervously. She looked down at her hands, trembling now as she tried to concentrate on slipping into her persona. "A girl I used to know," she explained.

"You usually call me Martina or Carlotta. Are they not important anymore?"

"Just fantasies," she assured.

"You can call me what you want, honestly. Giada isn't even my real name."

"I like Giada just fine," smiling pleasantly.

A cigarette found life, smoke curling through the private room.

They had entered with lips locked, hands tearing at the fabric, her vail slipping to the floor, the door almost forgotten.

Giada rose from the couch, rubbing ash off her breast. "We

have time." She wrapped her arm around Cecilia, placing a soft kiss against her neck.

The hotel catered to their repeat business, the bed uncomfortable, the barely level couch their preferred mode.

"Anna," she had whispered.

"Huh?" breaking away from business.

"Please," Cecilia choked. "Please be Anna."

A nod, "I will be anyone you want me to be."

Now, in the mirror, her pious form embraced from behind by the prostitute, she suddenly found disgust in herself. The mask she wore had become too tight, her ability to breathe restricted as if she was being crushed by the righteous hand of guilt.

"Why did you pick the church?" Giada asked, slipping the cigarette into Cecilia's mouth.

"Because...I am guilty."

"Huh?" she had heard her correctly, she merely could not grasp the concept.

"I am forever guilty. Perhaps, I can harbor goodwill. Collect it. Comfort others as I never had." She inhaled, filling herself with the fragrant tobacco. "A father who will not strike me," she muttered.

"What are you guilty of?" She was no longer the familiar acquaintance from the bar. "What are you guilty of?" Anna asked again.

"*This.* Rejecting normalcy."

"This is happiness. This is truth. Why do you run from such positivity? How can we truly know what sin is until we reject it?"

Cecilia stared into the mirror. Would she reject it now? Would she end her guilt without her love by her side?

Anna pressed her lips to Cecilia's ear, the follicles on her neck prickling, frigid water spilling down her back. She had no choice but to return, spinning, her tongue leaping for Anna's mouth. They moved quickly back to the couch, the cushions separating as damp clumps of straw and hay burst through the frame.

She had lost her in the yellow stalks, her muscles exhausted of will. She lay buried, warm in the grain and chaff, a flickering torch streaming between the crisscrossing layers. Metal squeaked as darkness entered, come to frisk her away.

The unprepared Mistress screamed.

▽△▽△

The ring of fire simmered, match shaken to extinguish the excess. A flat, ceramic sheet scraped against the metal rack of the oven, settling into the growing warmth. Flour, water, oil, salt, whipped and rolled, flattened against cold steel, measured into large coins and separated so they did not stick to one another. da Medicina admired his culinary skills, casting the unleavened bread into darkness.

More flames, whipping from wick to wick, the anointed setting the stage. As they lit the ceremonial candles, they were followed by a vial of dye, three droplets in each recess. The mixture swirled with the warm wax, each successive tear upon its surface to present itself in delicious black, blotting the white.

Clusters of towering incense had been bound, shoved into gilded tubes to keep their shape. They too received a bath of flame, the sweet smell of hazel wafting towards the swaying corpses.

Like a matador, a congregant waved a fresh sheet of black velvet across the altar, smoothing the imperfections, tying the excess to the undercarriage.

A jug of wine was tipped liberally into stubby chalices pounded from silver, etched with the symbols of the ancient language. They had prepared eight, an empty ninth remaining so.

Platens of oak maintained a manageable temperature under the heat of the unleavened bread as da Medicina shifted each piece carefully with a cast iron spatula.

Those who had grown under the dark tutelage had donned a blood-red, shedding their black robes and their lack of celebrity. Each of these chosen slid the filthy head of a Goat over their faces.

The assembled remained standing in their pews, waiting silently as the maestro took to his bench. The Songbird had no need for sheet music, the melody floating through his fluttering fingers as the massive organ whistled the commencement. Layering a heavy, sustained bass foundation, he plunked an eerie high-pitched scale, calling upon a hidden frequency to entice the procession down the uneven steps of the mutt's esophagus.

Frankie's eyes fluttered, the shallow light allowing a bit of freedom, saving him from the cold shock of lucidity. The first to pass beneath him marched behind one another, slathered in red, the leader bearing a torch, the other swinging an iron thurible as it leaked the aroma of sage with every gasp of silver smoke. He shook his head, unable to loosen the liquidity that weighed him towards the unkempt floor. He looked down, his arms angled behind him, wrists unable to separate.

Panic drove him to clarify his vision, the rope at his ankles no mere sensory overload. The line spun as he wriggled, the knot looped around the thickness of a chandelier above. The other corpses proved less frantic, swaying gently as he attempted to release himself.

His head shot upward, the marbled floor interrupted by four congregants supporting an inverted cross, ferrying the headless, mocked body of Christ down the aisle. A tone of resistance thundered from his mouth, but a moist suction prevented him from speaking his peace. Tape had been slapped across his lips, tearing at the budding facial hairs around his cheeks as he stretched his jaw.

Another torch crossed below, leading the final Goat as he hoisted a flesh-bound gospel, pointing it towards the heavens in a gesture of rejection. Frankie moaned viciously, cursing in a string that was ultimately lost between the organ's violent key changes.

The white orator, the shining light of those who had gathered, remained last, hands folded, his bloody gown exchanged for one bearing cleanliness and fragrance. A curtain remained over his face, hiding his surgery, beneath a tiered tiara, each layer adorned with the plaque-stained fangs of bloodthirsty predators: animal and human alike. He walked along a thin line of exhaustion and death, the shuffling slag inching him tediously towards his post.

Those who had processed before him positioned themselves around the altar, the cross hung upon a hook, left to dangle. He bowed before his collection, signaling for the organ to cease. The whisper of the exhaling pipes gave way to Frankie's futility, threatening harm of imaginative torture beneath the muffling. The crooked handle of a wooden staff jabbed him in the shoulder, poking him like resistant cattle. He looked towards the shepherd, a single finger to the mask of a Sheep, silencing him, lest he required another bruise.

A congregant behind the altar clapped his hands twice, savoring the glorious echo of the palatial sanctuary. He twisted his fingers, pointing two to the heavens and two towards the bowels. "As above! So below!" he declared. "I will ascend to the altars in Hell."

The chorus responded with enthusiasm, "To Satan, the giver of life. *Veni, omnipotens aeternae Diabolus!*"

A fellow red produced a stole of equal tint, slowly wrapping it around Paolo's neck, adjusting its symmetry.

The standing began their praise, chanting in unison. "*Suscipe, Satanas, munus quad tibi offerimus memoriam Recolentes vindex.*" Repeating it did not nullify its effect, the sacred combination following Paolo as he accepted the leathered tome, his robe sweeping the floor as he ascended the pulpit stairs.

Frankie tried to identify his brother amongst the hidden, but the masks of nature rendered it impossible. He craned his neck towards the lectern as the holy book was laid to rest.

"May the gifts be forever with you."

"*Avē Satana!*"

"You may be seated."

They obeyed. The selected reds finding cushioned armchairs at the rear of the chancel.

Paolo opened the gospel before him, thumbing through the crisp and fading pages, each one blank. He held out his left hand, calling for his next ingredient. "Our selected Mistress...indoctrinated this night. *My daughter.*"

Frankie protested, fighting against the hemp, blistering a ring around his wrist. He begged for her to run but received a slap to the temple from the Sheep below.

A Crane and a Hog shoved her jellied legs forward from the shadows, their hands seizing her forearms, preventing her from succumbing to the floor. Stripped of clothing, a shroud had been draped over her head, cinched at the neck. A black rosary swung between her breasts as they approached the altar.

Horror spilled from behind the mask of a Dog in the front pew, his arms splayed outward, legs scaling the short wall in front of him. "Cici!" She flung herself towards him, mumbling underneath the cloth blockage, her fingers grasping at the air.

He was restrained by the flock, forced to remain seated. Frankie muffled his brother's name, the pup craning to acknowledge his presence. The inspector's ingenuity called forth another sting from the cane to keep him humble.

The Crane and Hog transferred their ownership to two Goats as they rose from their thrones. Despite her sedated cognizance, she tried to wriggle free, summoning the reserve to empty, the wilted strength defying expectations. They simply lifted her, swinging her like a prized and gutted hunt. Her back caressed the black velvet of the altar, hands at her sides.

"Praised are you, my King, by the defiant," Paolo continued, "Through our arrogance and pride we swallow your essence: let it become for us an elixir of life."

A Rabbit presented a tray of chalices to the Goats, each of the seven selecting the next in line, leaving the eighth and ninth behind. Their naked fingers plunged into the dark nectar, breaching slowly; soaking. They took positions around the altar and flicked morsels onto her body, the heavy beads slithering past her nipples, dripping into the crevices of her legs. The cold kisses tickled her exposed flesh, causing her to writhe in a bit of unexpected ecstasy.

The Goats assembled in a row at the base of the chancel steps, awaiting further instruction.

Spreading his arms like purified wings, Paolo addressed them once more. "With pride in my heart, I give praise to those who drove the nails, who thrust the spear into the body of an imposter. A useless tool to satiate, may their followers rot in their rejection and filth."

"*We do renounce the great deceiver and all his works!*"

"Then feast! Feast on the consecration!"

A cadre of black Rats processed from the shadows, each carrying a platen of baked, crude coins. The congregants exited their pews in an orderly fashion, waddling towards the eucharistic mockery. Each obeyed, lifting their masks to their noses, shoveling the flavorless treat into their mouth. The odor of wine filled their noses as they leaned into the alcohol, swallowing with delight.

A sudden weightlessness overcame Frankie as the rope around his ankles awoke, plunging him downward, the chandelier and his fellow decorations wafting in the wake. The Sheep, level now with his head, tore the tape from his cheek, searing a rash across his lips.

First pain, then the epithets: "*Zoccaro, frasca, merduso, piscialetto, sauteriello de zimmaro-!*"

He was muffled once more, an unholy Eucharist shoved into his gullet, his face splashed with consecrated wine, the tape returning as he gagged, blowing droplets from his sinuses. His eyes slammed shut as the rope ascended, tossing him to and fro as he tried to chew, swallow, and breathe without upsetting his bubbling gut.

David too imbibed with hands on his shoulders, keeping his range of motion limited. The congregation returned to their seats, the Rats of bread dipping into the shadows while the Goats of wine returned the chalices to the offered tray.

"We have gathered this night, in accordance with ancient testimony. Sons and daughters of Satan, born of selected wombs, you have become his army, his sword, his flame. Together we have held mass, have collected the necessary ingredients. But we have witnessed failure...after failure...

"Those of you who doubted have been thinned, the shepherded now before you only. Though we have summoned our Lord before, have seen his form, have touched his flesh, we dedicate this final mass to a new crusade! One thousand years of peace, under his influence. We are but knights in his service, growing our arsenal in order to fetch the boiling seas and the immolated plains. We raise our Lord tonight to guide him towards his ultimate, and final, throne.

"For centuries he has wallowed beneath the soil, his powers weak, stealing the souls of the bedridden and the elderly. We have assembled a vessel this evening, one that has led you into this new rebirth, one that will carry us into a new millennium. *Me.*"

"*Avē Papa!*"

"I am the vessel!" roared David, held steady, shushed by the hiss of the annoyed. "He cannot save you if you are–" The stock of a submachine gun caught his jaw, twisting his head aside, the Dog whimpering in the confines of his mask.

"We call upon a new mass," Paolo invited. "Incantations carved on the very columns of Cocytus. We shall not concern ourselves with petty creeds. We shall fill this sanctuary with howling delight! We shall fill this sanctuary with blood!"

"*Avē Papa!*"

"Tonight, I grant thee *your* desires. Satan is fickle! He demands your sacrifice. I declare that you have sacrificed enough for an eternity! Lust, pride, greed, gluttony, whatever you require, I will bestow. I will assume the role that has become stagnant, a role that will finally strike fear into those who waver, those who hide behind precious charms. Assemble my sons and daughters, whisper your desires, then you shall consecrate yourself with the blood of our Lord as I consecrate our portal."

Leaving the blank pages behind, Paolo closed the sacred text for the final time, turning carefully and descending to the end of the aisle. Commanding his dead muscles, though his decomposition was no secret, he began to kneel with vigor. A righteous Goat came to his aid, offering his arm for guidance. But Paolo refused, genuflecting before his followers.

"Come, my sons! Confess to me your desires."

Just as they had accepted the tainted body and blood, they proceeded down the aisle in an organized hush. To mask the whispers of each man, the Songbird struck up a Theremin-like waltz. Waddling the keys, his eyes to the trapped souls squirming within the pipes, he played with divine intervention, contorting his body like a composer in the midst of his opus.

One by one they knelt before their Father, mouths pressed against his ear, whispering their fantasies, describing flesh they wished to covet, money to stuff their pocket, the slain blood of enemies and friends alike.

"It will be so, my son," he returned, nodding with approval.

Some spoke of simple pleasures, others railing with anger, screaming for the heavens to blanket those who dared cross them, in this life or the next. Each man was allowed their turn, the confession to last until each voice had made their peace, satisfied that it would be rendered in due time.

David remained standing, refusing to approach.

"You are angry," Paolo deduced. "Call upon it. Rectify it. Whisper to me what I know you desire."

He shrugged off his handlers, gliding cautiously forward. He stood above his father.

"I kneel for thee. Will you not kneel for me?"

David scanned his fellow congregants for assistance, the shimmering wicks suddenly too bright beneath the black lenses of his mask, the air stale and rising with a rotting odor. He ripped at the decaying flesh, unsheathing himself from the Dog's anonymity.

He turned towards Paolo, unwilling to meet him on his subservient level. "You bred me to be the vessel. I raised you for this purpose. Allow me to be the vessel. That is my request. You cannot deny it. *You promised.*"

"Yet, I do not run off into the woods, shying away from responsibility. I grant you your request and you flee. You believe that I would allow you to wield such power?"

"*I did not raise you for this purpose!*"

"I did not ask you to raise me."

"Then what have you been waiting for?"

"*You.* You have weakened enough for my liking."

"What...?" it was childlike, completely dyed with shame.

The black sea rose, enveloping him in musk, dragging him safely away, trapping him at the base of the chancel, forced now to gaze upward at the never-ending sadism.

The Songbird's solo transitioned seamlessly into a rousing hymn of praise. Risking injury, Paolo pressed his hand to the cold marble, pushing himself upright.

"*Sanctus Satanas, Sanctus!*" they sang in tune, filling the head of Cerberus with celebration. "*Dominus Diabolus Sabaoth!*"

Paolo approached the supple, pale skin, running his thin fingers along the shivering and pimpled leg.

Frankie mumbled her name, screaming above the holy incantations as best he could. The slack of his thread dipped as he met the Sheep's hollow stare once more. His scalp burned, a handful in the shepherd's grip, a pistol to his head, forcing him to watch.

"*Satanas - venire! Satanas - venire!*"

His father pulled her legs towards the edge of the altar, spreading them so that all may witness. She offered little objection, arms fluttering across her chest, tugging on the rosary. Paolo parted his robe.

"*Avē, Satanas, avē Papa!*"

With each labored thrust, Frankie turned from the rape. A slap from the Sheep and a burrowing of the barrel of the pistol returned him to the destruction. David hung his head, unable to stand the wet slap punctuating the rousing hymn like a bass drum.

"*Tui sunt caeli, tua est terra, avē Satanas!*"

A manger of olive wood, overflowing with straw, navigated down the sanctuary steps, two congregants on either end. The child seemed unaware, plump cheeks warm and tinted, mouth muttering nonsense as he drooled.

From his peripheral vision, Frankie caught the blur, the tiny fingers taking shape as they peeked from beyond the crevice of the bed. He followed their progress, keeping the Sheep happy as he remained obedient.

David too saw the child, the manger brought to the base of the altar, within his very grasp.

"Valentina!" he screamed, his mouth clamped shut by a woolly hand; a shotgun to his temple.

Paolo groaned as he climaxed, thrusting deeper, remembering the long-lost feeling of ejection and shame. The Songbird too finished, ending with a sickening tone that faded slowly, haunting those in attendance as Paolo removed himself, lowering his robe down to his feet. He stepped away from his pride and nodded towards the red Goats.

Two took to the child, one to scoop him into his arms, the other to fetch the sheathed knife laying beneath.

David clenched his jaw, biting into the heavy palm, freeing himself to argue. "That is *my child!* I have bargained for its ownership!"

"The child must be sacrificed!" a Fox screamed, the others in his vicinity agreeing with muffled exclamations and nodded heads.

"A child for a child?" Paolo whispered.

"How will we continue this sacred mass without blood!?" exclaimed a Horse.

"Have you forgotten my words!?" Paolo screamed. "This shall be our *final mass.* We shall strip each other of our symbols, of our anonymity. This sanctuary will crumble. The spoiled, rotten guts of the rat shall cease their production."

The animal kingdom huffed in unsure whispers, wondering where this spark of rebellion had been lit.

"Have you forgotten our creed? Have you forgotten our mission?"

"Have you!?" a voice from the rear questioned.

"We must not concern ourselves with petty ceremonies anymore. This pomp sickens me!"

The restless began to rise, their threats buzzing in a hive of underappreciation and rage. They clustered in the aisles, howling epithets at their former Lord.

"Why now?" Paolo wondered. "After all I have given you? All that I have promised, *delivered*?"

A handgun rose, a Beaver galloping forward. From the right, a Tortoise dove over a pew; to the left, a Cat, hands fumbling into his robe to draw flame. The Goats drew first, cutting down the uprising, disabling the Beaver at the knee. The Cat received a carabiner round in his shoulder, the second shearing the biggest toe from his foot. A shotgun blast launched the Tortoise back into his pew, the rampant buckshot chewing through the wood in a cloud of sawdust.

Smoke poured from Paolo's pack, a warning shot *pinging* off the ceiling, shoving the rage of the defiant congregants back further.

"Take the child!" he commanded, pointing furiously at David. "Drain these men! Prove to the others the punishment for mutiny."

Those still loyal rounded up the wounded, dragging them through their own blood towards the manger. Forced up their knees, their masks were removed, their heads wrenched back with fistfuls of thinning strands.

A Goat granted David the use of the knife, the military issue sheath sliding from the old war relic.

"Show me who you really are."

A well bucket was placed before each of the transgressors, a terror beyond their seeping wounds suddenly beating their hearts faster. The former Beaver lost natural color, the sight of the blade numbing his fingers. He struggled against the vice that shackled him, hyperventilating, the inhalations a mixture of hazel, blood, and sex. He released a chilling declaration of regret as the blade entered his neck, the wail gurgling with obstruction and evacuation. David made quick work of the sacrifice, dragging the knife outward, severing the windpipe and emptying his arteries into the bucket below.

Frankie averted his gaze, the Sheep allowing for a bit of privacy.

The congregants held the spewing mess as steady as they could. The Beaver continued to gasp, unable to free his hands to close the gap.

David approached the Tortoise, his fingers granting darkness to the anxious eyes, the knife plunging inward and snapping out, filling the second bucket.

The Cat wept, repeating requests for his mother to flutter down from Heaven. David gazed upon the newborn in the cold hands of a Goat, weighing the pact he had committed to. His decision came swift, slitting the throat of the final mutineer.

"You who have submitted your desires," Paolo declared. "I pledge to grant thee all that you have asked. The ancient texts dictate that we beg our Mistress for these carnal and valuable treasures, so that Satan may grant them to us. Tonight, all we ask of our Lord, is an audience. Prepare the portal!"

As the congregants drained the remaining blood, a Goat retrieved the knife from David's hand, quickly marching towards the altar.

"Cici!" he called.

Frankie opened his eyes, focusing towards the continuing madness.

"Restrain him!" Paolo ordered. David once again fell victim to the black sea of pale arms.

The Goat dragged the blade across her neck, opening her veins upon the chancel in a sickening wave. Three more joined him, holding the gyrating body as the vivisection began.

"Cici!"

Frankie could barely contain his composure, the need to vomit impeded by the mouthguard of tape. He shook violently, kicking his feet and swinging the chandelier in an unsteady routine. The Sheep beat him with his staff, threatening to end him with a bullet.

At the base of the neck was where they began, working the knife through the muscle, sawing the obstructing organs of gushing fluid, chipping the annoying density of bone. Each inch required a reseating of his grip, the others doing their best to steady the sickening resistance. Finally, through the stomach he carved, ending at her crotch.

Hyperventilation seized Frankie, a tingling bliss injected into his limbs as he swung between planes of consciousness, losing swaths of time as the ceremony proceeded despite his illness.

No longer able to endure, she expired, flooding the altar with urine. The Goat dove inward, separating the interconnected tissues from the pumping valves, throwing the wet slop into the manger.

Wicker baskets overflowing with currency appeared from the rear of the sanctuary, the volunteers emptying the collection atop the harvested entrails, layering the new deposits with hundreds of wasted bills.

A torch waited patiently as the body was excavated, an empty cage remaining, soiled with a layer of blood and excrement. The flame leapt upon the paper money, boiling the ink, caramelizing the lungs and heart. Higher and higher it stretched, feeding off the frenzy of greed and gluttony.

"*Dominum nostrum a mortuis resurrexit!*" Paolo said, waving his arms forward as the buckets of collected blood were emptied into the cavity, filling it like a baptismal font.

"*Magruser. Satana invicta.*"

They repeated his instruction. A hum from the organ joining them.

"*Magruser. Satana invicta.*"

"*Magruser! Satana invicta!*"

Frankie watched the harvested body through a wall of saltwater, his tears plopping at the Sheep's feet.

"*Magruser. Satana invicta.*"

"*Magruser. Satana invicta.*"

"*Magruser! Satana invicta!*"

"*Magruser! Satana! Invicta!*" The congregants began to raise their hands to the ceiling.

"*Magruser! Satana! Invicta!*"

The Songbird added a new layer, a third, a fourth, working his fingers across the possibilities.

"*Magruser! Satana! Invicta!*"

"*Magruser! Satana! Invicta!*"

The first to buckle was the stained glass of opulence, the windows exploding in violent shards, spiraling into the crowd below. Green and red debris impaled a Stag to his pew, ripping through his chest. The others hurried into the aisle, the unaware weighed down by the dangerous debris as it slit through their robes, shearing limbs from torsos, spraying the fleeing in arterial black.

The vaulted ceilings followed, the marble and plaster *cracking* in a spider's web of panic, depositing the heavy burden. With the resurrection chant still spilling from their lips, the organ blaring with respect, they dove, avoiding the crushing stone as it flattened their brethren, destroying the hand-carved benches and reducing them to mere splinters.

The Songbird paused in the shattering tremors, eyeing the bending copper pipes as they too buckled under the pressure. The heavy cylinders buckled under the supervision of the crumbling sanctuary, pulverizing the organist, splashing his keyboard with blood. The lingering notes fizzled, punctuated by the falling souls now freed from their organic prison. Their numbed dispositions chimed as they crashed upon the still operational keys, haunting the room with ghostly wails.

A column moaned as it lost its will, chipping the chandeliers above as it plummeted onto the pulpit. Frankie slammed his face into the bloodied floor as the counterweight collapsed, the drained souls littering what remained.

The limited light of the inky candles found no comfort as a cold breath snuffed them all, plunging the sanctuary into total darkness.

Flashlights found their use, awakening a yellowed clarity in the thick evening. They trained their beams upon Paolo as he recovered from the dust and confusion. To the portal now, the bloodied pond, waiting for their Lord.

"*Magruser. Satana invicta,*" they whispered.

Her toes flexed.

"*Magruser. Satana invicta.*"

Nothing now. An illusion in their minds.

A bubble, in the blood. One, surfacing slowly, exhaling, peeling open and disappearing.

Another.

Another.

A boil rising.

The vessel twitched as the cavity stirred, a vortex forming beneath the surface.

A bony, sunken finger pierced the barrier. Upward, a hand. A forearm. It gripped the split ribcage, using the leverage to rise.

The sickly, coated visage burst upward, spraying blood across the stained floor. Gnarled teeth hissed as the demon rose higher, snarling and retching at the bright beams of the flashlights.

The Devil, frail and pathetic, had risen, his form gangly, malnourished and bordering on transparent. He stepped forward, resting his feet upon the chancel, hunched against his protruding spine. His veins moved with purpose just below the festering layer of skin, each lane throbbing with progress as green and black fluid galloped throughout his body.

He hissed once more, his form flaccid and pathetic, a shriveling husk. He surveyed the remaining flock, huffing disappointment. "I have risen for this paltry collection!?" His cadence wobbled with hysteria, his tone a foundation of a churning river of pitch underneath a shrill and menacing growl.

"*Avē Satana!*" the congregants chanted.

"Silence! I will not be treated with such ceremony. Such filth! Hiding sanctimoniously behind your veils once again. Pathetic! I come to you as a King, yet you honor me as a *prince*. As a peasant!"

"We have brought you a vessel," Paolo assured.

"A vessel!?" the demon leapt from the steps to his feet, shoving his dripping fangs into his face. "Have you learned nothing!? You raise me from my post, serve me under glass in the drippings of sin, yet you offer me no gilded cloth. You beg for your dreams and your needs to be fulfilled. *You use me as a puppet!*"

Into the crowd of hungry onlookers, he rocketed, parking his jaws around the neck of the unlucky, his mangled display ripping through the skin and spraying a nasty streak amongst the darkness. To the next, ripping the arm from the socket. Another, dragging him to the ground, the mask of a Bear slipping free. A swipe from the demon's hand and the lower half of his head severed, leaving dangling strips of flesh.

The flashlights scurried, leaving those without clarity as the evil rampage continued unabated in the void. Brave souls fought through their fear, tracking the Devil as he hopped from sacrifice to sacrifice, ridding them of their anonymity and peeling their flesh.

Frankie, his head throbbing in a continuous spiral of light, tracked blood as it streaked across his field in a brief flash of clarity, hoping now he would not be chosen next.

"You have only decimated your own seed!" Paolo screamed.

The Devil paused, slowly *cracking* his neck as he turned toward the high priest. "You lie!"

"I have assembled your sons for this night. You only postpone your desire."

The Devil breathed heavily, looking down at his bloodied claws, strips of skin caught on the rough edges. He would not believe the declaration, charging towards Paolo, fangs bared, arms akimbo.

From his robe he produced a crucifix, the despised Lord, casting the Devil to his back in an invisible wave.

"The Son! The putrid Son!" he cried, casting his arms over his eyes.

"You have infected this society with your timid display," Paolo said. "It is time to knight your sons and daughters as your successors."

"My sons and daughters serve only their Master!"

A Goat handed Paolo his knife. "I drank of your blood on the battlefield. I received more than I was promised. Now, I will claim the years you have stolen from me!"

RITUAL

He lowered the crucifix, allowing the Devil to release his guard. Paolo struck, dragging his knife across the evil throat, emptying an egregious flow as the beast collapsed to his knees.

The eighth chalice was presented, the ninth tipped to the gurgling neck as it filled to the brim.

"Prepare the vessel."

The others shared concerned glances between their expressionless veils.

David was led forward, planted in front of the wheezing Devil.

"You must drink," Paolo encouraged.

His son stared into the fading, subterranean eyes of the beast, the lips unable to stretch over the chipped and infected teeth.

"*No.*"

"What is this nonsense!?" a voice questioned.

"*You* must drink," they pointed, choosing Paolo. "David is weak!"

"I thought you wanted to be the vessel?" he asked David coyly, smiling through his own surgery. "All I have done is drain you of hope. Fattened you with lies and empty promises. You cannot stand in my way if you are fragile; *if our Lord is weak.* Protect me now so that I may reign supreme."

The Goats forced David's mouth open, the chalice tipping like a massive ocean wave into his throat. He choked on the horrible stench, the taste of copper making him retch. Paolo imbibed from his own chalice, swallowing the sweet nectar easily.

David began to convulse, his eyes rolling into the back of his head as his arms shook violently. His torso contorted, rotating to its zenith before it yielded.

The Devil felt the same urge, his neck pumping as his muscles were seized with a violent spasm. The pair spewed blood across their chests as they found the unforgiving bounce of the cold, wet marble.

The skin of the demon bubbled, the white mixing with the thick dye of his opening veins. He was devoured by the viscous paste, leaving a paltry stain in his absence.

"You have deceived us, Paolo!"

A second mutiny brewed, but the Goats charged their weaponry, halting any sort of meaningful attack.

"Do you believe I would allow our Lord to control me? What power would we gain? He would rule as he saw fit, not as we have trained. David is simple, to be prodded and pushed as we declare. Soon we will rid our pages of Satan's ways and we will progress into the moonlight, reborn under my guiding hands."

A protest rose again, fists beating the air. The echo of a cadre of shotguns ceased their chattering, bathing them in silence as Paolo released his first true order as their new Lord.

"Bring my sons to their quarters. Allow them to rest. The night is still fertile, my brothers. By sunrise, we shall all bathe in satisfaction of our new trinity."

The Stag. The Woodpecker. The Dog. The Cow. They starred, vacant, watching as David held tightly to the iron knob of the cabin door in the misty, overcast light of the mid-morning.

They were early.

He ran, pivoting quickly, reaching for his rifle. The horde overpowered his escape, tackling him against the kindling, their arms groping as they slipped underneath, finding leverage.

"In the cellar!" David cried. "Take him! I have kept him alive."

The Stag threatened with a furious jab, upsetting the flow of information from his brain.

"Not me! I am not the vessel!"

A cylindrical cage slammed down around his head bruising his shoulders, a padlock sealed his struggle. Shackles *chimed* around his wrists as he was hoisted forward, positioned properly on his heels.

"Take *him*. He will be the vessel! In the cellar!"

The Woodpecker grabbed David's rifle as they escorted him from the cabin and down the shallow hill. The congregant tossed the weapon to a waiting Eagle as she flicked aside a half-ingested cigarette. The sharp-eyed hunter popped the bolt and counted the remaining ammunition.

A velvet hood splashed over the cage as David was cast into darkness, his legs anemic, his protests futile.

"Why do you think you lash out?" The question was warranted. The smug expression pushed circular glasses back against his face, the crease in his nose irritating him.

David hugged his knees, somehow fitting onto the tiny armchair without tipping it over.

"*Dottore*, I–"

RITUAL

"David, we have gone over this before. You must not be so formal. You may call me Bonifazio."

"It's my birthday today."

"I am aware. And how would you like to celebrate?"

He hid behind his legs, bumping his forehead slowly against the bent bone.

"David, please, sit properly."

He complied, pressing his bare feet onto the stained wood.

The private office had been lined with accomplishments, framed and tacked; the comforts of alcohol, assembled on a cart flush with clean tumblers; the appearance of intellect, leather bound, creased volumes coded by color, date, and size; the incessant ticking clock, *tocking* to an almost incomprehensible beat, every second divided, then divided again, again, *again*.

David could barely concentrate, tugging at the sleeve of his emerald wool sweater, his thin pajama suddenly too itchy. "I want to see my sister. I want to see Valentina."

"What about Cecilia? What about her?"

"She's gone. She's gone...she's gone. F-for good. Frankie says she went to the Americas."

"Gone? Do to what?"

The ball of his right foot ground into the floor as he bent it, pumping his heel rapidly, counting each rise and fall.

"Why has she gone so far away, David?"

"I want to go back to my room now."

Peeling back his laboratory coat, the doctor inspected his gilded watch. "We have only fifteen minutes. Perhaps we should talk about things more pleasant. It is your birthday after all."

He was afraid to ask, a sheen hovering across his eyes. "*Dott...*" catching himself, recomposing the sentence. "*Bonifazio*...do we pay for our sins?"

"How do you mean?" he leaned back in his chair, following carefully down the line of questioning.

"Do sons pay for their father's sins? If-if-if my father did something...if my father did something...if-if-if my father did something-something, but was not punished, would I be blamed?"

"Do you feel as if your stay here is punishment?"

David nodded emphatically.

"Can you explain?"

"They said that he did something...that he made a deal. But he never paid them back. He never paid them back. Now, I must pay for him."

"Who told you this?"

David *cracked* his neck, tearing his gaze from the doctor. "The Messenger," he whispered.

"And when do you talk to the Messenger?" his pencil scribbling quickly in the thick file, capturing the breakthrough.

"At night. During the day. Whenever he feels like it. But...not anymore. Not since *he* found out."

"So, he initiates the conversation? The Messenger?"

"No. Not him. Not anymore." His heel found the rhythm, tapping loudly.

"How much does your father owe?"

"They won't tell me."

"I see. And they expect you to pay?"

"I am already paying."

"By being here?" he clarified.

"It is not enough, though. They want what they can't have."

"Not money?"

"No...no...no...no..." he repeated, finding the sound it made to be quite pleasant. The power to refuse. "They want her, but she is dead. I saw her. Frankie saw her. He lied. He said she was fine. That she needed her rest. I know what blood looks like. She was dead, right?"

The glasses found the peak of the session notes, an angled finger to clear away the dried mucus in the corners of his eyes, another to massage the nose. "Yes, David," the doctor sighed, your mother is dead."

"I know that."

"Then why did you ask?"

"To see if you were lying. Sometimes...sometimes you lie to me. Others lie to me. You said I could leave soon, but that was fourteen years ago. *Fourteen years ago.*"

"Treatment takes time, David. Have you not learned that? Have you not seen that in your friends that have come and gone?"

"They all leave me. Maybe not today, maybe not on my birthday, but they leave eventually."

"Just because they leave does not mean that you aren't important."

"I'm less important."

"What gives you that impression?"

Frustration boiled his skin, insects crawling between the roots of his blistered hair. He tugged in clumps, rocking forward. "I am still here! If I was important you would have released me already.

RITUAL

You would have cured me!"

"It is not as simple as chemicals or surgery or even meeting face to face. This is an attempt to understand how you became this way."

"*This way?* What way...whatwaywhatwaywhatwhatwhat way am I? I am," counting quickly on his fingers, "*uno, due, tre, quattro, cinque, sei, sette, otto, nove, dieci,*" faster now, slurring, repeating fingers he's already counted, "*undicidodicitrediciquattordiciquindicisedicidiciassettediciottodiciannoveventiventiunoventidueventitreventiquattroventicinque. Venticinque!* Others have been here *half* the time I've been here. In and out, in and out, in and out! I've never even had sex!"

"David, we caught you and Bianca fornicating on multiple occasions. Do not spin this as if you are the victim here. You are getting the help required."

"*It's not working.*"

"If you do not try, it will never work. You must meet us in the middle. You must believe you can become better and recognize what you've done. Acceptance, David, is key. This will help you forgive yourself."

David stood, tipping back the armchair onto the floor, walking past it unaware. "I have done nothing! I have been forgotten since I was a child. Always overruled. They made promises they could not keep. Why am I being punished for their sins?"

"David, I-"

"I want that medication again." He turned his back on the doctor and walked towards a broad, paned window, each frame revealing a serene landscape of pine, the backs of the mountain towering above. "The ones that drive them out. I don't want to see him again."

"Who are you seeing now?"

"The one who blames me for my father's mistake. He is punishing me too. I must find my father, so he can explain. He didn't do anything wrong. He didn't do *anything* wrong. The Messenger knows of a place. Men...men who will help me."

"Our time has expired, David. Perhaps we can talk more about a medication strategy next week."

"You know," he sighed. "He said I could leave at any time. I know the grounds pretty well. I'm pretty strong. Not as strong as Frankie, but I'm pretty strong. He was always much stronger. I could just-j-just slip free, into the woods. That's where it all started. It's the perfect meeting place. Just a misunderstanding. They will clear it up, then they can keep their promise."

A hand on his shoulder, he had not heard the doctor approach.

BELOW

"We must get you back to your quarters." A warm smile, gesturing towards the door.

"You're right..." defeated. "I'm sorry I knocked your chair over." David bent down, lifting it upright. He spun quickly, smashing it against the doctor's back, forcing him against the edge of his desk. Disoriented, he felt his jaw spreading as David wrapped it around the tiered lip of mahogany. Before he could protest, a heel smashed the back of his skull, excavating the teeth from his gums, the splintered calcium lodging in his throat.

Blood erupted from the empty cavities as he crumpled to the floor, his cheek splitting at the corners of his lips.

"This way," David whispered, curling his arm. He dared not linger, tugging at the door and bursting into the hallway, the shuffling wings of the Messenger at his back.

He had spent the morning in a cold sweat, the soil compacted, hardened from the frigid temperatures. Snow had already fallen the previous night, a bounty for those wishing to remain indoors. Only he had disturbed the precious white blanket, his footsteps to be covered by grazing animals unlucky to spend their winters without warmth. More wisping cotton appeared from between the gangly branches, twisting silently into the hole he had already begun. His shovel speared the heavy earth, chopping away, collecting small deposits that were flung to the surface.

As he wiped away the sheet, he had not expected the suction to have outlined the body, the sight pushing him back against the far wall of the grave. The bloody imprint of their hands remained, the top of the fabric crusted in red as the neck had emptied completely.

He slipped in the thick powder, the body too cumbersome to raise, unwilling to leave the comfort of its eternal resting place. A rope around the upper torso proved useful, the edges of the pit working against him as he shimmied from side to side.

Collapsing onto his back, his father's corpse crushed him, but together they rolled awkwardly to freedom. The stench filled his throat with bile, trying desperately to release the sensation and tolerate the necessity.

He began with the rope, dragging him from the dig site, using the packed snow to avoid the obstacles of roots and rocks. Along the bed of the stream, frozen solid, his father over his shoulder, bobbing against his back with each foothold. The crest of the valley, overlooking the fields of birch, winged lumberjacks pecking away at fragile branches, sorting them carefully in their full nests.

They had rested here, his father leaning against a tree, bobbing slightly with every gust that caught them. He feasted on stale bread, water from a canteen, he desired little else. Down the hill, meeting the valley, walking through the obfuscation for hours, knowing only that forward would reveal more, that turning, even in the slightest, would set him off course. He cradled his father like a newborn, his back beginning to fuse as the muscles tightened. He moved too quickly, anxious to remove the burden.

The waterway, flowing beneath the arch, at the base of the mountain, his face plunging within, rubbing clean the elements of his journey. The stone tower drove a stake into the clouds, the ancient wall puffing its chest, for it would not be bested; no need for prickly vines of neglect.

The partially headless body clambered up the staircase, slapping each tread as he tugged and wrestled against the incline. The trees stood proud and rigid, their spines far from encumbered, allowing fruitful air to flow. Despite his exhaustion, his traversal proved uneventful, dragging his father to the peak easily, pausing in the shadows of the gate.

Spewing condensation like an ancient dragon, David lifted Paolo into his arms and approached the massive wooden doors. His heel banged against the iron accents, chiming three times, hoping that his simple prayer would be answered.

He awoke like a frightened goat, straw stuffed down his throat, grinding against his molars. A wet cloth had been pressed against his forehead, mopping up the perspiration of hellish nightmares. Frankie adjusted his vision, blinking through the moisture, smoke spewing from a wall of wax forming an artificial grotto around a ragged desk, horizontal wicks chewing down the paraffin. A figure hunched over a typewriter, pecking, mumbling as each sentence slowly spilled onto the page.

"David?" he mumbled, spitting free the dry stalks.

The correspondence ceased as the blur turned from the stool, the ancient wood swearing under its breath.

"David?" he tried again, hoarse and tender.

"Frankie? I didn't expect you awake so soon."

David tended to his brother, kneeling with a ceramic bowl of water and leaning towards his parched lips. Frankie obliged the cool liquid, his throat burning from the non-alcoholic flavor. He waved it off, he had had enough. David removed the washcloth, setting it across the rim of a bucket. He pressed the back of his hand to Frankie's head. "You don't seem to be running a fever."

"Where's Cici?"

Bewilderment painted itself across David's face, unable to understand. He scoffed, mixing it with a twinge of laughter. "Y-you were there. Don't you remember?"

"I can't...I can't remember."

"You just need more time," he smiled, patting Frankie's face. "Rest, now, I have a few things to attend to." He retreated to his stool, snuggling it closer to the desk, eyes rereading what he had already committed to paper.

A mobile of souvenirs twinkled above them: frayed lengths of twine wrapped around porcelain figures, punched through the borders of photographs, lynched around the necks of stuffed rabbits and bears. Reconnaissance had been tacked to the walls, the faces bright, unsuspecting, the mundane activities of their fruitless lives becoming David's fuel. Cecilia's face beamed as she left the confines of the convent, Frankie's nervous lips sucked upon a cigarette as he cocked his head away from a crime scene. *His* crime scene.

Behind David, the ambiance of his personal space faded quickly, the room heavy with black, no chance to determine depth.

"Imagine," the voice huffed. "*Us. Again.* This family...this repulsive excuse for a bloodline."

David continued his hunt for the perfect grammatical conclusion, his lips sealed, eyes squinting, thinking.

Frankie eased onto his elbows, wiping the confusion.

"I am tired, Francesco."

"David?"

"Don't look to him. He is busying himself. No need to intervene." A long shadow bled from the pit, a delicate finger that tapped David on his shoulder. He shrugged off the annoyance.

"Not now! Papa will be expecting this soon, I need-I need...I need to finish."

The vampiric appendage slipped away.

"What do I have to gain now? Huh?"

"Who are you?" Frankie pressured, struggling to sit upright, his back sliding against the brisk stone.

"I am what little David has to hold on to." In the darkness, outlines began to slowly adjust, a cutout approaching, feet scraping across the ground. "He drank of my blood. Choking on the stench, the ancient corrosion." Closer now, the fabric tattered, concealing the gaunt construction. "We are one now."

It appeared as David.

The shape of the face, the strong chin, the raised nostrils.

The color had been stained white as baby powder, the veins slightly raised, pumping dark fluid around battered cheeks. His lips had peeled, the corners swollen, sprouting pustules. His mouth could not contain the chipped and infected teeth, pushing them towards the center, the dominant fangs forcing the others to sprout jagged tails in a twisting smile.

"Jesus..." Frankie stared.

The grin faded, the upper lip snarling. "Fucking savior. You revert to *him* in times of need?" He drooled a viscous glob of pitch at Frankie's feet. "Pathetic."

"I'm not the one trapped in a man's body."

A sarcastic applause, the bones practically ripping through the paper-thin caul as the hands peeked from long sleeves. "A humble vessel, I suppose. Not even my own Father is as cruel."

"Then leave. Leave us to sort our own business."

"Francesco!" he growled. "I cannot benefit if I were to take flight."

"I don't understand what you need."

"A womb! *A fertile womb.*"

"There is no shortage elsewhere."

"Do you truly believe that I am that naïve? That I would stake my position, *my power*, on the crusted fields of *one*? Of *your mother*? Your sister? I have spawned many heirs. The ceremonies, the follies of *men*. It is tedious. I am presented with child, with man. I can do nothing with these. The soul requires too much intervention, too much energy." He peeled back the thick robe, his chest caved, ribs crisscrossing, an enlarged, beating organ pulsing laboriously just below the surface. "I am destined to be but a legend. My seed lives on, others to take my place. My services matter little. What do I honestly provide? Lust? Greed? Gluttony? These are the pleasures of men only. I feast little on these. Your time is brief, Francesco. Mine...mine has no end. Though, it appears that there is a greater plan ahead of me, one which I did not suspect."

"Why do you feel the need to father a child?"

"Do you not want to be remembered after you perish?"

Frankie averted the inquisitive gaze, pondering the question. "I am not old enough to require an answer."

"Youth?" a smile. "*Divine.*"

"What is your name? Are you still David?"

His brother turned from his typewriter, "Satanus."

"Bah! The nomenclature of a people too oblivious to my tragedies."

"What do you prefer to be called?" Frankie offered, the cobwebs clear now from his brain, focusing him towards the interrogation.

"Do not answer for me, child!" the disfigured commanded.

"I'm only trying to help!" David screamed.

"Please," Frankie pleaded, "allow him to answer."

His brother flung back his stool in defiance, marching towards the wooden gate that prevented his escape, screaming into his palms.

"I *like* him," the devilish smile admitted. "I was once knighted as a *morning star*, by those who have misinterpreted my existence. I have been branded Satan, Lucifer, Beelzebub, paltry descriptions that are thrust upon me, the stupidity of creatures stamping my name to random acts of betrayal and violence. It is true that I fell from favor, it is true that I dared to defy my Father. It is ingrained in us all to rebel, to seek justice and responsibility on our own. Am I not guaranteed that right? But rather than comfort me, rather than ingrain in me true virtues, I was cast from His light. Forced to grapple with my own kin! I was once in charge of the regiments, blaring the trumpet of peace. *Michele. He* was given my power. He was given my responsibilities! I wallowed in darkness, no promises of ever returning from exile. Michele...this would anger him so. To be referred to by his precious, glowing student. I suffer for our Father's sins, Francesco. I have been chosen."

"He-he is innocent!" David cried, pacing now between the door and his soul. "Papa did not mean the things that he said. He did not mean to hurt us."

"A whisper alone does little. But add to it, compose a symphony of wailing, *infest* the brain with suggestions, then a man will drive himself to commit what is necessary."

"No! No! Frankie, he was scared. He was scared! He always said he was brave, that all soldiers were brave. He was just scared. Once they talk, once they talk, it will be over, it will be worth the effort."

"I will speak with no one!" Michele screamed, rushing back into the darkness.

David stomped forward, "Papa just needs some time to speak

with him. He just needs time to explain that he doesn't need him anymore."

Frankie struggled to his feet, grunting as his knees buckled under the sudden pressure, the flow of fresh blood tingling his nerves into a frenzy. David stabilized him, pressing him up against the wall.

"I'm fine. I'm all right," he assured, his cheek to the refreshing rock. "What did Papa do? What does Papa need to explain?"

"He bargained," David whispered. "He-he-he was injured, during the war. His leg, his leg *gone*. Stranded, in the middle of the forest. He asked for help. He asked for help, that's all. God did not come. Satan. Satan came to him. He exchanged Mama for his leg, for his health. As if nothing had happened. He wanted a child, he wanted a child for himself. He did not give us up. Not you, not Cici, not me. He did not give us up."

"Valentina...?" he realized.

A nod; a hush overcoming his volume. "Satan took Valentina. He took her. But it was not enough. He wanted more, but Papa had no more to give."

"A lie!" Michele ejected, fuming from the shadows. "She was offered unto me as a bargain! A ruse to prevent my desire."

"Then Mama...she took Papa from us. She stole him away. He did not mean the things he said, he was only doing what he thought Satan wanted him to do. He thought it would repay his debt. But she killed him; killed him before he was through. I was chosen, Frankie. He chose *me*. He told me I must continue. I must continue to serve, to complete the debt. That is why I raised Papa. I brought him back. I brought him to renegotiate, to...to finish the debt."

"Is that why you killed those people?"

"I cannot defeat the armies of Heaven as one," the unholy grunted.

"They were sinners," David explained. "They needed to be punished. Papa says they needed to be punished. That they needed to be sacrificed in order to please him. To cure the world of sin, so that Satan would no longer have his army."

"His children..." Frankie whispered. "The ones you killed, they were his children."

"Simple minded, eh?" Michele chuckled. "To think using my own flesh and blood against me would diminish my anger or my strength."

"You are here now!" David screamed. "You will have only your soul to bargain with."

"That is not what Papa wants," Frankie explained. "All of this,

this is what the Devil wants," Frankie explained.

"Wrong!" both sides shouted, pointing their indexes at Frankie, accusing him of betrayal.

"God does not punish!" Michele assured. "God does not punish the wicked! The unclean! He leaves the penalty to *me*. He forces me to harm, he forces me to conjure disgusting penance for vain socialites and the thieving destitute. The sinful sicken me. I must rid my conscience of them."

"Why gut them? Brand them as sinners?" the inspector in him seizing an opportunity to delve deeper. "You can wipe them out, can you not?"

"To raise the spirits of the dead," David said. "An empty shell must be provided so that Satan may rise from the very belly of sin."

"Nonsense!" Michele batted. "Decorative playthings. I am not to be honored, I am not to rise from slumber into the mouth of blood."

"Papa needed their organs, he needed their flesh, to repair himself. To shroud those in attendance with anonymity."

"Razed over and over, reanimating dead tissue. Each piece of the magnificent clock working in unison. *Because of my hand!*"

"We needed to praise Him. Each night, reborn to praise his name until Papa could speak. Until he could protect himself. You saw how many came, Frankie. They love Papa. They will protect him, in case the Devil turns against him."

"*Each time* I am weakened," throwing his pale hands into the air. "I am drained of what little patience and opportunity remains. I am not this form. I am cursed! My wings, stolen! My armor, split, smelted into the foundation which traps me. My youth, my anger, my strength. It has been siphoned. I return to renegade fields of those who believe that mutiny will flow when I am beckoned from my duties. I am exhausted, bringing order and punishment, never to sit upon a throne and sleep!"

"Does a man who beats his children," Frankie offered calmly, "a man who sacrifices his daughter, who haunts his son, who coerces and lies and drives him to madness...does this man deserve to be praised?"

"I cannot rule over the labyrinthian chaos that exists below the crust of reality any longer," Michele begged, his form succumbing to guilt and pressure. He bowed to one knee, staring up at Frankie as tears streamed from his sorrowful regret. "I cannot endure this nightmare. My lineage is thinning, I cannot continue without confirmation."

"Why Anna?" Frankie glared, removing himself from the pitiful protest.

David panicked, folding his lips inward, moistening them over and over, inhaling more than he released, causing his own hyperventilation. Dust clouded his eyes as they moistened, attempting to wick away the intrusion.

"David!" snapping his attention. "*Why Anna?*"

"Because it is Cici's baby!" he cried.

His voice ignited a firestorm of wailing. David wiped his tears angrily, hurrying into the far end of the room, dipping his hands into the darkness and pulling free the howling child.

"Shh...shh..." he whispered, gently rocking it in the warmth of a wool blanket. "Valentina, you mustn't worry. It will be over soon."

"The child is a boy," Michele hissed.

"David, he is not yours to keep," Frankie explained.

"Cici committed a sin," David lectured. "She kissed this child's mother. She put her inside. Papa did not approve. But now, we have Valentina back."

"You traded Antonio," Frankie suspected. "You held your own ceremony, in the warehouse. You used Anna and you traded Antonio for the baby."

"The Devil would not leave me alone! I was tired of him always whispering, always telling me what to do! I thought if I could make him disappear, if I could pass it on to someone else, then maybe, I... maybe, I...I could get some sleep. I promised to take care of Valentina in exchange. *I promised.* Cici would not be punished. She would not be punished by raising the baby. I would do it. I would take her sin. I have seen it, Frankie. I have seen what they do to mothers! They bolt them to burning crosses, spear them into the sand. They watch their unbaptized children across an ocean of purity, begging for the mother's that will *never* come. I chose to keep him from Cici. I kept my promise. I wanted Valentina back. *She liked me*, Frankie. She looked at me and she laughed."

"What can I give you, Francesco?" Michele proposed. "What earthly delights would convince you to end this bastard's existence and grant me peace?"

The genuflecting demon was powerless without his agreement, a pathetic worm who could barely hold court unless his coffer contained a guaranteed contract.

"You have no power over me," Frankie spat confidently. "I reject you. I reject your attempt to draw pity upon yourself."

"My hands perform the work that none of you have the stomach for. You squirm from responsibility, you shy from acceptance. You could not pass judgment on the fallen, flay their flesh with your bare hands. Your bravado fails to impress me, so many righteous zealots who believe that they can cast me aside. I have collected your refuse for millennia. I have created order in this world, have struck fear into those who do good. And for *this*? For *this* you are punishing me? Your father made a mistake by trapping me inside the walls of this simpleton. I am giving you a way out, Francesco. Set me free. Do not tempt me to pollute your brother, to drive him further from you."

"Prove to me my brother exists somewhere inside of this imposter. That he has not become my father's puppet."

"You wish to measure his worth?" Michele stood, *cracking* the ancient joints, muscles dried and powdery, sifted over shivering veins. "The meager scraps are yours, I will only devour for the sport."

He slammed his hand over the back of David's neck, eliciting a terrified *bleat*. The child encumbered him as he slammed his knees into the stone floor. Frankie lunged, grabbing the blanket and reeling the baby into his care as David attended to the vice.

"Frankie," he breathed, using Michele's own inflection and timber. A cough, a lump at the back of the throat. Dry heaves released the tension, a familiar pitch returning, one that he had not heard in some time. "Frankie...judgement must come to these men. They have used me." His lips quivered as he wept. "The cabin... bring me to the cabin. You promised me we would finish. In the cellar. You promised. *Then we will kill them all.* Kill them all!"

"No!" Michele yelled, using his clenched fingers to raise David, his knees straightening as he hovered. "My sons and daughters will not be sacrificed for your vendetta! I am legend. I am eternal!"

David's eyes began to cloud as they rolled backwards, the bright veins replacing his brown pupils. His neck *snapped* as the bony wand conducted him. From the pit of his stomach, a chorus of the damned cried out.

Michele assimilated, his shadow banished from the room as David dropped to the floor, his skull slapping against the rigidity. Paolo stood in the frame of the open wooden gate, his rotten smile parting the stitched lips.

"*Avē Satana.*"

It felt painted on, as if the window had been installed with a sprawling canvas. The meticulous work of a determined artist dotted every tree with shadow, smearing the purple mountains with toxic white, ever so slightly dragging the thick paint across the stretched material.

But it was real.

Even when allowed the one hour per week of outdoor activities, it still seemed real. Between the latticework of metal, framing the beauty in a round-edged parallelogram, he would stare, freedom within his view, the taste in his lungs of the mountain air, separated by a mere fence. Though they had topped it with barbed wire, it mattered little, he would do what was necessary to escape.

"He speaks so little."

"Never! He *never* speaks."

"I've heard him mumble."

"Crying at night, the pitiful thing."

"David? Time to come inside!"

A hand on his shoulder, the wicked eyes of the Devil. "You heard them, young one."

He turned to face the cadre of nurses, finding their eyes gouged, a vortex of black tentacles spewing from the holes, screaming at him in undead tongues.

Awake now. In his private quarters, knees to his chin, huddling at the corner of his bed, back to the graying wall.

"What is to be done with your father?" The Devil croaked. "Drowning now in a pit of feces, choking on the bile and excrement of his fellow man. Dragged from the shores, stripped alive by hideous beasts, his skin blistering in the heat and flames. David, David, David, you are all alone here. Just a boy, now, locked inside, deserted, banished from your own family. And what do they grant you? Nothing. They refuse you a voice; relegated to red, blues, and yellows, popping them in your throat to make the voices go away. Do not think that I enjoy this. The punishment was not earned by you, but you will certainly pay the price."

A droplet of black liquid, thick as ink, splashed against his bed. The circumference stretched, forming a small stain. Another, near it, slightly bigger, growing upon impact. He craned his neck at the dark puddle languishing in the ceiling, slowly widening. Two more formed on the opposite side of the room, an army of beads marching from the edge, weighed down by a heavy, continuous flow.

His room exploded in a brutal monsoon, the rain pooling

quickly, the tide rising towards his mattress.

David screamed, tucking himself under the top sheet as the white layer became drenched, the light of the afternoon blotted. The bed began to shiver as the waves picked him up, tipping the mattress towards starboard. He kept his head buried beneath the black as he swayed, the motion uprooting his stomach, a metallic taste forming in his mouth.

Indentations appeared in the top sheet, a hand grasping the flat sail and ripping the protection from him. It was tossed over-board into a smoking and neon river of souls, their hunger tearing at the material, shoving it into their mouths as they bobbed along the surface. David huddled at the bottom of the wooden vessel, his featherbed long gone, the heavy stare of the Messenger turning to-wards the distant shore of embers as he paddled with the blunt end of his weapon.

The boat wrestled with the storm, socking the rim with a snarling gale. The Messenger pushed forward, necklace twinkling, his robe of burlap soaking the incessant water. Mucus-slathered hands pawed at the boat, those who had had their fill of punishment threatening to come aboard. He beat them back, slicing them off at the wrist, shoving their faces into the liberal, black waters.

"David," the towering beast spoke. "David, please, open your eyes."

The cowering child refused, shaking his head, covering himself with his arms, blocking out the fury of the damned and the roar of the storm.

"You must face it. You cannot fight it unless you face it!"

A woman flung herself from the froth, sinking her fingers into David's arm. His eyes opened into the dripping snarl, but the danger was instantly limited as the notched blade of the scythe tore through the intruder's head, the spliced skull sinking into the arms of the sea.

"Look," the Messenger directed, "towards the shores of the capital city. Keep your eyes open. I will protect you."

David nodded, crawling towards the bow, fighting back against the disorienting undulation, the beast's gloved hand clutching his back. He fixed his eyes on the tiny glow, the ochre heat wisping into dark fog that filled the sky with raging clouds.

The storm suddenly broke, not full stop; peeled aside as if a massive curtain, the intensity continuing behind them unabated. They sailed into calmer waters, still no closer to land, but free from certain danger. The Messenger turned from his duties and sat, with much discomfort, along a wooden beam, offering his hand towards another, reserved for David. The boy obliged, wiping his face free of water and ink.

They sat in silence, catching their collective composure, the water dragging them tediously in one direction.

"Who are you?" David mustered.

The skull cocked, a hand to the chin, contemplating the philosophical nature of the question. But David had not meant to be so deep.

"What's your name?"

The Messenger's clarity surfaced, an index in the air, "Oh, where are my manners?" He spoke in a dull, almost preprogrammed droll. It was pleasant, the rhythm of an older man who neither rushed nor procrastinated, each word deliberate and purposeful. "A century ago, I was christened Samael, but my Master now calls upon me as the Messenger."

"Why?"

"I must bring a message to those living and dead, that they are to be ferried deeper into the rings of punishment."

"Do you kill people?" eyes staring intently at the trophies around the Messenger's neck and waist.

"No. It is forbidden, lest I desire to face my own punishment. I merely assist their journey. Sometimes they will not come willingly, so I must intervene, but I mean no harm in doing so." He held forth the string of teeth and bones in his hand. "Merely decorations that I have collected. My Master insists that it will drive fear into those who refuse."

"Why does he visit me too?"

"My Master?"

A nod.

"Because your father has turned against him."

"Papa was not mean. He loved me."

"I do agree that you are not to be blamed, but your father promised my Master he would assist him. He went against his word and now you must provide where your father could not. He has chosen you, David."

"Did he choose you too?"

"I..." he stumbled, the thought crossing his mind for the first time in centuries. "I suppose you could say that."

"Why did he choose you?"

"I too was exiled from my home, forced to flee as they confiscated my belongings, my writings, my life's work. They burdened me with false charges, insinuated that my writing contained libelous accounts that threatened the lives and livelihood of rival families.

"Two of my children faced the same penalty, but we were separated in the following years. I could not bear to be apart from them, to exist in a world that would steal them from me. I received word that my enemies had slaughtered what family I had left behind. They mocked me, slandered my own name, forced me to disguise myself, become a man I was not.

"I blamed God for my misfortunes. How could He have allowed such a tragedy to befall such a loving person, a proud family? I cursed Him, I screamed at the heavens for an answer. I had dedicated my life to Him and he cast me into despair. I never received a reply, no matter how hard I tried.

"I journeyed into the woods...intending to kill myself. But I was prevented...in that final moment...by my Master. He showed me the horrors that await those who take their own life. He told me that God did not punish me. He walked me through the very gates of Hell, into the burning pits, the pus-spewing crevices, the lake of eternal ice. He gave me a choice: to become a messenger, to take the knowledge I had gained, the intricacies of death, and offer it to those who wished to sin; or, become a lost soul, to endure the torture, the punishment of this terrible hole. I wish to prevent others from coming here, from adding to the never-ending assembly of regret and tears."

"You don't like your job very much."

"It brings failure where I seek success. When my Master is called from his duties, the hounds of hell rise in protest." The Messenger angled his head towards the shore, calculating the distance. "Do you see the mountains, David?"

He leaned around the mass of bone and burlap.

"No, no," The Messenger assured. "From your window. Can you see the mountains from your window?"

He nodded, returning to the bench.

"When the time is right, when your strength has grown, I will lead you into the mountains. It is there that I can help you. I have seen the sons and daughters of my Master's seed. I know their names, I know their faces. I protect them. I watch over them carefully so that no harm befalls them. He cannot hear us now, so you must listen carefully. *I am but a pawn.* For almost a thousand years I have carried sadness and pain and delivered it to those who do not deserve it. I wish this fate upon no one, especially a child as innocent as you.

"You must understand that he cannot hurt you now. He cannot touch you. But you must *resist.* He will tempt you, he will provide for you, but you cannot, you *must not* become your father as he was. He will offer you a way out, but it is only a shackle to tether you. My Master is fallible, he relies solely on others, but if we resist, if we turn our backs against him, he will wither. Promise me that you will not become as I have. You must promise me this."

"Papa is dead."

"Yes, but that does not mean he has vanished. He toils here, in the circles and caves of torture. When you have the strength, come to the mountains, there I will save you from the darkness."

The vessel bucked, the bow craning skywards. The shore had come upon them, shambling, groaning sinners coated in flames aimlessly littering the beach as the storm grew volcanic, splitting open the magma-thick atmosphere. Their flesh boiled, bones steaming into ash as they knelt, collapsing into the black, salted sands.

"I can take you no further. You do not belong here," the Messenger hurried. "Promise me, David."

"Will you help me find Papa?"

The brittle bones rose from the perch, climbing over the side of the boat and into the heated minerals. "In time," he assured. "Your father has undergone a transformation, undeniably far from his fault alone, but he owes much to my Master. Perhaps there will be a way forward. Perhaps together we can solve our collective problems. He must not know that I have spoken to you. Do not allow him to grow wise. Do you understand?"

David nodded with purpose.

"Resist him. Do not become as your father was." He heaved, casting the boat back into the dark waters.

"How do I get home!?" David shouted, hands cupped around his mouth as he drifted.

A spouting flame pawed at the Messenger, gathering his attention briefly before being shoved into the sea, extinguished into a bleeding crust.

"Home?" A foreign concept.

The boat began to take on water, a gash suddenly appearing in the hull. The ocean's ravenous tentacles ensnared him, dragging him deeper. The Messenger waded into the shallows, arm outstretched, watching the bubbles rise to the surface, popping with David's horrific lamentations.

The sinners watched silently as they bid him farewell, grief oozing from their veins as they contemplated the atrocities that a child must commit to gaze upon their damnation.

$$\triangledown \;\triangle\!\!\!\!\triangledown\; \triangledown\; \triangle$$

The elegant fingers were barely a half centimeter long, curling inquisitively at the large being that hovered over her. Her feet danced playfully as she smiled, shaking the wicker bassinet.

"Papa!" he squealed, "she likes me!"

Paolo curled the newspaper away from his face. "Of course, she is your sister." It was matter-of-fact, no real sympathy towards the excitement.

"Can you say, David? Hmm? Day-*VID*."

"She cannot speak," Paolo grunted.

"Here," David suggested, holding the newborn's hand steady. He poked out his index finger and counted the tips of her fingers. "Val-en-tee-NA. V-a-l-e-n-t-i-n-a. Nine! Almost all ten!"

Valentina cooed, slipping her hand free and waggling it into the air.

The crowded hall buzzed with an annoying drone of forced whispering, the visitors trying to respect the other patients mere inches away. A cart in need of significant oiling squeaked down the aisle, glass jars of cotton balls and antiseptic rattling against the impatient pace.

Like the frames of the beds, the mattresses, the sheets, the scratchy down blankets, the nun had draped herself in white. An apron of old, bodily stains had been wrapped around her waist, just below a dangling rosary. She attended to the adjacent and thoroughly wounded, the poor soul bandaged around the head, torso, and legs, dried blood seeping through the pockets in the gauze.

David sought his father's side. "Papa," he whispered in his own interpretation of volume, "what happened to that man?"

The paper shuffled, catching a glimpse of the squirming patient before turning back to the printed word. But, he had seen something. Identification tags, around the neck.

"He was a soldier," he muttered.

"Was he brave?"

"All soldiers are brave."

"What about you?"

The redressing of the infected wounds ignited fear in his young daughter, her screeching escalating quickly. Alessandra rustled, rolling her head away from the sound, drifting once more into sleep. Paolo folded the newspaper quickly, reaching into his pocket and wrestling with loose change. He shuffled the coins into David's hand.

"Go find something to eat. Your mother needs rest."

"What about Valentina? She is crying."

"I will hold her, make sure she is happy." A smile tore through the stone facade, convincing the now second-youngest to shove off. He greedily stuffed the coins into his trousers, skipping happily through the den of recovery and past the double doors, much to the annoyance of the staff.

Paolo approached Valentina with fear, barely peeking over the shade of the bassinet. She was an unexploded piece of ordinance, his hands moist as he retrieved her, clutching the frightened head against his chest.

"Would you like me to call someone?" the attending nun asked as she threw the bloodied bandages of the soldier into a wastebasket.

He shook his head, "My fourth; I will take her for some fresh air."

Valentina began to hush as he swung her gently, "*Ninna nanna, ninna oh. Questo bimbo a chi lo dò?*"

They passed the infertile, the invalid, the impaired, the imperfect, the incurable, the indisposed, the infected; all once perfect bundles, wailing because they had soiled themselves, that the temperature in the room had changed, that they were lonely; now, returned to that state, unable to leave because they were too heavy to be ferried from the smells and the brimming sun, all jealously watching as Valentina road in the comfort of her father's carriage, his voice soothing her anxiety.

"*Se lo dò alla Befana, se lo tiene una settimana.*"

Through the swing doors, a casual right, away from the lobby, away from the bright warmth of the still rising morning.

"*Se lo dò all'uomo nero...*"

He had walked this mile before, the hallway stretching infinitely, growing tentacles sticky with bed frames and rotting corpses.

"*...se lo tiene un anno intero...*"

The white service door *clicked* as it swung open, the long coat over the dress shirt, a wide, black tie beneath.

"*Ninna nanna, ninna oh...*" he deposited Valentina into the doctor's waiting arms. A nod, devoid of sympathy. Quickly turning, hurrying downward, Valentina descended into the subterranean levels. The well door echoed behind Paolo as it closed. He craned his neck upward, caught in the dizzying funnel of the spiraling stairs as it met the glass tower above, sparkling in the white heat, drawing him towards the heavens.

But curiosity, an anxious need to know *now*, to confirm beyond all doubt, lead him downstairs, careful not to add to the faint echo of the doctor. The air grew stale, damp, chilling his breath as he released long streams of white. The electricity weakened, barely enough arc to reach the stationed bulbs, the dim yellow casting nasty shadows against the plain door at the bottom of the stairwell.

Pulling his jacket off, he unscrewed the buzzing globe, casting himself in black. The door opened easily, edging inward, a small slit big enough for himself. Two rusted, industrial boilers had nestled side by side in front of him, the odor of coal mixing with hazel as a dense cloud settled. Candles of midnight called him forward, a woman moaning against the slap of perspiration. He slipped between the pill-like vessels, avoiding the web of pipes that summoned and deposited water throughout the hospital. A coal locker prevented him from moving further, the latticed cage half-full, enough to duck against and take part in the proceedings.

A blast door at the far end of the room rolled open, unraveling a length of rope against its pulley, blasting the dark engine room with a yawning beam of sunlight. The masked Dog paused, mid-stroke, the girl's shrouded head hanging loosely from the altar, her naked flesh brimming with beads. A final congregant stood in the doorway, the crude, paper and wire masks of winged, pawed, and gilled creatures staring back at him silently as he slipped into a disfigured Crow of his own.

The steel panel shut with much difficulty, the darkness returned, the fornication renewed as the pent-up soul released himself, moaning with relief, clutching the girl's legs around his neck.

"So, you have sown," she spoke, "and from your sowing gifts may come if you, obedient, heed these words I speak."

Those assembled began to chant in unison, "*Dies irae, dies illa. Solvet Saeclum in favilla. Teste Satan cum sibylla.*"

The girl clung to her breasts, forcing the tingling sensation of the moment downward, pressing hard against her stomach.

Two interrupting *claps* stymied the chanting. "I know you, my dark children," she continued, her voice pierced by ecstasy. "You are sinister, yet none of you is as sinister or as deadly as I. I know you and the thoughts within all your hearts: yet not one of you is as hateful or as loving as I. With a glance, I can strike you dead!"

A Hog stormed towards the altar, black stole flung forward, wrapping it around the neck of the girl, squeezing tightly as she thrashed. Others flocked, a strong-headed blade brandished from beneath a robe.

"You may not disturb the sanctity of this mass!" roared a whiskered Cat.

"We have been compensated!" the Hog protested as the knife entered just below the sacrifice's neck, slitting downward, banging against her ribs. Paolo forced a hand to his mouth, the wretched slurp of blood spilling over the side of the altar, pooling quickly on the coal-dusted floor, formed a lump of regret in his throat.

This needed to happen.

"We present the child!" a voice surged. Valentina's sharp-pitched wail flooded the boiler room. "No guilt shall bind you here; no thought restricted. Feast then and enjoy as we remember that you are the Wind that snatches our souls!"

A pickaxe struck the stone floor, *pinging* like a monstrous church bell. *Again*, it struck, as Paolo was tempted to watch once more. The muscular form pounded into the foundation near the base of the altar, clearing a small hole. A Tiger knelt and placed a tetrahedron of clouded crystal into the earthly wound, covering it carefully with the debris.

"*Aperiatur terra, et germinet CHAOS!*" he screamed.

The Hog released the vice from around the girl's neck, her body still now, organs exposed to the moldy air. The gathered stepped away from their masterpiece, forming a semi-circle, a blanket muffling Valentina.

A lull sank into the basement. Condensation slid over their homemade masks, soaking into the glue-slathered paper.

The vessel began to twitch, the bloody cavity bubbling slowly, far, though, from becoming a boil. Paolo gripped the cage, refusing to flee as the Devil rose from the between the folds of the tightly packed organs, *cracking* the rib cage and clearing the remaining obstructions.

Drenched in blood, the fragile presence lifted his head, vomiting what he had swallowed. He sniffed the air, clenching his teeth in disgust. "Christ! Christ's holy stench is amongst us. You summon me in the festering hole of his purview! For what reason should I allow you to continue to live?"

The blanket over Valentina was lifted, the lost soul kneeling before his Lord as the newborn screamed. "A repayment of debt, on behalf of Paolo Zampa."

"I rise for this!?" He snatched the child like a goblin of tall tales, his teeth digging into her neck as he chewed angrily, spilling her blood down his gaunt forearms. He tossed Valentina's corpse aside, unsatisfied. "He has strayed far from our agreement. He wish-es to deceive me, to convince me that I am not who I say I am. I gave him *life!*"

He pawed at the hood of the nearest congregant and swung his fingers against his neck, slicing through muscle and bone, decapitating him. The robe remained around the head as the naked body collapsed beneath.

"I have been called to this horrid land for vanity! For fear!"

He dropped the cumbersome prize and leapt forward, tackling the Cat. He swiped at the insulting mask, clearing a chunk aside before bearing his teeth.

Paolo stayed hidden, clutching his knees to his chest as he listened to the chaos, sneaking his exhalations. The gathered pleaded with their Savior as he devoured them, gnawing their flesh, stringing their internal mechanisms across the filthy layer. He relished in their blood, each ejection bathing him in pleasure.

The Devil stood before the altar heaving with the growl of a threatened mountain bear. "Paolo...you have disappointed me. You have avoided me. Polluting that foul womb!"

Paolo shoved his palms against his ears, a deafening tone splitting his skull down the middle.

"I will punish you. I will return for your flesh and the flesh of your offspring. Your Alessandra will bear my child. She will bear the captains of my armies! Paolo! YOU! YOU WILL–"

The blast door rolled open, the cleansing light of day framing the Devil in a sanctuary of pain. The nun of virginal white stood in the doorway, too frightened to speak, heels glued to the stone. The crucifix around her waistband mocked him, his veins bursting beneath the skin as it cracked like a dry riverbed, singing into a volcanic black, flakes rising upwards into the musty air.

The Devil screamed as Paolo matched his agony.

Upright, leaving the drenched pillow, heart racing. Thick beads of perspiration oozed through the roadways of his scalp, trickling past his ear. He stared directly into a wall of bleached stone, the finish rough and dotted with veins. The bed had been pushed into the corner, his feet huddled beneath an inverted crucifix. He pressed two fingers gently against his face, running the callous edges over the crude stitching. Pulling away, he patiently watched as a glob of tissue and blood slid down his index.

He whipped his head to the right.

David stared excitedly, leaning forward in an armless, wicker chair. A semi-circle of black-robed creatures flanked him, a silent reverence cast over the assembled. da Medicina placed bloodied forceps onto a tray, shooing away the spindled ends of wasted silk and eyed needles. He cleared away a pile of stained gauze into a fuming bucket, a wet rag wiping off the top of a bureau.

"Papa?" David smiled.

They ground the beggar's meat against their molars, chomping, shredding the tough cut. Their lips slapped, munching, refusing to tighten their jaws to allow a bit of peace. Another slab, too big for the growing mouths, the tough skin eliciting a winking eye, a raised cheek, working through each morsel.

He had lost his appetite, the cud-chewing cows somehow syncing their attack, diving face first into the slop. Looking across the hungry, bruised faces of his children he could not release the sinister voice that whispered.

"Fucking diseases," the Devil breathed. "*Rats.* Vomited from a venomous womb to feed off your hard work." Twisting to his other ear. "Listen to them. Jaws clicking a week-old hunk of beef sliced around the maggots. They draw from your well, Paolo, they suck you dry."

Paolo stabbed a hunk of garlic and munched on the fried aroma, a giggle rising from his youngest.

"He laughs. He mocks. He knows you are cowardly. Even at that age, he knows. Knows that you are a fool who made an arrangement. Teach him you are no fool. Show the others that you are no longer a slave to their needs."

Paolo's chair shaved a thin layer of lacquer from the hardwood as he stood, slamming his napkin upon his uneaten beef. He marched to the far end of the table, palm open, and swung against David's supple cheek.

The chewing ceased, juices dribbling down the corners of the stunned lips. His son, face red in the outline of the massive hand, stared straight ahead, pinned at the angle his neck had turned to absorb the blow. He inhaled swiftly through his nostrils, a frustration angling his brows into a scowl. He picked up his fork and inserted it into the remaining meat on his plate, ripping the dull blade across the bias, plopping the cut into his mouth. He chewed silently, his cheek burning like an iron brand.

Paolo shook violently, inspecting his fingers, the blood and heat turning his palms bright red. He knew not what had come over him, the time between sitting and standing passing in a mere breath. A single tear wilted from David's eye, dissolving from the warmth of the bruise, but he refused to utter more, fixated on nothing in particular.

Returning to the head of the table, Paolo did not offer an apology. His appetite had emerged once more, his knife slicing the red meat. But he could not control the anxiety in his hands, the motion inaccurate. He shoveled the piece into his mouth, barely able to chew as David's expression of defiance burned a hole through his forehead. The Devil's claws squeezed his son's tiny shoulders, a pleasurable smile bearing his gruesome teeth.

Manure. The rancid smell.

She felt a pair of fingers scurrying up her calf. A torch burned beyond, allowing a bit illumination, just enough to watch the cockroach scurry from her skin. Cecilia tucked her legs into her chest, a tremor radiating up her back. She touched her torso; bare flesh. She had been stripped nude.

She sat up, shooing the straw, forcing the agile insects to depart.

Her ribs roared from the sudden movement. Her fingers grazed a swollen and discolored bruise, the iron vest no longer draped over her. She averted the pain, shoving herself into a sensible breathing cadence.

The iron gate.

She looked up. *Open.*

To her feet, hands to the stone frame, peeking into the arena of cells. They had been padlocked, filled with the yellow and white grain for comfort, a bucket once filled with water now steamed with vomit, the unpleasant side effect of their cooperation.

A prisoner stirred, her hand slipping underneath the incongruous metal bars. Cecilia knelt, cupping the dirty fingers, the purpled tracks of a needle traversing the forearm. The woman refused to squeeze back, instead vacuuming herself beneath the safety of the straw.

"Can you move?" Cecilia whispered, caressing the cold metal.

A mumble of nonsense.

"What's your name?"

Consonants and tiny vowels bubbled over drool, sleep once again finding the captive woman. She surveyed the others, turning over in their pathetic beds, speaking only under their breath, slurring in their unsettling dreams.

Cecilia slid the torch outside her quarters from its steel cage, tossing it quickly onto the dry stalks, locking the gate behind it, containing the distraction. She darted across the arena, scuttling into the darkness, shoulders against the far wall, settling into a cove only a foot deep. She was caught between two staircases, both winding up to the second level.

The footsteps came quickly, the smoke pluming, galloping from the blaze. From her left, the dark robes emerged, quickly streaming past her camouflage. A Hawk and a Bear glanced at each other, unsure of how to proceed.

"The well. There's a yoke in the cellar."

"Grab the keys, get the Mistresses out of here."

They nodded, understanding their duties. They fled in opposite directions, leaning down a distant hallway to fetch supplies.

Cecilia made her move, ascending the stairs, keeping her back flush, her head cocked towards the landing above. Guiding herself slowly, she reached the upper level, angling towards the familiar square, a sliver of light cast against the threshold of the wooden door.

The old man's curved spine faced her covert inspection, an exit directly adjacent to his station. His blade stormed down upon a thick specimen, a second and third chop needed to split it. Cecilia edged herself into the cookhouse, pausing with every gain, proud of the veteran wood for revealing little as she carefully pressed inward.

Enough room to slip through, she crouched, huddling behind a sack of flour as the door returned to its state. A tenderized cut slapped the cutting board, oozing what blood remained. She ducked her head, peering through the bottom of a metal cart at a velvet sack at his feet. da Medicina pulled on the material, allowing Sister Elena's severed head to gawk in the glowing light as it poked out from the rim of a crusted, beige pail, silenced by heavy black tape across her lips.

Cecilia slapped her own mouth shut, the fantasy of the catacombs burned in the flames she started, her sister in God sacrificed for the greater good.

da Medicina lifted the white handle, retrieving the nun's head for preparation.

His useless nose had somehow caught the scent. Like a loyal pup, he craned his neck, breathing the ash with short, calculating inhalations. To the boiling stew, using his palm to waft the delicious aroma towards him. But this was not the odor he was searching for.

The door to his sanctuary crashed inwards, the Hawk's scalp singed, a Crane assisting him as they deposited the burning corpse of the Bear onto the metal cart in the center of the room.

The elder threw his arms up in bewilderment.

"The Mistresses, one of the cells caught fire."

Off, he gestured. *Off with his boots.*

They yanked the heavy soles from his feet, tossing them towards the supplies, the sack of flour stained with black treads. The pink flesh of his toes was all that had survived, little else to save. The robe had fused with his skin, the intricate weaves of the burlap bleeding as he tried to pull air into his lungs, his mask oozing across his cheek, staining his neck.

Go! Go! Contain the fire.

"What about him?"

da Medicina sought his cleaver, wiping it clean across his rubber apron.

Go, he insisted. They would not want to witness his mercy.

The Crane seized the upper arm of the Hawk, urging him towards the flames. "The Mistresses."

"You make it quick," the Hawk demanded, shoving his finger into the old man's chest.

They made haste through the door, the tossed boots of their comrade snaking into the shadows as they headed into the draft.

da Medicina pulled upon the burnt shoulder, shifting the Bear to the rim of the table. He called an empty bucket with his foot, sliding it underneath him. Placing the cleaver along the neckline, he measured, raising it skyward.

The condemned lifted his fingers, lips muttering of some vision of hope. But death overcame him, his hand suddenly limp, cast over the edge. The old man wiped his brow, leaning heavily over the body, silent in his prayer of thanks. A sigh of much relief whistled past his lips as he reset the blade over the exposed neck. The cleaver sang, slicing through the bone and dropping the head into the bucket, blood cascading from the incision.

A scream bellowed from the prison; a woman, howling in staccato rhythms. He waddled to the door, blade in hand, cursing at the nonsense that unfolded, his attention needed in all matters.

Rising from behind the haphazard stack of supplies, Cecilia scanned the kitchen, the fireplace brimming with boiling delights, but of little help. On the opposite side of the room, a wall rack had been occupied with aprons, beneath it a pile of soiled robes. She tore past the guillotined soul, shaking off the top of the pile and slipping into the disguise. With the hood seated over her head, she bounded for the separate exit, pulling back on the iron ringlet.

Sister Elena beckoned her.

There was a protrusion, forcing the tape to bulge. A glance towards the whipping shadows of the fire in the arena, calculating the screams of assistance that wafted inward, buying herself a moment. She placed the stolen boots on the bloodied cutting board as she reached for the head.

With a hand on the top of the skull, she steadied Sister Elena, peeling back the tape. Flecks of adhesive stuck to the corners of the burned lips, a field of hives dotting her cheek. The crucifix of her mother's rosary slipped out in a stream of warm saliva.

Cecilia tugged on the crimson beads, slowly pulling the necklace free and stuffing it into the pocket of her robe. She returned the tape, patting it cleanly. Stowing the boots under her arm, the door closed behind her softly, darkness greeting her once more.

The knuckle came into focus, blood across the bow. Alessandra had turned away, legs splayed, facing the bottom of the mattress, cupping her nose. Paolo lumbered over her, breathing through angry snorts, examining his fist.

The six candles plunged into the buttercream frosting had been lit for some time, the wax congealing over the surface. David had chosen to stare at the depiction of Christ above the waist-high hutch, the frame askew, the nail barely able to balance the hanging wire. His hand, wrapped abundantly in gauze, throbbed with pain, though the injury had been nearly a week old.

He pretended to remember little. His mother simply wanted to baptize him, to bring him into purity in the eyes of the church. Paolo had refused, they had not the money for simple expenses, let alone a donation to the church for vile water. She had wept, protesting that it was the right thing to do. His hand had struck her down, the same one that had wrenched David into the heat of the kitchen, his tiny fingers searing in the boiling pot.

"*There,*" he had screamed. "*There is your sacrament.*"

A door slammed above, breaking David from the rehearsal.

Marching now, across the buckling boards. The children followed the anger, leaving the cake untouched. Their father screamed, threatening between bouts of eerie silence.

"I will kill myself! I will slit my throat, I will put a bullet in my *fucking* head."

The Devil sat patiently in an oak rocking chair, squeaking the curved base as he relaxed. "You keep such an empty shrine," he sighed. "Little Valentina, such a waste."

"Eighteen years..." Paolo replied, "Eighteen years you have been threatening me. Take what you want! Leave me alone!"

"*Now?* Now you wish to bargain, hmm? You know exactly what I require."

"Then take it! Take it! Just fucking take it from me!"

"Paolo, Paolo...where is the sport? Where is the triumphant splendor of victory?"

"You make me lay my hands upon my family. And for what!? They avoid me like I am a leper. As if I am unclean." The energy to defend himself had been exhausted, his eyes to his boots, lost in defeat. "They have suffered enough. Take what you need from me. Quickly. Return to your hovel and let us die in peace."

"In the north," the Devil chirped, "you will find the services of lost souls. Bring Alessandra to them. They will take care of the rest."

The dust at his feet rippled as he wept, the top of his shoe splashed with tormenting guilt. "W-what will you do to her?"

The demon rose to his bare feet, shuffling closer as he attempted to contain his joy. "The Messenger will bring her to the sanctuary. They will summon me to this realm and I will plant my seed. Another of my heirs will be thrust between her legs, destined to join the others as they praise my name. When my army has risen, I will finally be able to close my eyes, to rest my aging soul in a barrier of ice. My legacy will live on so that I may not. Do you understand!?" Anger now beset him, a frustration streaming through his veins. "Bring her north and allow us to devour her. I cannot remain awake in this *limbo!*"

"And our agreement?" he looked into the bloodied eyes, the sickly, powdered flesh.

"Null and void, of course," he grinned, waving his arms outward.

"My children?"

"None of my concern."

"Yet you haunt them."

"Only precious David!" he gleefully sang.

"You leave him be!"

"I rather like his disposition. He is becoming quite adept at ignoring your heavy fist."

"*Do not take him.*"

"To protect our agreement, I will hold on to David. Perhaps he will be useful. There are few I can trust among my own. Driving him away from you should not be too difficult."

"You have Alessandra!" he whispered, pointing an index into the face of evil. "That was our deal."

"And you have desecrated it! The terms are my own now. I am willing to let our extended dance take a final bow. Bring your wife to the north. There she will become my Mistress and...perhaps, David my servant. The others will be spared. Or shall I take them too?"

Paolo's fingers curled into his palm, threatening to burst through the clenched muscles. But he restrained himself against the war he could not possibly win. "You will have them," he sighed.

The desert of coarse stubble felt good against the old man's numbing fingers, the sensitivity reminding him that there was an ounce of sense left in him. The poorly healed scar, though, lingered, drawing his hands back. He licked his chops, blowing an uncertain sigh.

The barrel had been once stored his precious concoction. It had not been long since he had wrenched the thick cork from the bulge, inserting a vial into the sloshing nectar.

He deposited the haul into a wine glass, swirling the dark liquid until oxidation had completed, the smell invigorating.

But his lips would not taste of the age, a raucous whistle filling the cavern of the cellar, ducking between the stacked and elevated rows of barrels.

"Polizia!" came the familiar tone of a servant. His terror was overrun quickly with machine gun fire as uniforms stormed the manor.

"da Medicina!" They had spotted him, their fingers extended, rushing down the infinite aisle.

He dropped the glass, letting it shatter as he slipped behind the end of the row, raging through a swing door into another hive of barrels. He looked back, the swarm yet to catch his fleeing scent.

"Medi!" He thrashed into a perspiring figure, the helping hands steadying him. "*Bene, bene, bene!*"

da Medicina looked up into the kind expression. "Carlo," he choked, calming himself. "We must run."

Carlo smiled. His hand shot upward, plunging a dagger into the old man's neck. "For my brothers!" He dragged the handle across the circumference, emptying the flow onto his feet.

Hands squeezing his throat, da Medicina lurched forward onto his knees, the river bursting through his impromptu tourniquet. Carlo grabbed the remaining follicles of graying hair and pointed the knife accusingly.

"You believe you have exacted your revenge. Taken what you are owed. Your words damned my family, marked them with a scent that they cannot clean. Your empire has fallen Medi, sold to the highest bidder. Now, I will relieve you of your ability to find us once more."

The knife curled around the bridge of da Medicina's nose, dissecting the cartilage, sawing through the instrument until he had collected his trophy.

Left in an ejection of maroon, da Medicina laid still in the pool as Carlo walked towards a flurry of flashlights, the officers passing him without incident, their muffled directions surrounding the old man.

The thickness swirled, the vial filling once more, the glass swirling in his hand. He looked upon the bloodied sheet, dotted with flies, the knees curled, arms stiffened at an almost impossible angle. He turned from the corpse sticking out of the top of the barrel, a relic from his former empire, stamped with his family name. He buried the memory of that scalding summer morning, a vendetta a century in the making finally coming to collect. He nodded his approval to the young girl in pastel, slipping the glass to his lips as he drank of the sweet, fermented liquid.

The servant wiped her greasy hands across her apron as she departed, carrying the message. Around the circumference of the arena, watching employees roll barrels of wine into arched storage cellars below, the temperature perfected for aging the delicate juices.

Up a winding staircase, through a hallway wrapped in stained glass, into the anteroom of a greenhouse, down the aisles of local flowers and herbs, past the gardener, onto the gravel carriage path. She passed stone vases flush with cypress, their shaved figures wrapped in burlap to preserve them in the winter slog.

To the Prussian blue gates, a pair set into the middle of a cobbled fence, opening the wicket, the unannounced guest turning towards her, a bleeding sack draped over his shoulders, a bolt action rifle slung across his back.

"*Signore* will see you now," she smiled.

▽☆▽△

Trapped.

The glowing frame of the kitchen bubbled at her back, the walls of the corridor cinched towards each other, growing intimate as they peaked at a tiny square of red haze. She slipped the oversized boots over her cold soles, the warmth of the blaze still pulsated over the tongue.

No choice but progress. Straight ahead, into the depths of the passage, leaving her shadow behind. da Medicina had the stupidity of the congregants to occupy him, yet she twisted, eyeing the exit, making sure she could continue with a still heart and composed breath.

The illusion of the shrinking corridor shook free as the inviting light sized itself appropriately through the porthole of the door, her face seeking the wooden border as she drew herself inward.

The peaked, towering ceiling guided the exhaust through copper pipes of disproportionate sizes, the width of oil drums running alongside strings no thicker than a drinking straw. Dabbed with soot, the bolts that secured each bracket to the next had begun to loosen, peeling with rust, shaking like a frightened snake as debris coughed towards the surface. Disappearing into the trusses of the roof, the pipes stuck to deliberate groups, their humble connections rising from the tops of domed furnaces, their latticed grills clamped shut, sealing the weakened souls within.

Cecilia grabbed the iron ringlet and broke the barrier. Into the machine she clopped, admiring the passageway of monstrous ovens, steel teeth chomping as the next in line was slapped to the pan, sizzling in a stream of seven jets, spewing unimaginable heat. A trio of cauldrons, assembled in the shape of a pyramid, hung next to each furnace, boiling the waiting sinners, submerged up to their necks in blood.

The groan of ancient metal spawned to her right, as the pots rotated, the peak of the triangular formation tipped aside, the contents sliding through a tin chute. Blood splashed across the oven's cast iron slate, the sinner slamming his head into the burning metal. Without ceremony, before the pain could set in, the flames devoured him, a pathetic gasp of blood and air left in his wake.

The empty cauldron suddenly shifted as the mechanism continued its content pace. Blood refilled the vessel from a coagulated spigot, settling over an open flame until it had reached peak temperature. Cecilia kept her distance at first, fearing the inquisitiveness of this zoo would take pleasure in adding her company. Risk foolishly shoved her a few steps forward to peer over the rim of the still plasma.

A woman appeared, breaching the surface as if she had been cast overboard, a harness or raft to soon rescue her. The boiling point came upon her, correcting her posture and leaving her arms flopped over the side of the cauldron. Her torso twitched achingly as she lost all feeling below the waist. Bliss seemed to wash across her eyes, slowly leaning back in the warm tub, waiting for her turn to burn.

The sinner who had entered the furnace had been reduced to mere ash, the pile washed away by the blood of the next roast.

Cecilia turned to her left, the same tragedy playing out in syncopated time. As the network reset, she saw a familiar face, lips parting to speak. She took to Father Endrizzi's side, his temple gouged, the blood dry.

"*Pater noster, qui es in caelis,*" he leaked in stagnant exhales. "*...sanctificetur nomen tuum.*"

The prayer could not prevent the penance, his face rising out of her view, dumped into the shaft and cooked efficiently.

She retreated, reaching into her robe and snatching her rosary. A sharp pain, though; her finger throbbing with electricity, arm flinching as she scowled. She cupped the intruder: the necklace had tangled with an ornate needle, the plunger gilded, a dragon's mouth swallowing the chamber of a honey-like liquid.

"Cici!"

Ahead of her, a flailing arm.

"David!?"

He hung over the side of the steaming kettle, reaching for her. She ran, feet sliding from toe to heel against the nervous perspiration. But she was too far, his body suddenly dragged back into the bubbling mixture.

"David!" She reached the pot, the surface suddenly cold, clumping like ice. The automation rotated, pushing a fresh soul in front of her. She gawked as Petrisone's dull stare welcomed her, his wired jaw ripped open, jagged and frayed wires leaping from his bloodied mouth.

A gasp of hot air, a splash against stone. She spun towards the commotion, watching David emerge from another bath further down the assembly line. Catching his frantic swing, she held tight his slippery hand.

"Pull, Cici!" he begged, her grip loosened as he was sucked once more into the red sea. "Valentina!"

Cecilia stood bewildered, the name frightening her, the syllables so foreign coming from his mouth. There was little time to acknowledge it as he appeared behind her, "I will raise her, Frankie! Please, do not take her away from me!"

She locked onto his shoulders, tugging hard against the suction.

"Papa, stop!" His head slipped back into the thickness.

Spinning, trying to find the next empty cauldron, she raced ahead, parking herself in front of a spigot as it belched.

The growl echoed through the filling chamber: "You are but a stain of feces compared to the empire that I control!"

She leaned into the mouth.

David's head bobbed to the surface slowly, twitching, "End this," he mouthed, eyes shut. "End this!"

The flow ceased as he plummeted.

"Prepare the altar," he whispered from the depths.

Cecilia stepped back as the queue continued, taking away the half-empty sacrifice. She hurried forward, eyeing the other filling vessels, waiting for David to appear.

"You lied! You lied to me!" It burst from each oven's flame, overlapping. She spun, trying to identify the origin. "A contract has been struck!" The final outburst, his resistance drowning.

The factory returned to its normal operation.

She had run out of furnaces, deposited in front of two steel plates stacked atop one another. A gap between the floor provided a foundation for her fingers as she guided the panel upward. With little effort, it rose, the spouting flames brightening the interior of a freight elevator, a wheelbarrow left behind, occupied by a rotting corpse, its limbs hung over the sides.

Cecilia slipped underneath the bulky door, a dangling power box at the rear of the cab activating the lift. The massive doors squeaked shut as she rose, the factory droning onward, the futile protests drowned by the whine of the constant immolation.

Twenty-one, brightly lit, little columns of intertwining blue and white. The buttercream had been piped on in thick roses across the top, the sides dusted with crushed peanuts.

"Why this one?" he muttered, spinning a multi-colored pill around the bottom of a disposable cup.

Frankie tapped a half-finished cigarette into an empty ashtray. "I can't visit you on your birthday?"

"I didn't say that," David spat bluntly. "Why this particular birthday?"

"I was promoted," he smiled, "*Inspector*."

"Where's Cici?"

"*Come on*, you know that. She's off to Brazil or Chile, or one of those *puttanata* ghettos."

"That's not very respectful."

"She's doing the *Lord's work*, I suppose." He sucked on another cigarette, scratching a dry flake from his eyebrow.

"Why did she leave us?"

"Cici?"

"She *hated* mass."

"We all did. But, something called her."

His attention focused like a deer suddenly interrupted by a predator. "What do you mean? Did someone call her on the phone? S-s-someone is calling me too, Frankie." He set the medication down. "Someone calls me...and we talk. She must talk to him too. I don't need a phone, though. I've never even heard Cici's voice over the phone."

"No, just...mmm," he searched for the word. "*An intuition*. A feeling. She just felt as if she had to go. No one told her to leave, she made that decision."

"Oh..." defeated once more.

Frankie departed, two slices removed from the cake, a pat upon his brother's shoulder.

The door closed silently, the orderlies to fetch him soon.

"Is this my calling?" he said, picking at the moist pastry with a plastic fork.

The Messenger did not speak, wings adjusting their position to maintain comfort as he stood on the opposite side of the room.

"Voices speak to her," David theorized, leaning forward, elbows against the cold metal. "Do you think God sends his angels to speak to those who worship him?"

Again, the Messenger failed to respond.

"What is the matter with you? *Talk to me.* Suddenly we've run out of things to discuss?"

"Though the deliciousness of a secret is too tempting to avoid," came the unwanted hiss, "I do despise when they are kept from me." The Devil strolled along the bulge of the tin ceiling, avoiding the domed lamp and its impenetrable cage. "The ability to speak is the tool of those whose hands have been bound. The writer relegated to flapping his sanctimonious lips. There is no need for such things anymore, his past finally catching up to him."

The Messenger hung his head in silence, guilt projecting through the expressionless skull.

"You cannot outrun the offspring of those you have wronged. Eh?" He chuckled at the Messenger's misfortune. "Hiding, masking your face, cloaking yourself in filth. They will find your *stench.* Is this your calling?" he posited, looking upwards toward David. "My slave has grown tired and irritated, the work unfulfilling. Perhaps, a novice would have more glee in their work. More *loyalty.*"

"What would happen to him?" eyes darting towards the Messenger.

"To the rivers of pitch, the tarred fingers of his dirty secrets dragging him forever into the depths, a mighty sword to strike should he decide to find his voice above the surface."

The Messenger raised his head, presenting his gnarled, gloved hand.

David swung his arms against the boxed cake, plastering the walls in buttercream.

"I refuse! I will not become indebted to you!" He grabbed his medication, sucking down the single pill dry. He crumpled the plastic, snapping it into the corner. "Give him his voice! You are not allowed to punish others because of what I had done!"

Alone now, the room grew tall, the heavens so infinitely far away.

David drooled as his head twitched, *snapping* from side to side.

"There will be little time for such theatrics," Paolo preached as he stepped around his elevated son.

"You have imprisoned me!" Michele echoed, his voice seared with flame and gurgling bile, erupting from David's mouth.

"Come now! For days and nights on end you would appear to

me, projecting images of your vast domain. Men and woman eaten alive, cut down by iron, buried with dirt in their throats, immolated, frozen, hung, shot, raped with instruments of searing lead. You showed me my own flesh, ripped and dissected over and over. You forced my hand against my family, begging me to beat them, to turn their days into a bleeding nightmare that you controlled. You fear irrelevance, my Lord. You fear that the Messenger will never come for you. I will grant you this desire."

"Such petty morals!"

"If I could not negotiate, then why have I summoned you?"

David squirmed as the spirit punctuated his retort. "Your silent heart will never beat. You seek my hand to bring meaning to your miserable stench."

"I would be lying if I did not express my displeasure with my appearance. Spreading your gospel has become a clandestine affair."

"You assemble *my* sons and daughters! Slaughter the rest! You allow them to worship you! *You!?* What more of my soul do you wish to steal?"

"You believed our deal was fair, that my poor wife was a worthy hole for your seed. But you pushed this family too far. You endangered my children!"

"And Valentina!? I suppose my followers mistook me for a fool!?"

"You chose to punish her. I gave you a vessel."

"You refused to uphold your end of our contract. You believed you could summon the courage to satisfy me with a meager prize. You were afraid of admitting you were responsible, that you chose yourself before others. You feared to beg for forgiveness, genuflecting and asking for others to dismiss your guilt. You are weak, Paolo!"

"We have the means to keep David alive; to keep you imprisoned."

"You threaten me with damnation!?"

"*You*, my Lord, are *weak*. I have summoned you with the open corpses of those who have sinned, who carry your blood. I have followed the doctrine of da Medicina, the words of the old way. I have feasted on their mechanisms, swallowed their blood, just as I had been instructed to keep my failing body from fading. Each time you are drained. Each time I summon your strength, your kingdom descends further into chaos. Without their King, how will they keep your reign controlled? Imagine now, the fields of sinners rising to the surface, fusing with the world of the blissfully ignorant? The fields of sheep, waiting to be shepherded? Francesco has witnessed it; Ce-

cilia too. The blasphemous hand of her lover and her brother's incestuous child festering in that womb, another of your bastard offspring
to join your army. You have what you begged for, you always have."

Frankie gazed down at the child in his care as Michele barked
back. "Anna's womb was a gift by your own son; control of Antonio
merely a pleasurable distraction. David's penance was raising the
child."

"Valentina!" the milky pupils drained their opaque mist, the
color returning, a memory of David emerging. "I will raise her,
Frankie! Please, do not take her away from me!"

"Return to me, Satan!" Paolo screamed, grabbing David's
sweater and pulling him downward.

His eyes rolled back once more, the color diluted, oozing away
from the center as the trapped face snickered.

"I am no hound! I will not come at your beckoning!"

Paolo wrenched the material deeper into his fist, their faces in
danger of colliding like two celestial wonders. "You have ruined my
existence. You have forced me to rise in this decrepit form. You have
made me into a preacher of the unholy. I do not want this. *I do not
want this.*" Closer now, trading the odors of death. "I will ruin your
empire. I will take what you have built and I will crush it. I will bury
the very face of evil beneath my boot."

"*Release me.*"

Despite his disadvantage, Paolo shoved David backward into
his desk, rattling the clutter aside, his typewriter chiming as it bent
against the stone. Among the fallen, Frankie noticed the rectangular
box, the chipped corner splattered with dried blood.

"Stand up!" Paolo urged. "*Michele?* Pathetic! Hiding behind
your brother's accomplishments. You are Lucifer! You are Satan! You
are the Devil!"

"You will not kill me," the Devil hissed. "Not your own son."
He departed, curling deep into David's psyche, biding his time as
clarity returned.

"Papa! Please!"

Paolo slapped him hard across the cheek. "Return to me Satan!"

Again, across the face, harder, an emphatic grunt to encourage
the kinetic abuse.

Again. Again. *Again,* each time David returning to his father's
rotting eyes.

"Papa, stop!" He stiffened his arm, blocking the next wave. "I
brought you here to end this."

"If you do not return to me, I will plunge you into darkness!"

"Papa!" David shoved him back, a stumble, but not enough to drop him to the tepid rock. "*Enough!* I did not bring you here for this! I did not want this for you, Papa."

"You awaken me, funnel me into this sack of mismatched meat and you expect me to believe that you are righteous!?"

"Did he not torment me? Did he not raise his voice at me? Bring me visions such as you? I spent fourteen years in that hospital because no one would believe me. Not Mama, not Cecilia, not even Frankie. But you, Papa. You would believe me. There was not a day that would go by that I did not think of you, that I was not reminded of what you did. The Messenger protected me as best he could. He helped me rebuild you, helped me give you what you needed, no matter the cost. He knew that you would protect me, pass the torch so that we could live again.

"Despite all of it, despite my guilt, I forgive you, Papa. I forgive you for what you did. In your final moments, you chose to save yourself so that Mama would not have to cry; so that she would never be lonely. *I understand!* But you made a mistake. You-you-y-you gave up more than you wanted to, and you tried to hide, tried to make it better on your own. You were afraid, you were afraid that you would be judged.

"I love you, Papa. I brought you here to end this. I brought you here so that you would finally admit that you were wrong, that you would give him what he wanted so that we could be a family again."

Paolo, stunned by his son's simplistic, yet noble, mission, began to doubt even the air he breathed.

"Isn't that what you want?" David pressed. "For this to all be over? I miss home, Papa. I just want to go *home*. Give him what he wants."

"Release me!" the Devil warbled, scrambling through what remained of David's belongings, clawing at the wall, ripping down the carefully selected photographs.

"I will not be reduced," Paolo shouted. "I will not sacrifice what I have built!"

"What you have built?" the demon roared, pouncing forward, hand pulsating around Paolo's neck. "You are but a stain of feces compared to the empire that I control."

David fought through the rage, peeling back his hand, shoving his wrist downward. He retreated from his father, holding back the Devil's charm. "End this!" he cried.

But Paolo refused, thrusting him against the wall, both hands crushing his windpipe. "You will give me your kingdom, or I will imprison you. I will dry your bones and I will crush them into ash."

"Crush me," the Devil urged. "Kill your son. Set me free."

"This will be only the beginning of my torture. I am prepared to drag you to the very precipice if I must. The longer you wait, the more lost souls will rise. You will perish without circumstance. *You will fade, forgotten for all eternity.*"

David felt the sensation now, the Devil allowing him to witness his father's power. He grasped at Paolo's tensing forearms as blood began to pool at his neck, the oxygen stale in his throat, unable to proceed.

"What...do you want...of me?"

"Grant me your power. Give to me all that you own and all that you owe." He loosened the vice, mercy granted for a pleasing response.

"And in return?"

"You will serve me, your loins to flourish within my daughter."

Frankie cocked his head at the offer.

"She will bear the princes and princesses you desire. Alessandra was too easy. You wanted filth, you wanted sin that would tear apart a family. You shall have it, the womb of your enemy. Your daughters will become yours as well, to breed for as long as David shall live. When you expire, when you fall victim to the weapon of the Messenger, then, you will be at peace. *I* will continue your legacy."

"You believe you will grant me death?" the Devil whispered.

"I guarantee it."

An expression of uncertainty and relief mixed against David's complexion. Frankie stared, transfixed on the proceedings, unable to quantify the emotions that forced him to sideline his intervention.

"Prepare the altar," came the verdict, quiet, defeated, willing now to let go.

But David would not cast his vote in favor. His eyes flipped from the darkness of his skull as he wrestled his father away.

"I brought you here to save you, Papa!"

"You *are* saving me, David. This is what I want. You will be by my side, your sister your bride."

"You lied! You lied to me!"

He lunged, attacking with a whipping haymaker, casting Paolo to the ground. With a raised heel he clocked him across the forehead, opening a gash in the stitched skull.

"A contract has been struck!" the corroded voice bellowed, David seceding control once more. Paolo fumbled across the wall, using the leverage to help himself upright as David retreated. He struck the wooden gate, his head banging hard against the iron accents, but refusing to acknowledge the pain.

His father approached, hand inspecting the thick release from his own wound.

"You will restore my youth," Paolo instructed. "Fix these festering bruises, my veins which refuse to clot."

Frankie tiptoed towards the box on the floor, bending down and unbuckling the face.

Paolo closed the gap, wiping his blood across David's face, forcing him to inhale the toxic odor.

"*Get away from him,*" Frankie commanded, his right hand gripping the spine of a silver crucifix, his left cradling the bastard child. Paolo cocked his head. Nervous fingers drenched the holy relic.

"You could never keep your mouth shut, Francesco," he smirked, pushing towards his firstborn. "Always wanting the last word. Standing up for yourself only when it was convenient. When the luster had died down."

Frankie thrust his hand forward as if magic would spawn from the delicate Christ.

"Charms and symbols do not frighten me, Francesco, they are merely empty." He motioned towards David, his eyes shielded, growling like a wicked beast, blinded from the heat of the cross.

His back against the wall, Frankie confronted the intricacy of Paolo's face, the stolen flesh somehow forming into that familiar landscape. The crucifix slid from his care into the hand of the immune. "These will not save you," Paolo lectured. "There is a place for you in my heart, but you are making the case f-"

The typewriter *pinged* as it crashed against the back of Paolo's skull. He slumped to his right, hands tapping the floor as he attempted to steady himself, his face ultimately skidding across the rough stone. The crucifix flew from his grip, sliding into the darkness as David straddled him, driving the machine deep into the crevice he had opened.

The typebar snapped, the keys left behind in the slop as he pounded bone into matter into bone. He ripped the remaining pieces free, flinging blood against the wall, slamming down the internal mechanisms into what remained, leaving them to sink into the crimson pool. David huffed, sweat popping through his dirty pores, unafraid of the mess he had made.

Shadows trotted down the hallway, jiggling across the door, growing as they approached with haste.

David turned to Frankie, his father's blood splashed across his face. "Please..." he sobbed, "h-help me..."

The shaft groaned as the elevator ascended, the darkness unchanged, the landscape fertile and unexplored. The cab stuttered, the brake clamping down upon the steel cabling. The steel plates split horizontally as she descended a short ramp onto the gums of the rat. Mounds of human fuel had been piled in loose structures, hands bound, clothing stripped. Frail bundles of arms and legs had been fastened like kindling, ferried easily into wheelbarrows and carts for the journey.

Cecilia shielded her mouth and nose from the nauseating stench that combined with the leaking of the factory below, funneled passed a shriveling uvula, sucked and vomited through the rodent's crusted nostrils. She escaped the jaws, the sky no longer shrouded in gray, a paltry helping of stars glimmering in the young evening.

The grounds remained cluttered, the congregants seeking shelter and the warm comforts of sleep. She scuttled down the incline, reaching the gravel walkway. Passing the sunken reservoirs of black liquid, she eyed the abandoned carriage. She crossed into the dry grass, ducking behind the damaged spokes.

Finding the compartment door locked, she boosted herself using the kickstep, fishing into the decapitated roof, the familiar material of their supplies tickling against her fingertips. With some difficulty, she pulled the rucksack from the refuse, settling onto the ground and taking stock of what she had left behind.

The esophagus of the dog glowed, the ribbed layer throwing long shadows into the arched coves of the sanctuary. Like fireflies they rose, single-file, stomping up the steep treads, kicking the bleached posies without regard. Disoriented Mistresses, hair matted, faces slathered with soot, had been struck of their shame, wrapped in loose blankets of wool, shoved forward and kept in line.

Cecilia pulled on the hem of a sleeveless, ankle-length habit, adjusting it over one of Frankie's dress shirts, the cuffs rolled up to her elbow. She shifted her knees, unable to gain much mobility in the tight cut. She peeked through the debris around her, shifting the lid of a loose crate, finding dry soil and damp scraps of rice paper, the beginning of a garden failing to take shape.

She spotted the handle, angled outward, the head of the blade buried into the side of a barrel. Jiggling the hatchet, she freed the tool, using the tip to fray the bottom of her dress. She tore against the stitching, removing the restrictive material at the knee.

Torches met the stone-rimmed reservoirs, igniting the flammable material, surrounding the gathered congregants in ten, brilliant flames. The majority had attended, a throng of forest dwellers, jungle kings, and aerial creatures. Pallbearers laid the burnt offerings of those who had perished in Cecilia's blaze in front of the others, exposing their charred flesh to the crisp air.

The animals clucked and hawed amongst themselves, peering through black lenses, waiting for a voice to silence them. A Fox raised his hands, obliging the dissenters.

"We are no longer privy to our future. What has transpired here tonight has gone against our principles, what we have strived for these many decades. Those who hold this truth are present, over a hundred strong."

Cecilia snuck towards the windows of the carriage, throwing her robe over her head, peering through the gaps in the greasy smudges at the coven.

"You did nothing to stop it!" shouted a Raccoon. A chorus of agreement.

"And you?" the Fox noted. "Did you raise your voice? Did you push past your brothers and remove the vicious hand of our Master?"

"We cut our losses," suggested an Owl. "Take the Mistresses, perform the ritual in the woods. Release the binds that Papa has shackled us with."

"If we allow David to be released, he will wreak havoc upon the world. We will be left with nothing. We must sacrifice him, spread his blood among the trees so that they will contain him." chimed a Viper.

"It is not David who concerns me," the Fox steadied. "Papa controls David in essence and in blood. His connection to him is one that none of us could imitate. But he alone does not grant us mortality! Lust and greed! David now owns this responsibility, the very blood of Satan flowing through his veins, with the power to resurrect any one of us. To spare us from an eternity of his devilish torture. Satan believes he can manipulate man, but he is imprisoned. He must bow to us!"

The gathered cheered, shouting their enthusiastic agreement.

"We shall decide his fate! Papa siphoned power from our Lord. Who is to say that he will truly lead us forward? You are just as loyal as I! Collectively we can bring about the change we have sought, that our father's fathers have sought."

"What if he bargains?" The question dampened their spirit.

"Satan bargains only as a means to keep himself alive," a Cougar interjected. "We will listen to his propositions, for he will provide in exchange for his freedom."

"David is simple," the Fox reminded them. "A knife across the throat will end him. Another vessel to hold our Lord easily obtainable. We will rid ourselves of Paolo Zampa and his tyranny."

"The burning pits of the rat's stomach!" came a suggestion.

"Yes! He shall burn like our brothers have this evening! Fetch them! The Zampa bloodline will kneel before us tonight so that we may finish this tedious chapter."

The Fox nodded towards a pair of Rats, "Bring them to the sanctuary, lure them with promises of libations and fertile wombs."

Cecilia tiptoed from the carriage, darting between the wreckage as she spied the scurrying rodents trotting towards the mouth of the goat.

"Deposit those who have died this evening into the furnaces. The Mistresses will be cleaned and pruned. Keep watch on da Medicina, his loyalty lays with David, he will be the first to revolt."

She crouched low, shuffling from obstacle to obstacle, sliding eagerly towards the shadows of the surrounding forest.

"Prepare the incense and wipe clean the goblets. And fetch the child! His blood will be nourishment this evening, a proper mass to finally guide us."

Through the thicket she stiff-armed aside the lascivious branches, watching the Rats disappear into the goat's yawn. Above her, the slope had been created by the massive girth of an uprooted tree, its stiffened tentacles squirming through the forest, searching for a hand to right them and pull them from the insanity. The trench left by the tree had widened, a descent slick with soil, leading into abject darkness.

She had no stomach for the unknown pathway, instead, creeping behind the base of the tree. Her boot struck an unnerving chord, her sole pivoting as she revealed the broken remains of a newborn, the tiny hand crushed by her weight. In the darkness, she could barely make out the dotted soil, the skulls of sacrificed children curling towards the delicate bones of their mangled torsos and legs. She could not count how many had been tossed aside, only that she feared any number would upset her.

Forcing herself away from the burials, she hiked up the remaining rock that clung to the massive trunk. She found the top of the mound, looking down on the loyalists as they collected their dead, the Mistresses fawning over their new masters. Cecilia hopped into the goat's warm musk, skipping underneath the gentle swinging of the chandeliers, skirting the formations of wax. She refused to abandon hope as she followed the scent of the Rats, the delicate thread of her family taught and waiting to be gnawed.

Their disgusting heads cast frightening shadows against the wall, the whiskers wiry, wobbling as they rushed towards the rear of the cellar. Using a skeleton key, they prepared themselves to unlock the thick security. But it had been completed, the padlock dangling from the metal rung of the portcullis.

A confused glance came between the rodents, but they continued, stowing the keys and descending further. Down a corridor, to the dead ending, the slide bolt recessed, the gate loosened.

David's eyes curled backward, the milky white undercarriage sapping the rest of the color. "No more bargaining, Francesco. The bastard is dead. Now I will take what I want!"

The gate swung, the Rats storming the quarters, one snapping to Paolo's bludgeoned skull, the other to David's cocked inquisitiveness.

Cecilia grunted, lodging the hatchet into the back of the distracted skull. The Rat squeaked, gasping as pain coated him, blood showering his face, seeping down his back. As he toppled, he found his knees, the axe free to extract.

The still-standing rodent lunged, Cecilia's fingers meeting his as they tugged at the shaft of the weapon. David charged, arms akimbo. Her left hand shot from the darkness, palm flat, their mother's crimson rosary wound between her fingers, the crucifix dangling in the center.

David shaded himself, turning quickly from the charm, the backs of his hands beginning to sear.

Frankie angled his shoulder down, plowing through the Rat, releasing the valued grip on the hatchet. The newborn announced a shrill exclamation of displeasure, drawing Cecilia's attention.

"Vile corpse!" the Devil protested.

She threw off her hood as she loosened the blade, allowing the dead Rat to meet the stone, keeping the necklace facing David's tantrum.

"Cici!?" Frankie beamed, laying a heel into the chin of the

downed congregant, knocking him unconscious.

"How dare you bring my filthy brother into my kingdom!" David howled. "I have control of this husk!" But he refused to rise above the blinding heat.

"Jesus," Cecilia swallowed, breathing heavily as she watched the pathetic shell consumed by the demonic spirit cower against her might.

"Do not speak his name!"

"Jesus! Jesus! Jesus!" she screamed, approaching quickly, forcing David to retreat. "*Bastardo!*"

"We can't stay here, Cici," Frankie warned.

She cocked her head, leaving David's gaze.

"*The cabin.*" They both spit out the same conclusion, a confusion shared across their faces.

"David said something about a promise. In the cellar, I had promised," Frankie hurried. "He wanted to kill them all. Weapons; food; something! Something is in the cellar that he needs."

"It's a place he is familiar with, one that will ease his mind."

"You can get it out of him, right, Cici?"

Her eyes avoided his, tongue moistening her response. "I don't know." Panicking now. "*I don't know.*" She fumbled in her robe, pulling out the gilded needle. "Give him this. It will calm him. We cannot transport him like this."

"I'll trade you." He exchanged the child, helping cradle him in the crook of her arm. "He's been waiting a long time to meet you."

She gazed upon Anna's creation, admiring the buoyancy of his cheeks, the pursed lips, the tuft of hair threatening to sway over his brown eyes.

Frankie approached the possessed, thumb steady on the plunger.

Cecilia tore her attention from the baby, keeping the crucifix angled.

"David? David, can you hear me?" Frankie asked.

"I have swallowed David." The blank eyes appeared beneath the parting shield of fingers. He swiped, grabbing his brother's tightened wrist, forcing the needle away.

Cecilia marched, slamming the rosary into the emerald sweater, pressuring him to release Frankie. David cried out in a chorus of ancient terror as his chest began to singe, an imprint tearing through his clothing and branding his chest. He forsook Frankie, turning to Cecilia and grabbing her hand, muscling the steaming cross from his skin.

The needle bit into his neck, the serum leaking quickly into his vein. A trail of blood trickled from the injection site as David mouthed his annoyance, his saliva thickening, the pressure dissipating from his protest.

He freed Cecilia, one hand following the other, burdened as if submerged in water. Frankie tossed the syringe aside, cradling David as his legs jellied, collapsing underneath the unexpected high. He laid him gently on the straw bed, turning his head against the cool stone. Hatchet secured, Frankie slung it through his belt.

"Do you know how to get back to the cabin?" Cecilia asked, concerned now that their plan hinged on too many factors.

"We either head back the way we came or circle around the rear of the property and try to link up with any water that feeds into the lake. We can follow the tunnels back up."

He knelt, reassembling Cecilia's kit, placing the sacramental oils snugly into their molds.

"Is that...?" she stared at the typewriter, the mangled materials replacing Paolo's head, the stitches along the neck frayed.

He shoved the box into her chest, distracting her. "Take care of the baby, I'll take care of David."

She nodded, slinking away from her father's corpse a second time, prodding the corridor for a search party.

Frankie pushed David's legs upward, bending his knees. "If and when...maybe make the dog..." He tugged his right arm forward, lifting him off his back. Crouching, he dipped into the limp lean, wrapping his arm through David's legs and positioning him across his shoulders. Using the loose arm as a scarf, Frankie draped it across his chest, linking his threaded hand to the wrist, locking the luggage into place.

With a grunt, they rose, the weight distributed as evenly as he could manage. Cecilia waved them through.

"Do you know the way?" he whispered, leaning close as they hurried forward.

"Through the gate ahead," she indicated, keeping her motions to a minimum to pacify the child.

She held the portcullis still as he ducked underneath, maneuvering David through the claustrophobic gate. They met a trio of tunnels, a lonely torch occupying each of the far corners, each one undetectably identical.

"*Merda!*" she spat, eyeing her options. "I-I don't know which one leads back to the surface."

A feather sank between them, wafting effortlessly, riding the subterranean breeze, landing delicately at their feet. Skyward, the shadow plummeting. Frankie's arm shot across Cecilia's chest, shoving them backward.

The Messenger crashed into the dust, lifting a crest that splashed against them. Cecilia coughed through the wave as Frankie loosened the hatchet, twirling his wrist, begging the beast to attack. The butt of the scythe pounded the ground, the gesture purely ceremonial as he knelt before them, bowing his head, his wings stretching from end to end.

"W-w-why is it bowing, Francesco?" she stuttered. "*Why?*"

He tested the subservient nature, holstering his own blade. "You may stand," he ordered.

The Messenger obeyed, folding his wings against his back and returning to a position of attention.

"Who are you?" Frankie asked.

The Messenger held his weapon across his body, carefully spreading the jagged instrument, encouraging a detailed inspection. Frankie shuffled, craning his neck, the sharpened curve notched from intrusion and resistance, each impurity marked in an unfamiliar symbol. The scythe snapped shut, reeling him back, a sharp, giddy sigh blasted from his lips.

"Can you show us the way out?" Cecilia asked.

The Messenger nodded. His robe scuffed the floor as he cornered Frankie. "*Waitwaitwaitwaitwait,*" he pleaded, free hand issuing a full stop. The gangly, gloved paw of judgment rose, cradling David's head from below, rubbing a bony thumb across his cheek. Frankie exhaled, hanging his head in relief.

"He's going to be okay," Cecilia assured, placing her hand on the elongated forearm. "We just need to get him out of here." The Messenger sensed the urgency, stepping towards the center of the intersection, an index revealing the fruitful path.

"*Grazi,*" she said, taking the route. Frankie paused, acknowledging the Messenger a final time with a nod.

David's sedated face slipped into the shadows, fear settling in the pit of the robed belly. Angling his skull towards the sky, the Messenger watched as the Moon slipped into the frame of the well's mouth, the choice to stay and fight within his capacity; the chance to flee, painfully overwhelming.

Despite the moistened air, the trudge had suited them, the pathway slick but manageable. Cecilia fought the dirty incline, leaning into the slope. The dehydrated tentacles of the uprooted tree instilled a helping of confidence, the child shuffling with each gain.

She turned towards Frankie, offering her hand, locking around his wrist. Ducking under the stump, they freed themselves from the lasting breath of the catacombs.

"Which way?" she breathed.

He turned towards the gates of the manor, congregants huddling with torch and bottle, preparing their consciences for another night of brutality. The Goats of blood red knelt at the mouth of the dog, a firing squad at the backs of their skulls. Shotguns and automatic weapons lit the night in fire and blood, their heads gored and dissected as their torsos were kicked into the moat of hunger, the dead devouring them further.

"Any way," Frankie grunted, shifting David across the wet patch seeping down his back. "They will be after us soon. We just need to keep moving."

The night was still upon them, the forest laughing maniacally knowing it was their only option. Curled fingers of thinning bark invited them into the thicket, tapping their shoulders as they shuffled past. The tops of the trees fluttered as wings appeared between the seams, ducking, swooping onto another perch.

Frankie and Cecilia stared up into the swaying sea, their exhaustion allowing for easy persuasion. They were certain the fragility of the sky would buckle, the celestial beacons raining down across the mountains. For now, they were content to remain standing in reverence, praying the Heavens would hold steady and prevent them from being dragged back down below.

BINDING BY OATH

VI

They could not help but continue to stare.

Dawn had broken hours before, the sun free of the thundering cumulonimbus.

"He's following us," Frankie noted, unable to tear from the illusion.

Cecilia dragged the back of her hands across her eye, massaging free the tiny molecules shed from the army of pine. The distance confused the vibrant green needles for the hidden wings that had been charting their progress. "If it wanted to kill us, it would have already." She broke away from the conspiracy, straddling a downed branch as she continued, leaving Frankie to ponder the beast.

"Mmm...pffff..." David drooled.

"How long is he going to be out like this?" Frankie chased, trying to catch her as he boosted himself forward with the help of the sap-stained trunks.

"I don't know. It was a lot of heroin."

"How did you know it was heroin?"

She stopped. Annoyance in her tone, eyes loose. "I'm not a good person, Francesco. Is that what you want me to say?"

"I'm not here to be judgmental," his face widening like an innocent fawn, uncertain why she had chosen to fight back so quickly.

"No? What then? Curiosity? Is this the routine you play when you interrogate actual criminals?"

"Cici, I-"

"What?"

The child began to stir, stiff arms bending and straightening as it sought an excuse to gain their attention, huffing a high-pitched warning.

"Cici, I-I barely know you."

"That's not my fault."

"I'm not saying *it is*. You just...*disappeared*."

"I wanted to. I wanted everything different in this world, nothing that reminded me of home."

"And that includes us."

"Yes." She blurted it too quickly, too confidently.

The mistake was wholly realized, but Frankie refused to allow her to backpedal. "I'm sorry I dragged you into this, then."

"Do not pretend as if your sympathy means anything."

The first flakes danced, catching the umbrella of the upper boughs.

"Do you think I wanted all of this?" Frankie argued, sweeping his free hand across his body. "That I wanted us to all grow apart?"

"We cannot fix *this*. We cannot return from this."

"Run from it again, eh? Is that your solution?"

"You are not better than me because you stood and fought."

A dusting now, the crystals sticking together, forming clumps of sparkling white.

"*I* fought for David! *You left me alone.*"

"I didn't leave because I hated you. I left because I did not want to become you. I did not want to be another in a long line of Zampas. *Nonno*, fleeing the *mafioso* in *Sicilia*. *His* father ferrying illegal goods to the East. Why do you think we never spent time with Mama's family? Why do you think they did not come to her funeral? They would rather spit than speak her name. She was an outcast to them because she married into a line of *bastardos*. I did not want to become her, or you, or Papa."

"Converting a few villages on the other side of the world was going to change what they've done."

"Of course not! But it made me feel *good*, Francesco. It made me feel as if I still had something to give, that I was *worth* something. That I wasn't a pound of flesh waiting to be beaten."

"You think I've become Papa?"

"I did not say that. We are still a product of our mother."

"I am not perfect," Frankie choked.

"*No one asked you to be.*"

The snowstorm had snuck between the thick limbs, clumping on the edges of the needles until the weight was too much for it to bear. They began to take notice, a hand out to ensure the frost was indeed cold, that it pillowed in their palms like the winters of their youth.

"We have to keep moving," he insisted, brushing past her, the forest floor beginning to collect the powdered deposit.

"Francesco?"

He pivoted, misjudging his width, David's head *cracking* against a snow-laden branchlet. She laughed, spitting out a stomached giggle she had not intended to ever share.

Frankie too could not help from sharing in the stupidity of the moment, attempting to wipe free the pine dust and sleet from his brother's face.

"Sauce...fish," mumbled David, his upper lip snarling as if served a detestable meal.

They only laughed harder, the joy spitting between their attempts to close their lips, hands masking the tears that would surely come if they continued. They found a gap in their silliness, slowing their gallop from a frenzy, sniffling against the dropping temperatures.

"Frankie, I just...want you to know that you can still know me without knowing me. The other things...they'll just take time."

The Messenger retreated from his perch, wings fighting against the mountain's swell as snow rained from his commotion. Cecilia shielded the child as Frankie beckoned her, urging them to continue. Between the sinking cotton, he spotted the hungry: a quartet of black hopping through the rising drift.

"*Cazzo*," he muttered. She saw the distant pack too. "Go! Go!" he ushered, his hand guiding her lower back.

Boots pounding the snow, they tore through the confusion, following only the clarity of the tree ahead. Frankie's knees *snapped* with each extension, David's weight guiding him closer to the ground, unable to raise an advantage.

The congregants shouted against the muffling breeze, elbows bent, weapons held high above the obstructions.

Cecilia cocked her head, eyeing Frankie's sudden performance. He genuflected, the unconscious torso slipping from his control. She stomped to his side, hiking David's pants, using the belt loop to shift him back into position.

Bark exploded above her as a rifle shouted, showering her with shards of wet pulp. She retreated, wrapping her hands around the child, the sudden impact enveloping the forest in his terrified wail. Frankie steadied himself against a trunk, rising slowly. Buckshot tore through a leaning bough, coating them once more, but leaving them unscathed.

Further now, into the thickening tree line, the storm masking a sudden slope. Cecilia slipped, her back slamming into the snow, the angle dragging her downward, depositing her onto a fragile layer of ice. The boy wept, shivering with each inhalation of the frozen air. Frankie slowed himself, gripping a bulging stone as he surveyed the expanse. The hounds barked behind him, releasing a volley of errant gunfire.

Cecilia moaned, her back stiffening from the bruise, a satisfying numbness overtaking the pain as she lay splayed. She turned her head aside, *cracking* the air in her neck, loosening the action of the muscle.

"I am innocent..." the soul whispered, his hair painted in the falling snow. The chattering head wriggling above the ice as his legs paddling against the dangerous temperatures of the lake underneath.

Cecilia screamed against the introduction, kicking her feet, squirming free of his proximity.

"I too am innocent!" another trapped sinner confessed.

"As I!"

"Release me!"

A field of punished had been locked into the lake's surface, eyes turned towards a possible savior, some forced to read only the expressions of others.

"Cici!" Frankie cried out, fishing for her status. He could make out the charging loyalists: a Hare, a Beaver, a Bear, and the Eagle, pushing efficiently through the snow, their accuracy improving.

"Forgive me," he whispered, unholstering David and laying him in the bed of powder. He sat behind him, bending his knees tightly. With strength, and grace, he shoved his brother down the embankment, watching the angle roll him like an empty barrel, sliding him out onto the lake. The momentum dragged him further onto the sheet, *pinging* off the heads of the entombed. Cecilia crawled towards his side, avoiding the threatening and *snapping* jaws of those who would rather eat than free themselves.

Frankie followed, a streak of youth flowing from his mouth as his rear bumped the frozen edge, upending him, his shoulder stabbing the ice, breaking a window into the erratic waves below.

The Beaver arrived first, his balance fooled, the others unable to prevent him from tumbling. He slammed into the decline, bouncing against the energy of the height, toppling onto his back. He skidded to an awkward, burning halt. Frankie twisted himself onto his knees, gritting through the pressure on the developing bruise spreading across his shoulder.

He stumbled towards the downed animal, eyeing the pistol in the swelling hand. He leapt against the glistening shell, straddling the robe with his knees. The Beaver thrust his free hand upward, creating a stiffening barrier as Frankie pawed for the weapon, pinning the occupied wrist to the ice.

The congregant pressed hard against his chin, easing his head back. They shuffled, arms flailing, the pistol drifting away from the surface only to be slammed back as the advantage waffled. Frankie scrambled, pinning his knee against the Beaver's bicep as he absorbed the unburdened fist's fury that stung his ribs. Despite the attack, Frankie was able to rip the hatchet from his belt.

The angle was not perfect, waylaid by the force attacking his chest, but he sliced through the Beaver's wrist, severing the hand and the weapon. The congregant screamed through his thick facade, blood spewing into a sensu pattern, the useless nub caught under the pressure of Frankie's leg.

He was suddenly uprooted, the black robe rolling over his head as they pushed the pistol out to sea, skidding against the divots of travelers' past. Frankie knocked the Beaver off of him, the hatchet falling from his wet grip. He kicked hard against the mess of flailing plasma, buying an extra stride. Onto his knees he slid, grabbing the severed hand and prying the pistol from the clutch. He spun, forced to his rear to stabilize himself, the black cloud diving, the weapon exploding in a manic punctuation.

The Beaver vomited a thick streak as his head fell, the bullet tearing a gash through the mask.

The cocky echo of a rifle swung past him, the round streaking through the forehead of a wriggling sinner, the aftermath coating those who had been stationed near him. The remaining trio of congregants had moved south, descending a more manageable crag. The marksman had knelt, racking the iron bolt and loading a fresh cartridge, eyes peeking through a magnifying scope.

Frankie fired a warning shot, nicking the rock high above the Eagle. He found solid footing, navigating around the pleading heads.

"Protect us!" they wept, tears freezing to their cheeks as he ignored them.

"I think we knocked him out again," Cecilia admitted as Frankie knelt by her side.

"You know what to do," he assured, grabbing one of the limp arms.

She followed, ensuring the child was secure, locking her thumb against David's, clenching tightly.

The rifle spouted once more, their heads shrinking. Frankie retorted, aiming near the ice as the Eagle led her comrades onto the surface. They paused, briefly, allowing the chipped ice to wash away in the wind.

Against the bumpers of protesting heads, they dragged David's body, weaving around the snarling, cursing sinners with the help of the intermittent blast of the pistol. The Eagle took to a knee, steadying her shoulder against the wind. Their shotguns were useless at this distance, but they sprayed buckshot anyway, coating the helpless in searing pellets, staining the lake with streams of blood. The barrel of the rifle fought the bullying breeze, the scope unreliable in its disturbance.

The trigger moved easily, the jump exquisite. Cecilia released David, heat pulling them apart, leaving a searing glue behind. Chewing through the back of her hand, the flattened round had deadened in the center of David's palm, a protrusion shifting his knuckles. She collapsed, the oar left in Frankie's care as he unloaded his magazine, striking the Hare in the shoulder, his feet upended as he banged his head against the crystal.

The bolt action *chimed* as the Eagle frantically ordered her remaining brother forward, waving her arm with insistence. The Bear chugged, pumping his shotgun as he maneuvered through the transgressors.

The pistol *clicked*, refusing to spit.

The Messenger made little pomp despite the anger that spewed from his nostrils. The black feathers pounded the air, casting aside the whipping snow. He slid across the surface, scythe activated as it carved a swath, flaying the faces of the immobile. He presented himself in front of the trotting Bear, wings flexing their own gale, knocking him off balance, the barrel of his shotgun steadying him like a crutch.

The Messenger twirled the stock of his weapon, slamming it through the top layer and dragging the serration in a jagged line through the water.

"What is he doing!?" the Bear shouted, looking back at his partner.

The incision complete, he rammed the butt of the handle into the weakness. A massive plate shifted, the ice *cracking* as the rear of the iceberg rose, the Bear caught now in the shift. He screamed, falling backward into the sudden incline. His weapon discharged, tearing a chunk of the Messenger's skull and wounding the beast.

The congregant plunged into the freezing lake, the plate of ice floating peacefully as it returned upright. Bubbles streamed from the Bear's mask as pale hands ferried him into the void. The Eagle took her retreat, slinging her rifle over her shoulder as she bounded for the embankment, passing the fallen Hare.

The Messenger shook off the grazing, his fingers pointing towards the opposite shore. Frankie nodded as their guardian flung himself skyward, soaring above the tree line, following the Eagle's escape through the forest.

Tearing the frayed hem of Cecilia's robe, Frankie measured out two equal lengths. He collected the gathering snow from the lake and packed it together. He called for her hand, the wound only a few centimeters long, but completely bored through.

"In and out," he assured, slapping the bleeding hole with the snowball.

She screamed, trying to wrench her hand away, but he refused.

"Give it a moment, it will go numb."

She cared not to watch as the snow began to melt, a thick red dye seeping upward. Frankie layered the burlap, crossing underneath and tightening with each revolution.

"Tight?" he asked.

"Tighter," she grunted. He obliged, squeezing the knot over the back of her hand, adding a second to secure it.

"How's the baby?"

She peeled back the blanket, a confused and enraged expression stuck to the child's sleeping face. "I think he passed out from sheer exhaustion."

"Him too," Frankie quipped as he pressed on the back of David's bulging wound, squeezing the bullet through the entrance, the bulbous head scraping against the muscle. The slimy round clattered to the ice as he layered the other bandage, gliding it between the limp fingers, around the wrist, and back over the palm.

"Frankie?"

He looked down at David, his breathing shallow, but still stable.

"Frankie?"

It came from the edge of the condemned. The Hare removed his mask and tossed it aside.

"Tomasso?" Frankie spat.

The wounded waved him over impatiently.

"Stay with David." He released the pistol's magazine; still empty. He hoped Tomasso did not realize.

Frankie took a circuitous route, tapping the loose iceberg, navigating around the buoyant raft. He shuffled towards the editor, pistol trained at his head.

"I'm not going to shoot you, Frankie!"

"*Cazzata!*" He picked up the pump-action, holstering the expended pistol. "Get up!"

"Frankie," hands raised in innocence. "They want David. They want to enslave him."

The shotgun erupted, punching a hole into the ice at Tomasso's feet. A childish *bleat* spewing. "*Bene, bene, bene!*" as he cowered from the reloading weapon.

"Turned against me!" Frankie dictated, widening the gap, chambering another round. "You brought us to the fucking table!"

"Hypocrite!"

"Hypocrite!"

"Hypocrite!" A symphony rose, the shivering mouths calling for Frankie's attention.

Tomasso ran.

The blast ruined his spine, the crippling twinge lunging him face first, scraping the skin of his cheek as he wilted. Frankie towered above him, listening to the soaked inhalations, blood bubbling past his lips. Tomasso's head erupted, the close range expanding his skull outward, the warmth splitting the ice, dunking what remained in the bobbing current.

The Bear suddenly stuck his helpless fingers through the hole, swatting for assistance. His snout rose, black lenses staring up into the equally dark barrel, the light of a fiery sun adding his blood to Tomasso's contribution. The Bear sunk into the abyss, guided by those who had yet to contemplate their own sins.

The pump snapped towards Frankie, ejecting the spent shell.

"Hypocrite!"

"Sell our souls for your own!"

He ignored the repentance, the guilty trying to save face.

"Why are they yelling at you?" Cecilia asked.

"They're trying to stop us, we have to keep moving. Head for the shore. I'll handle David." He seceded the shotgun to her as he prepared to hoist the unconscious.

"Honesty is reserved for those who bare it!" the heads taunted.

Cecilia pulled the hood of her robe over her ears, unable to drown out the incessant chatter.

The souls gnawed at David's legs, teeth wrestling with his trousers. Frankie kicked the material free, bashing the sides of their skulls as he snaked towards the forest.

"Hypocrite!"

"You shall be held accountable!"

"Lies beget lies!"

Finally, solid earth beneath him. He laid David down properly, collapsing near him, knees boring two holes in the fresh snow. He ran his fingers through his hair, clearing away the wet sensation, but the grease and perspiration only oiled his hand, spreading the mixture more thoroughly across his scalp.

"We..." he huffed. "We have to keep moving." He swallowed hard, lazily pointing deeper into the woods.

"We've been walking all night, we need to rest."

"The cabin," he coughed. "We need to get to the cabin." He pushed off the ground and stumbled upright. He shoved David's legs inward, bending the knees. Tugging the limp arm, he leaned into the rubbery disposition, securing his arm through the dangling legs and settling him across his back.

"Francesco, we need to take a moment. Just to breathe."

He was already marching away from the lake, mumbling to himself. "I have to get away from the voices."

"Run you bastard!" they shrieked. "A bed of lies awaits!"

"Wait! Francesco!" she called, shotgun dragging at her side, the child dipping in the other.

"Hypocrite! Hypocrite!" chanting, as if a ceremony had begun.

The tiny feelers of the forest dragged across his face as he plowed through the deciduous aisles.

"Wait!" Cecilia begged, the oversized boots too loose, each step adding snow to the interior.

"Hypocrite! Hypocrite!"

"Leave me alone!" Frankie screamed, saliva launching in thick beads.

Cecilia practically hugged the trunk of a pine, leaning her face against the cold bark as sweat streamed into her eyes. "We need to stop."

"We're close to the cabin, Cici. We just need to follow the mountain, just like we did before."

"*Will you give me one fucking minute to breathe!?*"

He held his tongue, waiting for her to finish.

"You never know when to stop. Just because you can keep going doesn't mean you have to drag others along with you."

"Cici w–"

"I know we're close! *I! Know!* I haven't exactly been asleep this whole time. *Fuck!*" She slammed her head into her forearm, praying the tree would hold her exhaustion. "Even as children, you took it too fucking far. You could never read our faces; when we had had enough."

"*I'm trying to save us.*"

"Us? Or you?"

His silence confirmed her suspicion.

"Why were they calling you a hypocrite?"

"I don't know."

"Did you know those people?"

"No."

"*Francesco?*"

"No! Jesus!"

"You push yourself *too hard.*"

"Maybe because I want to make a difference."

"And I don't?"

"*I'm different,*" Frankie asserted, tapping his chest.

"No, you haven't changed at all, you're just now realizing what you really are."

"Do you think I wanted us to end up the way we did? Don't you think that if I had stopped Papa, we would have grown up with a support system?"

"Mama took care of him."

"But before that."

"You cannot change the past. You think by putting away these criminals, by stopping abuse and rape and thievery that you are making a difference? The crime has already been committed, you simply sweep up the remains. Just because Papa died doesn't mean I have forgotten what he did to us. I will have to live with that for *the rest of my life.* And you will too. Stop trying to save everyone else. Save your family. Open your ears."

"*You neglected us.*"

"This again!" she sighed. "I explained this to you. I didn't turn my back because I don't love you, or David, or Mama. You must understand that we may be of the same blood, but our minds, our emotions, operate separately, unequivocally. We process these events differently, we cannot begin to understand how. You just have to trust me. Trust that I know how to heal my own self."

"You didn't talk to us for years. When was the last time you visited David?"

"*I was afraid!* I was afraid of seeing Papa in David's face. Of remembering what he did to him. I was afraid that all the progress that I made would be torn apart in an instant. That I would return to being weak again."

"Why didn't you come to me?"

"Because there are some things that you are not equipped to

handle. I came back from Honduras broken. The things I have seen, Francesco, the things that I have *heard*. No one deserves to know those things. I could not come back broken, not to you, not to David. You would have seen right through it. I had to come back on my own terms."

"Then why did you call me?"

"Because you are the most familiar thing I have in this world. I needed something to buoy me, to remind myself that on the other side there is something so much better than what I'm fighting inside."

He stomped the ball of his foot into the wet soil. "I'm sorry. I'm just trying to help."

"I know. I left for selfish reasons, but it's acceptable to be selfish, especially when you neglect yourself all the time. You help people for a living, no? There is sacrifice in that. Out here, we have only each other. Our dependency rests in our strengths."

Frankie nodded, turning his head, covertly wiping his eyes with his fingers. He snorted, sucking up the mucus into his sinuses, erasing his own moment of insecurity.

"How much further?" she asked.

"Not much," clearing his throat. "I think. *Fuck*, I don't know."

"Do you need more time to catch your breath?"

"I feel like I'm about to come apart at the seams," he smiled, sheepishly. "You?"

"I'm ready whenever you are."

David opened his eyes.

The stinging stone floor. Stomach boiling.

Down becoming up becoming down.

Darkness. Heat; a flame. Darkness once more. Ears popping, the elevation clenching his jaw.

The scent of pine. Nails across the face, caressing, like a kitten pawing at a giant.

Water. Endless water. Dribbling through the follicles of his scalp, the aqueduct sensitive, his arms too numb to scratch.

Pausing now. Spinning. North?

West now, away from the sun. An old acquaintance. Wave, from across the street.

They scream. They scream at each other. Mumbling gibberish.

The air freezes, his throat dry, the saliva drawing the moisture. Each motion scratches, his hands too big to reach.

Forehead exploding, the flock whipping his face clean. His lips move, he has freedom. The void taps him.

His stomach boils once more, the white flipping into black, then back. Then back again. His spine stiffens, shoulder blades burning with rash.

The pain increases, a firecracker bursting on the horizon. Light and circumstance.

They scream even more, thousands of them. Rats chew his ankles as his trousers soak.

All they do is scream.

The sun. Vomit. Neck tilting, the rest dropping behind, the cold powder welcoming in the heat of a fever.

The cabin.

The cabin. At the peak of the mount. The cabin. His throat bulged, expelling more than he wanted to.

Bile on his tongue.

Frankie slapped the vomit-stained cheek in quick successions. "David?"

"We should get him inside," Cecilia suggested.

"David, we're almost home."

"H-h-ho..." he mouthed.

"Come on," Frankie grunted, pulling him upright.

David's head hung between his elevated arms, nodding slowly. "Home..."

With little resistance he was upon his heels, leaning against Frankie's underarm, the crutch guiding him. Up the pathway, dragging against the snow, towards the memories of his youth.

The snout of the dead Pig hovered above the white dust, a frozen droplet of blood staining the nostril. Ripped from the hinge, the front door had been chucked outside, the hinge still gripping the frame. The Wolf had been censored by the draft, the open doorway allowing the wind to bury half of his exposed skull.

Frankie guided David past the corpse, navigating the holes he had opened in the floorboards, peeking in on the layer of corpses they had left behind. To the mattress, the iron frame squeaking as he deposited David and helped him curl into a comfortable position.

A blanket from beneath unfolded into an appropriate size, clumps of dust and hair lingering in the air as it flapped. Cecilia sought refuge on the stale cushions of the couch, laying the heavy pump action at her side and exposing the child from the wool prison. He fought the brightness, squeaking a shivering yawn, drool smacking between the gums.

"If he wakes up..." Frankie started.

"Where are you going?"

"To the cellar." He picked up the shotgun, inspecting the breach. "If you hear *anything*..."

She knew.

He nodded, hiding a bit of shame as he yanked the iron ringlet and raised the cellar door.

Skipping the collapsed riser, he avoided the prone congregants, ducking under the lower joists. The archway still lay cloaked in black, the hanging slab of faceless meat waiting near the rear, begging to be thrown out with the others.

Frankie began to his right, shuffling underneath Cecilia and her gentle humming, trying to encourage the baby to find sleep once more. An empty tool bench had been drenched in dust, no markings of recent use. A shelf beneath held a rusted coffee can, a collection of nails and a few cracked bolts rattling inside.

To the opposite end, a pipe affixed to the wall running from the basin above. A long, walnut handle in the corner led to the familiar curved head of a shovel. He had thought his mother had left it in the growth, but perhaps that would have been too incriminating. He inspected the metal: a fleck of dried blood clung to a small tuft of hair.

He returned the relic, preferring to ignore the memory for now.

Beneath the stairs, a steamer trunk, the skin peeling, the edges sanded from dragging. He released the latches and eased the cover open.

His father had hidden from them his actions during the early war, the bravery of others his preferred topic of conversation. His uniform had been folded neatly, the collar ironed, not a single scratch nor frayed fiber. A pair of trousers completed the set, the artifacts set aside, along with his combat boots and a pristine helmet.

A map of the north mountains tucked into a leather portfolio had been marked with red circles and black crosses with a thick grease pencil, the offensive targeting the most advantageous of artillery positions. A leather waist holster had been crumpled into a ball, the stock of a sidearm poking from the mess. Frankie released the weapon's magazine: two rounds remained, some forty years old now.

He tucked the pistol into his waistband, rummaging through the mess below: documents of discharge, a few folded German bills, but little else useful. He stacked the loose papers together, shoving them off to the side.

Underneath, a sheepskin bound notebook, the fluffy wool edging on gray. David's name had been embroidered in bright blue thread across the face. He opened the stiff spine, little hand-scrawled notes occupying the cover page: a fearsome dragon ejecting rancid flames from his mouth as a brave knight held steady; his shield of steel fought back the heat, his sword raised, the cowering form of a princess at his rear pointing towards the horror.

A cast list. Props. Sets. Dialogue.

The silly notions of children. He had remembered participating in the farces, heckled by the director. Eventually, frustrations boiled over, laughter turning to tears and the performance closing on opening night. Pages had been torn free, the final act whittled down to a handful.

He returned the book along with his father's belongings, letting the lid drop. A gap between the wall called his attention, an object caught in between. He slid the trunk forward, tipping its weight from side to side.

His fingers slipped along the surface of the mystery, the lacquered case fighting his excavation. Enough revealed itself, a handle to hoist it atop the trunk. Two gilded buckles popped open as he discovered another relic.

He allowed himself time to run his fingers over the barrel, the black metal so frigid, once burning with revenge. The thick oak stock had seen a few blemishes, the grain interrupted, but otherwise beautiful.

The double-barreled shotgun slid from its satin coffin, the butt to his shoulder. Even for him, it proved heavy, his mother handling it with grace. He snapped the barrel forward, finding the chamber empty. A pouch at the front of the case held three shells, two finding a home, the third settling in the breast pocket of his dress shirt.

A mucus-laden cough blared from beneath the archway, the weapon swinging towards the dark passage.

"Francesco!"

Bounding up the stairs, he found David's head leaning over the bed, blood spewing from his mouth as he vomited.

"Jesus." He set the shotgun on the butcher block and knelt at David's side, his hand rubbing his back.

"Release me from this form!" His eyes had clouded, his lips drooling.

David pounced, reaching for the shotgun. Frankie's hands clasped over his as the barrel jockeyed between them, the trigger pulled innocently as a round punctured the ceiling.

"Cici!" Frankie demanded.

Her rosary dangled between her fingers as she approached, flashing the burning antidote. David screamed at the heat, releasing the weapon, crashing against the carving table. The unit buckled as he collapsed to his side.

"In the name of the Trinity," she blared, "I command you to speak the truth! In the name of the Trinity and of the Most Blessed Virgin Mary, speak the truth!"

His arms wrapped around his head, shielding the torture. "I am perching in him, inside him, because he has been damned!"

Frankie flipped the shotgun, aiming loosely at his brother, waiting, his hands fluttering, drying the anxiety.

"Do it!" the Devil urged. "Kill him, kill him! Burn the body, bring him to me so that I may continue!"

"You continue to lie," Cecilia accused. "You are continuing to lie. I command you, unclean spirit, to speak, in the name of the Father and of the Son and of the Holy Ghost."

"I am no unclean spirit! I am the Lord of Flies, I am no prince. I am the fallen. I am the one you mock so openly!"

He unfolded himself, scrambling upright in a flailing mass. Frankie shoved the stock of the shotgun into his gut, directing him towards the bed, his head slamming against the mattress.

"Pain is nothing!"

Cecilia shoved the crucifix forward. "You will not find peace here!"

"You will hold me prisoner? *You!?* Little Cecilia, so many failures, so little time to grieve."

"Do not think that I will believe your simplistic performance. An actor of lies, bending and snapping the truth. You are poor and weak, a life no longer worth redeeming. By order of the Guardian Angels and by order of the Queen of Angels, speak your truth! I command you in the name of the Father and of the Son and of the Holy Ghost!"

David's shoulders *cracked* as his arms bent, his sweater bulging with bloat.

"You may not stand, Lucifer!" she ordered. "I have not given you permission!"

He planted his throbbing hands onto the mattress, his veins expanding as black ran through the opaque flesh.

"I will not bow to such pathetic sinners."

"On your knees!" Frankie threatened, the barrel rising with David's head.

"Drag me across my oceans, across my beloved sands of fire, only to set me ablaze, paint this cabin with the matter of father and son. A crooked bastard, a diseased bitch, shall not be at my side!"

"Let us speak to David," Cecilia said. "Let us speak with our brother."

"He is in here. He is with me."

"Release him then. Give him back to us."

"You wished your own death," Frankie interjected. "You agreed. You took my father's deal."

"I manipulate as I see fit."

"Then you do not wish to end? You wish to keep your king-dom?"

Cecilia glanced at Frankie, unsure where this thread was drag-ging them.

"I..." the Devil stuttered. "I...wish..."

"You take control," she started. "You take control of vessels that only propel you forward. You have no power here. You cannot conjure pestilence, nor war, nor famine, nor death."

David held out his hands, fingers clenching like the claws of a beast, curling towards the center of his palm.

"You only speak influence," she said. "You guide your tongue into the ears of man. You alone have no power here. When will you realize this?"

"I...David...I..." David swung his arms, sniffing for the bed, his face hitting the down pillow, the gesticulations fading, his eyes closing.

"We need to restrain him," she demanded.

"With what?"

"Rope..." David breathed. "The clothesline..."

A quiet glance of hope between them.

"Watch him," Cecilia said as she hurried through the doorway, leaving the child to rest on the bent springs of the filthy couch.

"David?" Frankie tested.

"Let me rest..." he mumbled.

Cecilia tugged at the side of the cabin, dislodging a metal hook and releasing the thin hemp. As she spooled the line into her care, she caught movement, the boughs of the tree line waving. The chipped skull observed her closely, silent, unsure of whether to approach or not.

David kept his eyes shut, the pores on his neck plumping as he shivered.

"Keep the blanket on him," Cecilia suggested as she tossed Frankie the rope. "We need to bind his hands and feet to the bed."

"Why?"

"This is only the beginning. He will grow stronger as David grows weaker. We must prevent him from expelling too much energy when he returns."

Frankie rolled David onto his back, hoisting his arm out and curling the rope carefully around his wrist.

"Where did he go?" Frankie asked.

"Deep inside him...somewhere."

"You don't know?"

"No one can be certain. The brain is a sensitive organ."

Frankie paused, cocking his head towards her. "You believe this is in his brain?"

"If one wanted to corrupt another, wouldn't the brain be the perfect place to begin?"

He pondered the observation, finishing the knot, the excess too much to snake through to complete it. His head darted, looking for a sharp angle. The knife roll, askew atop the butcher block, proved useful as he selected a simple paring knife.

Frankie sliced through the clothesline, testing the strength against the barred headboard. It was certainly taught, though how long it would hold against the strength of a grown man would be proven in time. To David's right leg, threading the line between his shin and ankle, meeting above the tongue of his boot.

"What happens when we get David back?" Cecilia asked.

"We go home." It was obvious. Wasn't it?

"I meant, what happens to David? Where does he go?"

Frankie kept his fingers busy, playing with the swooping knots, his eyes losing focus as he stared. He fought through his own conviction, the sense of justice he had strived to provide.

"Is David going to prison?"

"I don't know," he replied, eyes brimming with moisture to encourage him to blink. He returned to the hemp. "What would you do?"

"I think he belongs at the hospital."

"You believe that will cure him?"

"No."

"To keep him occupied?"

"I don't know what to believe. If David committed these horrible crimes under his own influence, he is guilty. Is he not?"

"Whether his mind or the minds of others pushed him, he is still the one who carried them out." Moving to the opposite leg, Frankie swallowed the conversation, preferring not to think about the aftermath.

"What did you find in the cellar?" she asked.

"Mostly nothing. Just that."

He nodded towards the double-barreled shotgun. She took control of the weapon, marveling too over its weight. "Do you think it felt good?"

"Huh?"

"Killing Papa."

"In the moment, perhaps. But it is a memory that you must relive, no matter the satisfaction. The act is just the beginning. I remember the burial much more vividly than when she finally pulled the trigger."

Cecilia lowered the barrel, worried her finger would slip. "What could have drawn David to want to return here?"

"Just a little white lie..." the Devil whispered. His arm shot forward, swiping for Frankie. He avoided the intent, scrambling to restrain David as he clawed. Pressing on the wound in his palm, the Devil howled, the arm turning to jelly as it limped into Frankie's care. Using the remaining rope, he secured it to the bed as David thrashed.

"So primitive! Have you no other methods!?" The thin line held as he looked down at his tethered legs. "Intending to fuck me?" he chuckled.

"Hold this," Cecilia said, transferring the rosary into Frankie's hand. "I need to prepare the blessing."

Frankie dragged the rocking chair from the corner of the room and parked himself next to the bed. Cecilia placed her consecration kit on top of the desk, the double barrel leaning against the wall.

"We have some time to talk," the Devil smiled, limbs wriggling as if he were being bounced about by the currents of a gentle ocean.

"You love an audience, don't you?" Frankie teased.

"A labyrinth of misery must hear my pathetic sermons. It is much more interesting to convince the single serving."

"You made a deal with my father. You begged to be cleansed and set free."

"True. True. I promise many things."

"What is it that you truly want?"

"Do you believe me when I say that I wish only to die?"

"Not particularly."

"Hmm. Why?"

"You are the Devil, are you not?"

The beast growled, eyebrows angling into a fierce and unexpected anger. He barked, saliva streaming down his cheek.

"Tell him," Cecilia said, refusing to turn from her duties as she removed a vial of wine, placing it upright next to a metal flask embossed with a silver cross.

The Devil writhed, shifting his wrists against the wound thread.

"What is he doing?" Frankie asked.

"He is in considerable pain. He will not speak his own name. It would admit he is simply and utterly one and only."

"Are you afraid of simplicity?" Frankie coyly teased, turning back to the writhing spirit.

"Do not peg me as simple! I reserve this for your *brother*."

"You asked me to call you Michele. Do you remember?"

He giggled, turning his head back towards Frankie. "Of course! I am no fool!"

"Michele?" Cecilia repeated.

"Is there a problem, Sister?" he hissed.

"Why do you take the name of your brother?" A cylindrical tube popped open against its hinge, a communion wafer sliding outward, the mechanism offering the sacrament, chambering another behind it for easy access.

"Brother!? No, brother!? My enemy!"

"But he is still your brother, no?"

"*Troia!*"

"I am correct, no?"

"*Troia! Troia!* You speak like flame."

"Tell us about Michele." She set three decanters next to each other filled with an increasingly darkening golden oil, her initials stenciled in faint white across the face. "Why do you have so much disdain for him?"

"You are not allowed to hear such a confession!"

"So, there are sins to confess?"

"No! You are powerless!"

"Tell *me*," Frankie insisted. "I am here. Tell me."

"You are no clergy!"

"Then I will have no reason to judge you. Tell me about Michele."

"The preferred of my Father! Little bastard. He excelled, huh? So did I."

"But you were vain."

"I was made in his image! Am I at fault? I strived to do better. Kept my loyalty. Always content with second-in-command."

"You did not have a voice," Frankie observed.

"Precisely. It fell on deaf ears. I must *trust* in my Father to provide. To light our way. Fuck! Fuckfuckfuck! Not our kingdom! His! His alone."

"Why did you rebel?"

"There was no choice. I would not be listened to. I would not be trusted. I blared a trumpet of hatred, for I would not be unraveled. I would not freeze in the shadow of my brother."

"And you were cast out?"

"Punished! I was given no chance to recant, to beg for forgiveness. I lashed out because of his inabilities and he has the gall to beat me. To thrust me below the very soil and torment me. To turn me against my inhibitions, to burn and tear at the flesh of those who too have simply voiced their unhappiness."

"Is this why you wish to die?"

The colorless eyes began to well, the saline dabbing the mattress as it spread through the worn material. "Yes..." he whispered, choking slightly on the mucus building up in his sinuses, dripping down the back of his throat.

"Then why do you struggle? Allow us to free you."

"And return home? Tail tucked between my legs?" he sobbed. "No. I must find another way."

Frankie leaned forward, David's head shying to hide his shame. "If David were to die, what would happen to you?"

"I would ascend the throne once more."

"What is Hell without a King?"

"Chaos," he mouthed, his voice barely audible.

"Then let chaos reign!" Frankie suggested.

"Then I will be a failure."

Cecilia could not help but crane towards the confession. Frankie met her eyes, sensing a breakthrough, or at least a part of the antidote, was taking shape. She nodded, allowing him to further the interrogation.

"What would it matter?" Frankie pressed.

"It matters to me!" his voice *cracked*, losing the thorny timber. "What do I leave behind, Frankie?" David turned back towards him, opening his eyes, the brown pupils shivering as he tried to focus through the tears. "I am nothing. Will I even be remembered?"

"David..." Frankie reached out.

"W-why!?" The rope worked against his wrists, his ankles twisting, trying to break free of the incarceration. "Why did you do this!? Ar-ar-are you taking me back to the hospital?"

"David...no. *No.* You are not going back to the hospital."

"He's still inside of me!" he whined like a child, squirming and oozing a pathetic mewl.

"Cici?"

She refused to participate. "Leave him be, Francesco."

He rose, marching to her side.

"Frankie, where are you going!?" David lurched.

"This is our opportunity," Frankie begged to her in a whisper. "We need to free David."

She looked away from her tools, though refusing to make eye contact. "David will appear to us. He will have moments of clarity, of truth, but he will sink back into the arms of the Devil. We cannot trust what either of them says. If David lied about the cellar, then he will lie about anything. He wanted us to come here, and we obeyed, now he needs to give us something in return." She finally met Frankie's concerned expression. "You need to trust me. This is not the first time I have seen this. It is painful to watch the struggle, but you must follow me as I followed you into the forest. I will lead us home."

The conviction in her assertiveness had not been expected, but, somehow, he was not surprised. He slowly nodded, placing his hand on her shoulder and squeezing.

The Devil shook the frame of the bed, stamping against the hardwood, grunting as he flexed his pelvis towards the heavens. "My children will spread my seed!"

"He will tire," she said. "Leave him be for now."

"Do I bore my siblings?" he squawked

"I will be in the cellar," Frankie sighed.

"Retreat into the dark! Perhaps to spill his own seed." A cackle filled the cabin, like a machine gun rattling.

"*Guarda!*" came the muffled warning from the cellar.

Cecilia pivoted against the stool as the rosary sailed upward through the shotgun blast in the floorboards. She swiped, securing it and slinging it over her neck. "*Grazi!*"

"*Grazi! Grazi!*" the Devil mocked.

She lifted the layer of molds inside her kit, a tight compartment beneath suctioning slightly against the tight fit. She retrieved a small circular compact of black plastic, reassembling the kit and latching the lid tightly.

Sliding out of the coarse, black robe, she tossed it onto the floor, glad to be free of its stench.

The Devil flicked his tongue into the air, tasting the molecules like a reptile, moaning in ecstasy. "A little too thin for my taste, but it will have to do."

Cecilia opened the compact, allowing the granules of salt to settle. "O salt, creature of God," her eyes closing, palms turned towards the ceiling. "I exorcise you by the living God, by the true God, by the holy God, by the God who ordered you to be poured into the water by Elia the prophet, so that its life-giving powers might be restored."

"Useless! You are not allowed!" the Devil screamed over her prayer.

"I exorcise you so that you may become a means of salvation for believers-"

"Utterly useless drivel! Nothing will come of your blessings!"

"-that you may bring health of soul and body to all who make use of you, and that you may put to flight and drive away from the places where you are sprinkled; every apparition, villainy, turn of devilish deceit, and every unclean spirit; adjourned by him who will come to judge the living and the dead and the world by fire."

She remained silent, allowing the words to settle like flakes of whimsical snow.

"Say, *Amen*, Francesco!" she called.

"*Amen!*" he responded through the cellar's portholes.

"Let us pray."

Frankie tugged at a dead congregant, rolling him off the machine gun tucked beneath his arms. As he wiped it clean, he listened carefully to Cecilia's sincerity.

"Almighty and everlasting God, we humbly implore you, in your immeasurable kindness and love, to bless this salt which you created and gave to the use of mankind, so that it may become a source of health for the minds and bodies of all who make use of it."

He ejected the magazine, turning it over in the limited light, squinting to count the cartridges.

"May it rid whatever it touches or sprinkles of all uncleanness and protect it from every assault of evil spirits. Through Christ our Lord."

"Amen." Frankie assisted.

"This displeases me!" the muffled anxiety croaked.

"O God," she continued. "for the salvation of mankind, you built your greatest mysteries on this substance, water. In your kindness, hear our prayers and pour down the power of your blessing into this element. May this, your creature, become an agent of divine grace in the service of your mysteries, to drive away evil spirits and dispel sickness, so that everything in the homes of the faithful that is sprinkled with this water, may be rid of all uncleanness and freed from every harm. Let no breath of infection and no disease-bearing air remain in these places. May the wiles of the lurking enemy prove of no avail. Let whatever might menace the safety and peace of those who live here be put to flight by the sprinkling of this water, so that the health obtained by calling upon your holy name, may be made secure against all attack. Through Christ our Lord."

"Amen." He had stripped the dead of their weaponry: a machine gun, stock elongated; a pistol, newly issued and stamped with the Beretta name; a black revolver, four rounds remaining; his father's sidearm; two pump-action and one double-barreled shotgun; and a bolt action rifle, the scope shattered with buckshot.

"May a mixture of salt and water now be made, in the name of the Father, and of the Son, and of the Holy Spirit." Cecilia tipped the container of salt into the mouth of the silver flask, allowing the surface to rise to the brim. She screwed the lid into place and shook the two elements together, the tiny crystals swimming in the clear sea. She set the compact down, crossing herself, kissing her thumb gently as she whispered, "Amen."

"Ancient words of no consequence!" the Devil reminded her. "You believe he speaks to one *man*? That he can change doctrine with the flick of his pen?"

Cecilia rose, bringing the consecrated water with her. She sat carefully in the rocking chair.

"Speak! Speak!" he demanded. "You rush to slip over the sacred words, but you will not converse with me?"

She unscrewed the flask, his eyelids widening around the white spheres.

"Vile sewage! You intend to bathe me? To baptize me?"

Swinging against her lazy grip, she teased him, ticking it from side to side.

"Vile water! Vile! You would not dare."

To her feet, dangling the threat over the bed.

"I have made a mistake!" innocence reshaping his lips. "There is room, perhaps, for niceties?"

Back to the rocking chair, squeaking the curved frame, leaning away and drifting forward with grace, the holy water taunting the Devil.

"David!" he exclaimed. "You would like to speak with him?" Suddenly he was unable to breathe properly, his chest expanding but little streaming from his nostrils.

She shrugged, jiggling the flask.

"Yes, you would like to speak with him. I will prove to you that he is still here." He shut his eyes, huffing shorter and shorter exhalations. "David?"

"Cici?" David mumbled, his voice still crinkling with churning gravel.

"David, tell your sister. Tell your sister you are fine," the Devil encouraged.

"I'm fine, Cici. My hand hurts a bit, but I'm all right."

His left eye peeked, making sure she was still paying attention.

"See!" the evil smiled. "A little lamb snuggled in its own warmth."

"Cici, I don't want to be in any pain," the ruse still speaking in a horrid tone, imitating David poorly.

"David's right," the Devil interjected.

"*Grazi.*"

"Look at us! Learning to coexist. Are you proud of us?"

She was far from amused, jamming the mouth of the flask past his lips, counting, "*Uno, due, tre.*" He twisted against the drowning, turning his head away. She gripped the side of his scalp, threading through the thick follicles as she eased him straight. Removing the blessed water, she slapped her hand over his mouth, forcing him to swallow.

"We cast you out," she grunted, fighting against his unwieldy resistance. "Every unclean spirit, every Satanic power, every onslaught of the infernal adversary, every legion, every diabolical group and sect, in the name and by the power of our Lord Jesus Christ. We command you, begone and fly far from the Church of God, from the souls made by God in His image and redeemed by the precious blood of the divine Lamb!"

David vomited, angling away from her, a putrid mess of clear liquid and festering bile.

"We cast you out!" she screamed, pouring the water into her hand and splashing it across the bed. "We cast you out!"

The Devil roared, the frame of the bed pounding an indentation.

Again, she sprayed him. "We cast you out, Satan! Return to a slumber so that you may weaken, so that you may rise a pathetic insect. We cast you out!"

Frankie stared at the dust as it rained down with every thundering heartbeat.

The ferocious onslaught ceased.

"Amen," Cecilia sighed.

The oversized boots *clapped* against the floorboards as Frankie followed her route. She marched down the staircase, finding a seat against a tread.

"He's asleep."

He resisted momentarily, watching her breathe. "Now what?"

She rubbed the beads of her mother's rosary against her thumb and index. "Now we can begin."

The splintered bucket rose with slushing clarity, the rope squeaking against the pulley's resistance.

A flame-streaked pot proved a perfect vessel.

Kindling had been chopped sometime before, David anticipating a brutal winter. Beneath the basin, hidden behind a checkered curtain, a thin crate of meager supplies. A tablespoon or two of soluble coffee, unmarked, churned in the boiling water. Dried meat tore easily against their exhausted jaws.

The small curtain provided the filter, a mug shared between them of almost digestible caffeine.

"Tastes like oil," she remarked.

He wrestled with the jerky, finally tearing a manageable sliver. "Better than what they gave me at the convent."

Frankie guided the handle of the bucket over the stabilizing hook of the well. Despite successfully freeing it, he felt resistance. He raised the pail, following a length of twine running from the base to a plastic cocoon dangling into the well, itself attached to another cocoon. And another.

He carefully cut the plastic wrapping using the paring knife, the layers blossoming as he extracted a small, dented tin of butane.

Another produced a swollen billfold of sweaty and stiff currency.

A set of unmarked stationary, an unsharpened pencil, a single ribbon of typewriter ink.

Packaged seeds of hand-labeled herbs: patchouli, hazel, sage; rubber-banded together.

A cluster of prophylactics.

Unscrewing the metal top of a glass bottle, he inhaled deeply, convincing himself to take a sip. He hacked, face blushing, as the homemade brew seared his throat. "Jesus! We should add this to the coffee." He handed it to Cecilia.

"Smells medicinal."

"Reminds me of the awful potato liquor that Papa used to boil for his friends."

The final item forced him to retreat from the carving table, the white wings unfolding. But it was not a deceased bird as he had first assumed, though they *were* wings. Cecilia watched them bloom fully, having been bound for so long in the water-resistant plastic. She comforted the fussing child as she slogged through her memory, wondering why they seemed so familiar.

Frankie shoved the butcher block into the open doorway, giving them partial coverage. The carving table would act as a useful backup.

The nails that had been abandoned in the cellar withstood the force of the small, wooden meat tenderizer tucked inside the knife roll. The split beams of the front door barely fit across the smashed window, the nails long enough just to lock them in place.

Frankie banged hard against the aged metal, accidentally bending the spike. "*Stronzo!*" He dug through the old coffee can, selecting a replacement.

"How long is this going to take?" he asked as Cecilia dipped her finger into a cup of water, dangling the drip over the newborn's mouth, trying to provide some form of sustenance.

"There is no telling. Sometimes within a few hours, perhaps a few weeks. A child I attended to was stricken for 84 days."

Peering through the slats in the window's new protection, Frankie scanned the tree line. The sun still roared overhead, the snow thick, the air whipping in short spurts, but he found no movement, save the brave flakes who wandered from the collective.

"Don't tell me we have limited time," she scolded. "I am aware."

He picked up the unfastened end of a plank and raised it into place, hammering until it remained stiff. "Is there an abridged version?"

"There is no version to begin with. It is not an exact science."

Satisfied with his work, he stepped away, counting the weapons he had leaned against the wall below for easy access. "David was coerced into drinking the blood. The others, I assume they did not have such a chance to refuse."

"No. Most began with a fever, a few dreams of unexplainable origin, but no different than a sudden illness. Boils would form, rashes, bleeding from sudden small wounds. They would perspire, shake their beds until they exhausted themselves. They would not eat. They would never drink. And if they did, they would vomit, almost immediately. The vitriol would start soon after, screaming horrible things at people they loved. Recalling events beyond their knowledge. Speaking in rhythms and tones unfamiliar to the local people."

"Why were they chosen?"

"I don't know," her face wilting slightly with shame. "I worked with a priest, Father Vincenzo, who once told me, that those who are inhabited by Lucifer and his minions do so because they believe they can relate. That they are so similar that the host cannot resist being tempted, easily giving in to their promises."

"Is that what you believe?"

"I refuse to believe that the children who have been afflicted all share in the agony of the Devil."

Frankie looked at David, sleeping with elbows bent, one knee edging upward, content in his confinement.

"David is different," she dismissed.

"Is he? Are any of us so different? Perhaps, just a bit more adjusted?"

"He was so young."

"He's been haunted for years."

"How so?"

"The last time I saw him at the hospital...it was his birthday. He asked me why you had left us. I told him that you had found your calling, that something had spoken to you. He didn't understand, he thought someone had called you on the telephone or something like that. I think...I think that he was under the impression that he heard a voice too. Just like him."

"He would not even cry when Papa beat him. He spoke so little after that."

"Something else wasn't allowing him to."

Cecilia slammed her fist onto the desk, rattling her accouterments. "*Zoccola! Testa di cazzo!*"

He allowed her to simmer, to seethe in peace.

"We cannot change it," he declared. "We cannot return to a time before Papa made his mistakes." He knelt before her, clasping her loose hand, the other still rattling from her punctuation. "What we can do now is to rid David of this spirit. We can break this chain. Even if he must return to the hospital, even if he must confess to what he has done, he will know that his mind is his own. Will he not?"

"The thought of him condemned to live forever in a cell makes me want to run, to leave him here."

"What we are doing truly cannot save him. It will only make him comfortable. But we must accept that."

"What if we run?" she theorized. "We flee with David, take him far away from here, where they cannot find him."

"And live life with our heads cocked? Looking forward and back. Always? That is no way for all of us to live. And David has already been punished enough. You've already run, Cici. You ran and found a bit of excitement and you found some difficult truths, but, in the end, you are here. Back to where all of this started, where all of this must end."

"They are coming for us," she whispered, eyes darting, trying to focus on his simultaneously.

"All the more reason we need to start."

"I..." she swallowed. "I..."

Frankie encouraged her to speak.

She cleared her throat, looking away briefly to collect herself. "How long has it been since your last confession?"

They sat with their backs barely touching, Frankie's legs splayed out, facing David should he stir. Cecilia crossed her feet as they tucked under one another, her hands resting together in the pocket created by her posture. The child was near too, a chrysalis of congregant robe providing a warm nest as he drooled and mumbled, infatuated by the ceiling above.

The heat of the fire at their side warmed the trio, David in no discernible discomfort. Cecilia watched the clogged doorway as the wind pushed the snow in dazzling miniature tornados.

Frankie cleared his throat, "I'll go first."

"Everything, Francesco," she warned. "He will know everything."

"H-how do I begin?"

"*In nomine Patris et Filii et Spiritus Sancti,*" she crossed herself, he followed clumsily. "How long has it been since your last confession?"

He looked away, searching. "Since I was eight. Jesus, twenty-eight years ago."

"The time does not matter, only that you recognize the scope."

He nodded, preparing himself as the kindling shifted, the dry wood *snapping*. "When I was ten...I killed an alley cat. A kitten, really. It had fallen from a window, I think. It was crying, bleeding, I didn't know what to do. I held it in my hands until it went cold."

"Then you didn't kill it."

"I suppose not. I just felt as if I could have done more." He played with his fingers, combing the archives. "When I was eleven, I smoked my first cigarette. A week later I stole my first one. A year later, I was selling them, a few coins here and there. I would give half to Mama, just slip it into her purse. It wasn't much. I got caught a few times. *Signore Russo* beat my back with his cane when he found me fishing through his overcoat. It was at that restaurant, on the corner..."

"*Sopra.*" She knew it immediately.

"Yeah!" he exclaimed gleefully. "I-I was making a delivery, I can barely remember why. I just know that he smoked these long, cigars. They reminded me of cinnamon sticks. They smelled like sulfur and fruit, just a disgusting combination, but I knew they were expensive. I could sell them at a markup to the neighbors who could only afford a single. I thought I was sly, that I blended in like a spy in those junk books David used to read. He had left his overcoat on a hook, near the door. I pretended to tie my boot, turning a little bit at a time to make sure he was preoccupied, shoveling bread into his mouth.

"When I was confident, I reached for his gilded case. But my wrist turned to fire," he mimicked the handcuff. "I don't know who he was, but I assumed he worked for the *Signore*. He had seen right through my ruse. He brought me to Russo and he took the curve of his cane and throttled my back." He thrashed his arm about, conjuring a graveled, stuttering timber. "*Frocio! Piccolo bastardo!*"

Punctuating it with his own laugh, Cecilia wondered aloud, "Why do you find this so funny?"

"It was harmless. It didn't really hurt, to be honest."

"Do you feel the punishment was just?"

"For who? *Signore* Russo, they put two bullets into the back of his head a few years later. He was washing his money; pimping heroin into the alleyways. He was a frail, old troll, and he got what he deserved."

"But did you?"

"A pathetic beating?"

"A poor punishment does not signify that you are absolved enough to continue sinning."

"You knew I committed a few petty crimes. I was a far cry from the Nencini brothers or Almici and his father. I was acting out. Mama had just died. I needed an outlet for my frustrations. I fought a little; tried my hand at dice. Nothing stuck. I saw how the others lived, checking over both shoulders, always tapping their feet, never satisfied.

"Right before David was sent to the hospital, I was coming home late. I worked...remember, I worked for the tailor, *Signore* Staccione?"

"Vaguely."

"He washed and folded, but he mostly repaired men's garments, coats, trousers, whatever you needed. I used to mark the adjustments so he could fix them in the morning. I would close the shop, this pathetic hovel. It was below street level, a staircase so thin that almost everyone tripped. I think that was on purpose, so they would tear their asses and they would have to pay him to fix it." He smiled, trying to extract the more relatable aspect, but he continued, his tone somber. "I took the same route home every day. I knew a few of the crooks in the area, we had sold cigarettes together, but they knew who I was. They wouldn't try to tackle me or steal what little money we had. I heard a woman crying out. Wailing like some sort of a banshee. I knew these kids would set traps, lure men of tough disposition into the alleys and beat them for their watches and billfolds.

"I hid...just listening to her scream." He rubbed his hands together, the center moist with guilt. "I forced myself to look, just once, before I ran. They slit her throat.

"I recognized the pair. I knew *exactly* who they were. The next day, an Inspector came by *Signore* Staccione's asking if we had seen anything. He was confident they would catch them. I knew there was a possibility that they would come after me if I talked. So, I kept my mouth shut. I let it rest." He shifted his legs, easing the muscles awake, leaning his back forward to fight the tension. "My first year coming out of the academy, I had a witness who I *knew* had seen more than he was letting on. I was far from becoming an inspector, but we hated the upper-class officers, and we all were afraid of becoming drafted, so we had to fight for attention. They were all cocky, tearing up the work we had done and starting over as if we wouldn't someday be in their shoes. The witness, he just... he was scared. I recognized that same anxiety. He was pouring over each scenario, trying to find a way to slip free of the punishment, but perhaps contain a bit of glory.

"I beat him. *I beat him*, Cici." He jammed his fist into his palm, simulating the punishment. "I broke two of my knuckles; his jaw. I left him a bruised, swollen mess. He looked like a slab of beef, marbled and swinging from a hook. He gave me the information that I wanted. He was eventually picked up later for his own petty crimes, but he put a murderer in prison. I justified my tactics and I got what I wanted."

Frankie fell silent, trying to control his breathing. He huffed an exasperated sigh, hoping Cecilia could take no more.

"Why did you do it?" she pressed.

"*Because...*" he chuckled incredulously, "I wanted to put someone in prison. I wanted someone to *suffer*. For the rest of their life. To rot in a cement casket; to listen to the others crying and screaming that they too were innocent. Criminals carry their own code, they wipe each other out. Drawing blood in the middle of the street is such an undeserving punishment. They suffer only in the smallest form."

"But their families suffer. *Forever*."

"To me...it was about making the perpetrator languish in his guilt. To laugh at him for being so fucking stupid. To know that daylight would come to him only once a week."

"You enjoyed it."

"It was a drug, Cici. It was addicting. But...eventually, it becomes sickening. The adrenaline does not fuel you enough. It exhausts you, it clouds your judgment. You stop. You stop for what seems like an eternity. It comes screaming back to you, like a feral beast."

"Is this still how you conduct yourself?"

"No...*no*. I...stopped. I stopped when I got married."

"Francesco!" scolding him with delight and curiosity, needling him with her elbow.

"I know, I know!" he smiled.

"You *hated* relationships."

"I was always working! Always trying to hustle the neighborhood for weak links, for a few coins. I never had time or money or fashion sense to court anyone."

"Well!? What happened?"

He chuckled nervously. "Her name w-was Juno."

"Ah! A Greek olive!"

"From the coast. Beautiful. Short, dark, dark hair. Perfect smile. She was a singer, mostly traditional, busking in the bars and restaurants that would even take her. The war had ended, the fascists driven from the streets, but prejudice remained. I married her right away, though. I lost all thought to my career. I just wanted to spend my time with her. I would show up for work, put on my uniform one button at a time, and make myself unremarkable. Risk suddenly became my greatest fear. Why would I want to be away from her for even a moment?"

"You could have quit."

"I wish it could have been that simple. She became ill. Throwing up blood, crying until all hours of the morning. Her mother would stay with her during the day while I ran patrol; I would come home and she would be unconscious on the couch, drenched in the sweat of constant care.

"Juno remained in bed, curled into a ball, unable to find comfort." Frankie had bored to the center of his heart, a rocky stretch that seemed impenetrable a short time ago. He inhaled the mucus that threatened to leak from his nostrils, his voice quivering, tongue moistening his lips over and over as he pressed them together, flexing his muscles to stave off the rush of sadness. "She died. Shortly after that."

"Francesco...I'm...I'm so sorry." She too held back her own emotions, wondering how he could have kept them locked away for so long.

"I was promoted to inspector a month later." He refused to wipe away the tears for fear Cecilia would know he had broken. "That was the last time I visited David. On his twenty-first birthday. I told him about my promotion. I told him I would see him again soon, that I would have more money to make the trip up north. He believed me. I believed it too. I thrust myself into my work, I buried myself so that I would not have to face the emotional weight of the city. I wanted nothing to do with everything that had come before.

"I hate to admit it...I'm sorry that I came on so strong before. I-I ran too. Just like you. I was afraid to poke my head out into the world and have it blow away in an instant. I understand what you did. I understand why you buried your head in the sand. My guilt far exceeds yours, I have so much evil in my bones. I dumped it all on you because I felt alone. And I realized that I *hated* being alone.

"I'm sorry that I have carried this-this expectation of you around in my mind, that you somehow deserved more scrutiny. You know how much I hate being wrong." The last admission made him giggle.

Cecilia remained in a stunned, weeping silence.

"I faltered twice more," he continued, breaking the chilling spell. "As you know, I took the bribe of a lovely young woman."

She remembered their conversation, a grin breaking through the tears. "It's not so shocking anymore," she joked.

He shrugged, "I don't even remember her name."

"And the other?"

"You know this too, but I broke that fucking rat Petrisone's jaw." He cocked his head, looking down through the shotgun blasts in the floorboards. "And I suppose I'm responsible for all those men down there. So, maybe I faltered a bit more than twice. Oh," he remembered. "And I was the one who told Arturo Giordano that you had breath like a dog."

Cecilia slapped at his side in jest. "You!? I can't believe you told him that!"

"He wasn't right for you."

"*Bastardo!* I was so in love with him."

"I'm sorry, I was just trying to protect you."

"Ah!" she squealed. "I cannot believe that was you! He was so handsome."

"He had a lazy eye! And he used to bring two slices of bread for lunch, with nothing on them."

"At least he had lunch! You were right, though. He grew up to be a tremendous *segaiolo*."

"I hope you're not mad at me."

"My ten-year-old self would be. But, I should be thanking you, even though I too hate to admit when I'm wrong."

They both shared in the clarity of the memory, leaning now against each other for support.

"That's all I have to say," Frankie finished, hanging his head, picking at the seams in his dirty trousers. "What is my penance?"

"You have to kiss Arturo Giordano on the lips."

"*Cazzo!* No!"

She drew her knees close to her chest, laughing at his enthusiastic disgust. "I cannot dole out penance. Only a priest is obligated."

"Then why did you make me say all those things?"

"Because the Devil will play us against the middle. He will use what we know to deceive and split us from a unified front. We must unburden our mind to be of clear conscience."

Frankie understood. "I trust you."

"I suppose it's my turn now. *In nomine Patris et Filii et Spiritus Sancti*. It has been one week since my last confession."

"A repeat offender!"

"I have only one thing to confess. Though, the men who have died on this mountain have certainly fallen under my wrath."

"They don't count, Cici. Self-preservation."

She huffed, slightly amused. "I've never told anyone this, Francesco. Not Father Endrizzi, not Father Barahona during our mission trips." She took what she needed, staring at her lover's child. "I am... *anormale*. The others assumed I might be a bit of a *frociarola*, but I conversed with those men because I enjoyed them as people. I cared not that they consummated with each other. It was simply a bit of fun. We are taught, very rigidly that what they are doing...what *I* am doing, is sacrilegious. That we are somehow spitting in God's face because we do not follow simple rules.

"I snuck away to Honduras to escape the prying eyes. There, I found more like-minded women. Women who could share their experience, women who I could love emotionally and physically, judgment far from their mind. This is where I also found the Devil. He taunted me. He would scream from the mouths of children how my fingers smelled of womanly musk. He would accuse me of sinning against God, that my torture would be the rape of my body by vicious, throbbing men.

"The families assumed that these were merely empty threats, a demon trying to provoke and assault their senses with foul language and imagery. But he meant every word. I knew what was ahead of me when I entered the postulancy. I took my vows, fingers crossed, pledging my poverty, my obedience, and my chastity. I walked a dangerous line, fooling those around me, charging my goodwill by dedicating my time to reaching into the mire and saving those who could not save themselves. It was an ever-changing scale. Each act I committed a weight to offset my lifestyle.

"When I returned home, I promised myself that I would take my vows seriously, that I would bury my urges and focus the poison into an antidote. But...I met Annamaria De Sio, and suddenly, my heart and my flesh were all that mattered. We met over a year ago, during a fundraising performance at La Fenice. We had sex in the back of a coat closet. I thought perhaps it was a rare crack in my new facade, but it proved to be a massive hole. It was like having two occupations, the amount of planning and secrecy involved with each meeting. We did not mind much, it was all for a greater good.

"Under the guise of providing counsel, I was called to her home. She had been crying for some time, her eyes bloodshot, face swollen. The police had been called too. She had been raped, the suspect slipping into the night. You know about her father. You know how much power he wields. The investigation fell off immediately, they never caught him, never even lifted a finger. Several weeks later, she was with child. I stood by her side, visited her often. Her brother, Antonio, seemed suspicious of me, always finding an excuse to spy on us, to barge in unannounced.

"Despite the circumstances, I wanted her to keep the child. I wrote letter after letter to Orders in the city, begging for them to take the baby, to raise it, to give it a better home than it would receive under the De Sio umbrella. Anna was, unsurprisingly, nervous about the entire situation. She grew rather distant in unanticipated ways, her concern drifting from the baby, making plans for us for the summer. She was almost...*excited* to release the child. As if he were some sort of evil presence, a creature forming in her belly. She no longer wished to carry the shame."

Frustration attacked her, an anger directed at ghosts unbeknownst to Frankie. "You...you know what happens next," she whispered.

"Is that who you saw in the mountains?"

She nodded. "She was knocked about by a terrible wind, forced to share the hand of her brother for companionship. Even though this child is not mine, even though he shares none of our traits, or even a drop of our blood coursing through his veins, he is half of Anna. And I love him. As much as I did her. He is what I will live for, to raise him to be everything that I am not. I am a liar. I am a thief. I am a fraud. *But he will not end up like David.* I do not care that I am unclean. I will face God someday and I will plead my case. That is my responsibility. Perhaps, today, when David awakens, free of the Devil's influence, God will see the good I have done."

Frankie could not help but stare at his brother's peaceful state, the confession he had uttered in the catacombs of his father's madness vomiting now from his own lips. "Antonio is the father."

"What...?" she croaked.

"I'm sorry...I'm sorry that you have to hear that from me. That you have to hear that after everything you have said. Everyone that

David murdered...they were all children of the Devil. He was trying to weaken any power that he had in order to give the advantage to Papa. He traded Antonio's soul for the baby. He performed his own black mass. He did not want you to be blamed for Anna's rape, to be punished for what he perceived as your sin. David bargained for the child."

"Anna..." barely a whisper, the color vacuumed from her face.

"I don't know what to believe anymore, Cici, I'm only telling you what he said."

"Then...this child. He...he is a spawn." The newborn felt a tremendous bout of boredom, crying out in a shrill, pig-like terror, hungry, wet, and utterly alone.

"You will give him a better life, one free of all of this."

"Evil can find you no matter where you are." She refused to blink, wishing her own heart would suddenly clog, stopping instantly and without pain.

"Then let's stop running. Let's stay and fight."

The Devil's son flooded the cabin with the awful lamentations of neglect.

The opposite end of the bed frame slammed into the ground, bouncing suddenly upward, tipping the entire collection over. Frankie grabbed the edge, fighting against the sudden strength of the inanimate steel, trying to straighten it onto its side.

"Free me! I have little time to spare!"

Cecilia shoved her end forward, righting the mattress and re-settling David onto his back. She splashed him with the salted holy water, driving pain across his face.

"It burns! It fucking burns! *Puttana!*"

"Are they always this strong?" Frankie asked, wiping his forehead free of his labors.

"At first," she admitted.

"David is tender, he shall last long into the solstice!"

"Why is your time limited?" Cecilia pressed.

"The others will come."

"The worshippers?"

"My congregants. My beloved few."

"Then they will rescue you, no?"

"No!" His legs kicked angrily. "Your breath rots with the piss of another woman! *They will take me.* They will make me their slave."

"As you did to them," Frankie noted.

"No! No! No! They chose willingly. They *chose* to bring me here. I did not choose their fat, disgusting forms."

"What is the hurry, then? Maybe we want you to be tortured."

"It is David they will torture! They will slap his flesh with leather whips. Bind his hands and feet in iron. They will defecate upon him and ravage him."

"Under the assumption that they will be doing it to the Devil," Cecilia reminded him.

"You will be humiliated," Frankie said.

The Devil croaked, *thumping* the mattress with his frustration. "They have no right!"

"We've been over this before, tell us what you want!"

"You know! You know! You know! They will call upon me again and again until I have lost my will. Until I have faded from obscurity. My seed must live on! I must die a proper death!"

"You have already spread it!" Cecilia screamed, backing her anger with Antonio's sin and Anna's suffering.

"More! More sons, more daughters. I must have an army of young. Papa promised me the wet mound of my sister."

Frankie slapped David across the face, stunning both Cecilia and the bargaining demon.

"You strike me as a defenseless dog. But you were witness to his ransom. Grant me her fertile womb and I shall leave David."

"I would rather put a bullet through your skull."

"What is he talking about, Francesco?" she asked.

"Papa promised you in exchange for power. To become youthful, to lead the Devil's domain."

"*And I agreed!* If you cannot deliver what I have been promised..."

David's eyes rolled forward, his pupils gyrating as he adjusted to the cabin. "Frankie! Cici! You have to get me out of here. I cannot go back. I cannot go back!"

Cecilia leaned onto the bed, grabbing his head and keeping it still. "David, listen to me. What do you see? When he takes over, what do you see?"

He blinked through the squirming sweat that rolled across the wrinkles in his forehead. "I see only pain. Fields of torture. Oceans of frightened souls. A piercing wind that knocks me down, presses my face into burning sands. He visits me, tells me he has had enough."

She looked back at Frankie, his eyes fixated on the account.

"What does he want?" David whispered.

"I don't know," she admitted.

"Why did you bring us to the cabin?" Frankie asked, moving closer.

"We found what you left in the well, but nothing more," Cecilia reported.

"No!" he cried, thrusting his head away. "We were supposed to finish what we started. You promised me, brave knight!"

The sun had sunk. The night proved impatient, thickening now, masking the forest. Torches provided the necessary advantage they needed.

The grave had been shallow, thin, and marked with crisscrossing branches and wet hemp. The congregants had tossed aside the monument, their tools piled together as rope slithered against the dirt walls, the wooden coffin rising, crashing hard into the snow.

A crowbar pried open the lid, their greedy hands devouring the stockpile of weapons inside.

His tongue received the Eucharist, yellowing teeth slowly munching. A vial of wine tipped into his limited range of motion, the sweetness buzzing against his dry throat.

"The body of Christ."

Frankie took the spring-loaded wafer and followed the ceremony, sipping the alcohol. Cecilia whispered to herself, taking her own communion and making the sign of the cross.

"Is he usually gone for this long?" Frankie asked as she returned the lid to the vial.

"Ceremony often befuddles the Devil. He cannot stand its rigidity. David will no doubt regurgitate what he's swallowed, but to accept the body and blood of Christ, he is acknowledging the presence of something more."

"I believe in God," David stated with the confidence of a child, a filter torn from his conscience that ran to his mouth, the world at his lips with no consequences.

"Of course," she nodded. "Just as the apostles broke bread in

Jesus' last meal, so shall we." She leaned towards Frankie, lowering her voice. "We need to get to the core of David's emotions. If we can figure out what is making him so vulnerable, we can drive the demon out by reversing those expectations."

"Can you loosen my wrists? It's beginning to chafe."

"I'm afraid we can't," Cecilia regretted. "Not for a little while."

"I have to help," he insisted. "The others, they will come."

"Which is all the more reason to hurry," she smiled. "We need you to be strong, David. We need you to tell us what you are feeling inside."

"I'm just glad that we're all back together."

"Is that why you brought us here? So that we'd be together again?"

"I...I think so."

"Why did you leave supplies in the well?"

"For Judgement Day. Papa said that there will come a time we would cast judgment on all those who have wronged us and that we should be protected. I buried what I collected. *Guns.*"

"Who knows about the weapons?"

"E...everyone."

Frankie tried to blanket his frustration with temperance. "Why didn't you tell us?"

"I just forgot." David rolled his lips together, a child's shame driving him into the corner of his mind for punishment, though he told the truth as he saw it.

Frankie rubbed his face, wiping away what he had allowed his expression to conjure. "What about the butane?" he asked.

"For warmth."

"The stationary?"

"To write letters to others who have survived."

"The seeds?"

"To grow sweet smelling herbs."

"The condoms?"

"I don't know," he looked away, blushing, unable to censor his smile. Cecilia chuckled, shaking her head.

"The money?"

"To buy goods. I'm not sure what sort of currency we will accept once the hammer has fallen."

"Where did you find it? The money."

"In the pockets."

"Whose pockets?"

David dared not speak his sin.

"Did it come from the people you killed?"

"Papa needed it."

"For what purpose?" Cecilia interjected.

"To call upon his Master."

"He left behind enough to perform a final mass," Frankie realized. "The ingredients in your letter, you kept some in case something happened to Papa. The body, in the basement, he was to be a vessel too."

"I didn't want to disappoint him. Papa *always* prepared."

"Do you remember anything after the ceremony?"

"Of course. I remember talking to you."

"Do you remember what you said?"

"When?"

"When Papa told you about his plans."

David swallowed, unwilling to make complete and accurate eye contact.

"David, Papa lied to you," Frankie sighed. "You said it yourself. You screamed at him. You beat him to death with your typewriter."

David refused to accept the account, shaking his head in disagreement, tucking his head deep into the mattress. "No, Frankie," he wept softly. "*That didn't happen.*"

"I was there, David. Would I lie to you?"

Mouth agape in confusion, David bucked with trend. "*Yes.*"

"What did I lie about?"

He came alive, awakening into a rambling burst of excitement, the foundation a slab of resentment. "Y-y-you said, you said, you-said, you would visit me in the hospital. Remember? *I remember.* You didn't visit me, Frankie. You either, Cici. You didn't visit me. You know who did? *He* did. He visited me almost every single day. The Messenger, he took me across the ocean. He told me that I should resist. That I was being punished for something that Papa did. They made a deal, and Papa did not deliver. Now he wants me to take the Messenger's place. I told him Papa would explain everything. That's why they had to meet. That's why they needed sacrifices. That's where I got the money. They were going to burn it in the ceremony. *I didn't do anything wrong.*"

"How old are you, David?" Cecilia asked.

"Six. Sometimes I say seven, but I think its six."

"What if I told you that what the Devil is doing is wrong. That he has no reason to keep you his prisoner."

"Don't lie to me, Cici."

"I'm not lying to you. Papa made a mistake, but there is no reason that you should have to suffer. Francesco and I did not suffer."

He was upset, fighting back tears before the tantrum erupted once more. "*I was special.*"

"Of course you were," she comforted, smoothing out his hair. "But that doesn't mean you should be punished."

"Why did he do it?" he sobbed. "Why did Papa allow this to happen?"

"Because Papa is not a good man."

"No! No!" he insisted. "Papa made a mistake, he is not a bad person."

"He hit you, David. He hit me. He hit Francesco. He hit Mama. Would you ever hit Mama?"

He reluctantly shook his head, eyes drooling with long beads. "I don't want to hit Mama."

She placed her hand in his incarcerated palm. "No one wants to hit Mama. You must accept that Papa is a bad person. That he is the reason that we are all here right now. That he is the reason why we all had to go away."

"You didn't have to go to a hospital," he shot back.

"No, but I was ill," Cecilia explained. "I had to find out who I was inside. I tried another form of treatment."

"Is that why you went away?"

"Yes. I had to. I needed to get stronger. I needed to have the strength to come home and face what Papa did. To face the world so that it did not overwhelm me."

"Frankie didn't run."

"No..." he sighed. "I didn't run halfway across the world, but I ran. I buried myself in my work because I was afraid that I would have to remember everything that has happened to us. And I didn't want to."

"But we are here, now," Cecilia reminded him. "Together we are strong enough."

"Papa used to hit me," David whispered like a mouse.

"I know," she said. "I am so sorry that he did that to you. I am sorry that he hurt you and that you could not do anything about it."

"Mama shot him, didn't she?"

Cecilia nodded.

"She did it to protect me. But she didn't know the promise he had made."

"None of us knew."

"I tried to save him. I tried to bring him back, to fix everything. But it didn't work."

"But that's okay, David. You did it because you love him. And we love *you*."

"Does Papa love me?"

Cecilia and Frankie exchanged concern, unsure of how to proceed. She chose the truth. "No. He does not love you."

He nodded in silence. "I have done what he has asked." His tone matured, aging rapidly. "I put his thoughts to paper, I grandstanded with him. I stalked, and I tortured, and I killed at his request. *At his will!* I wanted him to take this illness away from me. I wanted him to treat me like his fucking son!"

The room exploded with gunfire.

Round after round pumped through the walls, boring miniature tunnels as they crossed inaccurately. The wooden slats nailed to the window's frame ripped easily as buckshot tore the pulp, splitting them, ends collapsing.

Frankie dropped to the floor pulling Cecilia with him.

"Stay down!" he ordered as the onslaught continued, dust and splinters spiraling through the air in a brutal sandstorm. The bastard child screamed, waving his arms, *bleating* as the noise clogged his ears. Glass erupted as the carafes of oil shattered across her father's desk, the consecration kit *pinging* as it waddled against the buckling wood's downfall, the legs easily chewed.

The doorway lumbered forward as heavy fire eased the butcher block inside, shoving it onto the floorboards. David howled as sawdust coated him, the ceiling dripping with shards of searing wood. His ejection ceased, the attack momentarily stymied.

"Grab the baby," Frankie said.

Cecilia could barely raise her head in the choking cloud that had been left behind. Frankie crept to the window, keeping out of its sight line. He selected a machine gun and held it to his shoulder.

"Grab the baby," he whispered again. "Cici?"

She shook her hair free of the dust, pushing her attention towards the screaming newborn. She nodded, fighting against the debris as she crawled.

Frankie stood carefully, peeking through what remained of the window's face.

They had been surrounded. Again.

A hundred torches glittered in the forest, the advance wrapping around the cabin, out of view. In unison, they released their magazines, squeezing fresh rounds from the cache they had unearthed. Not all of them had been blessed, others cradling axes, cleavers, weapons of the blue-collared.

Cecilia slithered next to the child, snatching it into her care, rubbing his face free and unclogging his nose. She cloaked him further into the robe, retreating to David's side.

"David?"

"They've come for me," he coughed.

"Deliver us our Master!" It had risen from the Fox, his black robe traded for the blood red of former and blessed Goats. He savored the opulence, his fists full of a shotgun's stock and barrel as he commanded the congregation now.

"*Who?*" Frankie teased.

"Francesco!" Cecilia chided.

"Keep David talking. I will hold them off as long as I can."

"We will take you by force!"

"Usually, I like a little meal before I get fucked!" Frankie rose, *popping* the machine gun into the gathered. The targets scattered momentarily, little Rats and Squirrels foraging elsewhere.

"David?" Cecilia asked. "How old are you?"

"Old enough to fuck," he groaned, his head flopping from side to side. She swept his forehead of splinters and rust.

"We will not negotiate!" the Fox assured him.

"I'll put a bullet in his fucking head!" Frankie offered.

"What?" David clarified, trying to find the source of the threat, tugging against the rope.

"He's pretending," she said, patting his shoulder. "He's just pretending."

"He was always good at that," David sighed, relieved. "Remember when he used to pretend to be the brave knight?"

"I don't remember," she said. "Tell me more about the knight."

The Fox swept his arms outward. "We have an army at your gate! We will burn it to the ground if we have to."

"And if David dies!?" Frankie rose again, throwing a barrage into the reformed, nicking the arm of a Crane and disabling him.

"*Bastardo!*" the de facto leader swore. "Give us, David! We will not hesitate to kill you and the child."

"I don't remember much either," David confessed, suddenly shrinking, a simplistic timber returning, the child rearing itself once more. "The knight traveled on horseback, all day and night," the synopsis somehow rehearsed; called upon easily. "He was scared because he was not the strongest or the bravest. But he volunteered to defeat the dragon."

The Fox instructed an infiltration group of four to scale the shallow hill. Frankie spied them through the peepholes absorbed by the cabin's exterior.

"He crossed streams and fought against hideous creatures that lived in the forest. Even though he knew nothing about the dragon, he still volunteered, because he needed to prove his bravery to a woman he loved. *Valentina*."

The search party pressed themselves to the outside of the cabin, a Wolf sneaking his head around the corner.

"But the knight, he was confused. He became lost in the woods for hundreds of years, unable to find the dragon or the way home."

The Wolf scaled the toppled butcher block, stomping into the empty cabin, finding only David secured to the bed.

"He gave us hope after his horse died, refusing to go on because he realized that he was alone, that he would never defeat the dragon in his state."

The floorboards brightened, a volley of buckshot streaming through the hole in the floor, cutting into the neck of the Wolf.

Frankie hugged the trigger of the machine gun, rotating the barrel as he aimed upward, mowing two more across the chest. The fourth, a stumbling Beaver, tripped over the butcher block, retreating towards his brothers.

Throwing open the cellar door, Frankie tore up the staircase and bolted for the rifle tucked under the window. He rested the barrel against the sill, tracking the fleeing builder. The muzzle flash sparkled as he opened the back of the Beaver's skull, forcing his face into the ground, his weapon rollicking away from his care.

"He came upon a swamp and the dirty cave of an old witch."

Frankie collected the discarded weapons of the search party, leaning another shotgun against the wall, tossing the pistols with the rest.

Cecilia ducked under the staircase, laying the baby onto the ground and settling the robe into a makeshift bassinet. "I will be back for you," she promised, kissing his forehead. Looking down upon the seed of David's tormentor, she wrestled with his origin, hesitating momentarily before she dragged the steamer trunk in front of him, roping off the corner.

"The old witch, she hated the dragon too. She had once been young and beautiful. She had entered the woods to find her love, but she too became lost. There was a special flower, protected by the dragon, that would restore her beauty. But she was too old and frail to fight the dragon. She needed help."

Cecilia carefully ascended back into the cabin as Frankie leaned into the doorway. "Care to try again!?"

The Fox urged another group forward. A Pig shook his head, refusing to sacrifice himself, speaking for the cluster. The Fox raised his shotgun and blew the swine back against the trunk of a pine, practically splitting him in half. "Bring me David!"

A Bear volunteered, grunting as he trudged through the snow, rifle swinging from side to side.

"She would give the knight an elixir that would make his sword pierce the dragon's skin. If he was brave enough, he could defeat the beast and give her the flower. In exchange, she would help him escape the woods."

Frankie spun from behind cover, machine gun screaming in the quiet evening as he ripped through the burly shins, the bone *splitting* and piercing through the thin flesh in a blanket of spewing blood. The Bear fell forward into the powder, his pain muffled by the ice.

"I've got all night!" Frankie chuckled, crouching low as he tossed his weapon aside, cradling a pump-action and returning to his position.

"The knight found the horrible dragon and...he found the horrible dragon and...the knight found the–"

David's chest bucked, rising towards the ceiling.

"*Avē Satana!*" it was faint, from behind the cabin, whispered from the mountain. Just one brave enough to praise their dark Lord.

"*Avē Satana!*" Another.

"*Avē Satana!*" A group now, their chorus not yet unified but growing.

The Devil howled as the moon yawned behind the glowing, tinseled clouds.

"*Avē Satana!*"

"*Avē Satana!*"

"*Avē Satana!*"

David was magnetized, his ribs *cracking* as he rose, dragging the frame of the bed from the safety of the floor. His binding dug into his flesh, a rash developing, droplets of blood trickling down his ankles and wrists.

"They're encouraging him," Cecilia decoded as she crouched next to Frankie.

"What do we do?"

"Disable as many as you can."

Frankie sought the rifle once more, racking the bolt and chambering a new round. Cecilia slid to the broken desk, searching underneath, keeping an eye on the open doorway. She grabbed the flask of holy water and the black compact.

David rose higher, dragging the bed with him, snarling, barking, refusing to speak.

Cecilia emptied the compact of its salt, running the lip up the face of the broken desk, scooping the leaking oil inside, avoiding bits of glass.

"*Avē Satana!*"

The punch arrived almost simultaneously with the shout of the rifle, the congregant gurgling as he was thrust back into the brush, arms hooked against innocent branches. The choir halted, eyes staring at the dead Bull. The gap closed, black robes shuffling to dam the leak.

The Eagle leaned softly against the stock of her own rifle, head resting behind the magnifier as she followed Frankie's reload, the muzzle popping as he emptied into the crowd to her left. She had cleared away a few gasps of the brush, cloaked in enough foliage to remain undetected until the weapon discharged.

Cecilia shoved the flask and compact into her breast pocket, sneaking towards David. She reached upward, grabbing onto the bottom lip of the bed frame. Stiffening her forearms, she pulled, hoisting herself slowly off the ground.

"*Avē Satana!*"

Frankie took out another of the chanting creatures, the Possum limping into the darkness, the roar of those remaining echoing down upon him. The Eagle held her tongue, pausing in the raucous waste of her peers.

Elbows to the straw mattress, Cecilia adjusted herself, digging into the forgiving stuffing. She swung her knee upward, boosting herself forward. Her leg cleared the frame and she pawed for the taught line bolting David to sanity.

The trigger swung, but the well had run dry. Frankie popped back the bolt, staring into an empty chamber. A bullet struck the top lip of the destroyed window, dousing him in dust and shoving him backwards, the rifle falling from his grasp. The Eagle racked the iron bolt, loading a fresh round.

"*Avē Satana!*" It was on top of Frankie, a Goat roaring through the doorway, hurling a woodsman's axe across his body. Frankie stepped back, allowing the blade to catch the wall.

As the barnyard glutton struggled to free the handle, Frankie dipped down, hand slapping a shotgun. He released a blinding fury, severing the leg, tipping the Goat backward. Wrenching the pump, he leaned away, clearing the front of the mask with a blast, sheering the face from the bone.

The shotgun jammed, the breach catching on the spent shell. A Hawk swooped forward, chopping with a serrated hatchet. Frankie jabbed a heel into his stomach, shoving him back momentarily. He extracted the pistol from his waistband and raised it, cupping his hands together.

A Lion stepped through the barrier, taking the first bullet against his shoulder, the Hawk steadied his wounded comrade and shoved him away. Two more bursts and the feline slammed into the floorboards, a healthy spray coating Frankie's trousers. The Hawk stared just long enough, his hesitation painting the wall behind him. As the pistol's slider locked into place, begging for a fresh magazine, the congregant slid to his rear, leaving a slug-like trail of blood in his wake.

Frankie tossed the empty weapon out the window and grabbed the jammed shotgun, banging free the loose shell.

"Avē Satana!"

Cecilia popped open the compact, holding steady as the bed teetered. "Lord God almighty, before whom the hosts of angels stand in awe, and whose heavenly service we acknowledge; may it please you to regard favorably and to bless and hallow this creature, oil, which by your power has been pressed from the juice of olives."

Frankie forced another handgun into his waistband, peeking through the window. A stream of congregants labored forward, torches in one hand, weapons in the other. From her scope, the Eagle flung a volley of covering fire, dropping him out of view once more.

"You have ordained it for anointing the sick, so that, when they are made well, they may give thanks to you, the living and true God."

A blind warning from Frankie's shotgun thinned the herd by one, but the indoctrination of their chanting gave hope to those who remained.

"*Avē Satana!*"

"Grant, we pray, that those who will use this oil, which we are blessing in your name, may be protected from every attack of the unclean spirit, and be delivered from all suffering, all infirmity, and all wiles of the enemy."

A Snake ate snow as Frankie's pistol hugged the doorway, unloading until it could stomach no more. The unharmed returned fire, dropping him to his stomach, tossing the useless handgun aside.

Cecilia sought the fertile ground too, burying her head in the sweaty imprint of David's body. "Let it be a means of averting any kind of adversity from man!"

The black robes charged in a deliberate column, sheering the window frame away from the studs. Muzzles blared like trumpets of war, spent shells melting the high drift snow as they sank to the soil. The Eagle trudged to a new position, eyeing the remnants of the levitating bed, unable to find a tactically advantageous position.

"...redeemed by the precious blood of your Son, so that he may never again suffer the sting of the ancient serpent!"

Kneeling in the freezing mixture, the rifle took aim, Cecilia's wavering torso caught between the thin, black wires of the cross-hairs. The round disobeyed, the bed manipulated by David's violent refusal. It entered through the bottom of his foot, splintering the bone and exiting upward, snapping the line wrapped around his ankle. The Devil professed his pain, knocking Cecilia aside momentarily.

"Through Christ our Lord!" She dumped the oil into her palms.

The congregants ceased their chanting, their barrels steaming in the tepid mountain air.

"Amen," breathed Frankie.

Cecilia slapped her drenched hand against David's face, rubbing him thoroughly with the purifying ointment.

Frankie leapt, laying a base of fire into the cluster of waiting robes. They had little time to freshen their magazines as his forearm tightened, calling for shell after shell, the spreading pellets ripping the soiled fabric as it bruised their skin, boring like a flaming drill.

"Lord, have mercy on us," Cecilia grunted as she kept her slathered fingers across David's twisting snarl. "Christ, have mercy on us."

With the shotgun empty, Frankie discarded it, reaching for the Beretta. A platoon of buckshot thundered through the short wall, his left arm flapping forward. His already crusted dress shirt tore at the shoulder, a celestial bruise erupting. The tiny projectiles gorged on his muscle, ravaging the entrance wound, but refusing to rip off a healthy cut of meat entirely.

"Lord, have mercy on us. Christ, hear us!"

David wriggled his free limb as blood pooled in the sole of his boot, the overflow plopping onto the ruffled blanket below.

Frankie peeked through the newly formed porthole, watching as a Walrus snapped open the double-barrel and extracted the spent cartridges. A blur interrupted the reload as a Raccoon vaulted through the window frame. Frankie uncorked the axe from the wall and swung high, embedding the blade into the scavenger's neck before he could turn around.

The Walrus reset the barrel and took aim, the blast removing the top of the Raccoon's head, his torso colliding with the carving table, knocking David's supplies overboard. Frankie found the safety of dust and spent ammunition, avoiding the collateral damage. Scrambling back to the wall as their collective open wounds bathed the floorboards, he stuck the Beretta through the wall and wasted the magazine into the tusked ocean dweller.

"God, the Father of heaven!"

David's arms began to twist against their natural limit, the skin stretching, muscles rippling as they fought against the angle.

"God the Son, Redeemer of the world!"

He began to seize, a vile stench releasing from his mouth as bile poured from the corners.

"God the Holy Spirit!"

"I..." the Devil breathed. "Will...*break*...him."

"Holy Trinity, one G-"

The demon took offense, coating the walls with protest.

Cecilia realized the displeasure. "*In nomine Patris et Filii et Spiritus Sancti.* Holy Trinity! Have mercy on us!" She smothered his lips, forcing what remained of the blessed oil to drip into his throat. "Holy Trinity! Have mercy on us!"

A growling chorus of unsatisfied souls bellowed from David's gyration.

"Holy Trinity! Have mercy on us!"

The Walrus stumbled to a single knee, his weapon hungry, his pockets empty, his chest gushing.

"Holy Trinity! Have mercy on us!"

Frankie scooped up his mother's shotgun and marched through the doorway, into the fields of ice.

"Francesco!" Cici cried as he escaped her view.

"The Trinity shall be tortured in the trio of my holy jaws!" the Devil threatened. "I will chew with pus and bile and blood!"

"Holy Trinity! Have mercy on us!"

David shuddered, unable to speak against the prayer.

"Holy Trinity! Have mercy on us!

Frankie approached the heaving congregant, loading the barrel with the loose shell from his breast pocket. The Eagle tracked him, layering his head in the center of the glass. "How many more!?" he screamed at the thinning border of loyalists.

"As many as it takes!" the Fox declared, stepping from the

brush, blocking the sightline.

"Resist him, David! Holy Trinity! Have mercy on us!"

"H-have..." David spewed through the growing pool drowning his molars.

"Have mercy on us! Say it, David!"

"H-h-h..."

"Holy Trinity!"

"Have..."

Frankie ripped the mask from the Walrus, placing the shotgun to the sweating, middle-aged head. "What will you own when we release the spirit? You will have nothing!"

"We will have you!" a Dog screamed.

"I hope you don't disappoint easily," he smiled, his mind dumping a reserve of adrenaline, fueling a bit of bravado. He hugged the trigger, casting the visage across the snow, a smoldering crater remaining as the neck fluttered into the chill.

"Have...have mercy on us!" David choked. "Holy Trinity! Have mercy on us!"

"*In nomine Patris et Filii et Spiritus Sancti.*"

David blinked, a clarity returning, a realization of his height, the trusses within sneezing distance. His strength failed him as the bed plummeted. Cecilia lost her balance, sewing her fingers through the dense blanket, receiving no guarantees.

The back legs of the frame bent first, the rusted steel grinding against the sudden pressure. Cecilia's head whipped as they made landfall, the vibrations casting her overboard, jamming her shoulder into the floorboards. David met the moist reservoir of sweat, blood, and leakage, bouncing with the aftershock, his limbs calling for direction.

As he settled, he exhaled in an anemic moan, the oxygen sucked from his lungs, the fireplace doused, the cabin suddenly drowned in a black sea.

Frankie turned towards the snuffed and once-calming flame, convinced that he had failed. The remaining congregants charged, torches and blades thrusting into the calm night as they scaled through the tracks made by their fallen brethren. He simply froze, affixed to the stiffening layer below, watching as the balls of flame buzzed in attack formation.

Terrible wings, hulking and stiff with dry feathers, blanketed the light, wrapping Frankie in burlap layered with rot. The Messenger shielded him as the muffled ejections pelted the loose plumage. Frankie dropped his weapon, slamming his face into the material, wrapping himself into the folds and shutting his eyes.

The congregants exhausted their energy into the beast, finding no passage.

"Stand down!" the Fox commanded. *"Your Master is within these walls."*

The Messenger unfurled his protective span. He placed his arms upon Frankie's shoulders and peeled him away from the fibrous sea. He nodded towards the cabin, pointing encouragingly.

Frankie understood. *"Grazi,"* he whispered, stumbling towards the interior, drunk with exhaustion.

The torches retreated several lengths, giving the Messenger time to face them. With scythe unfurled, cocked at an offensive angle, he allowed them to speak.

"You will not stand in our way!" the Fox barked.

"He has turned against us," a Cat uttered.

"No!" The sly leader calmed the anxious crowd. "The Messenger is loyal. *Is he not?*"

Frankie scrambled to Cecilia's side, shaking her shoulder. "Cici?"

"Frankie?" It had come from David, slumped towards the broken angle of the bed frame.

"We have to get to the cellar."

"What's happening?" He peeked at the unfolded wings of his guardian as he stood in front of the threatening mob. "Da-Da..."

Frankie clasped the sputtering with his hand, shushing him. "David, we need to be very quiet. We need to get the cellar and regroup, *bene?*"

An understanding nod.

Frankie grabbed a blade from the knife roll and slit the remaining threads of David's restraints, tucking the sharp end into his pocket. "Help me with Cici."

David pressed his injured foot to the floorboards.

The Messenger cocked his head at the anger and rage that boiled from within the cabin.

"They torture your Master!" the Fox pleaded.

Cici bolted upright, hair matted with sweat and sawdust, eyes pulsating in uneven rhythms.

"Cici, David's hurt."

"Are they gone?" she mumbled, limping towards them.

"Our guardian is back."

"The cellar?"

He nodded.

"You cut him loose?"

"You have a better way to move him?"

She studied the pain in David's face. He needed a change of venue. Her arm slipped beneath his as they rose. "Grab what you can," she ordered. "I'll get him down there."

They hopped together towards the ringlet, Cecilia balancing him like a crutch as she flung open the lid.

Frankie examined the proceedings outside, collecting his father's sidearm and the remaining pump-action. He emptied the tray that had once contained David's meager rations and loaded it with the homemade brew, piling atop the stationary as he swept his arms across the floor. He stuffed the billfold into his back trouser pocket.

Snapping open the top of the butane tin, he began spraying the bed, coating the couch and desk, soaking the fireplace. He ripped the remaining sleeve from his bleeding arm and splashed it with the last droplets of fuel. Wrapping it around the edge of the axe's handle, he secured it with a tight knot. He discarded the empty can and slipped down the staircase, closing the cellar door behind him.

"Let's take a look at that foot."

The Messenger backed the ravenous crowd another length, fingers twiddling against the staff of his weapon.

"You cannot prevent us from proceeding. If we must strike you down, we will do so."

"Perhaps he is looking for gainful employment?" a suggestion rang.

The Messenger huffed an annoyed snort.

David turned his head away, grinding his teeth as Frankie slid his boot off. The stone floor twinkled as a stream of blood poured from the interior.

"Through and through," Frankie smiled.

"How do you know?" David spat, breathing in shallow cycles.

"Two holes," he pointed as he popped the lid on the clear homebrew, drenching his foot.

He writhed, fighting against Cecilia's calming vice. "Fuck! Fuck!"

The alcohol stirred with the blood below, clearing away the grime still sticking to his heel.

"Not exactly sterile," Frankie joked, taking a swig for himself.

"But delicious."

David giggled, calling for a sip. Cecilia granted permission.

The brew went down easily. "I can barely taste it," he confessed, drinking more.

"*Bene, bene,*" she tempered, grabbing the bottle, returning it to Frankie, exchanging it for the checkered pattern of their makeshift coffee filter. "This is filthy."

Frankie soaked it in the alcohol. "Better?" Frankie quizzed.

She furrowed her anger, accepting the nature of the antiseptic with reservation. She carefully wrapped David's foot in the stained bandage.

"Careful, *careful!*" he directed.

Frankie picked up the woodsman's axe and twirled it in his palms. He walked toward the middle of the cellar and picked a competent spot, calculating risk. He raised the blade over his head and jammed it into the joist, keeping the butane-soaked rag at a respectable level. He fished the crumpled matchbook from his pocket, tearing a bent stalk, leaving a single bulbous head to wallow in the grime of his trousers. With the flame limited against the short length, he tapped the axe's handle, watching as the heat leapt onto the noxious fumes.

The material plumed, brightening the cramped cellar, the smoke swirling through the shotgun blasts in the floorboards. To the first few treads of the staircase, he crept, finding relief. Spreading the wound on his arm he inspected the torn chunks. He splashed the exposed muscle with the stinging alcohol, clenching his fist against the pain. Rotating his shoulder blades, he could feel a catch in the motion, a pellet blocking mobility. Another wave of the liquid, his hand tightening into a pale, shivering mass.

His free fingers dove inward, slithering between the folds, the coagulation bursting as new blood squirted free. He groaned through the bubbling anxiety in his stomach, his eyes fluttering from the sudden onset of shock. A nail scraped against the steel sphere, rolling it between index and thumb. Freeing it in a wave of blood, he held it in his palm, disgusted at its pathetic form and its utmost power. He tossed it away, dousing the wound once more.

"Ten. To the basin of the river. Use the sewers." The Fox whispered to those willing, the volunteers escaping quickly into the darkness as the Messenger held his ground. "David has told us of your plight. Do you not wish to return to a semblance? To finally die?"

Cici carefully ripped the already torn hem of her skirt. She swung the holy gauze underneath Frankie's underarm. "How much longer?" he pried.

"Hmmm?" she concentrated on tucking the excess into the folds.

"How much longer do you think this will take?"

"I..." She offered an uncertain outcome, refusing to finish tending to his arm.

"Cici...? What?" His eyes darted, studying her timidity.

"I...*nothing*. I am afraid that he will outlast us...that is all."

"I can hear you," David mumbled. "Sounds like a bunch of wasps buzzing."

The gathered loyalists cocked their weapons, raising the cold barrels towards The Messenger.

"You have been warned! If you shall protest further, we will strike you down. We know you will not resist with violence, we know that you will not break your oath."

His bony fingers curled around the shaft of the scythe, determined to remain stoic, his size and determination to frighten them away. But the first volley voided all that he had pledged, his shoulder bucking against the force. He swung, removing the upper half of a Rabbit as the congregant unleashed a blast from his revolver. The Eagle tracked the swift and improbable motion, anticipating his targeting. Dangling amongst empty air, she rubbed the trigger.

The chorus sang, the hill blaring with a syncopated hymn.

David screamed, throat barely able to keep the pitch steady. Frankie and Cici rushed to his side, pressing him against the stonewall, his breathing erratic.

The Messenger threw his wings against the shelling, the rounds zipping through the coarse feathers, pelting his skull as they knocked him about like a novice boxer. He summoned an attack, thrusting the span outward, knocking back the first row of congregants.

The rifle blared amongst the empty frame as he slid into view, the round severing a curling horn, casting it aside as the Messenger rushed. He *cracked* through the line of huddling and reloading and devoured a pair at the neck. He pivoted, reseating the scythe as he maintained his ground, his robe fluttering in majestic shards as they kept up the attack.

"He is but a sinful man!" the Fox called as he steadied his shotgun and chipped away at the Messenger's face. "A liar! A murderer!"

David wept as he reached for the surface. "No! Leave him alone!" They held his torso, digging into his ribs as he wrestled for freedom.

"David, no! You have to stay here!"

He fought against his eyes as they curled into the white bath of the Devil's control.

"You have sold him! Sold him into a dishonorable death!"

"Why does it matter!?" Cecilia shot back. "You have others who are loyal to you!"

The Messenger fell to his knees, palms flattened, crushing snow into dirt. A blast ripped through his back, a wing shearing at the joint, fluttering free.

"He is the only one loyal to me!" The Devil shouted.

Cecilia glanced at Frankie, unsure of the meaning.

"You know all about loyalty, Frankie! You wavered between thieves and crooks, giving them what they desired. You trusted only one. Only *you*."

"David! Be strong!" Cecilia urged.

"You sold them out, just like you sold Da-"

Frankie launched his hand around David's throat.

"Francesco!" Cici blared, clawing at his wrist.

"You betrayed both sides," the Devil spat. "So, they came for the middle."

The Messenger turned towards the Fox as he loomed overhead, the cadre now encircling him. "Who are you loyal to?" The beast turned away from his captors, wheezing in agony.

"Who are you loyal to!?" the Devil sneered.

"What is he talking about?" Cici begged.

Frankie released his grip, turning his back on the taunting demon.

"Yes, Francesco," he mocked. "Tell us. Tell us about *Signore* Beneventi. About the Vecoli family. About poor, dead Juno. Her cunt ravaged."

Cecilia launched a weak hook into David's nose. She covered her mouth, yelping at her sudden act of disobedience.

"*Cazzo!*" the Devil sneered as a thin line of blood leaked from his nostril.

"It's true." Frankie sighed. "I made deals with the *mafioso*, I gave them information about raids, about checkpoints, investigations. I helped get their men out of prison; I dropped charges, lost paperwork in a minefield of other cases. In exchange, they would help me target their enemies, put them behind bars, pad my arrest record.

"I got greedy. I got *fucking* greedy. I pushed it too far. I was taking bribes from everyone to protect everyone else. I was pushed into a corner. It drove me fucking mad, I could barely keep my information straight. Suddenly, my friends had become my enemies. I distributed false information and someone important, someone with influence, was at the wrong place at the wrong time.

"They came for me. They came for Juno and her mother. So, I turned on all of them, sold them all out to my peers. We cleaned out the streets, one bullet at a time. We raided their distribution networks, the dockyards, the warehouses. We fought their flames with our own, steel against steel. They made me an inspector. I had finally made it, Cici!"

"You sold your soul for the sweetened taste," the Devil screamed. "Just like you sold out the Messenger!"

The final judgment came from the surface, a huddled mass of exploding barrels felling the last of their guardian. Their eyes clung to the woodwork above, listened as the last of the bloodied echoes died.

"You sold him to the cancerous betrayers! I will have no protection!" the Devil wept.

"He could have taken you and delivered you into the hands of these *freaks*! But he didn't! He chose David over you."

"Keep your tongue hitched!"

Frankie shoved his father's sidearm into David's forehead.

"Keep talking," Frankie encouraged, leaving a swollen indentation.

The Devil cringed as he tried to lean away from the threat.

"What else do you have to say!?" Frankie screamed. "Eh? I sold what I had to get ahead and I lost...I lost what mattered to me. I can fucking admit that. It ruined whatever is left inside of me. You are nothing but a voice. You can do so little it is fucking pathetic. I won't listen to your shit anymore!"

"But when will you turn on us?" the Devil teased. "When will your family become overwhelming? When will you forget what is right and what is wrong? When will up become down and an embrace become a loaded pistol? You make promises and you break them, Francesco. You cannot escape that. The question is, how long until you betray all of us? Huh, Cici?"

His lips moved purposefully, forming the correct vowels and consonants, but the voice seemed to echo only between her ears. His eyes had wandered back towards Frankie, but he was challenging her.

Only her.

"How much shall he weigh us down?" The air moved with much burden, the muscles pulsating slowly. "He dragged you here, did he not? Convinced you to leave the city behind. Those precious children, lamenting your absence. Take him, Cici."

A throbbing tone guided her towards the pump-action. "Just a feather to weigh it down, a lifetime of fear to vanish."

A spell of silence had been cast upon Cecilia, her eyes focusing once more on the straining veins of Frankie's face, the anger and guilt worming its way into his brain. "No," she huffed. "You will not build a wall between us. Not now!"

"He lied!" David thrashed his fingers, clawing at Frankie's face. "He lied to you. To *us*!"

"I have lied as well!" she said.

"No, Cici! *You are pure.*"

"We all have lied. But I refuse to leave their side. *You* are alone. The Messenger has chosen David over you. And so have I."

"You promised," David mumbled, closing his eyes to release the shivering tears. "All I have left is you. You promised me, brave knight."

Frankie removed the pistol, the barrel shaking uncontrollably, his adrenaline drenching his back in a garish stain. "I promised...?"

"Here. *Here.* You promised you would finish. *You never finished.* You left me with him. In the dark. I was alone. *I was not brave.*"

"Brave...?" Frankie whispered. "Fuck...fuck!" He ducked behind the staircase, throwing open the steamer trunk. He thundered through his father's belongings, grabbing the sheepskin binder. He paused, peering into the corner quizzically. He hurried to David's side.

"This," he shook excitedly. "Right? *We never finished it.*" He turned towards Cecilia. "There's a baby back there, by the way."

She bolted for the child, having forgotten him. He was in fine spirits, cooing and blowing bubbles as she cradled him.

"You kept this," Frankie continued.

"We were interrupted," David argued.

"Call it an intermission," a hand squeezing his shoulder. "A really, really long intermission."

Cecilia knelt next to Frankie, staring at the binder as he flipped through it. "What are you doing?" she whispered.

"We never finished," he reiterated. "Just the ending, that's all we need."

"I never even wrote one..." David admitted, smearing his sadness. "It doesn't have a proper ending."

Frankie dove for the stationary and the unsharpened pencil.

He handed David the parchment, tapping his pockets quickly. He giggled as he pulled free the knife, whacking maniacally at the flattened edge, forming a jagged point.

He blew away the shavings and handed over the acceptable utensil. "Tell us what we need to do."

"Francesco, have you gone mad?" she whispered, grabbing his healthy arm.

"You said we needed to find David's weakness. We need to reverse his expectations. *We never finished.* He's rooted to that moment before Mama broke the spell. He expects to never finish what we started because he was all alone, he couldn't do it himself. Let's finish his masterpiece. Give him the attention he lost."

Cecilia followed his logic closely, realizing the simple observation. "What do we need to do, David?" she asked.

David, taken aback, blinked through his confusion, looking up from his notes. "Uh...we need a sword."

Frankie dove to the corner, retrieving the shovel.

"An elixir."

The fermented alcohol.

"A suit of armor."

His father's infantry jacket.

"A dragon."

Frankie bounded from beneath the darkened arch with the disfigured mask of a congregant.

"Dragon's breath."

The final match, bent and pathetic, but nonetheless useful.

"The mean, old witch."

"I suppose," Cecilia reluctantly agreed as Frankie swept the robe that had adorned the child across her back.

"Wings, for the transformation scene."

"D-don't give too much away," Frankie said excitedly, peering through the many holes above. He saw the still, white wings peeking, cast to the cabin floor in the confusion. He snaked his arm through a gash, dragging them below as the first boots entered quietly through the frozen doorway.

David scribbled furiously across the pages, biting his lip as his brain surged with possibilities.

One by one the still-loyal congregants shuffled through the debris, forming a prayer circle. The Fox entered last, allowing one final glance at the Messenger's silent corpse. He nodded towards the Eagle as she sucked on the end of a cigarette, straddling the tree line; keeping a vigilant watch.

The bright green head of the papier-mâché beast roared with David's prepubescent pitch. He pulled down on two, thin streams of hemp, rubbing against the thickness of the maple's branch, raising the clunky arms of the dragon. He alternated each claw, swiping the air with malice.

A colander slung low over his eyes, Frankie lifted the rim slightly, eyeing the ferocious foe. Thrusting his cardboard sword, he jabbed, parried, and swung.

But the dragon would not be defeated.

David released one of his tethers and grabbed a handful of red and yellow leaves, tossing them awkwardly with his tiny hands at Frankie's struggling knight.

"His fire breath is too much!"

He fell hard onto his back, the sun streaking through the crowns of pine, blinding him momentarily. "*Vaffanculo!*" A breeze swayed the shadows, granting him relief as the old, unfriendly witch popped her head over his, bathed in a black robe, white moss hanging in ribbons.

"Remember our arrangement!" Cecilia snarled.

"I am not brave enough!" the knight whined.

"You have been lost in this forest for hundreds of years, yet you still live! Is that not bravery?"

"But I am without my love! Without my poor Valentina."

"I will guide you from the forest. But you must retrieve for me the flower I need."

"Without Valentina then what do I have to live for?"

"Slay the dragon, brave knight, and you shall see."

David roared, throwing more leaves at them.

"The elixir!" the knight remembered.

From her cloak, her father's flask. The knight climbed to his feet, loosening the lid and downing the sweet gold.

Frankie tossed the empty bottle of homemade alcohol into the corner of the cellar. He hoisted the dirty shovel into the air, his other hand grabbing the dog-eared, yellowing pages of the decades-old script from his waistband. "I have tasted the Elixir of Bravery!"

The congregants above exchanged glances of uncertainty, the slightly muffled performance, though, intriguing them.

"I will slay thee, dragon!" As Frankie poked the mask perched on Cecilia's hand, David feigned the beast's reactions, keeping the incestuous child close to his thundering heartbeat.

Cecilia struck the match against the coarse ridge of sandpaper, waiting until the flame had settled before tossing it at Frankie who avoided it easily. "Your flames cannot harm my precious armor," tapping his father's tight uniform and field helmet. He switched pages, nodding in agreement with the dialogue. He chopped at the mask again, forcing her to drop it to the ground. "I have slain the dragon!"

He trudged around the room, rummaging thoroughly through each corner. "But I cannot seem to find the flower the old witch needs."

David hissed, drawing his attention to the child. Frankie scooped up the baby, declaring victory. He checked the script, "With this flower, I will finally find a way out of the forest."

"That's Cici's line," David corrected.

She donned the black robe, swiping the script, clearing her throat. "With this flower, I will finally find a way out of the forest."

"Will you keep your promise?" Frankie wondered as David mouthed the words in perfect harmony. "Will you guide me from this forest to my Valentina?"

"Brave knight," she assured. "Your Valentina has been here all along."

She quickly shed the stench of the congregant's robe and slipped into the white wings. "For I have~"

"Twirl," David insisted. "Do a twirl, you have to let the audience know there has been a transformation.

Cecilia hesitated, unsure of the direction. Frankie urged her, opening his eyes wide. Her heels spun as she rotated. "For I have been your Valentina all along!" She looked back down at the script. "Uh..." turning it over, gliding over dialogue she had already delivered.

David held out the stationary fresh with his scrawl, shaking happily. They each took a copy and returned to their marks.

"I have been searching for you for over a hundred years," Frankie said.

"Brave knight, so have I."

"I am not brave. I simply drank an elixir to cure me of my fear."

"But, brave knight, this was no ordinary elixir. It was only water. You conquered your fears on your own."

"How?"

"You used your undying love for me to defeat the beast. Now, we can be together forever."

Frankie awkwardly shuffled forward, leaning in as Cecilia angled away from his disturbed expression. He gave her a peck on the cheek.

They both separated, eyeing David for approval.

"You can do better than that! This is the grand finale! *Everyone is watching.*"

Frankie slapped his palm over Cecilia's mouth, kissing the back of his own hand as he dipped her away from David's critique. He released a *smacking* effect, sealing the performance as they righted themselves.

David erupted into applause, brimming with satisfaction as he stepped over the slain dragon puppet, releasing his hold on the strings. Frankie and Cecilia bowed to their adoring audience as they giggled, the summer afternoon carrying their camaraderie high into the lilac peaks.

Laughter permeated through the floorboards, rising into the rigid ears of the Fox. A Rat reached for the ringlet, but a hand stopped him. A whisper through the masks. They began to quietly reload, fresh magazines summoned from their deep pockets.

Frankie and Cecilia began clapping, focusing their attention on the playwright. David bowed as well as he could in his suspended state.

"*Bravo! Bravo!*" they called.

David blew kisses to the masses, waving his injured hand as he blushed.

He vomited suddenly, a thick paste that jolted past his feet.

"Enough!" the Devil screamed. David's body began to seize once more, his jaw clenching, neck pivoting to fight their presence. "This Holy Trinity churns my stomach! Your laughter sickens me!"

They took to his side, clamping his arms down, preventing an easy escape.

"Do you fear love?" Cecilia asked.

"Love!? Love! A disgusting concept. Chemicals infecting the brain. Blood to the loins! Hard! Wet! Nothing more."

"You have never been loved, Lucifer," she teased.

"Wrong! Wrong! My followers raise me from my slumber, from my domain."

"They are not your followers. They are not loyal to you. They do not love you."

"*Zoccola!* They worship me."

"Because they fear you. They fear what you will do to them."

"*That is love!* The other princes have turned on me, relegated me to servant! My kin will rise, their sins will run rampant on the circles, then I will be freed of my obligation. No longer will I live in Satan's shadow. I will rule from the subterranean lake! Frozen, paralyzed, no longer bothered with the mundane, the cruel. I will take the throne from them!"

"Satan's shadow?" she whispered.

"No one will control me! I will rule supreme! My eternal death will come upon the layers of Hell and my children will rule above ground. I will no longer lift my hands in exhaustion. I will be free. *Free!*"

"Mammon?" she attempted, unsure if this particular tree would bear fruit.

"What?" The Devil paused, eyes widening.

"Beelzebub?"

"What are you doing?"

"Amon?"

"Do not speak their names!"

"Asmodeus?"

"The princes of Hell will come to my aid!" David bucked, pushing Cecilia away, grappling with both hands as Frankie tried to shove him against the stone.

"Belphegor?"

"No! I will not bow before the recollections of a-"

"Leviathan!"

David released his struggle, clawing at his own face, shaving a thin layer of dermis underneath his fingernails.

Cecilia stood, shoving her finger forward. "Leviathan!"

The hounds of hell growled in his throat as he banged his head against the wall.

"It is not Satan," she said, fumbling in her breast pocket for her flask.

"What?" Frankie's incredulous pause gave her no hurdle.

"It is Leviathan. One of the princes of Hell, guardian of envy."

"Stop!" Leviathan cried, his face stiffening as his lips peeled back past the gumline.

Cecilia grabbed David's face, angling it towards hers. "David, you must listen to me. You can defeat him. *You are brave.* He holds no power over you, he is merely pretending. He is a simple minion of Satan. He is Leviathan. An envious creature who preys on the weak. *You are not weak.* Drive him out. Drive him out with this elixir."

She dumped the flask into his throat, shoving the holy water into his esophagus. A whining signal began to invade their ears, as David screamed in a frequency they could not control. The alien *bleat* drove them to plug their ears, the congregants above dropping their weapons as they too were overcome with a similar tone, wrestling themselves to the ground for relief. As the demon sunk into darkness, he dragged David with him.

The sky threatened with rolling plumes of gray ash, curling in an approaching storm that rose from the peaks of the golden dunes. As the wall of horror crawled forward, the interior beckoned with streaks of flame and light, blood exploding from the electric arcs that punished the ground below. Thunder bellowed with the roar of a blacksmith, the embers spewing into the sand as the sky above collapsed, tearing holes of fire in the storm.

Leviathan stood alone.

Cloaked in black, his spine bent, he turned his pale visage into the shimmering heat.

A figure walked calmly, arms at his side, chest wrapped in emerald wool, unafraid of the heat.

"Begone!" the demon shouted, his bony palm flat.

But the figure continued; determined.

Leviathan hurried from the top of the dune, feet sinking into the fine grain. Hyperventilation prevented a smooth motion, his eyes fluttering as he tripped. The landing was soft, the descent exacerbated by his robe, rolling against the incline.

He was deposited at the foot, sand blowing into his mouth, his limbs suddenly too heavy. A hand gathered the material, cinching it upright, his buckling knees barely able to keep him afloat.

"You kept me imprisoned," David began. "*For twenty-six years.* You raised my father's hand against me. Against my family. The ones that he loved. The ones that *I* love. You struck fear into me. You threatened me. You controlled me. You convinced me that I am alone, that I have no one.

"You make me hurt those who do not deserve it and drag me into the black sea, drowning me over and *over* again. You refused to let me grow, stunting me, keeping me simple. *You lied!* A pathetic ruse to keep a child-*a child*-your plaything. You made me think that I had destroyed the only thing left in my life. You drove me from Frankie and Cici, you made me believe that I was wrong, that I was incurable!"

"I am abandoned by my brothers too," Leviathan sobbed. "They are praised! They are rewarded, yet I remain alone, charged with plowing these fields, a never-ending parade of pathetic sinners that I am forced to punish. I want to be encased in ice, to close my eyes from the madness. My armies, my kin would have risen. They would have overthrown the masses! The throne was mine! I would have been King!"

"You are a chess piece, a mere pawn for your brothers," David reminded him. "You are unloved; born envious, untrusted by those who claim your blood. You have been cursed to walk this desert alone because you refuse to wear a mask befitting of your role. You steal and mimic and coerce those into giving you what you want because you will never earn it yourself. This Hell shall remain your punishment: an eternity of choking in the dust that you have made with your selfish behavior."

Downward, his entire weight bending. Leviathan's face sifted through the sand as David pressured the back of his head, straddling the flailing torso, drowning him.

"This is not what I deserved," David wept, flattening his hands. "I am no longer envious, like you. My family returned to my side, just as we once were. I will finally return to those who love me. You will only sink to the bottom, buried below my happiness."

The demon's arms clawed the gold dust, fighting for dominance, scooping a mound into his fist. The pressure overpowered him as the last remnants of his power faded, his frail form growing silent and still. David admired the crystals as they swept over the robe. He investigated the distant storm, worried that he would not have time to revel in his victim.

Rolling off Leviathan, he laid his back against the warm surface, looking up into what remained of a crumbling, dying star.

David bolted forward, falling hard onto his knees. A viscous tar spewed from his mouth, gurgling in a fountain-like eruption that inched forward like hungry magma.

"David!" Cecilia called, gripping his shoulder.

He continued to vomit, back *cracking* as he heaved, throat singed with every wave that passed through. His eyes watered, veins creasing the white surface as his pupils returned. His cheeks ran red with effort as mucus slithered down his nose.

The last of the concentration slipped past his lips, his revulsion driving him from the puddle and into Frankie and Cecilia's waiting arms. The substance burst into a brilliant flame, the forked crown of red and yellow waves shooting upward through the floorboards.

The butane sniffed the heat, locking onto the inferno. The cabin erupted, the pattern indeterminate as the cloaks of those who remained roared with heat, the greed splashing to the others as they ran for the freedom of the night, clogging the doorway. They collapsed, trapping each other, the intelligent dragging those who had fallen.

"David!?" Cecilia inspected, curling his face towards her.

"H-he's gone...Cici. He's gone." A smile of relief, a beautiful angle of happiness.

Frankie helped them to their feet. "Grab the baby!"

"Valentina?" David asked as he leaned against his brother's crutch.

He drove them forward, ducking under the curling snicker of the blaze above. Frankie flung the cellar door upward, breaking the hinge and dislodging it.

Cecilia covered the newborn fully with the discarded cloak, storming up the staircase, avoiding the broken tread. The couch shifted, crashing through the rotting floorboards, spreading the flames to David's sheepskin binder, devouring his masterpiece.

They limped through the door, buoyed by the bridge of deceased, coughing ash through their noses, finding relief in a handful of snow.

The livid Fox approached, mask singed, his graying hair poking through the defects. "Our empire has been lost in-"

David tugged at his father's sidearm, removing it from Frankie's trousers, his retort pumping straight through the elder's skull, drenching the white in maroon, the useless shell sinking below the surface. He reseated his grip, daring the others to make their move as the flames reached the roof of the cabin.

"Leave!" he screamed, firing the last round they owned into the sky.

The loyalists flinched, retreating quickly as they discarded their weapons, snow fluttering from their fleeing boots. David tossed the pistol into the white void, basking in the heat. They watched silently as the cabin purified itself, bathing in the demonic envy.

David looked down at the tattered remains of the Messenger, refusing Frankie's help as he approached. To his knees, digging through the massive burlap flaps. He pulled back the fabric, revealing the frail, lifeless expression of da Medicina.

"He protected me," David snorted, fighting his frustration. "He was a poet. His family was taken from him." He delicately rubbed the blood free from the old man's forehead. "He would ferry the dead into Hell, distribute them as his Master saw fit, sworn to never lay a finger on the living lest he face his own punishment. He could not have known what he was doing. That he was just another son of his pathetic empire."

"He broke his oath to protect you," Cecilia observed.

"Leviathan told me I was responsible for the Messenger losing his voice, but I do not know what to believe now." To the cabin, watching the trusses collapse. "It was Papa...he made me like this," he muttered. "But...I must take ownership of my own actions."

A match scraped painfully against a rough edge, drawing the trio to their left.

She wriggled her wrist, shaking free the flame. The edge of the cigarette glowed as she inhaled. The rifle had been slung around her shoulder, the mask of the Eagle in her opposite hand, dangling at her side. She studied the corpse of the old man as she kept the cigarette in the corner of his mouth.

Her neck bore a similar judgment, the flesh torn free, the healing process improper, jagged crevices and scar tissue running a ring that slipped underneath her chin.

Whipping the rifle from her shoulder, she set the stock into the snow and leaned it toward David. At first, he misunderstood, drifting into her eyes blankly. She edged the barrel towards him again, encouraging him to accept.

With a meek paw, he grabbed the gift, nodding with a bit of

shame.

She puffed a steady stream of smoke from underneath her smile. They stared as she silently turned from their mourning, tossing the head of the Eagle into the rotting refuse of congregants.

Suddenly remembering the correct verbiage, she turned back towards them, placing both palms over her heart, mimicking a single heartbeat. She pointed her index, releasing another smile as she grabbed the cigarette and let it hang at her side. Into the murky night she vanished, brushing aside the limp branches of the forest that only wished their immediate and eternal exit.

Frankie and Cecilia shared confusion across their furrowed brows.

David inspected his weapon, running the tips of his fingers across the cold steel, transitioning to the lacquered wood. Meeting the trigger, the sensation suddenly felt alien, the action forbidden. He flung the rifle forward in disgust. "I need you to take me back to the hospital," he declared.

Stunned, looking now to Cecilia for clarification, Frankie stuttered through his response. "A-are you sure?"

He remained silent for some time, admiring the bravery of the silent knight. "Yes. Like him, I too must face my own punishment. He never knew death itself, yet the others feared his message, never realizing he was only preparing them for the journey ahead. I know enough to continue."

"What about the child?" Frankie wondered.

"I was driven to steal him, to atone for what Cecilia had done and protect her from the horrors that I was dragged through. She did nothing wrong. I was simply envious of her freedom, her ability to be loved so easily. You have every right to the child. I know that you will raise him with respect and turn him from the evil that he was bred for."

There was no response. No need for it.

"I love you both very much," David said. "I hope that you can forgive me...and that we can be a family once more."

The sun was beginning to stretch its spindly fingers over the horizon, using the sill as a hitch to vault into the morning sky. Musty ochres danced hand in hand with sizzling pink as the fuming giant cast its domain over the heads of the pine and maple. The snow had dissipated, the dead end road dry, though the rains had soaked it not a few days prior.

The skeleton crew limped from the brush, thumping towards Frankie's car, keeping the forest at their backs. They cared not about haste, reaching the vehicle each unsure of how long they had until they were tormented once more. David leaned against the trunk as Frankie tapped his pockets lazily, realizing he had lost his keys some time ago.

His elbow struck the driver's side window, covering the seat in nuggets of glass. He pulled the tab lock and wiped off the debris, settling into the seat. Unlocking the back and the passenger side, he allowed his siblings to crawl into the leather comfort. The underside of the steering wheel ripped away easily from the dash, exposing a mess of multi-colored worms. He grabbed a cluster and began tearing them with his teeth, exposing the wiring.

David reached under his rear, pulling out the discomfort: his father's flask. His fingers sketched the initials, admiring the craftsmanship before twisting the lid free and sucking down a healthy gulp of the elixir. He tapped Cecilia on the shoulder with the cold vessel, encouraging her to drink. She obliged, staring out the window as she swallowed the bitter liquor.

Frankie slapped the two bare ends of a blue and green wire together. The engine roared to life, the frays twisting around one another to keep the car idling. He closed the door and tugged the gear shift towards him, lurching the old junker forward.

David admired the sunset, licking his chapped and peeling lips. "What are you going to name him?"

Cecilia turned towards the rear, suddenly pulled from a daydream. "Who?"

David nodded towards the child.

"There are a few names I can think of that will not make the list," she teased.

"*Vaffanculo*," he smiled back.

Frankie admired the joke as a fit of laughter overcame them slowly. "*Polpette*," he added. He kept his eyes focused on the curve of the road ahead, delighting in the first joy they had all contributed to in decades.

David began to weep from the timely punchline, clearing his cheek as Cecilia peered through her window, wiping the same enjoyment free of her bloodshot eyes. They bathed in the lingering warmth, chuckling to themselves, slowly winding down their excitement and steadying their exhaustion.

She pivoted back to David, "What name do you think-?"

She just stared for a moment. She adjusted herself carefully, sitting straight, facing the glare ahead. Frankie held his tongue, refusing happiness. He checked the rearview, confirming his sister's silence as David's head hung limp.

Tears fell again, but they spoke no condolences; the trinity still whole in their minds as long as they looked forward.

"What will become of us?" she asked, fixated on the road.

"I don't know."

She offered him a final drink, he offered her the billfold that David had collected.

He accepted the vessel, waiting until the river ran dry to remove it from his lips. He read the initials to himself, the combination brewing an evil incantation in his gut. Cecilia studied the money closely, running her dry skin against the blood that had soaked through the cotton. The child pawed for the bundle, a boil beginning to brew in her stomach. Wanting to satisfy, she dangled her mother's rosary in front of him, the imperfect beads inviting his own version of play as he snatched them for himself.

Frankie tossed the flask out the window, watching in the side view mirror as it bounced to a pathetic stop, shrinking in their escape. The fear of uncertainty fueled his foot against the gas, but the ability now to outrun the sins of their father steadied the wheel.

As the sun rose confidently, they ventured further away from the clustered forest, leaving behind a rising cloud of putrid, black smoke. The cabin where they had cleansed their souls was reduced now to greasy ash, their unwanted memories buried in the cellar below.